Never a Dull Moment

The Chronicles of a
New York City Street Cop

By Detective Charles J. Longi (Ret)

Hummingbird Publishing

Published by *Hummingbird Publishing*
Concord, New Hampshire

Printed in the United States of America by Total Printing Systems
Newton, IL

ISBN 978-0-9833825-2-2

This novel is a fictional product based on the experiences of a
New York City Street Cop. The characters are fictional and any resem-
blance to actual persons, living or dead, is purely coincidental.

Dedication

This book is dedicated to my parents, Joyce and Chuck, who taught me from an early age, respect, loyalty, dignity and the value of hard work. The loving environment that they provided in our home, taught me and my two sisters the true meaning of family.

It is also dedicated to my maternal Grandmother, Nana, who always took the time to enlighten me with her wisdom. She was the matriarch of our family. My Nana always made everyone feel special and never had a bad word for anyone. She taught by example how to treat people, and to carry yourself in a dignified manner. She always made me feel special and loved. Although she had five Grandchildren and eight Great Grandchildren, I was her favorite. It was always our special secret.

Contents

Introduction

THIS BOOK IS A CULMINATION OF EVENTS that took place on the lawless streets of the Bronx as seen through the eyes of an NYPD street cop named Giovanni Franco. It chronicles events that occurred from the officer's childhood until the horrific events of September 11th 2001. The stories within this biographical novel are entertaining, funny, bazaar, and horrifying.

The officer, Giovanni Franco, who was raised in the Bronx during the 60s, encounters events in his life, like the mugging of his paternal Grandmother, that inspired him to dedicate his career to serve and protect.

Emotions run deep within this novel on many levels and Giovanni must make decisions that sometimes cause him emotional conflict. He goes on to be promoted to the rank of Detective Investigator, where he investigates some very unusual cases including that of the first murder 1 death penalty eligible case in New York City history.

This novel will captivate you, anger you, make you laugh, and make you cry. You will feel the full spectrum of emotions as you journey through this officer's experiences.

ENJOY!!

1

His Bike

GIOVANNI FRANCO WAS KNOWN in the squad as a Detective who didn't take
any shit. Perps knew better than to challenge him physically and if they
did, well, they paid for it big time. One time at a Caribbean Day parade,
a practically naked man wearing only a loincloth, and painted all green,
received a nightstick beating from Giovanni after he smeared him with his
war paint. This prompted a riot in the streets of Brooklyn. But Giovanni
was not a violent officer, and most skells respected him, and that was the
trick. Giovanni demanded respect. It's not that he was unreasonable or
unfair; in fact, Giovanni had excellent people skills and a knack for secur-
ing confessions better than most anyone else in the squad. He had a likable
personality that just naturally got people to open up to him, even when he
was attempting to get them to confess to something. Perps often left the
box (interrogation room) thanking him and feeling as though he was their
friend. He had a "GOOD LINE OF SHIT" as they say.

It is probably true that Giovanni's personal experiences growing up
influenced him to become a police officer and to take his vow to serve and
protect seriously. Giovanni definitely had his father to thank for his trait of
demanding respect. When Giovanni was only seven years old, he would
leave his Bronx home, and bike down Seton Avenue at the fastest speed
that he could, an early indication of his love of fast sports cars. He would
always return home by 5 P.M., in time for dinner with his family. Kids in
the Bronx in the '60s and '70s played outside most of the day. There were
no cell phones, no pagers, no instant messaging, no cable television and no
texting. If you wanted to be entertained, you went outside. If you wanted
to see or talk to your friend, you went to his house and you knocked on his
door, or better yet, you called him from the window. Parents didn't know
where their kids were most of the day, but they also didn't worry. The

community looked out for one another. If someone in the neighborhood saw you misbehaving on the street, you can be sure that your parents were going to be told. Families felt that their neighborhood was safe because the community looked out for one another and for each other's children.

Giovanni loved his bike and took very good care of it. It was a metallic, hunter green, Ross. It had a bell on it that rang as he flew down the sidewalk. He kept it clean and shiny and attached baseball cards onto the wheel spokes with clothespins so that they made a flapping sound as he pedaled. It was intended to imitate the sound of a motor. The cards were always of Boston Red Sox or Baltimore Orioles players. Giovanni was a huge Yankees fan even from an early age. He knew the cards would get messed up from the spokes repeatedly hitting them, so he would pick the cards of his team's rivals. Giovanni became a Yankees fan at first because of his family. His father and mother were Yankee fans, along with all his uncles, cousins, both grandmothers, and grandfathers. At that early age he did not know anyone who was not a Yankee fan. It was the only option. His family would all be gathered in the kitchen around the table at his Grandmother's house in the Bronx and someone would shout out, "Mickey's up" referring to the great Mickey Mantle. Everyone would get up and rush into the living room to watch Mickeys at bat. As soon as he was done they would all go back into the kitchen. At this time in his life, in 1967, seven year old Giovanni thought Mickey Mantle was a God. He was his first hero. He would imitate Mickey's swing, and how he ran around the bases after hitting a home run. Head down, elbows up. He would even practice signing Mickey's autograph and pretend to be him signing a ball or something for a fan. His mother would find dozens of Mickey Mantle autographs all over the house.

It was a beautiful October Saturday afternoon and Giovanni yelled to his mom who was doing her weekend cleaning, that he was heading out with his bike. "Be home for dinner" she called to him. "Your cousins will be here tonight." Giovanni had a very close family and it was not uncommon for his aunts and uncles to come over with his cousins just to visit. There did not have to be a special occasion. The men and women would gather in the kitchen talking over coffee and cake and the kids would be playing or watching the black and white TV in the living room. There was always a feeling of togetherness in Giovanni's house.

He decided to deviate from his usual route and started pedaling down Pitman Avenue; this would lead him to Pizzi's candy store where he could buy some penny candy before heading back home. Pizzi's Candy Store seemed to have everything, especially in the eyes of a seven-year old. There were barrels filled with sour pickles and everyone knew that you had to dig to the bottom if you wanted a fresh one that people hadn't poked and prodded at. But today was not a pickle day and Giovanni was trying to decide whether he would buy Bazooka Joe bubble gum, Good and Plenty, or Mary Jane's. He would get fifty cents every Saturday from his father after he cleaned the garage and picked up after their dog Venus who had a doghouse attached to the garage in their yard. His father taught him from an early age a work ethic, and how important it was to take care of your property.

When he came out of Pizzi's, there were three negro boys surrounding his bike, which he had left at the curb. All three were at least a head taller than Giovanni. "Hey white boy, we're taking your bike," they stated as a fact, as one mounted the bike and started to pedal away.

"Hey, gimme my bike" Giovanni yelled as he tried to grab hold of the boy. The other two boys, who were jogging alongside their friend, laughed and pushed him. "Go home you stupid guinea."

Giovanni had never felt so angry or frustrated before. His eyes filled with tears as he clenched his fists and walked home. "Ma!" Giovanni sobbed when he burst through his door. "They stole my bike!" He expected that his mother would hug him and console him, dry his tears and offer him some food. However it wasn't his mother who was home at the time but his father. And his father was not dishing out any sympathy. "Who stole your bike?" his father asked with a disgusted tone to his voice.

"Three negro boys" he answered.

"You let moulinyans take your bike?" his father angrily demanded.

"Why didn't you stop them? What's wrong with you? Go get your bike back now. Don't come back to this house until you get your bike back. Do you know how hard I have to work to buy things for you?"

"Daddy I tried," Giovanni wailed, "they were bigger than me and there were three of them. I tried, Daddy."

"You didn't try hard enough. Stop crying and go. Don't come back until you get your bike back."

Giovanni was stunned. He expected a hug and some sympathy, and maybe a cookie, but instead he got a foot up his ass and was shoved out the door. His sadness and frustration soon turned to anger. At first he was angry at his father. *What could he have wanted me to do?* Giovanni thought. *There were three of them and only one of me. They were bigger than me too. Why wouldn't my father just go get it back for me?* But after a while his anger became directed at the three boys. *I'm not letting them take what's mine*, he thought. *They're going to give it back.* And so Giovanni set out on a search for his bike, canvassing the neighborhood, asking questions of people on the street that might lead him to his bike. Little did he know that this would be some of the very same techniques he would use later in life as a detective.

"Hey, you seen three negro boys with a bike?" Giovanni asked his friend

Vinny. Vinny was sitting on his stoop, bouncing a spaldeen (a pink rubber ball made by the Spalding Company) back and forth between his legs. "Yeah, they just went around the corner. Hey, you wanna play skully?"

"Not now" he answered. Giovanni's heart was beating wildly and his mouth had gone dry. He knew he was about to face the boys who took what was his, and he knew he needed a plan to outsmart them. He looked around and picked up a large rock from the side of Vinny's apartment house. When he walked around the corner, the three boys were sitting on the sidewalk, with the bike lying on its side next to them. They had taken the baseball cards out of the spokes and were looking at them and passing them between them. Their backs were to him and Giovanni knew he had to act quickly. His heart was pounding as he raised the rock above his head and smashed it down as hard as he could, on the head of the largest boy screaming "Arhh" loudly. The two other boys scrambled to their feet while the boy whose head was hit, collapsed on the sidewalk. Blood ran down the front of the boy's face. Giovanni again raised the rock, turned to face the next largest boy, and charged at him, screaming again. The two remaining boys took off, screaming about a white boy gone crazy. Giovanni did feel a little like he was going crazy, but he also felt a great sense of relief wash over him. He wiped his nose with the back of his hand as tears of joy and relief ran down his face. He grabbed his bike and picked up his cards off the sidewalk as he made a mad dash for his house.

As he looked back at the bleeding boy he saw him stumble to his feet and run in the opposite direction. On the way home his thoughts again went to his father and how he left him in this situation without helping him. He could not understand why his dad did not at least come with him to get the bike back. *What if he had been beaten up, what if they stabbed him, what if they killed him. Didn't his father care?* As he was thinking this, he began to cry more intensely. He felt a feeling of almost hate for his father. A feeling he had never felt for him before. Giovanni loved his daddy and would look at him as super human sometimes. His dad was big and strong and no one in the neighborhood ever messed with his dad. *How could he send me out to get my bike after I explained the situation?* He thought. He was now determined to show his father that he did not need his help; he did it himself, and he made those guys understand that he too was not to be messed with.

It was just starting to get dark as he entered his house. His mother cried out and ran to him when she saw him. Although Giovanni felt like crying and hugging his mother back, he stifled a sob and stood still. His father was standing in the alcove of the living room.

"I see you got your bike back," his father said to him. Giovanni stood there with a cold stare directed at his father's eyes almost as if to tell him I didn't need your help. His father approached him with a large smile on his scruffy unshaven face. "That's my boy" his father said, as he cradled Giovanni's head with his large calloused covered hands. "That's my good boy." He again began to cry. The relief he felt from this ordeal poured out through his eyes. His father was proud of him, and he knew he earned that pride. "You go wash up for dinner, and we'll go out for ice cream later." Giovanni felt so proud that he thought he would burst.

From that day on, Giovanni lived his life based on principles not on convenience. He learned that it's better to do the right thing than it is to do the easy thing. His father taught him that you need to take a stand even if you're scared. That you need to face those fears, and deal with the situation. He went on to use these principles throughout his life, both on and off the job. There were times when he was working and was scared out of his wits, but he would refer back to that time as a child with his bike and it would give him strength. He would imagine his father there with him in some of these situations, and he would gain strength knowing his father would want him to stand up and make a difference. At the time he did not realize his father was teaching him a life lesson; he just thought he didn't care. As he grew older, he realized his father was preparing him to deal with some of the most stressful situations anyone could ever have to deal with, and he deeply loved him for it.

2

Hoe Avenue

POLICE OFFICER GIOVANNI FRANCO shivered in the alcove of a tenement on 174th and Hoe Avenue. The temperature on that December evening rose no higher than 15 degrees F and there was no where to go to escape the cold. As a rookie who only three days ago graduated from the police academy, he knew going in, he would wind up in a shithole due to the fact that the Neighborhood Stabilization Unit (NSU) could send him anywhere he was needed. This meant that rookies got sent to the shitiest areas with the most crime. But Giovanni still couldn't imagine this war zone being his post in the South Bronx. Crime statistics showed that the Homicide rate in one square mile around this particular foot post was the highest in the country. Desolation and despair didn't begin to describe what he was looking at. Across the street was a vacant lot and Giovanni noticed two pit bulls sniffing and wandering around. Both were extremely skinny and didn't seem terribly vicious. He had dogs his whole life and knew that pits were no different from any other dogs, at least when they weren't being used for dog fighting, but packs of them running on the street were another story. Pit bulls tend to be very territorial and in a pack environment could be extremely dangerous. Just two days ago, a few blocks from here, guys in his squad had rescued ten pit bulls from a filthy basement apartment that was doubling as a dog fighting ring. The apartment contained a 9' by 9' fighting ring, and bite sticks, syringes and pain medications littered the floor. Those dogs that were not savagely vicious were severely mauled, and one young female pup had died en route to the shelter. She had bites covering most of her body, and must have been used as bait. Giovanni would have to keep his eye on the two in the lot.

On the other side of the street was a burnt out building. Most of the Morisannia section of the Bronx was burnt out, destroyed by arson throughout the '70s. The lucrative drug trade, routinely produced gang wars amongst rival gangs fighting over turf. Murder was part of doing business in this god forsaken area. President Jimmy Carter had visited the South Bronx, specifically Charlotte Street, in 1977 and declared it the worst neighborhood in the United States. Well no shit Sherlock, thanks a lot for letting us know.

So that's where Giovanni started his career with the NYPD, on a street corner in the worst area in the United States. Just ask the former President, he'll tell you. There he found himself trembling in the freezing cold standing on a corner with a couple of possibly savage pit bulls eyeing him from time to time, and a view of burnt out buildings everywhere he looked. A few suspicious characters seemed to lurk in the street down the block, no doubt as aware of his presence as he was of theirs. There wasn't even a bodega nearby where he could go for a short time just to warm up. *It doesn't get much worse than this*, Giovanni thought.

"Psst"

Giovanni turned. The sound seemed to be coming from above him.

'Psst. Papi, jou cold?"

Looking out a window of a fifth floor apartment was a pretty Puerto Rican girl. She had long dark curly hair and thick juicy looking lips.

"Jou cold papi? Come upstair."

Why the fuck not, Giovanni thought. Besides, her face was cute. If her body was hot, this could be interesting. He looked up and counted the windows . . . "One, two, three, four, five. Five what?"

"5B," the girl said.

Giovanni took the stairs two at a time and arrived at the fifth floor landing to find the girl waiting for him. The heat of her apartment hit him square in the face as she opened her door and Giovanni was pleasantly surprised to see that she had a hot little body. Big tits, a small waist, and an ass that you could rest a drink on.

"Come inside, papi, I make you somethin to eat."

Giovanni cautiously entered the apartment, with thoughts of what he had learned in the police academy running through his mind. Danger could always be present, even if the situation seems harmless at the time. Police Office Franco let his instincts take over as he walked and looked around the apartment. He began looking behind doors and inside closets. As he opened the door at the far end of the apartment there was a young girl almost as pretty as the one who invited him up sitting on her bed watching TV.

"That's my seester Luz" Carmen said

"Hey, how you doing? I'm Giovanni. Is anyone else here?"

"No just me and my seester," Carmen replied.

Oh man, can this get much better Giovanni thought. *Sisters? Holy Shit*!

To Luz, Carmen whispered, "Mira este papi chulo."

Carmen went into the kitchen. The apartment was typical tacky Puerto Rican décor. Plastic beads separated the kitchen from the living room and the couch was a fake fur fabric of brown and orange. A cat lounged on an imitation leather recliner nearby. *Yeah there's a lot of pussy in this apartment*, Giovanni thought.

Luz said nothing but her smile spoke a thousand words. She kept her eyes on Giovanni as he walked back toward Carmen.

Carmen had returned with a mashed up concoction on a plate. "Jou like mofongo?" Giovanni had no idea what mofongo was, but he figured he should not insult her cooking skills and graciously accepted the dish. Carmen went to the stereo and started playing Fania All Stars, one of the most popular salsa groups.

Carmen started to dance and her sister Luz joined in.

"Jou like to dance? Come dance with us," Carmen demanded.

Giovanni hardly protested, but Carmen saw the need to get the party going. She took Giovanni's plate and placed it down on the coffee table and pulled him up by his gun belt. She ran her hands up his arms feeling his biceps. "Aye papi, jou feel so strong," Carmen said and turned her back and pressed her ass up against him leaving no doubt in his mind what she wanted. Her body was swaying to the music as she reached down with one hand and caressed his crotch through his police trousers. Luz was still dancing, but she started to caress her own breasts as she watched her sister grope Giovanni.

Carmen was wearing the typical tight jeans that girls in her neighborhood all seem to wear, so Giovanni slid his hand inside her waistband unbuttoning her pants and sliding her zipper down. He reached his hand inside her pants. He slid his other hand up her waist to her ample breasts. He felt her nipples hardening and reached behind unclipping her bra with one hand. Carmen pulled off her tee shirt, a white shirt with a picture of "Minnie Mouse" across her breasts. Carmen was wearing a red lacey bra. But that did not stay on long as Giovanni slid his hand under her bra and cupped her left breast with his left hand. He then removed her bra and spun her around to face him and they kissed passionately.

She pulled his hand out of her jeans and held it as she walked him into her bedroom. She did not close her bedroom door which Giovanni found interesting. They hurriedly undressed with Giovanni holding his gun belt awkwardly, looking for a place to put it. He decided by his feet would be the best spot. With that, he positioned the naked Carmen on the edge of her bed and entered her from behind. He saw something out of the corner of his eye move. He looked to his left and saw Luz standing in the doorway. He extended his hand to her all the while not missing a stroke behind her sister. Luz smiled back at him and slowly walked to him. He took her by the hand and kissed her deeply and passionately. He slid his hand inside her shorts and Luz immediately pulled her blouse over her head. She had an incredible body, and Officer Franco could not believe his good fortune. Luz pulled off her shorts and panties and Giovanni motioned for her to get alongside her sister. She was as wet as her sister and Giovanni just had to know how she felt, so he slowly slid himself out of Carmen and positioned himself behind Luz. Carmen looked back at him with utter disappointment on her face, but Giovanni assured her that it would be all right and began to finger Carmen as he entered her sister. Luz arched her back and Giovanni thought he was in heaven. This continued for several minutes and Giovanni was working up a major sweat due to the heat in the South Bronx apartment.

He then decided to get back behind Carmen, causing Luz to protest.

Being that the sisters were side by side, Giovanni requested that they kiss. At first Carmen protested, so Giovanni stopped what he was doing. He felt totally in control, and felt he could make them do whatever he wanted.

Carmen turned towards Luz and kissed her gently on the lips. Giovanni laughed out loud and began to slam Carmen harder and faster than he had before. He couldn't believe his luck, two hot Puerto Rican sisters side by side in the South Bronx in the middle of nowhere.

All of a sudden Giovanni heard the WOOP WOOP of a police sector car. He froze but did not remove himself from Carmen.

"Why you stop? Come on, no stop!" Carmen demanded.

"That might be my Sergeant." Giovanni said.

"Tell him to come up too" Luz said.

"No, No," Giovanni said. "Let me see." The window was on the other side of the room and Giovanni didn't want to remove himself from Carmen if it wasn't necessary. Maybe it was just a random patrol car out there.

"Umm can you, umm, just inch up a little?" Giovanni asked. He remained inside Carmen and walked her over to the window; she slightly bent forward with him pressed up behind her.

"Shit!" Giovanni said. "It's him." He removed himself from Carmen and ran over to his gun belt which held his radio, he didn't realize that he had lowered the volume and when he raised it his heart sank from what he heard.

"Post 6 come in, Post 6 come in," the central dispatcher stated over and over. Officer Franco in a panic answered, "Post 6 central go ahead"

"Go to channel 2, post 6." Officer Franco switched to channel 2 which was a direct connect to the sergeant's walkie talkie.

"What's your 20 post 6?" the sergeant asked.

Giovanni's hard-on was gone and his balls felt like they were in his mouth. "1701 Hoe Avenue," he replied.

"I need to give you a scratch," barked the sergeant. Police officers carry memo books that are periodically marked, or scratched, by their superiors as a check of where they are and whether they are all right.

Giovanni rushed to put on his clothes. His body was drenched with sweat, but his clothes were dry since he had stripped everything off. Maybe his sergeant wouldn't notice.

Like a madman, he raced downstairs. He saw his sergeant driving away from his location, towards the corner. He stepped out of the building and out into the street motioning with his hands. The RMP made a u turn and pulled up to Giovanni's location. A cop named Bobby, a rookie who had just graduated the academy three days ago, like Giovanni, was the sergeant's chauffeur.

The sergeant, a real tough cop with a thick Irish brogue, named Sergeant O'Malley, looked Giovanni over from head to toe. In a strong commanding voice, Sergeant O'Malley questioned Giovanni. "I was looking for you lad. Where were ya? I ain't got all night to waste on ya. I got 20 other youngins to take care of."

As Officer Franco saluted the sergeant he was sure the jig was up.

"I was up on the roof sir," he stated.

"And what might you be doin up there?" the sergeant asked.

"I was watching these guys dealing on the corner, Sarge. I was just about to come down and make a collar."

With that, Bobby, the sergeant's chauffeur began to laugh hysterically.

"What the fuck are you laughing at?" Giovanni demanded.

"Your head is steaming," Bobby choked as he pointed and laughed at Giovanni's head.

Steam was literally coming off the top of his head into the cold South Bronx night.

As officer Franco looked into the side view mirror, he saw steam coming off his head, and his face was red and flushed. *"BUSTED" there goes my career before it even started*, was all he could think.

"That roof must be very hot now, is it son?" Sergeant O'Malley proclaimed, pointing to his steaming skull. He motioned for Giovanni to lean in towards the window.

Giovannni was speechless and stared back at the sergeant with a blank expression. The Sergeant just shook his head and told his driver to drive off. As they did, Giovanni thought he heard the sergeant say to Bobby, "He'll never make it." Giovanni was not sure exactly what to make of the sergeant's comment, but for now he thought he 'dodged a bullet.'

From that day on, Giovanni would request that desolate, disgusting, horrible, crime ridden post on Hoe Avenue, and everyone in his squad thought he was out of his mind. But in Giovanni's mind, it didn't get any better than this.

3

Crotona Park

JOEY GIZZO AND GIOVANNI FRANCO were part of a 20 man squad assigned to NSU as rookies. There were approximately 50 posts covering four precincts in the South Bronx. Rookies were sent to the worst areas,
typically poor and crime ridden neighborhoods. The rookies were not yet
paired up as partners, but Joey and Giovanni were often assigned to the
same post or to adjoining posts, based on their last names in alphabeti-
cal order. Giovanni found himself thinking he wouldn't mind so much if
a guy like Joey wound up eventually being his partner. Giovanni, in his
mind, knew what type of characteristics made for a good partner, and Joey
seemed to possess most of them. He was loyal, tough and street smart. The
problem was, however, that Joey was also, at times, not too smart. To make
matters worse, Joey had a speech impediment: a serious lisp which made it
sometimes difficult to understand him, and to take him seriously. Giovanni
was not one to judge, though, because most of the friends whom he grew
up with were not educated, and many had some type of quirk. Some had
actually pursued a life of crime. He knew that he could have easily gone
in that direction himself if it were not for his father. He had no doubt, his
father would have literally killed him had he ever been arrested or brought
home by the police. Actually, Giovanni had many of the characteristics that
would have made him a very successful criminal. He was crafty, strong as
a bull and fearless. But, he also had one trait which would have made him
a very poor criminal; he had a conscience. When bullies picked on kids in
school, it was always Giovanni who stepped in to defend them. He was the
oldest of three children, having two baby sisters who he always felt protective of. As such, he believed himself the protector of the weak and this
was in large part the reason why he became a cop. But, the main reason he
chose law enforcement was the fact that when he was younger, his elderly
grandmother had been mugged. Although she offered the thief her money,

the mugger, in his junkie rage, had shoved his grandmother down a flight of stairs. It appeared, at least to Giovanni and his family; the police were not as motivated as they should have been to apprehend the perpetrator. He swore at that time that he would become a police officer to serve and protect the innocent in society. Children and the elderly held a special place in his heart. In some ways, this protective trait of Giovanni's extended to his feelings about Joey.

On one particular evening, he and Joey were working the night shift from 4 P.M. to midnight, assigned to Crotona Park. Crotona Park is 127 acres of supposed recreation for Bronx families. It has twenty tennis courts, five baseball diamonds, a 300 foot pool and a 3.3 acre man-made lake. It was named after the Greek colony of Croton, known for its Olympic athletes. But, in the '80s an Olympic athlete was the last sight you would expect to see, as Crotona Park was a haven for gangs, drugs, and prostitutes. It was a shame too, because the park itself was a beautiful place and could have been a great resource for Bronx residents. However, it was not uncommon to see members of the Bloods and the Crips, who were just becoming prevalent in the area, hanging out in the park. The Bloods and the Crips were causing a lot of tension since other gangs, such as the Latin Kings, Ching-A-Lings and the Savage Skulls considered themselves already established in the area.

They felt these new groups were trying to muscle them out. Black gangs occupied one section of the park while Hispanic gangs occupied another. But, their coexistence was far from peaceful as fighting over drug territory was a constant battle the officers had to contend with day and night. Most of these battles, or rumbles as they were called, occurred in Crotona Park usually out of the eye of the public in the middle of the night. It was not uncommon for a body or two to be discovered in the morning by a Park worker after a "RUMBLE" had gone down the night before. Of course, there were never any witnesses, and many times these cases went unsolved. When Giovanni and Joey were assigned to Crotona Park, they would patrol it on foot and demand that the criminals, or mutts, as police officers called them, who were loitering there, leave. Officially the park closed at dusk, so when the officers first took their post, they would observe who the players were and then by sundown, kind of like the Wild West, they would make their stand by telling them to leave, and in some instances forcing them by whatever means necessary.

It was a particularly cold night and one would think that Crotona Park would be empty, but that was not the case. Crotona Park was never empty. Officers Franco and Gizzo needed to chase off groups of fifeen to twenty skells; some were just mutts who were hanging out drinking and had no other place to go, but others were drug dealers, buyers, steerers (people who work for the drug dealers and direct and solicit customers), and lookouts. The drug trade was operated by gangs, and this made Crotona Park a very dangerous place. But, there was one particular individual who did not show the deference for the police officers that the other cast of characters did. Instead he chose to argue what he claimed was his right to stay in the park.

"I live here," stated a large man in a defiant voice. "Ya'll can't chase me out of here. This here is where I live." The man wore the typical homeless man uniform of layered coats, sneakers that were too large for his feet and mismatched gloves. He also wore a large fedora on his head which made him look a little like a pimp who was down on his luck. His body odor was extremely noticeable, even in the bitter cold. He was pushing a shopping cart filled to the brim with bottles, cans, plastic bags and newspapers.

"What are you thalking about?" Joey demanded. "There ain't no housth here."

"What the fuck you saying?" the homeless man asked. "I can't understand you. What the fuck is he saying?" the homeless man asked Officer Franco.

"Oh shit," Franco laughed. "Dude, he's fucking with you!"

"I'm gonna kick your ath, thath what I'm thaying, you thon of a bitch," Officer Gizzo began getting visibly agitated.

"I LIVE here," the homeless man continued through a large gap between his teeth, which ironically did not produce the lisp that Joey had. He pointed to a large cardboard box filled with layer upon layer of *The Daily News* and *The New York Post*. "This is my crib. You can't make me leave."

"All right, all right, take it easy" Franco demanded. "We're going to take a little walk. Keep your mess out of our sight and we'll leave you alone. C'mon Joey, let's get something to drink."

"YA'LL CAN'T CHASE ME OUT OF HERE!" the homeless man screamed once more for good measure as the officers were walking away.

"Hey, leth get thom beer. That guy pithed me off. I could use one." Joey excitedly suggested.

"Beer? Really? We really shouldn't be drinking on the job. I'd rather have coffee, I'm freezing." Franco said as he cupped and blew into his hands. "It's fucking cold tonight."

"Yeah, come on, thom beer would be great. Bethides, ith Friday," Gizzo begged.

The officers walked out of Crotona Park and over to Tito's Bodega on the corner of Charlotte Street and Crotona Park East. Tito himself was behind the counter and as always, was thrilled to see the officers enter his store.

Most of the food in bodegas is unhealthy crap, so it's not surprising that a large proportion of Bronx residents are overweight. Many do the bulk of their grocery shopping in the bodega where soda, chips, and candy are rampant and fruits and vegetables scarce. But who can really blame them? For about a dollar you can choose to buy either a large bag of chips, some cake, or two oranges. The chips or cake would last you longer and fill you up. You do the math.

"Good evening officers," Tito said in his thick Spanish accent. In the corner, two men were engrossed in a game of dominos. They looked up and nodded at the officers. The officers were a welcome pair here as their presence provided a very real sense of security. In reality, the police are the only reason gangs don't come into stores in this neighborhood and just take whatever they want. Robberies and murders happen literally every day. Tito loved when the cops would pay him a visit. He would offer them free food and drink and engage them in conversation to try and keep them there as long as he could. Tito had been robbed many times in the past and was roughed up a couple of times, which shook him up badly. Officer Franco had a feeling that Tito might have a gun lying around which he undoubtedly purchased on the street. Franco chose not to inquire knowing Tito was a good man and had been victimized numerous times. He felt if some mutt walked into Tito's store and tried to take what Tito worked so hard for, he deserved what he got. He also knew if Tito was tried by a jury of his peers, there was no way they would convict him. People of the South Bronx walk around their neighborhood in constant fear of being robbed, stabbed or shot and Officer Franco loved when he heard stories of vigilantism or what he liked to call, street justice. Although he kept those opinions to himself, deep down inside he loved to hear when a bad guy got blown away by a decent person, which happened often in the neighborhood he was patrolling.

"Hey Tito. How you doing? How's your wife and my kids?" Officer Franco asks with a smile on his face.

Tito gave out a big laugh and said, "Everybody fine. Gracias. But the keedz shoes are getting tight. Maybe jou could buy them new ones."

They both had a good laugh and Tito asked if the officers would like coffee.

"Please, por favor, toma café." Before the officers could protest, Tito pours them both a hot cup of Bustelo coffee.

"Shoogar? Meelk?" he asks.

Gizzo goes to the back of the store and returns with a six pack of Budweiser tall boys. The officers hang out for a while with Tito, and after finishing their coffee, they each drank a beer. Tito, not being a beer man, poured himself a shot of some concoction that had grass and roots in it. Tito offered some to the officers and when they asked what it was, he responded "mama juana." Officer Franco asked, "What is that. It looks homemade." Tito explains "Si, I make it in me bathtub. It make you a strong lover." With that, the officers look at each other and say no thanks.

The men share a toast to health and family as Tito puts the other four cans of beer and two bags of Doritos in a brown paper bag. After a half hour or so, it's time to return to Crotona Park.

"Tito, how much do we owe you?" Franco asks. Tito is notorious for trying to give the officers food on the arm, but Officer Franco, knowing how hard Tito works, knows he needs the money to support his family. He tosses a ten dollar bill on the counter, and says "Thank you Tito, have a good night."

As they are leaving, Joey leans in closer to Giovanni and complains, "I can't understand a fucking thing that guy thays." Franco laughs aloud. "Whath tho funny?" Joey asks, looking confused.

The officers can hear Tito protesting about the money as they leave the store, but they good naturedly wave good-bye and make their way back to Crotona Park now carrying a 4-pack of tall boys and a couple bags of chips. The park appears quiet, but the officers know better than to be fooled by appearances. They take a few minutes and tuck behind the park house to enjoy their beer. They each drink one, crush up the cans, and toss them in the garbage. The remaining two cans and two bags of Doritos they tuck underneath a park bench and resume their patrol through the park. They patrol on foot, harassing the locals, which seems like a never ending battle, kind of like pissing into the wind. Every now and then someone needs to be cracked in the shins with the nightstick to get the point. Then the word spreads quickly that it's probably a good idea to leave.

Once the officers get a feeling that the park is void of miscreants, they head back to the beer bench.

Gizzo reaches under the bench to find nothing but empty cigarette packs, garbage and a used condom. His beer is no more.

"That fucking guy. Ith him. I know he took it, that thon of a bitch" Officer Gizzo is again all worked up.

Sure enough, just a little investigation leads the officers to the homeless man, who is sitting up against a tree, sipping a tall boy and eating the Doritos. When he sees the officers, he raises his beer and toasts them before taking a swig. His fingers are orange from the chips and he very deliberately licks each dirty one. The other tall boy is in his shopping cart.

Officer Franco tells Joey, "That's your beer he's drinking, cuz I paid for all that shit. My beer is in the shopping cart."

"You scumbag, I'm gonna shove my thick up your ath," Gizzo screams as he charges at the homeless man and raises his nightstick.

"You aint hittin me with no stick," the homeless man screams as he attempts to push Officer Gizzo. But Gizzo holds his nightstick horizontally with both hands and shoves the homeless man backwards. The homeless man being at the edge of the manmade lake in the park slips off the concrete edging and into the lake. The officers hear a splash and realize what happened. The homeless man is now screaming for help, arms flailing, and head bobbing in and out of the water.

"Help me, help me," the homeless man screamed as he thrashed about in the lake. "I'm gonna drown. I can't swim."

Most of the lights in the park had been broken by drug dealers who prefer to sell their wares under the guise of darkness. So it was difficult for the officers to see the homeless man and to determine how much danger he was actually in.

"Aren't you gonna do something?" Franco asks, "You can't let him drown!"

"Thith is bullthit, I SHOULD let him drown." But, Officer Franco, knowing that this could turn into a major clusterfuck, told Gizzo that he better do something. With that, Gizzo kicked off his patent leather shoes, removed his gun belt, jacket, and hat and took three running steps jumping feet first into the lake. Due to the murky, slippery, lake bottom, Officer Gizzo started skidding and landed, with a swoosh, on his ass, creating a wave of lake water that splashed over his chest and hit him in the face. Immediately, the homeless man stood up to demonstrate that the water only reached his waist. He pointed and laughed at Officer Gizzo as Franco, realizing what had happened, started laughing hysterically.

"You asshole! I made you jump in the lake!" the homeless man screamed.

"Oh my God," Franco said. "He made you jump in that nasty, homeless people piss and shit water." Franco was laughing so hard that he couldn't catch his breath. Tears were running down his face and he envisioned going back to the station house and telling the guys all about it.

This was about all Gizzo could take. He began to chase the homeless man to the edge of the lake, grabbed him and proceeded to punch him several times in the head.

Franco, realizing he needed to say something, told Joey to cut it out and leave him alone. Giovanni extended his hand to Joey, helping him pull himself up from the slippery edge of the lake. The homeless man climbed out about twenty feet to Joey's left and started walking away, undoubtedly going back to his crib. The homeless man then turned to Gizzo and taunted, "I might be hypothermic so I should probably go to the hospital, nice worm bed courtesy of the City of New York."

With that, Gizzo became enraged again saying, "I'll thend you to the hospital you thon of a bitch," but most of the fight was taken out of him. He stood there drenched to the bone, shivering in the January night, in lake water that was used by bums both as a toilet and a washing machine. A homeless man had bested him, and Officer Gizzo knew he should let this battle go.

Franco yelled to the homeless man, "You can have my beer; you earned it." Joey gave Giovanni a dirty look and Giovanni just shrugged his shoulders sporting a big smile on his face. They walked to a park bench nearby so Joey could put his shoes on. He put his jacket back on as Giovanni handed him back his hat. He held his gun belt in his hand so as to not get the leather wet. After he got dressed, they started walking towards the park exit, with Joey squishing with every step.

Joey turns to Giovanni and says, "You ain't gonna thay nothing, right?" This request really disappointed Giovanni because he couldn't wait to tell the guys, but knowing that Joey was embarrassed, he stated, "No, not this time, come on. Let's get back to the house so you can change your uniform. We can put ourselves out on meal and then maybe they'll find us something to do at the station so we don't have to come back to the park." Rather than take the van that was available to pick up the rookies and return them to the house, the officers decided they would walk the 10 blocks to avoid exposing Joey to the bosses, forcing him to explain why he was drenched, dirty, and smelled like a sewer.

By putting themselves out on meal, the officers could take their dinner break and this would allow Joey to sneak downstairs to the locker room to shower and change, perhaps unnoticed by the guys.

The homeless guy was on his own, but when you think about it, in his mind, it was probably a pretty good night. He scored two beers, two bags of Doritos, a bath and got to pull a fast one on one of New York's Finest. Franco, although out ten dollars, laughed so hard at Gizzo that he felt it was worth every penny. For Officer Gizzo, it was a rough night, but it could have been worse. No one got hurt, and Franco never told the guys about the prank that the homeless man pulled. Therefore, the night's events definitely bonded the men for a future that could possibly include being partners.

4

Suave Sanchez

IN THE LATE 1970s THERE WAS a boxer from East Harlem who moved to the South Bronx and made it big. He won several New York Golden Gloves Championships as an amateur before moving on and turning professional. His nickname was Suave Sanchez and he could fight. In fact, after moving to New York from his native Puerto Rico as a kid, he found himself constantly getting into fights in his neighborhood. His mother put him into karate and boxing classes to try and keep him out of trouble. He was on the streets and trouble seemed to be his middle name. He was first arrested at the age of fifteen and was in and out of juvenile facilities during this time. His mother knew if he was to escape the mean streets of New York, boxing would be his way out. Once he won his first New York Golden Gloves Championship in 1978, at the age of sixteen, you would think that things were looking up for Suave, but he just couldn't control his wise-ass nature. He was immature and would start fights wherever he went. He did not know how to control the anger that seemed to burn inside him. He went on to win two more Golden Gloves Championships before turning professional in 1981.

Officer Giovanni Franco, assigned to NSU 7 in the South Bronx, was assigned a post on 3rd Avenue between 145th Street and 159th Street. It was a cool Sunday morning in April 1984 and the South Bronx Little League was having their annual Parade down 3rd Avenue. All the teams were dressed in uniform and marched down 3rd Avenue. holding banners for their individual teams. It was a day where civic pride and love for the local neighborhood children was evident. There were people lining the streets holding signs of encouragement and yelling to the teams in both English and Spanish. There were bands from various organizations along with the local high schools playing as the teams marched down the street. Franco, as he stood on the corner of 149th Street and 3rd Avenue, felt a sense of pride for the boys marching by, as he remembered when he was a young boy marching in his own little league parade. It was a welcome break from the posts and details he had been getting lately. Being assigned in the South Bronx, there weren't many assignments better than this he thought.

That thought was quickly interrupted as an elderly Puerto Rican woman came up to him and told him that there was a man riding his bicycle down the parade route weaving in and out of the marching children, causing all kinds of problems. She said people have asked him to stop but he wouldn't. The parade route on 3rd Avenue. bends with the contour of the street, so Franco could not see down the street far enough to see the bike rider. He started walking up the parade route looking for the defiant cyclist. As Franco made his way up the street, the jerk on the bike came into view. He was a tall, skinny Hispanic man who looked to be in his early twenties. He noticed Franco right away and turned and peddled in the opposite direction weaving back through the marching boys. This infuriated Franco, and he knew he would have to come up with a plan. He could have called Central Dispatch and asked for some sector cars but he did not want to make a big scene and have to stop the parade. He decided to handle this himself. He went around the corner and thought he could sneak up on the bicyclist coming up from behind, but the man was constantly looking for him and spotted Franco as he was just a few yards away. The bicyclist turned, hopped up onto the sidewalk and gave Franco the middle finger as he again sped away. Many in the crowd saw what was happening and Franco was livid.

"Mr. Policeman, make that bad man stop," sobbed a small boy. Franco vowed to the little boy that he would get the guy. He watched as the bicyclist made a right hand turn and left the parade route.

An old man came up to Franco and asked "Do you know who that asshole on the bike is?"

"Who is he?" Franco asked.

"That's the boxer, Suave Sanchez."

As soon as he heard the name, Franco recognized him. He knew he looked familiar. Franco had seen him on T.V. several times and even saw him fight at Madison Square Garden a few years back. Now he was more determined than ever to catch him. *How could he be doing this to these little kids? He is an asshole,* Franco thought. *These kids could look up to him as a role model. Someone from the neighborhood who made it big, but no he had to be a jerk.* He wanted him bad.

Officer Franco made his way across the street to the McDonalds and placed himself in the doorway entrance. From there he was out of sight from the street but he could see both ways up and down the street in the reflection from the glass windows that were on both sides of the entrance. *This is perfect* he thought, *because if he comes back he won't see me until it's too late.* He stood in the alcove to McDonalds for what seemed like forever with his nightstick in his hand and anger in his heart. As he looked up and down 3rd Avenue, he spotted Suave Sanchez coming down the sidewalk on the same side of the street he was on. *Please keep coming* he thought as he watched Suave looking back and forth as he got closer and closer. Just as Suave was almost directly in front of the McDonalds, Franco jumped out from his hiding place. Suave saw him at the last minute and tried to avoid him by turning back into the street but he could not. As he jumped out, Franco jammed his nightstick into the front wheel of the bike, breaking the spokes, and causing Suave to fly head over heels, over the handlebars of the bike landing with a loud thump as he hit the concrete. He immediately jumped up and assumed a fighting stance although both his arms, and one knee were bleeding, and Officer Franco was standing there with his nightstick in hand.

A large crowd had gathered and most knew of the situation with this jerk messing up the parade. The crowd was cheering Franco on and it had the feel of an old fashion street fight. Franco had to remind himself he was a police officer and needed to act accordingly. Franco informed Suave that he was under arrest and to put his hands behind his back. If he failed to do as he was instructed, he would be beaten until he complied. Suave Sanchez, although a professional boxer, and run of the mill street punk, could tell by the look in Franco's eyes that he was not playing. Therefore, he put his hands down and turned around. Franco cuffed him without further incident.

Franco called for a sector car and they removed Sanchez and his broken bike to the 4-2 Precinct. Once they got to the 4-2 Precinct, Franco had a long heartfelt talk with Suave Sanchez, whose given name was Santo Sanchez. He spoke to him about being a role model and how the kids looked up to him. He also told him how his own people were calling him a jerk and an asshole. He wanted Santo to understand he had the power to make a difference in many people's lives and that he could become a respected and valuable part of the community. Something happened during this talk that Franco found quite unexpected. The rough tough Suave Sanchez began to cry. He explained that he never had a father in his life growing up and his mother was too busy working to support her family, so she really did not have the time to teach him how to behave. Franco did not feel this was an excuse for the way Suave had lived his life up to this point, but he did see genuine remorse in Santo's eyes. He made Suave a deal. If Suave made a contribution to the local Little League, and promised to sponsor a team next year, he would let him walk.

"I'll do you one better," Suave told Franco. "I'll do all that, plus I will pay for a picnic at the end of the season for all the kids and their families." With that promise, the two men shook hands with Franco taking him at his word and let Suave go.

For every year since 1985 Suave Sanchez has sponsored the End of Season Picnic for the South Bronx Little League. It has become a tradition and is looked forward to by hundreds of underprivileged youth in the area along with their families. Now we don't know if this is a coincidence or not, but Suave Sanchez has never had another problem with the law since this cool Sunday morning in April of 1984.

5

Yankee Stadium

BEING A ROOKIE IN NSU HAD ITS UPS AND DOWNS. The cons were that you never knew who you were working with or where you were working. As a rookie, your assignments were always the ones the guys with more time on, didn't want. So not having a choice, you would get the shit post or shitty assignment. Rookies were notorious for being put on stinky DOAs or getting stuck with Alexander's holding one. In the Bronx, dead bodies would sometimes remain in their apartments for days before anyone realized that the person wasn't around anymore. It was usually discovered by the stink that permeated the hallways. As far as Alexander's goes, it was a large department store chain that possessed the most overzealous security staff known to man. So when they caught someone shoplifting a $5 dollar item, they would inevitably call 911 demanding that the police respond and arrest the perpetrator. When a rookie would hear "Alexander's holding one" over the radio, he would cringe especially if he had that foot post. The perp usually had a warrant for failing to appear in court on his or hers last arrest, so a DAT (DESK APPEARANCE TICKET) would not be a possibility. He knew for the next eight hours he would be stuck in central booking, processing a bullshit arrest. It only came in handy when the weather was bad or if you were looking for the pretty Assistant District Attorney whom you spotted down in court last week.

But Giovanni began to see that there were also advantages. For one thing, the girls in these poor areas were so anxious or maybe even desperate, to snag a decent, normal guy they would do anything, and that means absolutely anything, to pique a man's interest. Young rookies in uniform represented a prize that South Bronx women actively sought, and most of the times, the girls were beautiful. So far, being a cop had brought Giovanni a good deal of sex, and a feeling that he was in charge of the street. Yeah, he was young, but he knew how to command respect and these past months in the NYPD had given him greater confidence that he had made the right choice to become a cop and not to pursue the criminal life that many of his friends and family had chosen instead. But another unexpected benefit to being one of New York's Finest was the amount of bonding and camaraderie the rookies shared. Just a few months had gone by, but Giovanni already felt very close to his fellow rookies and enjoyed spending time with them, on and off duty.

One Friday afternoon, the rookies at the behest of one of their sergeants, were planning a barbeque after the 8 to 4 shift and a trip to Yankee Stadium. The Stadium, as everyone calls it, was mere blocks from most of the posts that he was assigned to as a rookie. Giovanni's sergeant, as a cop, was assigned to the Yankee Stadium detail, meaning through the course of the season he worked at the stadium every home game. He was then promoted to Sergeant and assigned to NSU, but he had many contacts and knew he could get his squad in to the game through the press gate. So the night was set; a barbeque underneath the Cross Bronx Expressway, and a Friday night baseball game against the hated Boston Red Sox. After an uneventful 8 to 4 shift, which was very unusual in itself, the guys proceeded to leave the 48th precinct, where NSU 7 turned out of. They went across the street and two blocks down so as to not be close to the precinct since there would be some drinking involved.

The party got started with Joey Gizzo, the consummate comedian, performing a strip tease to Stevie Wonder's "I got sunshine." With his pronounced lisp, it sounded more like, "I got thunthine on a cloudy day." He danced around holding a red plastic cup of beer and had everyone around him in stitches. Joey liked to be the center of attention and the guys really liked him. Giovanni stood off to the side with the other guys, shaking his head, almost feeling embarrassed for him. The beer started flowing and inevitably the war stories from a bunch of rookies who didn't know shit from shiola, were being told one after the other. A rookie cop named Tommy Lavin was cooking the food in a half cut open 50 gallon drum, filled with charcoal, with a grate on top of it. This was the first time all the guys actually got together in a social atmosphere and they all seemed so happy and at ease, a very different feeling from watching your back in the dangerous streets of the South Bronx. As time went by and the beer kept flowing, intoxication seemed to be inevitable. Sergeant Tom McFadyen got up on the bumper of his car and announced, "All you jerkoffs that can still walk better head down to the stadium." With that order, the guys dumped the charcoal and hid the barbeque grill in the corner, covering it with two wooden skids that were laying there with some other debris so that the skells in the neighborhood wouldn't steal it. They would retrieve it the next day and bring it back to the precinct before their shift began. So here they were, twenty or so rookies, feeling good on their way to the game.

Giovanni, owning a car he loved, and not wanting to drive it to the stadium for obvious reasons, decided to leave his car at the barbeque location and hopped a ride from Joey in his beat up yellow Ford Pinto. Giovanni made fun of Joey's car as they drove down to the Stadium and said that it smelled like the Fulton Fish Market. Joey cracked back at Giovanni, "That's because I fucked your mother in it last night," and all the guys let out a loud groan, knowing the way Giovanni felt about his mother. Joey, realizing that he shouldn't have said that, quickly added, "I 'm just kidding, I'm just kidding. Giovanni knows that I love his mommy and I would never do anything bad like that to her." Joey is probably the only one who could ever get away with saying something like that to Giovanni. He knew Joey was a little simple and a little drunk. Plus he really had affection for Joey.

The guys all met at the press gate and Sergeant McFadyen went over to the Lieutenant in charge of the Stadium detail and informed him that he was there with his guys. As the Lieutenant motioned for the guys to come towards him, he warned each and every one of them that their behavior was a reflection on him so they needed to act appropriately. Since the guys had no tickets, the Sergeant took them all the way to the upper deck probably to keep them away from sober, paying fans, as twenty rookies who had been drinking half the day tend to get loud and horse around. The game was great and, of course, the Yankees won 9-2. As they were leaving, someone got the bright idea they should head to a strip club. Joey in his funny way, yelled out. "Why didn't I think of that?' Giovanni knew he was in for an all-nighter at that point. So they headed over to *Hedz and Humpz* in the heart of the South Bronx where only the locals dare tread. All of a sudden 20 rookies enter this dump that mainly consists of ten to twelve over the hill stretched marked, saggy women whose main job was to beg for your dollars and make you feel sexy. Giovanni hated this atmosphere because he felt it was phony and not for nothing, but he could get a lot better pussy than what was offered in this dump. But he loved hanging out with the guys, especially Joey, so he put up with the occasional begging of a toothless hag. Most of his time was spent shooting pool off in the corner with Sergeant McFadyen all the while keeping an eye on Joey because he knew Joey was a little loose with his hands when it came to women. The locals in this establishment didn't seem to like the idea of cops being there, and you could feel the tension in the air. From the conversations the guys were having, it was evident they were the police which was probably not very smart to do in a place like this. But the rest of the night went off without a hitch and before you knew it, the owner was flicking the lights off and on, signaling closing time. The guys all piled into their cars and went their separate ways. Giovanni jumped into Joey's car for a ride back to his beloved 1977 black Chevy Monte Carlo. It wasn't a Ferrari but Giovanni had bought it with his own money, working construction with his father, before he became a cop.

Joey dropped Giovanni off on the corner so he could gain access to the Cross Bronx and not have to go around the block. As Giovanni walked underneath the Cross Bronx, he noticed for the first time how dark the area was. When they left for the game it was still daylight and Giovanni's car was the only one underneath the expressway sitting in the dark. A bad feeling came over him at that point but the car looked okay from a distance. As he approached the car, he put the key in the driver's door, unlocking it. He opened the door and immediately realized that there was a problem when the interior light didn't come on. As he looked into the car, he couldn't believe his eyes. The car's entire interior was gone. The front seat and the back seat…gone! There was nothing left but seat belts. He also noticed that his radio had been ripped out of the dashboard. The first thought he had, was that he wasn't as street smart as he thought he was. Why didn't he drive the car back and park it in front of the precinct? He didn't take it to the stadium because he didn't want anything to happen to it, but he left it unattended in the South Bronx, in a dark area, where it could be stripped. Giovanni walked over to the hood of the car and opened it. What he suspected became a reality as he saw that his battery had been stolen too. So Giovanni walked to the 48th Precinct which was only two blocks away. But when he got to the front of the station house, he realized that he couldn't go in because he had been drinking and could be found not fit for duty by the Desk Sergeant. Police officers must always be fit for duty, even when they're off. So now what was he to do? It was 4:30 in the morning, he had been drinking, and his car was all fucked up. Out of the corner of his eye, he noticed a metal milk box propped up against the outside of the station house. This box was used to keep tools in, like tire pressure gauges and wrenches to do minimal work on police vehicles parked in front. Giovanni grabbed the box thinking maybe the tools would come in handy. Then he got a better idea. If he could locate a battery, he could use the box as a seat so that he could drive the car home. He tossed the box into his car and walked around for several minutes, finding himself in front of the *White Castle* restaurant on Webster Avenue, a twenty-four hour fast food burger joint located in the slums and known for their famous murder burgers. Giovanni's first thought was, *Let me get some murder burgers; I'm starving,* but then he told himself, *Concentrate on the task at hand and find a god damn battery.* He observed a Spanish guy parking a beat up Chevy Nova in the White Castle parking lot accompanied by a pretty Spanish girl. Giovanni had some knowledge of cars and knew that the Nova did not have an inside hood release and could be opened without entering the vehicle. He watched the two walk into the restaurant and slowly walked over to the Nova. He could see the couple through the large windows of the restaurant. Never taking his eyes off the two, he went to the front of the Nova and felt for the hood release. He located it and slid it over, keeping his hand on top of the hood to prevent it from popping up. He never took his eyes off the couple as he slowly lifted the hood approximately a foot. He reached in and felt for the battery cables. He located them and wiggled them until they came off the terminals. He looked around to see if anyone was observing him and when he felt it was all clear, he reached in and removed the battery. A terrible feeling came over him at that moment, knowing he was committing a crime and knowing he was the one who was supposed to be preventing criminal behavior. But, he was tired, pissed off, mainly at himself, and just wanted to go home. So he put the battery on his left hip, put his shirt over it, and carried it off, all the while still watching the two on line getting ready to order their food. He ran back to the Monte Carlo and installed the battery. When he opened the car door and saw the interior light come on, he felt a sense of relief. He put his key in the ignition and turned it and the car started. His baby was alive! He positioned the milk box where the driver's seat used to be located and climbed into the car. It was awkward and uncomfortable but he used his left arm, putting it outside the window, and holding onto the door to steady himself. He drove all the way home like this knowing tomorrow he'd be in some junk yard probably buying back his own interior. He had to get the dashboard fixed and buy a new radio all because he made a rookie mistake by not anticipating what could go wrong when leaving his car unattended.

Like Giovanni's career so far, this night had its great moments and its pitfalls. The Yankees won; he ate some great tailgate barbeque, and he felt closer to his fellow officers than ever before. But, he also allowed his sense of invulnerability to cloud his judgment, which caused him to lose his personal property. He knew that he had made a risky decision tonight, one that could have ended his career in a heartbeat. He found it hard to reconcile the contrasting behaviors and emotions that he had experienced today. Was he the law or was he the criminal? Did he feel pride or guilt about his resourcefulness? Giovanni knew that his Bronx friends and family would always be a part of his roots and would influence his life's choices whether he liked it or not. But he also realized, as he turned onto the Cross Bronx Expressway and almost fell off the milk box, that he was now a police officer, one of New York's Finest, and he needed to hold himself to a higher standard than ordinary individuals. He understood he still had a lot to learn about life and about work; he was determined to absorb every aspect of his job, so he could become the best police officer he could possibly be.

6

Feeling Bloated

IT WAS THE END OF JULY IN 1985 and a heat wave was attacking the city. The temperature daily for fifteen days was in excess of ninety degrees. Humidity filled the streets and the air felt like a wool blanket smothering you. The city had opened cooling centers in the poorest neighborhoods where people had no air conditioning. These cooling centers found themselves full of homeless people, the elderly, and anyone who was attempting to escape the oppressive heat. In these centers, crimes sometimes took place if you left your valuables unattended. On this particular day, Officer Franco, having one such center on his foot post, was summoned by the director at the front door of an elementary school, because there was a problem. As he walked into the center, cold air rushed to meet him, and he thought to himself, *this is a good place to hang out.* He was directed to a row of cots set up in the school's gymnasium and was told two people were fighting over a pair of shoes. When he approached the two, one man with a long beard, who appeared to be down on his luck, started to walk away. As Franco motioned for him to come towards him, the man cursed at him in Spanish and continued to walk. The other individual, whom he seemed to be arguing with, told Officer Franco, "He stole my shoes and he's wearing them now. I need them back 'cause I have to walk to Fordham Road to pick up my son from his mother." The man was visibly agitated and was spitting as he spoke. Franco walked over to the gentleman wearing the sneakers and he could tell the sneakers weren't his, as they were the only things he was wearing that were clean. Franco thought to himself, *now I have to get this guy to take off these sneakers and I'm sure his feet stink. If it were me, I wouldn't even want them back.*

He approached the sneaker thief who was getting a drink of water at the fountain in the hallway and obviously trying to avoid the officer. He assumed that his nasty response would deter the officer from approaching him. Franco removed his nightstick from its holder and walked over to the sneaker thief.

"I need to speak with you," he told him, adding. "Don't walk away from me again"

"Que Paso?" the man asked with a crazy look in his eyes.

"Whose shoes are those?" Franco asked.

"Me shoes," the man shot back.

"No, no, no," Franco told him. "Take them off."

As he stood there with his nightstick in his hand, the homeless man looked him up and down.

"You no hit me with that stick," the man stated.

"I no hit you with this stick if you take off the shoes," Franco shot back, "and I'm not going to wait all day."

He looked into Franco's eyes and probably could sense that he was losing his patience. He sat down on the steps in the hall of the facility and slowly untied the sneakers. He pulled one off and Franco noticed that his sock was gray in color and had several holes. He could see through the holes that his feet were filthy. Franco stood far enough away to avoid smelling his nasty feet. He motioned for the other man to come over as the homeless man removed the second sneaker. That foot had no sock on it at all. Although he was a light skinned Hispanic man, his foot was black. As the original owner of the sneakers came over, Franco kicked them in his direction. The man bent down and picked up the sneakers. He looked at Franco and Franco just shrugged his shoulders back at him. Feeling that there would be a physical confrontation between the two if he left, Franco asked the director of the facility if there was security on hand. He was told that there was and Franco noticed in the corner an old man wearing a powder blue security shirt and jeans. He thought to himself, *real tight security.* He suggested they ask the homeless man to leave for fear of a future confrontation. The director asked Officer Franco if he could tell the homeless man to leave and they would watch out for him at the door and not allow him back if he should return. When he escorted the homeless, shoeless, one sock man out the front door, he told him not to come back. He reluctantly walked out the door with Franco, and stated, "muy caliente."

Franco responded, "Mucho. I know, I'm out here with you. Don't come back. If you do, I'll lock you up."

The man asked, "You got air conditioning in jail?" Franco just shook his head, knowing the man didn't care where he was as long as he stayed cool.

As Franco started to walk away, he heard the Sergeant calling his foot post over the radio. "Four- four post nine on the air?"

"Post nine." he answered over his radio.

"What's your location?" his Sergeant asked.

"One seven o and the conk," Franco replied. "The conk" is a nickname that the officers use for the Grand Concourse, a major thoroughfare that runs through the Bronx.

"Stand by," the Sergeant instructed. A minute or so later, the Sergeant drove up with his chauffeur, Billy Mulroy. Mulroy was in the same squad as Franco and they worked together on foot posts several times. Franco called him "Sunshine" because he was always tan and spent his days off in the Hamptons with his wealthy family, a very different life than Franco experienced. Franco had affection for Sunshine because even though his family had money, he elected to become a cop and from what Sunshine had told Franco, his father was dead set against it. Nevertheless, Sunshine was defiant to the point of possibly being disowned by his family. He respected the fact that Sunshine chose to live his own life when it would have been very easy for him to just ride the gravy train. Sunshine seemed to drive the Sergeant a lot, probably because the Sergeant wanted to spend some time in the Hamptons himself.

Franco saluted the Sergeant and inquired, "What's up, boss? You already scratched me." The Sergeant, who already had done Franco a solid back on Hoe Avenue, was about to fuck up Franco's day.

"Seems like we have a DOA in an apartment on your post, and I need you to go in through the window and open the apartment door for us. You're probably going to have to sit on the DOA until the ME comes."

Franco got in the back of the RMP and they drove a short two blocks to Sherman Avenue.

"You sure this is part of my post?" he asked the Sergeant, but he knew it was.

"I'm sure, Franco; I've been working the 4-4 for 19 years, any other stupid questions?"

He sat there quietly, breathing in the air conditioning from the RMP. He knew it would be the last moment of air conditioning he would feel for the rest of the day. Sweat ran down his back and he could feel it dripping down the crack of his ass. He thought to himself, *at least I'll be able to take off this vest, if I have to sit on this DOA.* He was trying to find the bright side of the situation.

They exited the RMP and the Sergeant told him the apartment was 4D. They did not want to force the door open, but the smell in the hallway was definitely death. If the police must force the door open, they have to prepare an aided card and the city has to pay for the door to be repaired, also they will have to secure the apartment until the door is fixed. So most of the time, they will try to gain access through a window. As the three climbed the stairs, they could smell the unmistakable stench of death even as they approached the first floor landing. The Sergeant told Franco to go up to the roof, go down the fire escape, and look through the window to see if anything or anyone was visible. Sergeant O'Malley and Sunshine waited at the door of apartment 4D while he continued up to the roof.

As he started to descend the fire escape, he remembered all too well his fear of heights. Fire escapes in the South Bronx are not in the best of shape. He thought to himself, *when was the last time this fucking thing was inspected by anybody?* It was rusty, very old, and seemed to be missing some important parts, like brackets that were supposed to be screwed into the building. Franco, being 6 feet tall and 220 pounds, wondered what his police funeral would be like and who would show up. He pictured his mother and father, grandmother and sisters, all carrying on in front of his casket. He also envisioned the guys from the precinct standing around making plans to go out drinking in his honor. *Fuck it*, he thought as he snapped back to reality. *I gotta do what I gotta do*, so he began his descent. He kept telling himself not to look down. He could feel the whole fire escape moving as he slowly and gingerly worked his way down from the six story rooftop. *Only two floors*, he thought to himself. *And you don't want the guys to think you're a pussy.* At one point, his radio holder caught on to the edge of the fire escape causing his entire gun belt to be pulled up towards his chest. *Shit*, he thought, *I'm gonna break my fucking neck.* But he made his way down to the fourth floor and felt a sense of relief. He couldn't wait to climb through that apartment window until he looked through it and had a rude awakening.

He could clearly see what appeared to be a very large black woman lying face up on a hardwood living room floor. He did not smell anything, and could not tell if she had been dead for a while from his vantage point. He radioed to Sergeant O'Malley that there was indeed a DOA lying on the floor. Sergeant O'Malley asked if he could gain access from the window. Franco attempted to pry the window open with his 007 knife that he kept between his gun belt and his holster. But the window was locked and no access was possible without breaking the glass. He really wanted to get off this fire escape and asked the Sergeant if he should break the window.

Sergeant O'Malley stated, "Break it with your night stick, but make sure you turn your face away when you do it. The girls on Hoe Avenue don't want to have to lead you around their apartment if you're blind." The Sergeant was making reference to when Franco, only having a few days on the street six months prior, was caught in an uncompromising position in a Hoe Avenue apartment with two pretty Puerto Rican sisters. Franco laughed aloud and thought to himself, *I love my Sergeant. He's always looking out for me.* With that, he tapped on the window, turning his head away, but the window did not break. *Ok a little harder*, he thought and the next shot shattered the entire bottom pane. Instantly, a disgusting, foul, rancid odor hit Franco in his face, as if the apartment was fighting back. *Oh my God,"* he thought to himself, *this is the stinkiest DOA I ever smelled."* He only had four others to compare it to, but this was surely the ripest. The apartment had to be 150 degrees with all windows being shut and filled with two weeks of oppressive heat. He pulled his uniform shirt over his nose and radioed back to the Sergeant that the window was broken. The Sergeant told him to clear all the glass from the frame, to climb in carefully and to open the apartment door. As he entered the apartment and walked past the woman lying on the floor, he noticed her skin was black but she looked to be Hispanic. The apartment was neat and nothing seemed to be out of place, but the smell was making him sick. There were several statutes of Mother Mary and Jesus set up around the apartment almost like a shrine. It reminded Franco of his paternal Grandmother's house, also located in the Bronx. He ran over to the front door, unlocked three Medico bolt locks, and opened the door allowing access for the Sergeant and Sunshine, holding his breath the entire time. Finally he was able to take a deep breath once in the hall and he told Sunshine, "Damn does it stink in there!" Sunshine shot back "You've had women that smelled worse!" Franco laughed thinking his shitty assignment was over. He told the Sergeant he was going to run downstairs and have a cigarette.

"Wait, wait, wait, me boy," Sergeant O'Malley exclaimed. "You need to search the body." Franco being sure the Sergeant was fucking with him laughed and took two steps towards the stairway.

"Didn't ya hear me, me boy?" Sergeant O'Malley repeated.

"You're not serious, are you Sarge?, search her for what, she's not under arrest!"

"Now, you know what they taught you in the Academy. Every DOA needs to be searched for property and identification."

With that, Sergeant O'Malley reached into his leather memo book holder and pulled out a pair of rubber gloves, handing them to Franco.

"Hey Sunshine," Franco asked, "This would be good practice for you. I don't think you've had a DOA, have you?"

Never a Dull Moment

"I'm the Sergeant's operator," Sunshine shot back. "It's your post, your DOA, plus the Sergeant and me are going to hang out at my Hampton house this weekend and he wouldn't do that to me."

The Sergeant looked at Sunshine, puzzled, and obviously had no knowledge of this Hampton weekend getaway.

"Your post, Franco," the Sergeant stated, "your job. Sometimes you touch pretty Puerto Rican girls; sometimes you touch old dead people." He reluctantly took the gloves from the Sergeant, put them on and went over to the dead woman. She was wearing a yellow housecoat typical of elderly Spanish women. She had no shoes on and her feet were swollen to the point that it looked like she was going to burst. Her skin was charcoal black and appeared to be almost leather-like, making Franco think that she had been dead for quite some time. Her entire body seemed to be extremely bloated. He didn't have much experience in this area, but it seemed to be common sense. There were a lot of flies in the apartment and he wondered where they were coming from. His skin was crawling as he reached down and stuck his hand into the right side pocket of the housecoat.

"Nothing there" he quickly said out loud, and then reached over to the left one. "No, she's good Sarge, "nothing on her."

He went to walk away, but the Sergeant, seemingly unaffected by the smell, walked over and told him, "What about her pants?"

Franco rolled his eyes, not understanding why the ME's office couldn't tell them if she had anything on her when they got her to the morgue. But, he didn't say anything, and ran his hands over the outside of her legs, feeling her pockets. He was getting grossed out and momentarily thought of that good time on Hoe Avenue to take his mind off of this. That was the best day on patrol so far, and this day might be the worst.

"No, nothing Sarge," he stated as he began to walk away again. He felt like he was holding his breath for so long that he could be a world class diver.

"Just one minute, Franco," the Sergeant exclaimed.

What now? Franco thought.

"You need to roll her over and search the back of her to see if she has any rear pockets."

He felt like he was going to cry. He couldn't stand touching this nasty body but the Sergeant reminded him that this was probably someone's loved one and that they needed to do the right thing by her.

Sergeant O'Malley told Sunshine to run down and get the super of the building to see if he knew her name and possibly her next of kin. As Sunshine exited the apartment, he yelled to Franco, "I'll smoke that cigarette for you while I'm downstairs."

Franco shot back, "Blow me."

So Franco bent down, took the woman's right leg and placed it over her left, put one hand on her hip and the other one on her shoulder and gently tried to roll her over onto her stomach. He remembered what the Sergeant said about her having a family and tried to treat her with as much dignity as he could but he really wanted to do this quickly, as he felt sick to his stomach. As he tried to roll her over, he found it difficult to move her. She actually seemed stuck to the hardwood floor.

"She's not moving, Sarge," Franco stated.

"Use a little elbow grease," the Sergeant shot back. With that, he gave a big push and what happened next was something out a horror movie. The woman's back and buttocks literally stuck to the hardwood floor causing her body to rip open, exposing thousand of maggots. Franco was horrified and jumped back and ran towards the Sergeant.

"Holy shit" he exclaimed.

"I actually never saw anything like that" the Sergeant said. "Maybe we should wait for the ME."

Good idea, Franco thought. The smell that came out of the woman's body was horrific and apparently all the gases that had built up inside of her had caused her to appear bloated. The super had a phone number for the woman's son, who lived in Westchester New York. He was a pharmacist and would visit her once a month or so. Sunshine called him from the super's apartment and he learned the son had just gotten back from a three week European vacation and last spoke to his mother two days before he left. She probably died shortly after that. Sunshine broke the bad news to him and he was extremely upset over the phone, blaming himself for not calling her while he was away. Sunshine assured him there was nothing he could have done and she probably had experienced a heart attack. As Mulroy returned to the apartment, the Sergeant directed both he and Franco to open every window and to go down to the bodega on the corner to see if they could get incense or scented candles.

The super arrived at the door and was visibly upset, having known the woman, Mrs. Maria Hernandez, for more than thirty years. He told the Sergeant she was a sweet lady who went to church on a regular basis and sang in the choir. The super asked if there was anything he could do and the Sergeant asked if he had a fan he could bring to the apartment. He did and returned with it. The Sergeant set up the fan to blow the air from the apartment out the broken window. Mulroy and Franco returned a short time later with incense and scented candles and strategically placed them around the apartment. Two detectives from the 4-4 squad arrived on the scene. They looked at Mrs. Hernandez, walked around the apartment for a minute or so, took a couple of Polaroid pictures of her, and told the Sergeant, "It looks like natural causes."

One of the detectives, wearing a blue sports coat, and a tie that came only halfway down his big belly, stated, "The ME will make the final determination." They didn't seem to want to stick around and Franco thought *who could blame them*? He envied the fact that they could just walk in, take a look, snap a couple of pictures and leave. He thought to himself, *One day that's going to be me. Have some schmuck rookie sitting here breathing in this nasty stink while I go back to my nice air conditioned detective squad room.*

Before the ME arrived, the Sergeant directed Franco to fill out a 95 tag (toe tag) and to complete the other necessary paperwork now that they knew the deceased's name. The ME arrived a short time later and the two morgue attendants had a hard time dislodging the body from the hardwood floor. One of them went down to his truck and came back with what appeared to be a large ice scraper attached to a long metal pole. One attendant attempted to lift a portion of the body while the other wedged the scraper underneath her. At this point, maggots were crawling all over the immediate area and one of the attendants made a comment that this was one of the worst ones this week. He was a tall skinny black man with a candy cane sticking out of his mouth. Franco found this odd being it was the end of July. He thought, *that candy cane must be really old; maybe it was some type of trick to keep the taste of death out of your mouth."*

He asked the attendant, "Why do you have a candy cane in your mouth?"

And the attendant, with a puzzled look on his face, shot back, ""I like candy canes."

Franco thought, *ask a stupid question, you get a stupid answer*. They finally pried her off the floor, put her in a black rubber bag and zipped it up. They were removing her to the morgue for an autopsy. The apartment was searched for any valuables, but there didn't seem to be any. The super assured the Sergeant he would get a glazer to fix the window and he would clean the stained floor along with the bugs, before her son arrived at the apartment. The son had told Mulroy that he was on his way and would be there in about forty minutes. Sergeant O'Malley didn't want the son to see the area where his mother died looking the way it did now. Word of Mrs. Hernandez death filled the neighborhood, as the morgue personnel carried her out of the building in the big black bag, people in the street, having known Mrs. Hernandez, stood on the sidewalk weeping. They made several comments, both in English and in Spanish, of how she was such a good woman and made the sign of the cross as she was carried past where they were standing. It made Franco realized that it's not just a DOA, it's someone's mother, it's someone's friend. He thought he had it bad, having to touch her, but it was still a lot better than being in her shoes. What the Sergeant taught him about dignity for a dead person stayed with him for the rest of his career.

7

Trust

AFTER OFFICER FRANCO COMPLETED HIS TIME IN N.S.U., he received his orders and was assigned to his permanent command, the 47th Precinct located on Laconia Avenue in the East Bronx. This precinct is huge and covers 5.2 square miles. It consists of multiple family dwellings and five different housing projects, one more dangerous than the next. These housing projects are: The Edenwald Houses, The Hillside Houses, The Gunhill Houses, The Olinville Houses, and the Baychester Houses. Housing projects are large groups of apartment buildings within a complex. Some of these complexes consist of twenty or more buildings and are usually ten stories or more. It makes for a huge population crammed into a very small space, which is not really conducive to peaceful coexistence. The Edenwald projects, the largest housing complex in the Bronx, consists of forty buildings that are fourteen stories tall on 49 acres. It has 2,036 apartments, housing approximately 8,000 people. It is divided into two parts, the north side and the south side and is located directly across the street from the Precinct.

On Officer Franco's second night in his permanent command, he observed a hand to hand drug transaction while on a foot post at the corner of East 226th Street and Laconia Avenue, right in front of the Edenwald projects. He gave pursuit on foot, and apprehended the seller a few blocks away. Some marijuana was discovered on the perp, and Officer Franco radioed for a sector car to transport himself and the perp to the Precinct. The amount of marijuana was small and Officer Franco, after checking for any warrants, issued the perp a desk appearance ticket. He would have to appear in court on a later date to answer the charges. Franco grabbed a honey bun from the vending machine and made his way back to his foot post. He thought to himself, *not bad for my second night in a new command.* He was hoping to catch a bigger fish but he had nineteen years to go so a marijuana collar wasn't so bad.

46

As he walked back to his post he observed a motorist go through a stop sign making a right hand turn. He jumped off the curb and motioned for the motorist to pull over. He issued the summons without incident and walked back to his post. The rest of the night consisted of moving some skells off his post and writing a few parking tickets. He got back to the command just before midnight, signed out changed out of his uniform, and went home.

The next day he received a call at home from the roll call officer asking him to come in to see him before he gets dressed for the 4 to12 tour. Franco asked what was wrong and the roll call guy assured him that everything was fine but he did not want to speak over the phone. It was approximately 1:00 P.M. and he did not have to be at work until 3:35. Franco's mind began to race; he could not figure out why the roll call officer would want to speak to him. The roll call officer is a clerical position within the precinct. He is responsible for assigning details, partners, overtime, and he prepares the roll calls. He is usually someone with many years on the job and can make your life miserable if he does not like you. Franco thought; *I've only been here two nights, why would he need to speak to me?* His stomach was in knots the rest of the day.

As Franco entered the precinct, he asked the desk officer where roll call was located. He was directed to an office in the rear of the precinct. The door was closed so he knocked. He was told to enter and he introduced himself and asked for the roll call officer. He was warmly greeted by an elderly officer sitting at a desk who introduced himself as Patsy Lombardo. He had a genuine smile and he extended his hand to Officer Franco. He did not know what to make of this show of friendship. He was always told that the old timers wouldn't even talk to a rookie for sometimes years, and here was this guy who looked like he had thirty years on, seeking him out and being rather friendly. He was definitely suspicious. Lombardo went on to explain that he was the union delegate and he had been in this command for over twenty five years. Franco stood there with nothing much to say except, "pleased to meet you." Lombardo went on to ask him if he had issued a summons for a stop sign last night. Franco's mind began to race, *what was this all about,* he thought? He answered "yes" and Lombardo proceeded to tell him that the person he gave the ticket to owns one of the local junk yards and he does the right thing for the guys. He further stated that he called him today and asked Lombardo if there was anything he could do about the ticket. Lombardo explained when the guys need parts he takes care of them. His mind was racing. *Is this some kind of integrity test? Is he being set up?* He could feel sweat beading on his forehead; he didn't know how to answer. Lombardo, sensing his uneasiness, told Franco "It's just a stop sign." That was not the problem as far as Franco was concerned. He did not care about a stop sign summons; he cared if this was a set-up. His head was spinning. He wanted to do the right thing and he wanted to be accepted as a good guy in his new command. He also knew the roll call guy could either take care of you or fuck you every chance he got. It was time to make a decision.

Franco leaned close to Lombardo and in the sternest voice he could muster for someone who was scared shit, he told Lombardo, "Okay I'll take care of the summons, but I'm telling you now old man, if this is a set up and I get fucked for doing the right thing you'll regret it.

Lombardo let out a huge laugh. "You have a huge pair of balls kid." Is that what you're worried about, a set up?" he asked. "I'll tell ya what," he said, "go around and ask the guys that have time on about me. I'm your union rep for God's sake. Then come back when you feel comfortable and let me know what you're gonna do."

"That's not necessary," he shot back. "I said I would take care of it. I'm one of the guys, and I'm a team player. It's just that I've been here two days and I've heard stories about integrity tests and being set up and I don't know any of you guys."

Lombardo, obviously feeling for Franco's situation, put his arm around him and stated, "I appreciate your honesty, and I assure you it's not a test, or a set up. It's just your union delegate asking you to do him a favor."

With that the two men shook hands and Franco exited the roll call office a little more grown up than when he entered. He made the ticket disappear and Officer Lombardo looked out for Franco until the day Lombardo retired.

8

Volkswagen

JOEY GIZZO WASN'T EXACTLY WHAT YOU WOULD CALL great partner material. For one thing, he was difficult to understand, and sometimes perps would actually mock his lisp when he directed them to do something. Giovanni would have to set them straight, and while he didn't mind being the "bad cop," he didn't like the lack of respect many of the general public displayed for Joey. He saw it as his job to correct them. Secondly, Joey couldn't drive for shit. He hit the brakes too hard, and worst of all, if the officers were in their sector car, waiting at a red light at night with Joey at the wheel, he would fall asleep or sometimes nod off. "Man, do you have narcolepsy?" Giovanni would ask. "Whath narolethy?" Joey would demand. So most of the driving fell upon Giovanni, which was actually a good thing because Giovanni was an excellent driver. He ranked second out of 3000 recruits in his Academy class at Floyd Bennett Field, an old abandoned airport in Brooklyn, where the driver training course is given to probationary police officers. He actually could not believe some other recruit had bested his time, if only by .08 of a second. But being that they worked together often in N.S.U. and now they found themselves permanently assigned to the 4-7, it was inevitable that they become partners.

Officers Franco and Gizzo were working a 12 midnight to 8 A.M. tour, and they turned out at 11:35. Police tours always overlap so there will always be police on the street. It was a freezing December night and the officers had handled a bunch of jobs already. There was a domestic violence job, two drunk gay guys fighting in their apartment over one of them flirting with the super, and an emotionally disturbed person, who apparently didn't take his meds and had to be sent to Jacobi Hospital Psych Ward. Luckily, Franco and Gizzo would only back up these jobs and didn't get stuck with them directly. Finally at around 3 A.M., the two officers pulled into Dunkin Donuts Drive Thru window and got two large cups of coffee. Franco asked Gizzo how he takes his, "I like my coffee black, juth like my women." Then the next thing out of his mouth was, "Get me three creamerth." Franco ordered his, milk, no sugar, smiled at the pretty Spanish girl giving him the coffee through the window, and then got annoyed when she charged him full price. "What'th thith world coming to? Doesth that bitch know who we are? No dick for her!" said Gizzo. Both officers laughed as they drove out the Drive Thru. They proceeded back to their sector, 4-7 Henry, hoping to pull over and drink their coffee in the RMP. It had just started snowing about a half an hour prior. A few minutes later the Central Dispatcher or Central, as the officers call it, gave 4-7 Adam a gun run. The job was: man with a gun, shots fired. Franco and Gizzo were the first ones on the back even though their sector was the furthest away. Other sectors stated they were also backing up the job, and the guys knew there should be plenty of backup. The Officers were at White Plains Road and 241st Street near *Pepino's Pizzeria* right under the elevated 2 train. Being rookies, they wanted to get to the job quickly, and headed south on White Plains Road at a high rate of speed. They both tossed their coffees out the window. There were no cup holders in cars back then. Gizzo commented, "That's two dollars down the drain." Franco told him, "What the fuck are you bitching about; I'm the one who paid for it." The two were flying down White Plains Road and could hear over the radio there was a sector car in pursuit. Central asked 4-7 Henry their location. Franco looked to the left and noticed he was passing 221st Street. He told Gizzo to tell Central 219th. The next radio transmission that the officers heard was the pursuit of a station wagon wanted in connection with the shots fired. Franco's adrenaline was flowing and he was determined to get there to help. The roads were very slippery due to the snow that had been falling now for more than a half hour. Giovanni, so far, was handling the sector car really well, despite the bad weather.

Gizzo asked, 'Giovanni, if we grab these guys before Adam, do we keep the collar?"

Giovanni shot back, "Only if you're a scumbag. It's their job, they get the collar."

When they get to 216th Street there is a fork in the road where the Gunhill Road train station is located. At that point, southbound traffic goes around the station and north bound goes to the left. As Franco approaches the turn, his car starts sliding. Franco knows how to handle a skidding car and cuts the wheel in the direction of the skid. But the icy roads and the rear wheel drive are too much for even his driving expertise and the RMP continues to slide. The officers see the car is going to crash into the el pillar and they are going to hit the pillar on the passenger side, exactly where Joey is sitting.

"Oh thit!" Joey screams as he jumps onto Giovanni's lap to avoid being hurt in the collision. The sector car fishtails and slams into the pillar. Officers do not normally wear seatbelts, as they sometimes need to exit the vehicle quickly and disengaging a seatbelt would slow down their exiting the vehicle. Luckily they are not severely injured. The car's ashtray popped out from the dashboard and hit Giovanni in the forehead, causing him to bleed. Joey is moaning that his leg hurts, but it doesn't appear to be broken and looks more like a contusion.

"Get off my fucking lap!" Giovanni yells at Joey.

Joey, ever the comedian, gives Giovanni a kiss on his cheek. But this is no laughing matter. They now have to call this accident in to Central and tell them they were involved in a 10-53, a collision. Central asks how many vehicles were involved and Franco cringes as he responds, "One."

Central asks "Are there any injuries?" and Franco looks over at Joey and asks, "You're not hurt, right?"

Joey states, "Yeah, I am, my fucking leg is killing me and I'm thuing you."

Franco shoots back, "Can you fucking be serious for one minute please, I have to give her an answer."

"Yeah Giovanni, my leg is really hurting."

With that, Franco tells Central, "one injury but its minor." Central states that she's dispatching the Patrol Supervisor to the location. Central tells them that they will send a bus (ambulance) and that the Duty Captain has been notified. The Duty Captain was basically known to be a scumbag. Officer Franco could picture it now. He would probably lose a week of vacation and be made to walk for months.

"God damn it, Joey, this is bad. What are we gonna say? We were involved in a one car accident. I don't want to walk for the next year!"

"It wathn't your fault, "Joey says as he tries to console Giovanni. "The road wath sthlippery."

"It makes no fucking difference. I was 100% wrong and I know it, and the Duty Captain is going to know it too! We should have never backed up the job being so far away." Giovanni's adrenaline, spiked from the speed of the car and the accident, is causing his brain to race. He's not the kind to go down without a fight, so he figures there has to be a way around this.

"Okay listen to me." Giovanni tells Joey as he is looking down, rubbing his leg. "Hey, are you listening to me? This is fucking important. It's my ass, not yours, on the line here. The Duty Captain will be here any minute!'

"I'm lithening, I'm lithening," Joey replies. "Why don't we tell the Duty Captain that we just hit the pole?"

"No, no we need a story about WHY we hit the pole. Okay, remember as we were driving, we heard them say something about a station wagon that was getting away. They said it was heading northbound, which would mean it was coming right for us."

"Yeah, tho? My leg hurth."

"Please can you listen for just a minute?" Franco begs. "The station wagon, it was coming right towards us. We can say we hit the pole to avoid the station wagon, and even better, to make it more believable, let's say that the station wagon had one headlight out."

Franco hears the ambulance sirens approaching. "Do you understand Joey? Tell me, what are you going to say to the Duty Captain?"

"Um um it wath coming right at uth. We hit the pole to avoid it."

"We hit the pole to avoid what?" Franco demanded. "Come on, tell me the story! We have to have our stories straight!"

"We hit the pole to avoid the thathin wagon. I know it. I know it. Ow my leg hurth" Joey complained.

"What was different about the station wagon?" Franco asked, his patience clearly wearing thin as the approaching sirens got louder.

"There wath a headlight out!" Joey screamed.

"That's right" Franco said, "passenger side headlight. Got it Joey? Please don't fuck this up. Now repeat it back to me."

"You're pithing me off," Joey said. "I underthand, I'm not retarded."

"Okay" Franco said and he repeated the whole thing for him again. "Remember, station wagon, one headlight, passenger side." With that, Joey gives Franco the finger.

The ambulance arrives and it brings them to the hospital. An officer has been assigned to safeguard their weapons while they were being treated. Officer Franco is in triage, receiving stitches, while Officer Gizzo is being seen by the Emergency Room staff. He is not able to talk to Joey again and is worried about whether the Duty Captain will buy their story or not. Sure enough, the Duty Captain shows up at the hospital.

Although Officer Franco feels that his story will hold up and be believable, he is also worried because the Duty Captain has a reputation of being a prick and as rookies might want to make an example of them. Franco is anxious to talk to him and get past this whole ordeal. Joey is in x-ray and Giovanni knows that the Duty Captain must have already spoken with him and he anxiously awaits his turn.

The Duty Captain approaches him and Franco throws him a highball (salute).

"Officer Franco," the Duty Captain affirms in a strong authoritative voice. "Tell me what happened tonight."

Franco tells the Duty Captain that they were backing up a gun run and that they came to a split in the road at 216th Street and White Plains Road when they saw a car coming right at them, head on. Franco explained that he believed that it was the same car that sector Adam was chasing related to the gun run, and shots fired that got away. To avoid colliding head on with the vehicle, he tells the Duty Captain that he attempted to maneuver the sector car around the escaping vehicle and wound up hitting the el pillar.

"What kind of car was approaching you, Officer?" the Duty Captain asks looking directly into Giovanni's eyes.

"A station wagon, sir, with one headlight out," Giovanni asserts as confidently as he can.

The Duty Captain squints his eyes at Giovanni and repeats, "What kind of car?"

"A station wagon, sir"

The Duty Captain crosses his arms over his chest and takes a deep breath. "A station wagon, huh. That's not what your partner said."

Giovanni's mind begins to race. *He's being a scumbag*, he thinks. *He's trying to trick me.*

The Duty Captain leans forward towards Giovanni and says in a quieter, but still very firm voice, "That's not what your partner said. Go talk to your partner. I'll give you a couple of minutes to get your story straight."

He's fucking with me, Giovanni thinks. "No sir, I don't need to talk to my partner. My story is straight." Giovanni stubbornly insists.

The Duty Captain sighs in exasperation, "you sure that you don't want to talk to your partner?"

"I'm sure sir, talking to my partner won't change anything."

"Okay" says the Duty Captain, as he brushes his hands together, as though washing himself clean of Giovanni's problems, "You want to stick with that story. Your CO will get my report and recommendation." With that, the Duty Captain gets up to go.

Giovanni is on pins and needles, and cannot wait to go in to talk to Joey, but he wants to be sure that the Duty Captain is out of the hospital. He asks the officer who is safeguarding his gun if in fact the Duty Captain is truly gone. He does not want the Duty Captain to see him run off to talk with his partner.

"Yeah, he's gone," the officer responds. "He didn't look too happy either."

He quickly makes his way over to see Joey.

"Joey" he asks, "Did you talk to the Duty Captain?"

"Yep," Joey answers.

He wants to strangle him already. "Okay, make believe I'm the Duty Captain. Tell me what you said?"

"Cut the thit, Franco; I thaid what you told me to thay," Joey replied as he lay on a hospital gurney in his boxer shorts.

"Just humor me please," Giovanni pleaded. "What did you say?"

Joey bobbed his head from side to side and said in a sing song voice, "I told him the guy was coming thraight at uth, the car was gonna hit uth thraight on, you cut the wheel real fath.'

"What KIND of car?" Giovanni begged.

"A Volkswagen, with one headlight out."

"A Volkswagen with one headlight out!" Giovanni repeated in disbelief. But his shock soon turned to anger. "I told you STATION WAGON, not Volkswagen!" They were chasing a station wagon. "The car that got away was a station wagon."

In the early eighties, there was only one Volkswagen, the round little two door car that when spotted on the road, kids would give each other punches, hence its nickname, Punch Buggy. By contrast, a station wagon was always a very long vehicle with four doors, it could hold seven or eight passengers. There could be no mistaking the two.

Joey shrugged and smiled his simpleton smile, "thathon wagon, volthswagen, what's the fucking difference?"

"The difference is I'm gonna have to walk in the freezing cold, on the fucking midnight tour because you're a fucking moron, that's the fucking difference."

So Giovanni left the hospital with three stitches in his forehead and a knot in the pit of his stomach. Joey had a wrap on his leg and a prescription for painkillers. As the two men were driven back to the station house, Joey turned to Giovanni and said, "thorry I fucked up, but I'll come by your foot post as often as I can. And don't worry; I'm not going to thue you." Giovanni just shook his head, knowing tomorrow he would learn his fate.

The CO found Officer Franco to be grossly negligent and he was made to walk for sixty days. This being the dead of winter the punishment was all the more cruel. To add insult to injury, Joey would frequently drive by with his new partner and hold a hot cup of coffee up to Franco through the sector car window. The problem was the window wasn't open and he wasn't offering it to Giovanni. As Giovanni would approach the car, they would drive off laughing. So for all his expert driving skills, Officer Franco did not touch the steering wheel of a sector car for the next two months, while Joey sat in a warm RMP. But this is an officer's life. You will be fucked with by your fellow officers and you will fuck with them too, whenever humanly possible. But at the same time, the officers always looked out for each other and so too then, Joey looked out for Giovanni. Whenever possible, he sat with Joey and his new partner in the sector car, at least while they weren't on a call.

Although he was a rookie, Giovanni had already established many relationships with seasoned cops and bosses at the precinct. During his punishment, the roll call officer would frequently find a post for him inside the precinct, or assign him the Station House Security post. This meant his post was right outside the front door, basically protecting the precinct from any type of attack or invasion which frequently happened in the Bronx in the early '80s. Sometimes an incident between police and civilians would spill back to the Precinct, and the Precinct would find itself under attack. The locals would sometimes attack the officer's personal vehicles parked around the station house. The Station House Security Officer was an important post during those times. The 47th Precinct wasn't called Fort Laconia for nothing.

9

How Typical

ONE 4 TO 12 SHIFT, FRANCO AND GIZZO, WORKING sector Adam, responded twice to the same address of a family dispute. It seemed the husband was somewhat drunk and arguing with his wife over anything he could think of. The first time the two officers arrived at the location, the wife stated that she didn't want to press charges; she just wanted him to leave her alone. The officers pulled the husband on the side and told him that if they had to come back again, they were going to arrest him. He was somewhat belligerent but seemed to get the message. They gave the job back, (10-91) Condition Corrected, and resumed patrol.

A short time later, Central dispatched them to the location again, stating that the wife had called back saying that her husband smacked her. Franco and Gizzo, when the job came over the radio, were in a bodega on East 236th Street and White Plains Road, talking to the owner's daughter who possessed a pair a 36 DDs and Gizzo seemed to be infatuated with her. Franco got a kick out of watching him trying to talk to her with his lisp. He knew Gizzo had no chance with her but found it very entertaining. The conversation went something like this:

"Tho what did you do thith weekend, thuthette?"

"Oh I just worked in the store," Suzzette replied.

"Tho your boyfriend didn't take you to the movies or out to dinner?"

"No I don't have a boyfriend," Suzzette replied.

"Thatth too bad," Gizzo sympathized as he stared at the cleavage before him.

Franco standing to the left of the counter with a cup of coffee in his hand chuckled as he watched Gizzo's lame attempt to pick up this hot young Spanish girl right in front of her father.

"So, Carlos," Franco exclaimed, "How would you like to have Gizzo as a son-in-law?"

"No fucking way!" Carlos shouted as he reached behind the counter and pulled out a machete and started waving it in the air in Gizzo's direction.

With a smile on his face, he told Gizzo, "My daughter is going to be the first one in our family to graduate college, and then she's gonna marry a doctor, not a silly cop who spits all over himself when he talks."

With that Franco and Carlos had a big laugh, but poor Gizzo didn't find it too funny.

Both he and Suzzette blushed as Gizzo's game was exposed.

"I'm not trying to pick up your daughter," Gizzo told Carlos. "I juth like her becauth thees a nice perthon."

"Okay Carlos," Franco said, "We gotta go to this call. We've been there already and this time the guy's going to get locked up for taking me away from all this fun."

Carlos invited them back for a cup of coffee if they got the chance. He then told Suzette to go in the back and do her homework.

The two officers left the bodega and headed over to the job on Barnes Avenue and 214th Street. Upon their arrival, they could hear loud arguing coming from inside this one family house. Franco banged on the door and announced "police." Surprisingly the husband opened the door and the two officers pushed their way inside. Gizzo took the husband into the living room and Franco went to speak to the wife in the kitchen. The wife told Franco that he smacked her in the face because she burnt his dinner. She did not feel it was burnt, it was just well done. It was some Jamaican concoction and when Franco looked in the pot he couldn't tell if it was burnt or not. He just knew it looked nasty and smelled worse. He thought to himself, *well he didn't marry her for her cooking and he didn't marry her for her looks, maybe she's a good conversationalist.* She was in excess of 200 pounds and had visible hair poking out from her arm pits covered by a dirty stained white tank top. *What a life* Franco thought as the woman pleaded with him not to arrest her husband. She had a visible welt on her face from where she was smacked and Franco had already warned the husband if they came back he was going to be arrested.

The woman sat in a chair and a young girl climbed up on her lap. She appeared to be no more than four years old. She asked her mommy if she was okay, because obviously she witnessed the whole fight. Franco asked her if she had any other children and she answered no. At this point Franco heard loud arguing between Gizzo and the husband and dashed into the living room. The two were fighting and Gizzo was attempting to hand-cuff the husband. He was a large man who stood approximately 6'4" and weighed 250 pounds. Franco came across the room holding his night stick across his body with both hands, slamming it into the man's back, causing him to be pressed up against the wall. He kneed the man between his legs from behind, and placed his stick around his throat in a carotid choke hold and took the man down to the floor.

As he and Gizzo attempted to cuff him, the wife was screaming to leave him alone. They had one wrist cuffed and were trying to get the other arm behind his back when the small girl ran up and kicked Franco in the side of his face as he was kneeling beside the suspect. Franco looked over at the wife and told her, "Get your kid out of this room." As Franco and Gizzo were applying the second handcuff, the young girl looked Franco right in the eye and told him, "Suck my dick."

Franco looked at Gizzo as they both knelt above the suspect with him fighting as they finally got the second handcuff applied. Gizzo got on the radio and called for backup as the man was still kicking and trying to bite the two officers. They held him down on the floor and the young girl taking both her hands and grabbing her crotch area, again told the two officers, "Suck my dick."

Franco again looked over at Gizzo and stated, "How typical. You can't make this shit up." Franco told the woman if she did not go back into the kitchen with her daughter, she would be arrested also. A short time later back up arrived and the suspect was removed to the precinct for processing. As the officers were leaving the house, the young girl making her hand into the shape of a gun, pointed it at Franco and made a shooting motion.

The Sergeant who had arrived on the scene asked Franco, "What's that all about?"

And Franco replied, "She's her father's daughter."

10

He Got Shafted

A RASH OF BURGLARIES HAD HIT THE 4-7 midnight tour for the last couple
of weeks. White Plains Road and Boston Road were especially affected. It
seemed that a group of burglars were entering through rooftops, making
their way down into a store, and then breaking through adjacent walls into
other stores that were all attached. Officer Giovanni Franco and Officer
Bobby Stutz had just turned out and were on their way to get some coffee at
the Baychester Diner. They heard an alarm come over and Central stated it
was the *Silver Chimes Restaurant* at the corner of Nereid Avenue and White
Plains Road. Officer Franco, being friendly with the owner Tommy, picked
up the job, even though it wasn't in their sector. He told Stutz, "Tommy's a
good guy and does the right thing."

They shot over to Nereid Avenue but the metal gates were down and
it seemed secure. There were tiny slots in the gate where you could look
through. They attempted to see into the restaurant with their flashlights,
but didn't see anything out of place. When Franco radioed to Central and
asked her how the job came over, she stated it was a 911 call. They didn't
hear any audible alarm and wondered who could have called this in. Central stated she had just gotten a second call and it seemed that the perp was
on the phone with her and she was having a hard time hearing him, but
he told her he was stuck in a metal vent. Central further informed them
she was still on the phone with him; somehow he was able to call 911. He
stated he was unable to move and having difficulty breathing. As Franco
positioned his flashlight again at the small opening in the gate, he directed
the light towards the grill. He thought he saw something dangling above it.
It was very hard to see so he asked Stutz what he thought it was.

"Oh shit," Stutz said. "It looks like two feet."

"Don't tell me this guy's stuck in the exhaust vent above the grill," Franco exclaimed.

They notified Central of what they thought they saw and she dispatched Emergency Service. Franco being friendly with Tommy the owner, had his phone number because Tommy had let Franco use his house upstate to go snowmobiling last winter. Tommy lived a short distance away in Yonkers, New York and although it was now one in the morning, Franco thought if they could get Tommy to open the restaurant, it would save them a lot of aggravation. He wasn't really concerned about the guy dangling in the vent, but he didn't want to get stuck on this job all night either. So he went to a pay phone, put in a quarter, and called Tommy's house. A woman answered the phone and she had obviously been sleeping. Franco explained who he was, apologized for calling so late, and asked to speak to Tommy. Tommy's restaurant had been burglarized several months ago and Tommy swore if he ever caught the guy, he would kill him.

Tommy was an old school Greek man with a hot temper and had the biggest hairiest eyebrows you have ever seen. Tommy got on the phone.

"Tommy, it's Giovanni from the 4-7. I think we got the guy who broke into your store."

Tommy sounded happy and assumed that Franco was talking about the prior burglary a few months ago. When Franco explained there was a guy stuck in his grill vent at this moment, Tommy exclaimed, "I kill him!"

Giovanni told Tommy to get to the restaurant right away before Emergency Service had to rip the gates off the front.

"Don't rip no gates,' Tommy pleaded. "I'll be there in five minutes."

Tommy and Emergency Service arrived almost simultaneously. When Giovanni saw Tommy, he couldn't help but giggle. He was wearing blue slippers, green pajama pants, and a white tank top with tufts of hair sticking out everywhere. He already had the keys to the gate in his hand as he exited the car, a big red Cadillac El Dorado. Franco thought to himself, *He looks like a Greek colorblind pimp.*

When Tommy saw Giovanni, he ran over to him with keys in hand.

"Okay open up Tommy and promise me you're not going to touch this guy 'cause you'll get me in trouble."

Giovanni had a sneaky suspicion Tommy might be armed yet he really didn't want to know one way or the other. Tommy opened the gates and by this time there were about six sector cars pulled up to the restaurant because they had heard of this rather unique occurrence. Tommy opened the gate and about fifteen cops rushed in. When Tommy went over to the light switch panel and turned on all the lights, all everyone could see were two feet wearing quite expensive Michael Jordan high tops, dangling above the grill.

Franco and Stutz walked over to the feet and Franco yelled, "Santa, what have you brought me for Christmas?"

All the guys laughed but the man in the vent didn't think it was too funny.

"Help me, help me, I'm going to die."

"You should die, you fucking malaka," screamed Tommy.

Malaka is a Greek slang term which literally translates to "wanker," but is used in connotations to mean asshole and jerk as well. It is derived from the Greek term malakos which means soft or spoiled. Using the term on a stranger is considered derogatory, but the word can be used between friends without fear of insult.

Franco grabbed one foot and Stutz grabbed the other and they attempted to pull the man the rest of the way out of the vent. He let out a loud muffled scream and his cell phone fell onto the grill. It was large and bounced, almost exploding. "I don't even own a cell phone" stated one of the cops who were looking on. "Me neither" said another, as several cops chimed in how a ghetto burglar had something as high tech as a cell phone. "I only have a beeper Franco chimed in." There was no way they were going to remove the burglar in this manner. The ESU Sergeant, who had about 35 years on the job, stated he was sending two men up on the roof to see if they could pull him out. They tried to lower a rope, but his arms were stuck in a downward position and he couldn't grab it. They asked the perp if he was wearing a belt and he stated he was.

"You should have hung yourself with it," Tommy yelled, but Franco motioned to Tommy to be quiet by putting his finger to his lips. At this point the Duty Captain and Patrol Supervisor were on the scene. The ESU Sergeant made a comment that the ultimate goal was to remove the skell without doing damage to Tommy's property. Tommy seemed appreciative of this. They asked Tommy if he had any grease in the diner and a few of the cops made comments about his cheeseburger deluxe. Tommy responded he had oil in the fryer that was just changed that night before he closed. The ESU Sergeant ordered one of his guys to bring a big bucket of oil up to the roof. They poured the oil down the grill vent from the roof onto the burglar. He was protesting but didn't seem to have much say in the matter. Franco, Stutz and Sergeant Rooney from the 4-7 grabbed a hold of his legs and attempted to pull him down again, now that he had been lubricated. But he still didn't budge. It seemed Plan B would have to be called into effect, so the ESU Sergeant lowered a grappling hook from the roof and was trying to catch onto the man's belt. Several times the man screamed, the hook had either hit him in the head, or was digging into body parts causing him extreme pain. Sergeant Rooney told him to press his body against the side of the shaft to let the hook pass by him. After several attempts and a lot of whining from this July night Santa Claus, they were able to hook his belt with the grappling hook. They attached the grappling hook to a portable wench and began to pull the man back up towards the roof. His feet slowly disappeared from sight as he ascended back up the shaft. One of the guys made a joke that he was going back up to his reindeer.

Franco and Stutz ran up to the roof for fear someone else would steal the collar. Giovanni was friends with Tommy and he wanted to make the collar. As they brought the man back down to the street, he was visibly shaken, covered in grease, and claimed to be injured. He stated his neck and his back hurt and he had every intention to sue Tommy. When Tommy heard this threat, he reached for a bat he kept under the counter by the register.

Giovanni stepped in front of him, and said, "Tommy, you're gonna get me jammed up. He's not gonna sue you. How the fuck can he sue you?"

With that Tommy apologized, thanked the officers and started to lock down the diner. Then they broke the bad news to him; Tommy would have to come to the precinct to fill out all the necessary paperwork to press charges. Tommy informed Giovanni he would have to get up by four A.M. to open the diner.

Franco, feeling for him, said, "Okay when we're done processing the arrest, I'll come by here and have you sign a paper called a supporting deposition. It just means that this person had no permission to be in your store."

Tommy thanked Giovanni and said, "I'll see you in a little while."

The burglar, claiming he was injured, had to first be removed to Our Lady of Mercy Hospital for treatment. Franco and Stutz, having a good relationship with the night staff at the ER, were able to get him in and out in a short period of time. They found he had no injuries other than a few minor scrapes and bruises. They brought the supporting deposition to Tommy to sign and the perp was removed to Central Booking for processing. They finished up at around 11:00 A.M. and when they returned to the precinct, they were told to go look in the muster room. They couldn't believe their eyes. There were three tables of every kind of food that you could think of such as trays of cheeseburgers, Reuben sandwiches, and of course Greek specialties of gyros and souvlaki. Along with it all was a note from Tommy that was taped to the table.

It read, "You guys are the best, especially Giovanni. Thanks for everything that you do, Love Tommy."

Although it might be considered an illegal gratuity, none of the bosses seemed to ask who Tommy was or why the food was there. Everyone ate lunch and the precinct seemed to be especially happy that day. Free food seems to do that or maybe it was the appreciation that was shown to the cops in the 4-7 that day.

11

My Guardian Angel

GIOVANNI FRANCO AND HIS PARTNER Mike Connelly were working an 8 to 4 tour on a Saturday in August of 1986 when a job came over the radio of a 10-30 in progress (armed robbery). Central gave out information alerting all units a liquor store had been robbed on East 233rd Street and the perps, three black males, had fled in a white Dodge work van. All three suspects were armed with guns, and one of them had fired a shot into the ceiling of the liquor store. The owner of the liquor store was not injured, but he was badly shaken up and couldn't give much of a description of the suspects other than that they were black males. The plate on the van was unknown along with the direction of flight.

Franco and Connolly canvassed the area along with numerous other units, but the van seemed to have gotten away. They drove by the location and saw numerous sector cars parked in front of the liquor store. Connelly was driving and when they pulled up in front of the store, Franco rolled down the window and asked one of the cops on the sidewalk if there was any more information on the suspects. The cop he was speaking to was a surly Vietnam veteran named Sherman.

Sherman answered "This guy doesn't know shit. You would think he wasn't even in the store when he got robbed. All he knows is its three black guys in a white van, maybe a Dodge."

Officer Sherman had about twenty-eight years on the job and seemed to have little patience for people's bullshit. Franco thought to himself, *this guy probably should have retired a long time ago,* but Franco knew he was a good cop just by observing him from afar. He was what was known in the business as "burnt out." Franco had heard some stories about him being exposed to Agent Orange and he was also aware that he was a

Purple Heart recipient. Sherman was a tough street cop who didn't take any shit and it seemed that maybe time was passing him by and he should probably retire to Florida, get a boat and go fishing. Franco nodded at Sherman and told him "We're going to canvass a little more, but they probably got on the Bronx River or the Deegan and are probably long gone by now."

"No, I bet they went into Mount Vernon," Sherman shot back. "That's where all the hamsters go to hide." So with that in mind, they decided to head towards the border of Mount Vernon which was a mile or so away.

An hour or so passed, and both Franco and Connelly figured that these guys were long gone. Franco asked Connelly to pull over at the corner of 241st Street and White Plains Road. He wanted to run into *Pepino's Pizzeria* for a slice as they had a 1300 meal and it was almost 1500 hours. They had worked through their meal, looking for these perps. Franco asked Connelly if he wanted anything, and he responded he had a date with his girlfriend Fiona and they would be getting off from work in an hour anyway so he declined. Franco went in and got a Sicilian end slice and made his way back to the RMP. As Franco looked across the street, he couldn't believe there was a white Dodge van parked in front of another liquor store. As Franco was walking towards the RMP, he noticed the driver of the van looking at him. He knew in his heart that these were the same guys who robbed the liquor store on 233rd Street. Franco tried to play it off as though nothing was unusual because he didn't want to spook them.

As he got back in on the passenger side of the RMP, he told Connelly, "Do not look to your left, just look straight ahead. But the van that did the robbery is parked right across the street in front of another liquor store."

"No fucking way!" Connelly exclaimed. "I have to look," he said.

"No no don't look, just drive down the street, I'll call it in then make a U-turn and pull up behind them." Franco instructed.

As Connelly drove away from the corner, Franco called in to Central they had possible suspects in the robbery of the liquor store. He called for a 10-85 (officer needs assistance) and he knew that within a minute, he would have plenty of help. Connelly made a U-turn about a block down the road and headed up towards where the van was parked. They didn't know if there was anyone else in the van beside the driver because they couldn't see the passenger side and there were no windows.

Franco stated, "I hope the other two are in the liquor store."

Connelly replied, "They must be or they would have drove away already."

Franco told Connelly that the driver looked right at him, but he played it off and hopefully didn't spook them. As the RMP was approaching the van, the van doors flew open on both sides and all three suspects jumped out and ran north on White Plains Road.

"Shit" Franco exclaimed, "here we go," as he jumped out of the RMP and gave chase.

He didn't even wait for Connelly to stop and stumbled as his feet hit the ground, jumping out of the moving RMP. Connelly slammed on the brakes, which allowed the passenger door to slam shut. He then proceeded to drive up ahead of the perps and tried to cut them off with the car. All three made a quick right hand turn and went down an alleyway between a *C-Town* supermarket and a Chinese restaurant. Franco gave chase and Connelly made a right hand turn at the next block in order to cut them off at the pass in case they came out on the next block. Franco could hear a parade of sirens getting closer to where he was as he chased the three down the alley. All of a sudden the perp closest to Franco turned and fired three shots at him. Franco was ready with his gun in his hand and returned fire as he ran toward the perps. Another exchange of gunfire between Franco and all three perps ensued as Franco took cover behind a large green metal dumpster located in the alleyway. His heart was pounding, and he had no time to say anything over the radio. He was in survival mode, and he seemed to have tunnel vision. He could hear the bullets making a high pitched noise as they ricocheted off the walls around him. Franco returned fire one more time, shooting twice and leaving himself with one bullet left in his revolver.

He then heard all three perps screaming, "Okay, okay no more, we're good you got us..." He didn't know if it was a trick because they were only about 30 feet ahead of him, so he positioned the dumpster in a way that he could take a peek. *Cover and concealment*, he kept saying to himself as he looked out from the side of the dumpster. When he peered out, he saw that all three perps were laying face down on the ground and he saw their guns had been thrown to the side. He couldn't believe that they actually surrendered. There were three of them and only one of him. They had semi-automatic weapons and he had a six shot revolver with only one bullet left. He thought there could only be one answer. *It must be my guardian angel.*

When Franco was in the Academy, his best friend Daniel was killed during a robbery while he was away on business in Baltimore, Maryland. Franco always carried the laminated card they give at the funeral home in memory of the deceased. This card had Daniel's picture on it along with a prayer about angels. Franco carried this card in the lining of his police hat and never went on patrol without it. He felt Daniel would watch over him and protect him from harm. Although he wasn't wearing his hat in the alleyway, he had it with him in the car and the first thing he wanted to do was read the prayer when he got back into the RMP.

Franco jumped out from behind the dumpster, gun drawn, as the other cops rushed into the alley. They were cuffed by the responding officers and Franco made his way back towards where Connelly was on the next block. As he walked towards the RMP his legs began to shake and he felt like he couldn't control them. He wasn't sure if it was obvious to anyone looking, but he needed to sit down. When Connelly saw him, he put his arm around him and asked him if he was okay.

With a big smile on his face, Franco responded, "Yeah just another day in the life of a gunslinger." As he sat back into the RMP, he reached in to the back seat, grabbed his hat, took Daniel's card out and read it. He gave it a kiss and put it back into his hat. The Patrol Sergeant came over to the car and told Franco to go to the hospital to get checked out. Franco stated, "I'm fine; I need to get to the house to process the arrest."

The Sergeant stated, "I'm going to have somebody process it for you. It's your collar, but you need to go have your blood pressure checked. You look a little pale."

"Okay Sarge, whatever you say," Franco replied, thinking he might get some sympathy from a pretty nurse. *It sure beats doing all that paperwork,* he thought. So they headed down to Miserocordia Hospital and Franco received the royal treatment. Cops were coming in and out of the emergency room to see how he was doing and to congratulate him on a job well done. He thought to himself, *the whole thing probably lasted only 30 seconds, but it could have been 30 seconds that changed his whole life.* At one point he looked up towards the ceiling and whispered, "Job well done, Daniel."

12

Avanni

IT WAS AN EXTREMELY HOT AUGUST DAY and Police Officer Giovanni Franco along with his new partner, Officer Rudy Nosdag, were in *the Silver Chimes Diner* on the corner of Nereid Avenue and White Plains Road. They were checking on the owner, a nice Greek man named Tommy, because the diner had been burglarized one night over the weekend. The officers, when they heard what happened and knowing Tommy for some time, went in to see if they could do anything for him. As it turned out, the Latent Print Unit still hadn't gone in to dust for fingerprints. It was hard for Tommy to conduct business and not have his workers touch the areas that were ransacked by the burglar(s).

As Franco was using the diner phone to call the Print Unit to find out what caused the delay, a man wearing a bus driver's uniform ran into the diner. He obviously noticed the sector car parked in front and was looking for the police. He ran over to Officer Nosdag and frantically explained there was a woman in the back of his bus having a baby. Officer Nosdag, who only had a couple of years on the job, pointed towards Officer Franco who was on the phone. Franco, noticing the agitated bus driver, and thought the bus driver had a rider that didn't want to pay his fare. After a brief conversation with the Print Unit, Franco walked over to the bus driver. He was visibly upset and in a thick Middle Eastern accent told Franco there was a big fat woman at the back of his bus having a baby. The two officers proceeded outside and saw the bus parked in front of the diner at the bus stop. As the two entered the rear door of the bus, they observed a large crowd standing around a very large black woman lying on the floor in the rear of the bus. They directed all of the people to leave the bus. Giovanni yelled at Rudy to call for an ambulance.

He also told Rudy, "This one is yours; I've delivered two already, and she's one of your people" with a smile on his face.

Rudy being black turned to Giovanni and stated, "She ain't one of my people; I'm American Black, she's Jamaican. Plus I have no idea what to do."

With that, Officer Franco told his new partner "Then go back in the diner and boil the water."

Franco attempted to ease the woman's mind, but she was in a bad state. She had a very colorful sun dress up around her waist, and she had no panties on. She had to be at least 400 pounds and Franco was totally repulsed by what he was looking at. He knew he had to do something, or at least make it look good. He got down on one knee next to her and then something happened that he never expected. The smell that was coming from between this woman's legs was sickening and repulsive. It reminded him of the petting zoo at the Bronx Zoo. He could feel his stomach turning but knew he might have to possibly deliver a baby. He asked Rudy for an ETA on the bus and when he did, he was told that all ambulances had been diverted to a multiple car collision on the Bronx River Parkway. An ETA was unknown. The woman was screaming loudly that the baby was coming out. There was a large puddle under her ass where her water had broken and in a thick Jamaican accent she repeatedly said "Oh Lord, me baby coming."

Officer Franco begged, "No, no, it's not coming yet."

"Yeah mon, I got four babies at home." The woman protested. "It's coming soon."

When he looked between her legs again, he could see her vagina opening and the head coming out. It wasn't easy to see, however, because she had a huge bush that rivaled Don King's head. He made the suggestion to the woman that they get in his patrol car and shoot down the hill to Misericordia Hospital which was only a few blocks away.

She stated, "Are you crazy, mon, me cannot move."

Franco thought to himself at that moment, *why does shit like this always happen to me?*

Having put the job over the radio, Officer Nosdag informed Franco the Sergeant and another sector car just pulled up to the scene. *Good,* Franco thought. *Maybe one of these guys wants to get on the news and they'll jump in for me.* The Sergeant, his driver, and two other cops, entered the bus. They took one look at the huge women lying on the floor with her legs spread and her dress around her waist and all four did an about face and walked off the bus. When Franco saw them exit, he knew he was fucked.

Never a Dull Moment

There wasn't anyone coming to help him and this birth was all going to be on him. At that moment, the woman let out a large scream and was panting. It reminded Franco of when he was a kid and his German shepherd had puppies, only his German shepherd didn't smell like a water buffalo.

The baby's head was almost all the way out and Franco knew it was time to do what he got paid to do. So he reached between the woman's legs and cupped the sides of the baby's head, inserting his fingers into her vagina on both sides. He told her to push and as she did, she defecated all over the floor of the bus. Franco thought to himself, *if I had a free hand I would surely shoot myself in the head. This is fucking disgusting.* He looked back for his partner Rudy but all he saw was the bottom of Rudy's feet as he exited the bus from the back door. Now he was there all alone with this woman who had just shit on herself while he was holding her baby's head. He told her to push again, all the while trying to hold his breath. She pushed and the baby's head came out. He now gingerly turned the baby's shoulders which were covered with slime. As he maneuvered the shoulders, the woman pushed again, and the baby slid out.

Franco noticed the baby wasn't breathing and opened the baby's mouth and slid his pinky in to try to clear the airway. There was a lot of mucus in the baby's mouth and that didn't seem to work. Franco turned the baby on its stomach while holding it with his other hand and tapped the baby gently on the back thinking that that would clear the airway. That didn't work either and he yelled out to the officers who were standing on the sidewalk.

"Get me an ETA on the bus, the baby's not breathing!"

When the woman heard this, she started to scream and carry on, "Me baby, me baby, save me baby," she cried.

At this point, Franco wiped the baby's face as best he could with his shirt sleeve, pinched its tiny nose between his index finger and thumb, and put his mouth over the baby's. He gently blew into the baby's mouth and the baby began to breath. He turned his head to the right and spit several times. He thought for sure he was going to puke.

He placed the baby on its mother's chest as she lay on the floor in the back of the bus crying. "You saved me baby," she said.

With that Franco could hear a siren in the distance coming close. His partner stuck his head in the back of the bus and cheerfully said, "The ambulance is here."

Great timing, Franco thought. A minute or so later, two ambulance attendants entered the bus, placed the mother and baby on a stretcher, and put them in the back of the ambulance. The Sergeant directed Franco to ride in the ambulance with the mother and baby and told Officer Nosdog to follow in the sector car. Upon arrival at Misericordia Hospital, mother and child were admitted and Franco was told both were doing fine.

The next day before going to work, Franco stopped by the hospital to see how mother and baby were doing. As he entered her room, she had visitors, several family members, including her husband. When she saw the officer, she gave him a big smile and motioned for him to come over to her.

She told the people in the room, "This be the mon who brought me baby into the world."

Everyone was shaking his hand and thanking him. Franco stated that he just wanted to see how she was doing. He didn't even know if it was a boy or girl because he never bothered to look. He was told she was a girl. At that point, the woman, whose name he found out to be Ullene, asked him his first name. He stated "Giovanni."

With that she looked at her family and said, "I think I'm going to name the baby Avanni, after this wonderful officer."

She held out her arms and she and Giovanni hugged. Everyone in the room said, "Aww." With that he thanked her and she thanked him, and he left to go to work.

As Giovanni was driving to the precinct, he thought to himself, *what began as something really disgusting, turned out to be pretty nice in the end.* He was glad he got the baby to breathe, the mother was truly appreciative of what he had done, and he felt that he had made a difference in one person's life

13

The Power of Suggestion

BESIDES A MARRIAGE PARTNER, A PARTNERSHIP in the police department is probably the most important partner a cop will ever know. Your life is sometimes held in the hands of your partner and you need to have total trust in that person to comfortably get through a tour. If you don't have total trust in your partner, and you hesitate to do certain things, it could spell disaster. Most times in the NYPD, partnerships are formed based on a prior familiarity with each other and a feeling of chemistry between the two individuals. Officer Franco, having recently lost his partner to a detail (Joint Terrorist Task Force), was in the market for a new partner and had been riding with several other cops whose partners were out for the day. They were either in court, out sick or injured. Having been promoted from patrol recently to a unit known as SP7, the pool of possible partners became smaller due to the fact that SP7 was an eight man unit within the precinct. SP7 stood for Special Patrol 7. Their ultimate duties were to make street level narcotics arrests in uniform utilizing unmarked vehicles. Just about everyone in SP7 had already partnered up and when Franco entered the unit, there was only one available person who didn't have a partner. So Franco wound up becoming partners with a cop who seemed to be a bit of a loner. He didn't go to many functions with the other guys; he didn't hang out after work, and he didn't seem to have many friends within the precinct. Franco, being a social kind of guy, was a bit leery of this partnership, but SP7 was a career path advancement and he didn't want to be on patrol his whole career. So he didn't see that he had much of a choice.

The Power of Suggestion

A couple of days went by without incident with Franco and his new partner, Jonathan Goldberg. They made a couple of low level drug arrests, but Franco still wasn't feeling comfortable with Goldberg. When they would approach large groups of possibly armed drug dealers, Franco didn't feel at ease. He couldn't put his finger on it, but there was still something that wasn't exactly right. With Goldberg being somewhat slight of stature, Franco always found himself watching Goldberg's back along with his own. There were several times, when individuals who were being questioning on the corner seemed to push the issue with Goldberg, and Franco needed to step in and sometimes physically correct the situation. His protective nature would often take over, but it just didn't feel right to him. He sometimes got the feeling that Goldberg was scared. Franco would observe Goldberg getting in people's faces, when speaking to them differently could have diffused the situation. He was feeling Goldberg was trying to make up for his lack of stature by being overly aggressive because he knew he would have his back which weighed on Franco's mind.

After about a week or so, Franco felt this partnership wasn't working and he was thinking about going to his friend, the roll call guy, to explain how he felt. But there didn't seem to be any solution because there weren't any other available partners in SP7. So it seemed he was stuck with Goldberg for the foreseeable future.

On one particular 4 to 12 tour, Franco and Goldberg decided to do some observations at East 228th Street and White Plains Road a known drug location. They observed an individual whom they each had arrested several times for drug sales, while assigned to patrol. He was a tall dark skinned Jamaican Rastafarian with dreadlocks all the way down to his ass. He used some of his dreads to tie back the other dreadlocks in a ponytail. On this particular night, the officers observed this individual approach several cars as they pulled up to the corner. The officers had their unmarked car positioned across the street and down the block and were making these observations through binoculars.

"This would be a lot easier," Franco said to Goldberg, "if we weren't in uniform. They have these fucking lookouts riding bicycles up and down the block and I think one of them spotted us."

This lookout, a young black boy who looked no older than twelve years old, appeared to make the officers and was riding his bike back to the dealers on the corner. He seemed to have said something to them. Franco felt it was time to move in before they all walked off. Franco was driving the unmarked car and proceeded to quickly speed to the location. Both he and Goldberg jumped out of the vehicle and they placed six individuals up against the wall including the dread they had observed approaching several vehicles. Franco was patting down one individual as he had the other four up against the wall at gunpoint. Goldberg was standing back a few feet to the right, with his gun also drawn: he had the guy with the dreadlocks up against the wall, frisking him. All of a sudden the guy with the dreads broke free from Goldberg and ran east on 228th Street. Franco thought that Goldberg was holding onto this individual and didn't immediately see him run as he was searching the others. When he heard the footsteps and looked to the right, he saw the Rasta running down the street, but Goldberg did not give chase. No one had anything on them and it was apparent that any drugs that they were selling were stashed somewhere in the immediate area, or they were on the guy that ran away. He felt like screaming at Goldberg, *Why didn't you chase him*, but didn't want to embarrass him in front of the five mutts who were left on the wall. The remaining individuals were told to disperse and not come back. They slowly and reluctantly walked away. Franco was pissed; in fact, he was fuming. He thought to himself, *I got five guys up against the wall, you can't control one?*

As they were walking around, looking for the stash of drugs, Franco slid his hand underneath the wheel well of a car parked on the corner. He discovered a large plastic bag sitting atop the wheel that contained 30 manila bags of marijuana. These were nickel bags that were sold for $5 apiece and each one was stamped "Love Machine" in blue ink. Love Machine was the brand that was sold on that particular corner. Franco couldn't contain his disdain for Goldberg any longer and as they got back in the unmarked car, with the newly found drugs, he looked over at Goldberg and said, "Now you're going to voucher this and explain why there are no bodies to go along with it."

Goldberg shot back, "Why don't we just dump it down the sewer?"

Franco looked at him and said, "I gave it to you. You do what the fuck you want with it. I don't know nothing. But I'm telling you right now, I'm not very happy with you."

Goldberg complained, "It wasn't my fault he got away."

Franco went ballistic. He told Goldberg, "I had five guys on the wall and they don't run and you have one off to the side and he gets away from you. I think you were scared to chase him."

Although he had no response, Goldberg seemed very insulted. As they drove away, Franco told him "I don't think this is going to work, I don't feel I can trust you." The tension within the car could be cut with a knife and you could feel the disdain between the partners. They didn't say anything to each other for the rest of the night and at 2000 hours, went into the precinct for meal.

Franco went to the lunchroom and hung out with the other cops. He had no idea where Goldberg was but he was happy he didn't come down to the lunchroom. He later found out he was upstairs vouchering the drugs while on his meal period. How he explained where they came from, Franco never asked. All he knew was, it looked bad to come into the precinct with drugs and no bodies attached to it. He seemed to always get his man and this really rubbed him the wrong way.

As Franco sat in the lunchroom with several other cops watching TV, he noticed a mop bucket in the corner that was giving off a terrible odor. It was no doubt left there by the precinct cleaner, whose nickname was Johnny Babo. Babo got his nickname because he was caught trading a case of Babo, a cleanser similar to Ajax, that he took from the Precinct. He traded it to the bodega across the street from the 5-2 Precinct where he worked for a ham sandwich. He was suspended, put on probation and transferred to the 4-7 Precinct. He was a huge, simple individual who always had a big smile on his face, but was as dopey as the day was long. He was also not a very good cleaner as the precinct was always a mess. Franco who had grabbed a slice a pizza from across the street and was eating it, found the smell from the mop bucket was starting to make him nauseous. He got up and removed it from the lunchroom and put it in the hallway. He continued to eat his slice and watch TV with the other guys when he noticed a black G.I. Joe with the Kung Fu grip doll dressed in camouflage on the table. He grabbed it and began imitating in a Jamaican accent, a drug dealer on the corner trying to solicit his wares.

"Yo mon, you want to buy some ganja mon, me got some good shit mon, me got the shit that made Ray Charles blind. If you don't believe me, ask Stevie Wonder, he was with him."

All the guys in the lunchroom started laughing and Franco continued to carry on with his doll in hand. Turns out a kid left the doll in the lobby. He was there with his mother who was making a complaint against his father. Somehow the doll found its way down to the lunch room. Franco thought to himself, *if this thing had dreads, it would look a lot like the guy who ran away from Goldberg a couple of hours ago. In fact that guy was wearing camouflage too.* He then got a brilliant idea. He went back out into the hallway, grabbed the mop out of the bucket, and using his 007 knife that he always had tucked in between his holster and gun belt, cut several strands from the mop. They were black, dirty and nasty looking. They looked a lot like dread locks. He went back into the lunchroom and started to tie them around the top of the head of the black G.I. Joe with the Kung Fu grip. It became somewhat of a science project as he sat there intertwining the hair onto this doll. One of the black cops commented that his wife pays a lot of

75

money for a weave and Franco seemed to be an expert as he transformed this doll into a Rastafarian drug dealer. After a half hour, his master piece was complete and he was showing everyone who walked into the lunchroom his creation.

Meal was over and it was time to get back in the car with his buddy Goldberg. He was dreading going back on patrol with him, but he knew he had no choice. He put the doll, which was approximately 6 inches long into his inside jacket uniform pocket and went back up to the front desk. There he saw Goldberg standing at the desk getting his copy of the vouchered drugs from the Lieutenant. They both walked outside towards the car and he felt the need to say something to Goldberg. They hadn't spoken for almost three hours and he knew it was no way to continue to work.

"I see you vouchered the pot," Franco said.

"Yup," was all Goldberg could muster.

"Oh so it's going to be like that, Franco thought. *Fuck this guy. He fucked up and now he's trying to make me feel bad? Maybe I'll just go back to patrol,* he thought to himself. *It's just not worth it to feel like this every day.* Goldberg was now driving and he said something to Franco that was totally unexpected.

"Let's go back to 228th and see if he came back. If we collar him, we could put the drugs on him."

"And if he runs, who's going to chase him?" Franco asked.

"I think we should both chase him," was Goldberg's reply.

"I'll chase him all day, as long as you're running with me," Franco promised.

The two headed back to 228th Street, and lo and behold the Rasta man was standing on the corner. When he saw the two officers, he froze like a deer caught in headlights. It looked like he was not going to run but they were ready to jump out, if need be. Then Franco had a brilliant idea. Knowing this individual from past arrests Franco remembered his name was Helmsley. He reached into his pocket, and revealed the newly created Rastafarian drug dealer doll.

"Yo, Helmsley, this is you," Franco screamed.

He then held it up and pointed to it with a crazy look in his eyes. He removed the pin from the back of his shield which attaches his shield to his jacket and thrust the pin into the doll's neck. Helmsley brought both of his hands to his neck and let out a loud scream.

"Argghh," Helmsley yelled.

"Oh shit!" Franco laughed as he turned to Goldberg. "He thinks I have a voodoo doll of him."

Goldberg laughed too, which was the first time that Franco had heard him laugh since they had been working together. Franco again thrust the pin into the Helmsley voodoo doll, but this time into his forehead. Helmsley clutched at his forehead, screaming, "Please officer, no more." At the same time, the other drug dealers who were standing at the corner, screamed and pleaded with the officers to leave Helmsley alone. Franco couldn't believe they were buying this act. He then stabbed the doll in the groin and Hensley fell to the ground writhing in pain. The two officers were laughing their asses off as Helmsley rolled around on the ground in pain. The other individuals on the corner ran off, but Helmsley seemed to be paralyzed. A few more thrusts with the pin and Helmsley was rolling around on the ground to the point where a crowd was gathering. The officers felt that he was punished enough for his misdeeds and drove off.

Franco turned to Goldberg and asked, "I thought you were going to collar him?"

Goldberg replied, "I think he suffered enough for one day." This made Franco feel a little better about his new partner. Although this whole situation was totally ridiculous, they seemed to have connected on some type of level. They drove around for about an hour and were contacted by Central to 10-1, the command. Ten one means to call the precinct by landline. Goldberg pulled over to a pay phone and Franco called the desk. The Lieutenant on the desk asked Franco if he had a voodoo doll of a drug dealer on 228th Street. Franco was shocked.

"A Voodoo doll?" he asked, repeating the Lieutenant.

"Yeah, a voodoo doll." Responded the Lieutenant.

"A voodoo doll?" Franco repeated. "Why do you ask me if I have a voodoo doll?"

"Because a guy was just here with long dreadlocks who stated he sells drugs on 228th Street. He claimed you showed up with a voodoo doll of him and kept stabbing it, causing him extreme pain." With that the Lieutenant let out a loud laugh and informed Franco this individual made out a civilian complaint against him.

"So he admitted to being a drug dealer?" Franco asked, trying to change the subject.

"Yeah," the Lieutenant shot back. "He seemed like an honest guy," he said with a chuckle. "This might be the funniest civilian complaint I've ever taken. You know some of these people believe in that shit," he went on to say.

"I wish I had a voodoo doll of Goldburg," Franco shot back, "but he's not Jamaican so I guess it wouldn't work on him."

They both laughed and Franco hung up never really answering the Lieutenant's question.

Never a Dull Moment

A few months later, Franco received notification to respond to the CCRB (Civilian Complaint Review Board) located at 40 Rector Street in Manhattan. He was told to bring his memo book from October 16, 1987. He looked at his memo book for that day but did not discover anything out of the ordinary. He was still working with Goldberg so he asked him if there is anything in his memo book that would refresh his memory. All Goldberg had written down on that date was that he vouchered 30 nickel bags, and the voucher number.

"Oh shit!" Franco exclaimed, "The voodoo doll!"

"Yeah that's right," Goldberg recalled.

"I can't believe the review Board entertained that bullshit," Franco added with a tone of disgust. "We gave that guy a play. He could have went for the 30 nickel bags and now I have to go all the way to the ass end of Manhattan and explain myself to a bunch of old ladies ,who would love to stick one up my ass." Franco was not a fan of the Civilian Complaint Review Board because he felt it was a kangaroo court who tried their best to screw cops every chance they got.

The day arrived and Franco had a post change to CCRB. Upon his arrival, he signed in and a few minutes later found himself under oath and being recorded as he was questioned. A middle aged black woman wearing a big colorful scarf was doing the questioning. The woman asked Franco if he had a voodoo doll in the likeness of a person named Helmsley Dixon.

He responded, "A voodoo doll? A voodoo doll! You brought me all the way down here to ask me if I own a voodoo doll. Do I look like a witch doctor?" He asked.

"Well, we have a complaint this individual made, and we have to investigate it," the woman stated.

"Well I've locked up Mr. Dixon several times for selling drugs, and so has half the precinct that I know of, so do you think maybe it's a way for him to retaliate and to keep us off his back?"

"No, I wasn't aware that you have arrested Mr. Dixon in the past Officer. But do you have a voodoo doll of Mr. Dixon?"

"A voodoo doll," Franco again repeats with a look of disgust on his face. "Do you know how many trains I had to take to get here?" He asked the woman.

"I'm sorry, officer," she responded, "but the complaint was made so we need to follow up."

"A voodoo doll? You have me here, asking me if I have a voodoo doll. This has to be the most ridiculous thing I've ever heard of." Franco kept shaking his head from side to side repeating the words "voodoo doll" over and over again.

"I guess that's a 'No,'" the woman finally surmised.

"Can I leave now?" Franco asked. "I have a long trip back to the 4-7."

"I guess you can go Officer. " The woman seemed apologetic without actually apologizing.

Franco never really answered the question. Although there was a voo-doo doll and several of the cops had seen it, he didn't want to lie, especially under oath, but really didn't want to explain his actions either that day. He felt it was a harmless prank and never thought "Mr. Dixon" would take him seriously. After all, he had given him a break and didn't collar him for the drugs. When Franco got back to the precinct, he took the voodoo doll out of his locker, cut off its head, and tossed it into the dumpster across the street behind the Chinese restaurant. He envisioned Mr. Dixon's head com-ing off somewhere on 228th Street and could only hope that his powers of suggestion were real.

14

Splat

OFFICER GIOVANNI FRANCO HAD BEEN WORKING in the 4-7 Precinct Anti-Crime Unit for several months now. He was working his way up the career path to Detective. He started out in uniform patrol, was moved up to SP7, promoted to SCAT (Street Conditions Apprehension Team) and now found himself assigned to Anti-Crime. Anti Crime is a plain clothes undercover street patrol unit. It is responsible for the apprehension of violent street criminals, robberies, assaults and weapons possession. It also involves undercover street surveillance in an individual or team setting. On this particular sunny cool day in October, Franco found himself on quite an unusual assignment. School was back in session since early September and it seemed a serial assailant was causing hysteria in the confines of the 5-2 Precinct. He was assaulting young elementary school children with a hammer as they walked home from the various schools in the area. Although Franco was not assigned to the 5-2 Precinct, he was selected as part of an anti-crime undercover task force that was told in no uncertain terms, this individual must be caught. Several children had been hit over the head by this psycho over the past two weeks and although no one had died, a few were still in the hospital with extensive head injuries. The community was up in arms and the media was running wild every day with the story. Mayor Koch called a Press Conference and the story was constantly on the news, both on TV and radio. The pressure to catch this guy was mounting by the hour.

Franco, being in this undercover unit for a while now, had grown his hair long, and was sporting a goatee. When he learned of this assignment, he decided to go to his locker and put on one of the many costumes he had at his disposal. Sometimes he would dress in a Sanitation uniform or Con

Edison uniform. He had over time, acquired many uniforms and costumes that he would wear depending on his assignment. Working in a predominantly African American neighborhood, he sometimes needed to blend in, and being dressed as one of these workers helped him to get up close and personal. He was particularly fond of his U.S. Postal uniform. There's a running joke in the Police Department that the safest man in the ghetto is the mailman, because he brings the welfare checks. Nobody messes with the mailman, and if they did, there would be a whole lot of people looking to kick someone's ass.

Franco stood in front of his locker looking at the selection of clothing at hand. He thought to himself, *the area I'm going to be in is mostly Puerto Rican so how can I blend?* Franco, with his long hair and goatee, could pass for Spanish as long as someone did not engage him in a long conversation in Spanish. He knew some words from being in the streets, but could not pull off a conversation. Therefore, he decided to dress like a bum. He wore ripped jeans, a dirty sweatshirt and some old sneakers he had at the bottom of his locker. He covered his head with a red bandana and took shoe polish off the top shelf of his locker and put some in the palm of his hand. He spread it around and wiped it as evenly as he could on his face looking into the mirror on his locker door. He wiped the remainder on his jeans and some on the sweatshirt. He removed a big brown wooden cross that he had on a piece of black string and tied it around his neck. He also took some rosary beads hanging in his locker around a picture of his son C.J. and slipped them over his head. He looked into the mirror and thought, *nice touch.* He tucked his 38 caliber snub nose into the small of his back and took a pair of handcuffs and placed them into the inside pocket of a very old and faded denim jacket. In the other inside pocket, he would carry his radio with an ear piece that ran up through the inside of the jacket, under his bandana and into his ear which was covered by his hair. So he was now ready, looking like a dirty, long haired Jesus freak. He figured a can of beer in my hand inside a brown paper bag and I'll be set.

It was now 1:00 P.M. and he needed to get to his post. He hopped into his own car, a white 1980 Turbo Trans Am and headed to the 5-2 Precinct where he parked his car in the precinct parking lot. He then took a slow walk to his post on Bainbridge Avenue, observing as many people as he could along the way. On the way over in his car, he stared at the composite sketch of the suspect given to the Sketch Unit by some of the children who had been assaulted. The perp appeared to be Hispanic and in his mid twenties to early thirties. He had light facial hair and in all of the attacks he wore a baseball cap. Trying to identify someone from a sketch is very difficult especially when the information is being obtained from children who were just hit over the head with a hammer and scared to death. He knew this guy would probably have to be caught in the act.

When he got to his post he observed that the area was mostly commercial. There were a lot of stores with apartment buildings off on the side streets. The schools in the area were only blocks away and there were three of them. He knew the perp would not hit too close to the school. There were a lot of vigilantes by the schools hoping for a piece of this guy. Fathers had stayed home from work to pick up their kids and the media was around with their news vans. Franco knew this guy would be looking for a victim off the beaten path, or maybe a kid whose mother or father could not afford to take off from work to pick their child up after school. A kid who had to walk several blocks either to get home or to get to the bus stop would also be a prime target. He knew it was going to be a cat and mouse game. He also noticed an increase in the number of marked police cars in the area and he became annoyed. He understood that it was to show a presence in the area, and he understood it was meant to give the community a feeling of security, but he also thought this guy was not going to strike again with all these fucking police cars going up and down the streets. He knew it would only make his job harder.

The area was flooded with undercover cops from other Bronx Anti-Crime Units. Franco did not know who they were, or what they looked like, he only knew the boundaries of their post. Each guy seemed to have approximately four blocks to cover. He walked to the end of his post and looked down the block toward the next post. He observed several people and wondered who the undercover cop was. He made funny scenarios in his head as to who it could be. There was one guy in a wheelchair in front of a bodega and Franco thought *what a great prop. If that's a cop no one would make him.* There was an Asian guy in front of a fruit stand. *That works, too,* Franco thought. He was amusing himself with these thoughts when he heard a job come over his radio's earpiece. Central was giving a 5-2 sector a jumper on Bainbridge Avenue. When Franco heard the address he turned around to see the building he was standing in front of and realized it was only three numbers off. He looked across the street and saw the address in question. Standing on the roof ledge of a six story building was a young, very skinny Hispanic man. Franco ducked into an alleyway as to not be seen transmitting over the radio. He informed the Central Dispatcher that he was Hammer Post # 9 and that the jumper was a confirmed job. He requested the Patrol Sergeant and Emergency Service Units. He then went into the street and attempted to engage the jumper in conversation until the troops came.

Splat

Franco looked up at the jumper, crossing his arms in front of his chest, "Yo whatca doing up there man? You're gonna get hurt."

The Hispanic man stood balanced at the roof's ledge, his body visibly trembling, "I'm gonna jump, I'm gonna kill myself."

"What? That's stupid." Franco yelled. "You don't want to kill yourself. Why would you do that?"

"I just found out that my woman has been cheating on me."

Franco waved his hand, "So what man! You can get another woman."

"No, man, you don't get it," the jumper wailed, shaking his head from side to side. "She cheated on me and then she got AIDS. I just found out she gave me AIDS and she's pregnant and our kid might have AIDS. I don't even know if it's my kid. So I'm gonna die, she's gonna die, and the kid is gonna die. I'm jumping before I turn into a zombie with all scabs and lose my teeth. Look at me!" the jumper demanded, "I lost twenty pounds already: I'm gonna jump, you better move."

Franco was positioned right under where the man was standing on the roof top and he felt the man's desperation. He thought maybe some reverse psychology was in order because he wasn't having much luck so far. He looked up at the skinny distraught man and said, "You know you're right. If I was you I'd jump too."

He figured if he could piss the guy off maybe he'd stop feeling sorry for himself and get mad at Franco. Kinda say *fuck you. You want to see me jump? I'm not gonna jump to entertain you.*

He didn't want to tell the guy he was a cop because he didn't want to blow his cover, and he didn't think it would help anyway. It might even make things worse. Again Franco looked up at the guy and said "Go ahead and jump."

As Franco spoke, a sector car pulled up right where he was standing. He looked away from the jumper momentarily to see who pulled up to the curb. When he looked back up at the jumper, he was approximately ten feet above Franco's head and coming straight for him. He gasped as his life flashed before his eyes. Then he jumped back and the man hit the cement street right at his feet. There was a loud splat and then the jumper bounced about three feet into the air, his body finally coming to rest less than a foot from Franco's feet. Franco held his hand to his chest as all the air seemed to leave his body. It was almost as if he had hit the ground too.

A young cop jumped out of the sector car and started yelling at Franco, "Why did you tell him to jump?" The young cop was driving the Patrol Sergeant and neither knew he was a cop assigned to the hammer detail.

Franco denied the allegation telling the cop, "I didn't tell him to jump."

83

"I heard you as we pulled up" insisted the young cop. "Sarge, I heard him; he told him go ahead and jump. We should arrest him."

Now Franco's head was spinning. He had good intentions because he felt the guy was going to jump and he was trying to use reverse street psychology. Certainly, he didn't want to see the guy jump, he felt terrible he had, but now this cop is making a big scene in the middle of the street with people gathering around. What was he to do?

The Sergeant, an older man in his late forties with salt and pepper hair, approached him and asked, "Do you have any I.D. on you? Empty out your pockets."

Franco knew if they searched him and found his gun it was going to be a mess. *This young cop will probably shoot me,* he thought, so he whispered to the Sergeant, "Sarge, I'm on the job. I'm working the hammer detail. I'm in Anti-crime in the 4-7 assigned to hammer detail # 9. Could you please tell this asshole to shut the fuck up."

The Sergeant looked at Franco and stated, "Get in the RMP."

He walked over to the back door of the sector car and got in on the passenger side. The Sergeant got into the front seat and pulled the RMP around the corner then turned around facing him.

"Show me your shield," the Sergeant demanded.

Franco pulled out his shield that he wore on a chain around his neck hidden under his sweatshirt. The Sergeant just nodded and Franco quickly tucked it back under his sweatshirt.

The Sergeant told him, "Go back to your post. The Duty Captain is going to have to interview you at the house. Do you have transportation?"

Franco stated his car was parked at the 5-2. The Sergeant told him, "Central will give you a 10-2 when the Captain wants to see you."

He nodded and then explained to the Sergeant. "You know Sarge, I was just trying to keep the guy alive 'til the troops got here. I feel terrible he jumped."

The Sergeant shook his head and said, "I know; I can see it in your eyes. Sometimes, no matter what we do, things don't turn out the way we hope. I'll talk to the kid. He's just a rookie; he has a lot to learn about life."

Franco went back to the other end of his post and waited to hear from the Duty Captain. He walked around and sat around and tried to blend in with the neighborhood. He was now more determined than ever to catch the hammer guy. He thought to himself, *If I get this guy it will be all over the news and there is no way they will try to fuck me for telling that guy to jump. Mayor Koch will be here kissing my ass.* He then started having thoughts of the skinny jumper. *What a shitty way to go,* Franco thought, *all because his woman couldn't keep her legs closed.* He wondered how the woman would

84

react upon learning her man had committed suicide. *How would it affect the unborn baby? Was it his baby or some other guy's? Sometimes this is a real complex and fucked up world,* He thought. He also thought, *you always think you have problems until you see the problems others face.* He then remembered what his friend Woody used to say repeatedly. "If you stood around with ten people and everyone threw their problems on the table, and you were told to pick one set of problems, you would take your own back." It made him think, *whatever happens with the Duty Captain, I know I had good intentions. I acted in good faith and like the Sarge said, sometimes no matter what we do, things don't always turn out the way we hope.*

About two hours later Officer Giovanni Franco was directed by Central to return to the 52nd Precinct to see the Duty Captain. He was interviewed as the first officer on the scene. The subject of telling the guy to jump never came up. The death was declared a suicide by the medical examiner, and Officer Franco had to go to the morgue the next day to identify the body, which was standard procedure.

Franco was assigned several hammer posts in the same area for the next several weeks. The assailant was still at large and had assaulted several more children in that time span. On October 31st, (Halloween) 1989, the hammer assailant was apprehended after he struck twice in a five minute span. His first victim, a ten year old boy, on his way home from P.S. 34, was hit in the shoulder as he waited for a bus on the same corner that Franco was assigned to the week before. The assailant struck again, hitting an eleven year old girl who was trick or treating with her eight year old brother just two blocks away from the first incident. A foot chase ensued and three undercover officers assigned to the hammer detail apprehended the suspect and recovered the hammer as evidence. Officer Franco was off that day, he had requested the day off so he could go trick or treating with his wife, and their infant son C.J.

15

On His Way

iT WAS JANUARY OF 1990, AND ALL THE HARD work, injuries and heartache seemed to have paid off. Officer Franco had been promoted to the Robbery Squad and was on his way to becoming a Detective. The Robbery Squad was a twelve man unit consisting of seasoned Detectives and police officers known as "White Shields" who were handpicked by their superiors for outstanding work over a long period of time. These "White Shields" had moved up the career path from patrol, to SP7, to the SCAT Unit, to Anti-Crime and now were assigned to the Robbery Unit. After twenty-seven months assigned to the Robbery Unit you are promoted to Detective and receive your "GOLD SHIELD" Officer Franco along with three other "White Shields" were now in the Robbery Squad. Up to this point in his career, Officer Franco had made hundreds of arrests, including many for gun possession, robberies, burglaries and violent assaults. He had taken countless drugs and drug dealers off the streets and had delivered three babies. He had been injured many times in the performance of his duties including being stabbed, bit and physically assaulted. Many of his fellow cops considered him to be a good street cop. Probably the best compliment another cop can bestow upon you is to say, "He's a good street cop" It means the cop knows what he's doing in the street under pressure. He knows when to be stern, he knows when to use force, and he knows when to let things slide. Most importantly he has your back, and he will fight with you to the end. You cannot only depend on him, but you can absolutely trust him. It has many meanings but when one of your peers says you're a good street cop, it's the best thing they could ever say about you. Officer Giovanni Franco prided himself on being just that.

Once assigned to the Robbery Squad many robberies were investigated over that twenty- seven month period. One such case that comes to mind was when he was working on a Pattern Robbery case. A pattern robbery is when one or more individuals commits numerous robberies over a period of time using the same M.O., Modus Operondi or method of operation. In this particular case a white male was mugging elderly ladies in the Woodlawn section of the 47th Precinct. He would usually sneak up on them from behind and assault and rob them as they entered their building lobby, or attack them at their front door. Most of these elderly women sustained serious injuries due to their age and the fact that the assailant would hit them over the head with a blunt object causing serious head trauma. Identifying this individual was very difficult because of many factors. The women were old so their eyesight in most cases was not so keen. He struck from behind in most instances so not many of the women got a good look at him. The sheer terror they experienced and the traumatic experience of being hit over the head tended to cause almost an amnesia type reaction. Many of these women sustained injuries that would take a very long time to recover from, if at all. In cases of this nature, a break in the case would be needed from an outside source such as a witness who might have seen the robbery go down.

One such break came in the case as the perp struck early one morning, and the robbery was witnessed by a younger male who gave a pretty good description of the perp and better yet his getaway car. The witness described seeing an old lady lying on the floor of her lobby on East 242nd Street. Upon further glance he noticed a male running away from the scene and getting into a tan Toyota Corolla. He further stated he would have been able to get the plate number but the plate was covered by a towel. Now Franco and his partner Tim Owney were at least armed with a good description of the perp. He was described as a white male in his twenties, approximately 5'10 and weighing approximately 140 lbs. He was further described as being unshaven but not to the point that he had a beard or mustache. It was described as kind of like a three or four day growth. The witness also stated he looked very dirty and appeared to be a junkie. Armed with this information, officers Franco and Owney alerted all units city wide through Central dispatch of the description of the perp and the vehicle.

Several more robberies were committed in this same area using the same M.O. in the next two weeks. The media was all over this case and Franco, who was assigned the "Pattern" was receiving much pressure to solve this case not only from the Chief of Detectives but from the Mayor's Office. Their big break came early one morning when the perp struck again just blocks from his last victim. This time a man walking his dog observed the robbery/assault go down and he chased the perp as he ran toward his getaway car. Again he used the tan Toyota Corolla and again the towel was covering the back license plate. This time the witness who ran track in his younger days at Mt. St. Michael Academy High School in the Bronx was able to catch up to the car as it sped away and grab the towel removing it from the license plate. He memorized the plate and gave it to the responding patrol officers. That was the big break Franco and Owney needed. All units were alerted and a city wide man hunt was underway for this individual and the car. The license plate was run through the DMV data base and the plates came back stolen. The vehicle that was described, a tan Toyota Corolla did not match the records for those plates. Those plates were stolen off a 1989 red Subaru, so the officers had reached a dead end.

That same day about six hours later the 3-4 Precinct Detectives called the 4-7 Robbery Squad and notified them that the vehicle wanted in connection with this pattern robbery was spotted parked and unoccupied on Broadway and West 190th Street in the Washington Heights section of Manhattan. Officers Franco, Owney and Detective David Rodgers responded to the location. They had asked that the 3-4 Detectives sit on the car until they got there. They flew to the location and arrived in a matter of minutes and were happy to see that the 3-4 detectives were "sitting on it" from up the block, avoiding spooking the perp if he happened to be watching the car. They had a brief conversation and they thanked the 3-4 guys. The 3-4 detectives would let the desk officer in the 3-4 and the patrol guys know that the 4-7 detectives would be in the area sitting on the vehicle. Since the 4-7 guys are in plain clothes and not from the area it is always a good idea to let the guys in the precinct concerned know you are there. If something goes down and you're running around with your guns drawn, you don't want to be mistaken for a bad guy and get shot.

Detective Owney was driving, Franco was in the passenger side, and Rodgers was in the back seat. Rodgers was a seasoned detective with over twenty years on the job. He had worked Robbery for many years and was very competent. Owney and Franco were still "White Shields" and although very good cops they were still learning the little intricacies of becoming very good detectives. After several hours observing this vehicle from across the street and down the block, Franco was not only getting antsy but very frustrated. He then got an idea. It was now four in the morning and most of these robberies had occurred early in the morning when the streets were still kind of empty. Being far from the suspect vehicle was making Franco uneasy. The car was parked in front of Fort Tryon Park on Broadway at West 190th Street, and Franco not only wanted to stretch his legs at this point, but he wanted to get a better look at the suspect's vehicle.

He told Owney and Rodgers he was going to walk by the vehicle to check it out and then position himself on the park bench right next to the car and lie there like a bum. He was dressed the part wearing old jeans, sneakers and an army jacket that came in handy in these types of situations. It was warm and could conceal not only his gun, but his blackjack and cuffs. It had a hood built in to the collar that he pulled close to his face. Before he left the car, they devised a signal if he needed them or if he spotted the perp and wanted them to respond with the car. He would reach down as if he was tying his sneaker. He exited the unmarked car and walked over to the area of the suspect's car and nonchalantly observed the vehicle. He could see the inside was a pigsty and he saw what looked like a couple of towels on the back seat. This really got his juices flowing as he lay on the park bench cuddled up for the evening. At one point he heard some strange noises coming from the park and as he peered over the stone wall down into the park he observed a guy in yellow pants and a hooded sweatshirt giving a blowjob to a guy who appeared to be wearing a bus driver uniform. *You can't make this shit up he thought.* A couple of hours past and the sun was just coming up. The activity in the street was increasing by the minute as people were beginning to come outside and started heading off to work. One passerby offered Officer Franco a dollar as he laid there on the bench. Another commented that "He should get a fucking job" he laughed to himself as he lie there with one eye open watching the vehicle and surrounding area.

At about 6:30 A.M. he spotted a white guy who looked like a skinny crack head walking across Broadway towards the car. His first instincts were to sit up but he did not want to spook him if he was the perp. The only way to be sure it was him was to wait until he got in the vehicle. As he got closer to the car Franco's heart was pounding. He glanced over to the unmarked car Owney and Rodgers were in. It was too far away to be able to tell if they were seeing the same thing he was, and there was a glare coming from the windshield due to the early morning sun. They had devised that signal before he left the car, but he did not want to sit up yet, nor did he want to give the signal if it was not the perp. He would just have to wait. Seconds seemed like an eternity as the dirty looking guy approached the car.

Broadway is a very wide street with several lanes going both north and south and watching the possible perp approaching was killing him. The perp got closer to the car and then as if to avoid oncoming traffic made a dash for the car and grabbed for the door handle. The car was unlocked and he opened the door quickly. Franco sprang up with no time to simulate tying his sneaker. He was approximately one hundred feet from the car and made a mad dash for the vehicle. As he got to the driver's side door, the perp spotted him and franticly tried to put the key in the ignition. He had already locked the door, and he glared at Franco as he attempted to nervously get the key into the ignition. In a flash, Franco drew his weapon and demanded the perp open the door. Since there was no immediate response, he smashed his gun into the driver's side window causing it to shatter. The perp almost simultaneously got the car started and attempted to put it in gear. Franco dove head first through the smashed window in an attempt to apprehend the perp and to keep him from putting the car in gear and driving away. Owney pulled up to the front of the suspect's vehicle blocking it from moving forward. There was a car parked behind, so it could only go back a few feet. There was not enough room to get away. At this point Franco's upper body is inside the broken window and shards of glass are ripping away at his midsection. The perp is violently fighting to escape, as he is repeatedly punching Franco in the face. He struck Franco several times as he was attempting to get out on the passenger side. Franco was holding on to him with one hand as he tried to remove the keys from the ignition with the other, all the while also holding on to his drawn weapon. At this point Franco got a grip of the perp's jacket and pulled the perp out the driver's side window backwards by his collar. Owney and Rodgers had run to the passenger side to head him off if he had broken away from Franco. The perp, as he was being pulled out the driver's side window, swung at Franco striking him in the throat. Franco, who still had his gun in his hand, smashed it down onto the perp's head splitting open his skull. At this point the perp stopped resisting and was cuffed and placed under arrest.

Franco thought, *how does it feel to have your head busted*, referring to all the old ladies that this piece of shit assaulted and robbed.

Blood was pouring down the perp's face and a large crowd had gathered. Some people in the crowd were talking violence towards the officers. They obviously did not know the circumstances and were not aware of how he was fighting with them or what he had done to all those old ladies. The officers thought it best that they remove the perp at this time and take him to the hospital instead of waiting at the scene for an ambulance. They removed the bleeding perp to Columbia Presbyterian Hospital on the corner of Broadway and West 168th Street for treatment. He received thirty something stitches to his head, and x-rays that were negative for any fractures to his skull. Franco was treated for cuts to his midsection, received a tetanus shot, and was given an ice pack to put on his face.

On His Way

The perp was then removed to the 4-7 to be placed into line-ups where, hopefully, some of the victims would be able to identify him. His vehicle was removed to the 4-7 by Detective Rodgers and searched and vouchered. Some contents were also vouchered like three dirty white towels and a pipe with tape wrapped around one end. This pipe was quite possibly the weapon that was used to strike the old ladies in the head. It would be sent to the lab and analyzed for any forensic evidence.

16

Line-Ups

NOW BEGAN THE LONG, TEDIOUS PROCESS of rounding up a bunch of women in their '70s, '80s and '90s and getting them transported to the 48th Precinct to view the suspect in a line-up. Franco and Owney placed the suspect in the holding pen inside the 47th Precinct Detective Squad Office and began making phone calls to the various victims. Out of the eleven victims they were aware of, six were located at the time, and none had transportation to the 48th Precinct where the line-ups would be conducted. The 48th Precinct is located on 174th Street and the Cross Bronx Expressway, and it's the home of the Bronx Detective Bureau and the Bronx Homicide Task Force. All line-ups in the Bronx are conducted in the Homicide Task Force office, except for the DA's line-ups which are conducted in the District Attorney's Office. A DA's line-up is conducted when the suspect has already been charged with a crime and is being housed in a correctional facility such as Riker's Island. If a suspect has not yet been identified as the perp, those line-ups are conducted at the Homicide Task Force.

Franco and Owney made arrangements to pick up the six victims but needed a form of transportation since all wouldn't fit in the unmarked car. After the arrest process took place, the suspect was transported to the Homicide Task Force at the 4-8 and put in a holding pen. Franco had made arrangements to borrow a patrol van from the 4-7 desk to pick up the elderly victims. It was the only way they could think of to get everyone at one time. With the perp tucked away in the holding pen, they made their rounds picking up each elderly women and transporting them all together in the van to the 4-8 for line-ups. The only problem was these women were elderly and most could not climb into the van because of its height. Therefore, Franco found himself picking up each one and lifting her into the van.

One particular woman named Agnes gave the Officers a hard time because she couldn't get into the van. She took exception when Officer Franco attempted to lift her into the van. She claimed she was a church going woman and hadn't been touched by a man in many years. This prompted a big laugh from Owney and a stunned look on Franco's face.

Franco responded, "I'm just helping you into the van; I'm not carrying you over the threshold."

He explained to her that this was the only way to get her to the 4-8 unless she wanted to get a cab, so she reluctantly agreed. It was explained to the women that they were all victims of a robbery and assault, and they were going to view a line-up. The process that would be taking place was explained, and how a line-up is conducted. Also, that the suspect could not see them, because they would be viewing him through a one-way mirror. It was further explained there would be six individuals seated in a room, and they would have to tell the officers if they recognized anyone. They were instructed not to discuss the details of their individual cases with each other. One woman had a cast on her right arm from the assault and three of them had their heads wrapped with bandages due to the blunt trauma inflicted upon them. Franco seemed to be visibly affected by these women due to the fact his grandmother had been assaulted and robbed in a similar fashion when he was a young child. It was one of the main factors motivating him to become a police officer. Although glad he had caught this individual, he was afraid none of the women would be able to identify him. Franco and Owney had also contacted the two younger male witnesses who saw the suspect flee from the scene on two separate occasions. The first guy got a good look at him, and he stated that he could identify him if he saw his face again. The second guy actually chased him and removed the towel that was covering the license plate. He also stated he could identify the suspect. One problem was the fact neither man witnessed the attack; they only saw him fleeing from the scene.

So off they went, Owney, Franco and six frail, scared elderly women. Line-ups are conducted at the 48th Precinct on the second floor. As Franco, Owney and the ladies entered the Precinct; Franco approached the desk and explained the situation to the Lieutenant. He informed the Lieutenant that the women had a hard time walking; therefore, they would be taking the elevator to the second floor.

"Bad news," the Lieutenant shot back, "the elevator has been broken for three days.'

"How typical!" Franco responded. It seemed to be one of his favorite phrases. "Now what do we do?" He turned to the women and asked if they could make it up a flight of stairs. Everyone stated that they could except for Agnes. She was a grumpy old woman, but who could blame her. She had been assaulted, robbed, and hadn't been touched by a man in many years.

Owney turned to Franco and stated, "Well, you carried her into the van; I guess you could carry her up to the second floor."

Agnes was not a happy camper as Franco informed her if she couldn't walk up the stairs, he would have to carry her. She reluctantly agreed and Franco promised not to get fresh. That statement brought a smile to Agnes's face, and Franco thought, *she's not that bad.*

Owney escorted the five other women to the Bronx Homicide Task Force office and put them in a room where they couldn't be seen by the suspect in the cell. Franco cradled Agnes in his arms, ironically much like you would carry your bride over the threshold. It was a long flight of stairs, and Agnes was by no means a light weight. She must have been pushing two bills and he tried not to show the strain on his face as they went up one step at a time. When they got to the top landing he felt a sharp pain in his lower back and knew his sciatica would be acting up for the next two weeks. A single bead of sweat dripped off the tip of his nose. At this point in his career, he had sustained four herniated disks in his back and two in his neck and seemed to always be in some type of pain. But the elevator was out and there seemed to be no other way to get Agnes upstairs.

Agnes was put in a room with the other five women and Franco went to find Owney. He located him in the Bronx Robbery Office which was on the other side of the building from Bronx Homicide. Owney was informing some of the detectives from Bronx Robbery they had possibly caught the suspect from their Pattern Robbery up in the 4-7. They would in turn check their cases to see if his M.O. possibly matched any cases they were working on. Owney and Franco then went to speak with the two male witnesses who had made their way down to the 48th Precinct.

Now they had to find fillers for the line-ups. Fillers are the other five people who will sit in with the suspect to be viewed by the witnesses. Usually the Officers hand pick these fillers at the Mens' Shelter located on Prospect Avenue. Fillers get paid ten dollars per line-up. If they do five or six line-ups, they can make fifty or sixty dollars. In this case, with eight witnesses, there was money to be made. Owney and Franco told the witnesses they would be right back and hurriedly went to the mens' shelter to find prospective fillers.

"I hope we can find five white guys in the shelter," Franco quipped.

"That might be a hard one," Owney shot back. "Five homeless white guys in their twenties in a South Bronx men's shelter might not be easy."

As the Officers pulled up in front of the men's shelter, the residents were hanging out in front. When they see an unmarked car, they know they are usually there for line-up fillers. It's actually pretty funny because they start yelling, "line-up, line-up," and charge the car.

Franco, who was on the passenger side, yelled out the window, "White guys" and they all stopped dead in their tracks prompting the officers to get out of their car and go inside to search the shelter for prospective fillers. The stench of feet and ass hit them dead in the face as they walk into the large open room filled with cots on the floor.

Franco screamed, "Line-ups, white guys," and no one came running. The two officers split up, one going on one side of the room and the other on the other side, each canvassing the rows for potential fillers. They were able to locate five potential candidates but had to explain to each one what was involved. They reluctantly agreed especially since Franco wouldn't take no for an answer. They were brought back to the 4-8 where the line-up process was about to begin.

The male witnesses went first, each viewing the line-up individually; both picked out the individual seated in seat # 3 as being the person they witnessed flee the scene of the robberies. Seated in seat # 3 was the suspect that they had arrested, John Reilly. Now it was time for the ladies to view the line-up. Out of the six who viewed the line-up, only two were able to identify the suspect. This was better than Franco and Owney had envisioned. The woman with the broken arm was able to identify him because as he swung at her head, she fell, and landed on her right arm breaking it in two places. She said she looked right into his eyes while he pulled at her pocketbook as she franticly held on to it. The second witness to identify him was dear, old Agnes. She stated when he struck her head with what she described as a pipe of some sort, she fought back, and it was not until he pushed her to the ground that he was able to get her bag. Agnes stated, in her younger days, he would have been no match for her. Somehow Franco believed her.

The officers had enough evidence to charge the perp with the robberies. It would now be in the hands of the Bronx District Attorney to decide how many counts of Robbery in the first degree and assault in the first degree he would face. DA's line-ups were also conducted a week later with the other victims, who were not available at the time Franco and Owney did their line-ups. Two more victims identified the suspect in those line-ups. After the ladies testified at the Grand Jury, the suspect John Reilly cut a deal and admitted to seven robberies. The Bronx Robbery Squad was able to close out eight additional robberies in the area based on his M.O. and the suspect was sentenced to twelve to fifteen years in prison. He asked and received drug counseling as part of his sentence and asked for the victims' forgiveness as he read a prepared statement at his sentencing. He spoke about the evils of drugs and how he had grown up a good Catholic boy who was overwhelmed by the power drugs can have over a person. As the court officers led him away in handcuffs, he turned to the victims who were present and simply said "Sorry."

17

The Promotion

IT HAD BEEN OVER TWENTY-NINE MONTHS since Giovanni Franco was assigned to the Robbery Squad. Fiscal problems throughout the city caused the delay in promotions throughout the NYPD. There were also contract disputes, so police officers and detectives had been without a contract going on four years. When Officer Franco arrived for work on a rainy Wednesday morning in June of 1992, he was told by the lieutenant in the Robbery Squad there was a message for him from the Detective Borough in the telephone message log. The first thing he thought was he was being reassigned for the day to some detail that would find him in the bag (uniform) and he was in no mood for anything out of the ordinary on this day. His father was in the hospital recovering from open heart surgery and Franco and his entire family had been sitting vigil at the hospital 24/7 over the past three days. He was sleep deprived and probably should not even have gone to work on this day. As he walked into the Lieutenant's office there seemed to be a lot of detectives from both the Robbery Squad and the Detective Squad eyeing him, and he thought whatever it is, it must really be fucked up because there appears to be a lot of guys interested in my reaction. He could feel many pairs of eyes on him as he approached the message log. As he read the message, everyone started to clap. The message stated, P.O. Franco Shield # 8126 is to report 0900 hours June 18th to One Police Plaza in dress uniform for promotion to Detective third grade.

He stood there for a moment wondering if this was a prank or really true. The guys in the Squad were notorious for pulling pranks like putting a dummy page in the log. He had never heard of anyone pulling a prank about getting promoted but he was the suspicious type. He turned to the Lieutenant and asked "Is this for real?" The Lieutenant nodded his head yes and walked over to him and shook his hand. Several of the guys at this point also walked over to Franco and congratulated him. It hadn't set in yet, and he was a bit stunned. The promotion was long overdue in his mind, but he really hadn't given it much thought. As he walked over to his desk in the Robbery Squad thoughts of his father entered his mind. The promotion was in two days and a feeling of utter sadness came over him as he realized his father would not be able to see his son get promoted to Detective. He was recovering from open heart surgery and was still in the hospital. When Franco left the hospital last night his father was very sedated and was constantly moaning due to the severe pain he was experiencing. This really put a damper on what should have been a very happy moment in his life. The first thing he did when he got to his desk was call his mother. He told his mom the good news and the first thing she said was your father will be disappointed he can't be there. She asked if they could postpone the ceremony and Franco thought *yea, the mayor, police commissioner, and chief of detectives of the biggest city in the world, in the biggest police department in the world will postpone a promotion ceremony for me.*

"No, Ma," he told her, "you'll just have to take a lot of pictures and we can show them to him at the hospital."

"He's not going to like that; you know your father."

"I know Ma but what can we do? He is too weak to come and it's in two days."

He begged his mom not to tell his dad, because he wanted to tell him that night when he went to the hospital.

His mother was very happy for him and then she passed the phone to Nana, Franco's maternal grandmother. Nana was his heart, and she always told him he was her favorite but that was their secret; he could not tell his sisters or his cousins who were her other grandchildren. She was his mother's mother and lived upstairs from his mother and father, which was common in Italian families. His Nana would carry him in her arms when he was young when they went on long walks. Giovanni was a big kid, and he is probably the reason his Nana developed a bad back later on in life. When he told Nana he was being promoted to Detective she was very happy; he even thought she might have been crying a bit. She told him she was very proud of him and that she loved him. After he hung up the phone, he called his wife, he told her about the promotion, and she was also proud. She put their four-year-old son C.J. on the phone and Giovanni told him the news. Although he did not understand exactly what it meant he knew it was a good thing and he said to his daddy "That's good right?"

"Yes it's a good thing baby," he told his son. He spent the rest of the day making phone calls to tell his sisters and other friends and family.

When he arrived at the hospital, he went to his dad's room and found his dad sitting up in his bed eating his dinner. It was a delicious look- ing concoction of slop that was no doubt intended to keep you sick and increase your stay. He asked his father how he was feeling and he stated "much better."

"That's good," Giovanni said. "I've got some good news Dad," he continued, "I'm being promoted to Detective in two days."

Giovanni's father's eyes began to swell up with tears and Giovanni became very uncomfortable. He had never seen his father cry before and he didn't know how to react. There was no one else in the room as the rest of his family hadn't yet arrived at the hospital.

"Come here my son," his father commanded as he motioned to him with his arms out stretched. Giovanni was afraid he would hurt his father as he hugged him, but he did as he was told. he always did what his father told him. As they embraced, his father whispered in his ear, "I love you my son. You have always made me proud that you are my boy. I will be there to see you get promoted."

"No, Dad," Giovanni told him. "The ceremony is in two days and the doctors told Mommy you will be here at least another week."

"Did you hear what I said?" His dad stated as he gave him a stern look. "I will be there."

Giovanni knew not to argue; he figured he would leave that to the doctor and his mother and sisters when they get there. A short time later everyone was in the hospital room and the nurse came in several times to tell everyone to keep it down. The room was located in the Surgical I.C.U. and the limit was two visitors at a time. Giovanni used his influ- ence to allow triple that amount. The nurse told him if you are all going to stay you must please keep the noise down. Giovanni's mother, sisters, and Nana were telling his father he can't possibly go to the ceremony. That was probably the worst thing you could ever tell his father, that he couldn't do something. As they argued about it for what seemed like forever, the doctor who performed the surgery entered the room. Giovanni's mother explained the situation to him and asked if it would be possible. He in- formed them in no uncertain terms that neither he, nor the hospital, would for liability reasons; grant him a discharge so soon after his operation. Not defeated, Giovanni's father asked him the magic question. "What if I just get up and leave? You can't keep me here against my will."

"No we can't!" the doctor exclaimed. "You can sign yourself out and that would remove any liability the hospital has if something should happen to you, but I don't recommend it."

"Okay doc, make sure you have those papers for me to sign on Friday morning and I would like to be out of here by 7:00 A.M." The doctor shook his head in disbelief as he left the room. Everyone in the room knew there was no sense in attempting to talk his dad out of the decision he had made. He was going to see his only son be promoted to Detective in two days, even if it killed him.

18

The Ceremony

THE BIG DAY HAD ARRIVED AND Officer Franco was meeting Officer Owney who was also being promoted at the 4-7, where they would drive down together to One Police Plaza for the promotion ceremony. As they dressed in the basement locker room, several well wishers came by and congratulated them. They were in their dress uniforms which are only worn for ceremonies such as promotions, parades, and funerals. As they made their way up to the lobby and went over to the desk, the Captain of the Precinct motioned to them to come over. He congratulated them and joked they sure had lowered the standards for detectives these days. They made their way up to the squad room and signed out an unmarked car to take down to the ceremony. Several Detectives wished them well as Franco sipped on a cup of coffee. Then he called his mother's house to make sure his father had been picked up from the hospital that morning. She stated he was, and that the car service was in front of the house, waiting to take everyone downtown. He asked who was coming and she rattled off nine names, "Well it's me, and Daddy, Nana, Cristina, Roger and Eric, Olga, your wife, and the baby."

"And you're all going down in one car?" Giovanni asked.

"Yes, the guy's outside now let me go 'cause we have to help your father. He can hardly walk and I don't know how he's going to do it."

"Well, let him hold onto Roger to steady him," Giovanni told his mom.

He was relieved knowing his whole family would be going together to the ceremony and he envisioned them riding in style in a beautiful stretch limousine.

As he and Owney drove down the FDR, the traffic was remarkably light and they arrived at One Police Plaza with plenty of time to spare. Franco was driving and he had a knack of getting to places quickly, even in bumper to bumper traffic. To the untrained eye, you might think he drove recklessly, but he actually was a very good "offensive driver." He figured if everyone was behind him, they can't hit him.

After they found a parking space near One Police Plaza, they threw the Detective Parking Plaque onto the dashboard and made their way into the building. They were to report to the head of the Ceremonial Unit in the auditorium. As they received their instructions, they were told to go to the 5th floor and report to the Shield Desk. At the Shield Desk they turned in their White Shields and were awarded their Gold Detective Shields. When the Sergeant from the Shield Desk took Franco's shield, he placed it into a mold to make sure it was the original assigned to him and not a "Dup" (Duplicate). After making sure it fit, the Sergeant tossed Franco's shield into a big cardboard box and it made a "ting" sound as it landed on the other white shields in the box. A sense of sadness came over him as he realized he would never see that shield again. They had been through a lot together and he felt like a part of him was being taken away. *If that shield could talk…*, he thought. But he told himself that he was moving on to bigger and better things, and maybe someday if his son C.J. decided to follow in his footsteps, he could request his dad's shield and he would see it once again.

Franco and Owney were told to get on another line to be awarded their Gold Shields. The N.Y.P.D. is very big on lines and you seem to spend a lot of your time on them. When they got to the front of the line, Franco was awarded Shield # 4328 and Owney was awarded # 4315. They were not officially detectives until the ceremony took place at 11:00 A.M. They made their way down to the Auditorium and Giovanni had time to canvass the crowd for his family. He spotted them in the second row and thought to himself *I bet my father gave someone a hard time to get those seats.* The auditorium was filled to capacity and there must have been two thousand people there. He walked over and kissed everyone hello. His mother commented how handsome her son looked in his uniform causing him to blush just a little. Other people sitting nearby heard her and he responded, "Ma." He asked his father "How you doing Dad?" and his father replied, "I'm fine." He could see the pain in his father's face as he sat on the metal folding chair. His chest was all bandaged and he clutched at his chest as he coughed. Giovanni thought, *He is one tough, crazy s.o.b.* He told them he had to go line up with the others who were being promoted, and his son C.J. asked if he could go with him.

"No you have to stay here with Mommy, but when it's all over we will go out for ice cream." That brought a smile to his face and Giovanni gave him several kisses on his belly as he held him up over his head.

"You watch for Daddy; I'm gonna be up on the stage in a little while"

"Okay Daddy," C.J. shot back, "See you later." With that Giovanni went to get on another line.

The ceremony began with all the pomp and circumstance that only the N.Y.P.D. could provide. There is an old saying in the N.Y.P.D, "The two things the N.Y.P.D. does best are Promotions and Funerals." Well, lucky for Giovanni he was experiencing the former and not the latter. The N.Y.P.D. Emerald Society Pipes and Drums Band started things off as they entered the auditorium playing the National Anthem. Everyone rose and Giovanni turned as he stood and tried to locate his dad. He just knew his father would be standing, and sure enough there he was standing at his seat with his left hand steadying himself by holding onto the back of his chair and his right hand placed over his heart. He was a Korean War veteran and there was no way he would sit as the Star Spangled Banner played. He had to look away as he felt himself becoming emotional. He stood there at attention with the rest of the honorees saluting the flag in his dress blues and white gloves.

All the dignitaries who were present were introduced along with Mayor Dinkins, Police Commissioner Brown, and all the Chiefs of the various Bureaus. There were several speeches made and finally the time came when the Detectives were being introduced to the audience. As Giovanni's name was called he rose and marched up to the stage. Once on the stage he saluted the Police Commissioner and then the various Chiefs. The Police Commissioner congratulated him, shook his hand and awarded him a large certificate that stated he was promoted to the rank of Detective within the N.Y.P.D. The Police Department photographer took his picture as he shook the Commissioner's and Mayor's hands. The audience was applauding and Detective Giovanni Franco gave a quick glance over to where his family was sitting. He spotted them and they were all standing, even his father. He made his way off the stage and back to his seat. He sat there holding the certificate and glanced down at it every now and then. The ceremony ended with the Pipers playing several songs as they led their way out of the auditorium.

He met up with his family in the lobby, and they took several pictures. Each family member stood next to Detective Giovanni and posed for a picture. Everyone seemed very proud of him and he was extremely happy. They were standing in front of the wall with all the names of the officers who were killed in the line of duty. His mother noticed it and commented, "The names seem to go on forever." He suggested they stand near the statue of the police officer with his hand on a young boy's shoulder. He didn't want to spoil the moment by having his family thinking about him being killed in the line of duty. It was a happy occasion and he didn't want to put a damper on it. They took several more pictures and then he said he would walk them out to the car waiting for them outside. As they headed for the car, his father supported himself on Giovanni and he looked exhausted. When they got outside, He asked his sister Olga (O.J) where the car was parked and she pointed to The Avenue of The Finest. He was looking but did not see a limo or town car.

"Where?" he asked.

"Over there," she shot back" but he still did not see the car.

Now he was becoming annoyed.

"Where over there?" he asked in an annoyed tone of voice.

"The bus over there," she shot back.

As he looked out on the street he observed a yellow school bus parked at the curb with a tiny Hispanic man sitting behind the wheel.

"I know you're joking," he stated as a sense of embarrassment came over him.

"A bus, you rented a school bus, are you serious, why a bus?"

He began to look around to see if anyone he knew was looking on. He could not believe they had rented a school bus.

His mother shot back, "It's good, we had plenty of room and everyone fit. Your father was able to stretch out in the back and the man driving was very nice."

Giovanni began to laugh and everyone else laughed along with him. It might not have been luxurious or classy, but he realized at that moment, it really didn't matter. What really mattered was the fact his entire family found a way to get there to share in his special day, even his father who was five days removed from open heart surgery. All of a sudden he was not feeling embarrassment anymore; he was feeling pride. Proud that he had such a loving family who would do whatever they had to do to be with him on this day. He helped each of them onto the bus and said he would meet them at mommy's house after he returned to the Precinct and changed out of his uniform.

When he arrived at his mother's house, all of his relatives were there including his mother and father, grandmother, wife and son, sisters, brother-in-law, cousins, aunts and uncles. They had a big party and everyone had a great time. The smiles on everyone's faces made Giovanni feel lucky to have such a close, loving family.

19

West Indian Day Parade

LABOR DAY IN THE NYPD IS A DAY some cops dread. Although the rest of the country considers it to be a holiday, in the police department there's a chance you'll be assigned to the West Indian Day Parade in Brooklyn. As far as Detective Franco was concerned, this day sucked. The West Indian Day Parade takes place every year on Labor Day and is considered NYC's largest parade. Crowds of people hailing from Jamaica, Trinidad, Barbados, and Grenada line up along Brooklyn's Eastern Parkway and make their way from Utica Avenue to Grand Army Plaza. Although they call it a parade, most cops consider it a gathering of loincloth wearing, drunken, high, lunatics, and 400 pound women prancing down the street wearing barely a stitch of clothing. It's enough to make the average American male sick to his stomach. The city doesn't talk about it, but there must be a reason why it's held in Brooklyn and not on Fifth Avenue in Manhattan where the rest of the parades are held for other ethnic groups. There's a feeling of lawlessness that permeates through the parade route. The officers assigned to this detail are usually picked based on their lack of seniority or what's known as, ordered overtime. The senior officers get ordered in to work on their day off. There's no refusing it and it's one of the seven days that the city can make you work in uniform contractually, on your day off. Detective Franco had been assigned this parade several times before and hated it. This day, in 1993, Detective Franco, back in the bag, was again assigned this ordered overtime detail.

As he stood on the corner of Bedford Avenue and Eastern Parkway, he was already anticipating the worst. Not a good mind set to have when you'll be standing on a corner surrounded by drunken and high miscreants for the next twelve hours. His precinct, the 4-7, was predominately Jamaican in population so he thought to himself, *I'm not even getting a break on my day off*. There seemed to be an inherent dislike, not only for the police, but for all white people by Jamaicans, some of this, no doubt, stemming from Rastafarian beliefs that Romans are the cause of all ills known to man. Franco had been called the "White Devil" numerous times in his career, and he felt somewhat of a dislike or at least distrust, of West Indian people in general. He knew this was an unfair characterization as he realized there are good and bad in every ethnic group, but having worked with this population for some time gave him a different outlook. Ironically he had some West Indian friends, both in the police department and in his private life, but they seemed different. They accepted him for who he was, and they thought of him as an excellent man and father. He in turn, considered them dear friends and didn't view them by their ethnicity. It seemed the ones who didn't know him personally, would assume he was evil based on the color of his skin. He found this ironic, because when you think of discrimination, or racism, it's usually the other way around.

Here Detective Franco was, on a hot September morning, with steel drums blaring in his ears and a large crowd gathered behind the police barricades. Every now and then there would be a strong whiff of marijuana in the air mixed in with the smell of Jerk Chicken, and people seemed to be drinking alcohol everywhere without fear of reprisals from the police. It was an unwritten rule and obviously the people knew it, that the police would only deal with very serious issues, such as stabbings, shootings and thefts. The bosses who muster you at the beginning of the parade would let it be known that you needed to use discretion when it came to enforcing the laws. In other words, unless you are attacked or you see someone else being attacked, look the other way, because we only have a certain amount of manpower on hand and this so called parade can blow up at any moment.

Detective Franco had been on his post for about three hours and he could feel the sweat dripping down his back. He was wearing a double layer of Kevlar in his bullet proof vest which made it twice as heavy as usual. The added level of Kevlar increased the stopping ability of a bullet depending on the caliber. If one layer stopped a 38, two layers would stop a 9mm or a small rifle round. There was past history of shots being fired into the crowd and at the police at this parade. He actually witnessed a shooting right across from his post the last time he was assigned to this parade in 1989.

West Indian Day Parade

A collection of floats carrying various neighborhood big shots, such as the owner of the local carwash, made its way down the parade route. He was just starting to feel maybe this parade would go by without incident when suddenly he locked eyes with a very tall nearly naked man painted green and wearing a loincloth. He was carrying a spear and dancing alongside one of the floats. They seemed to look at each other from hundreds of feet away and Franco knew instantly that this man would be a problem. They did not take their eyes off each other as the man danced and pranced down the parade route towards him, apparently gunning for Franco. The music was blaring but he didn't hear anything as he focused his eyes on this person coming towards him. Their eyes never left each other as the man got closer and closer. He removed his nightstick from its holder and positioned it in front of him. As he looked into the green man's eyes he vehemently shook his head back and forth, telling the man, *don't come near me*. But the green man continued to dance, whirl and make a spectacle of himself as he came closer and closer. Once he got about 20 feet away, he smiled a big smile at the Detective and the contrast between his green painted skin and his yellow teeth was glaring. Franco could see his bloodshot eyes and he assumed the man was drunk or high. As he got within 10 feet of him, Franco again shook his head no, warning the man, without saying anything, not to come any closer. At this point the man took three large steps towards him and did a spinning pirouette directly in front of him. As he did this, his green back rubbed across the front of Franco's uniform shirt. He instantly looked down and saw a big green smear of paint across his crisply pressed uniform. Detective Franco raised his nightstick and brought it down on the top of the green man's head, causing a loud clunk sound, like a bat hitting a tree, or maybe a coconut falling from a tree. Franco thought, *here we go*.

People started yelling and screaming in the street. They began jumping off floats, pushing and fighting with the police. All hell broke loose on that one particular corner and you could say a riot ensued. Franco attempted to put his back to something stationary but could only find a light pole to use. There were people throughout the street, fighting with the police, throwing bottles, screaming in their native tongues. A tall husky man took a swing at him and Franco, holding his nightstick with both hands, violently extended it forward, hitting the man in the throat and knocking him to the ground. At that same time, he felt someone grab his shoulder from behind, and he was sure he was about to be sucker punched. He raised his stick above his head and spun around quickly. To his surprise, a two star chief was standing behind him. The chief, in a very authoritative loud voice stated,

"Take five Officer; go sit in the bus," referring to the city buses the cops were transported on from the precinct.

Franco, being pumped up from all the fighting and being somewhat defiant in nature, pointed to his shield, and stated to the chief, "It's DETECTIVE and I think I'll take ten!"

With that he walked away from the center of the riot and boarded a city bus parked on the corner. With his heart pounding, he looked out of the window of the bus and tried to collect himself, but he realized that he could not in good conscience stay there while his fellow officers were battling in the street. He felt somewhat responsible for the situation at hand, even though in his heart he knew he had warned the green man several times and he felt it was not his fault. He jumped back off the bus and ran back into the center of the mayhem. A city wide 1013 (officer needs assistance) had been dispatched over the airways and both the Brooklyn North and South Task Forces had been mobilized. The riot went on for approximately one hour before order was restored. There were numerous injuries both to civilians and to police and some in the crowd found it to be an opportunity to begin looting stores and businesses along the parade route. *How typical,* Franco thought to himself as he watched people running out of the liquor store carrying cases of cheap wine. When order was restored, he finally had time to reflect and thought for sure the Chief would have his ass. When he finally got back to his command (the 47th precinct) at 10 P.M. usually, the parade would be over by four in the afternoon. He thought, *well, I made fourteen hours overtime, but I'm sure that Brooklyn Chief is going to try to screw me.*

A week or so went by and he hadn't heard any repercussions from the parade riot. Is it possible the Chief never caught his name? Being from the Bronx, maybe he had no idea who he was. Or better yet, maybe he didn't even realize the whole incident started with him in the first place. He never heard anything more about the incident and it was the last time he was ever assigned to the West Indian parade. Maybe it was a coincidence or maybe it was fate.

20

Large Moe

LARGE MOE GREW UP IN THE BRONX, a poor kid with a big appetite, his given name being Maurice Carmelo Cabrera. By the time he was eleven, he already weighed 200 pounds. Moe's father was Cuban and his mother was Puerto Rican, but Moe identified with his mother's ancestry since his father was never around and he had no memory of ever meeting him. From an early age he was into rap music, and the spoken word. Although his music was severely criticized by the majority of the American public for its gross use of obscenities and lack of respect for women and authority, Moe still had his followers. He also had a dark side and a need to get some street cred, which he tried to fulfill by rapping about killing cops and disrespecting women. He would sometimes break the law in front of his entourage just so people would think he was a gangster.

One day in 1994 Detective Giovanni Franco and Large Moe's paths crossed. There was a shooting at a nightclub on White Plains Road called Act III and Franco was the lead investigator. It seemed that a skinny underage Puerto Rican kid was shot several times at this local club and all fingers pointed to Large Moe. No one was willing to come forward and finger him as it is an unwritten rule to not rat people out amongst certain groups. So the investigation made its way back to the 47th Precinct Detective Squad interrogation room.

Franco had a lot of people on the street giving him information, and the word was that Large Moe did it. It seemed that the victim was himself an up and coming rapper who was talking shit in his music that he is the only true Puerto Rican rapper from the Bronx. Although not many people had heard of this new kid on the block, in the rapping circles he was considered very talented. People in the know told Franco that Large

Never a Dull Moment

Moe was not only very angry, but had told people on the street that if he got the chance he would make the skinny kid eat his words. Franco didn't have a witness who was willing to testify and the gun was not recovered, so he needed to try to get a confession. When the first officers on the scene attempted to interview the victim, he told them he didn't know who shot him and couldn't identify him. When Franco arrived at Jacobi hospital, he attempted to interview the victim but was told by his mother that she did not want her son to speak to the police. He was only seventeen years old and Franco shot back "your son should not even have been in a club drinking, he is under age." With that the mother responded, "fuck you, then arrest him and see how it looks to arrest someone who has just been shot, I'll have every news station here in an hour and I'm a very good crier." With that Franco knew unless he got a confession, this case was going nowhere. Franco and his partner Tim Owney responded back to the 4-7 where they were holding Large Moe and others from his entourage in separate pens downstairs.

He brought Large Moe upstairs to the Detective Squad interrogation room which consisted of a table with a chair on either side. There were four dark blue painted walls made of cinder block. He told Large Moe to have a seat and went behind him to remove his handcuffs. He then began to question him. Large Moe admitted to being at the Club and in the general area where the shooting took place, but stated that he had nothing to do with it. His entourage, who were also taken to the 4-7 Precinct, were being kept downstairs in different holding pens. At one point during the questioning, Large Moe became agitated when Franco told him he knew he did the shooting. He sneered at Franco, giving him what he thought was his signature tough guy look, but Franco wasn't buying it.

At that point, Large Moe stood up and pointed his finger at Franco stating, "Arrest me then, do you know who I am?" With that, Franco backhanded his big fat face making a very loud echoing sound within the room. Large Moe stood there, his mouth open and stunned, with a big welt on his cheek.

Franco stated to him, "Do you know who I am? I'm the guy who has your balls in my hand, and you don't want me to squeeze. Now sit your fat ass down and don't speak until you're spoken to."

The rest of the night the responses from Large Moe were "Yes sir, no sir, may I please get a drink sir? Can I please use the bathroom sir?" and so forth. Large Moe was allowed to use the phone after several hours and he called his lawyer.

A short time later, one of the guys in Large Moe's entourage confessed to doing the shooting and stated that he handed the gun off. He claimed that he didn't know the person he gave the gun to. He also stated that large Moe had nothing to do with it. That person was arrested even though Franco knew that he was taking the rap for Large Moe. The ADA assigned to the case stated, "You have no proof that Maurice Carmelo Cabrera did it, and this guy is confessing. So we have to go with it." The case never made it to trial because the victim refused to press charges and everyone knew that Large Moe had paid off the victim, and the guy in his entourage who took the rap. Large Moe even cut a record with the victim several months later entitled "5-0 CAN'T STOP THE CASH FLOW." 5-0 is slang for the police. What a beautiful thing, harmony amongst rappers. This case haunted Franco for the rest of his career.

21

I Like Dark Meat

THANKSGIVING, FOR MOST PEOPLE, means family being together, kids home from school, parents off from work, and everyone being able to sit around the table, enjoying each other's company, sharing laughs and, of course, good food. But this, unfortunately, is not what it means to a detective. Although corporations close down while their employees jet off to grandma's for some hot toddies, police and detectives are hard at work, protecting their cities and safeguarding their communities. Crime does not take a holiday. Homes being unoccupied due to travel are prime candidates for burglary and too much alcohol around the Thanksgiving table can often be a recipe for disaster, leading to violence or even homicide.

It was Thanksgiving Day 1994 and Detective Franco tried not to think about the fact he was away from his family. Thanksgiving was actually his mother's favorite holiday. It allowed her to cook up a storm, which she loved to do except for the stuffing, which was his father's job. His father along with his youngest sister had been making the stuffing for as long as he could remember. Unlike Christmas, there was no pressure on her children to buy her gifts, and she preferred they saved their money. The guys in the squad had ordered Chinese food; there was pork fried rice and General Tso chicken which came from the dump across the street. There always seems to be a Chinese restaurant across from every precinct. Franco knew it was a far cry from the lasagna, antipasto, turkey, Aunt Camille's chicken soup, mashed potatoes, stuffed artichokes, candied yams, sweet potatos, and everything else that would be passed around the table at home. He just couldn't bring himself to eat Chinese on Thanksgiving. He would rather wait until he got off from work.

At around 2:30 P.M., a call came into the squad of a man stabbed, likely to die. Franco looked up at the clock on the wall and thought to himself, *they're probably just starting to eat the antipasto right now*, making reference to his whole family who were surely at his mother's house enjoying a feast. He got up and walked over to the catching sheet to see who was up. Of course it was him. "Fuck," he said out loud. He was hoping to be out by four o'clock. Now there was no way that was going to happen. It was probably going to be an all-nighter. He would be lucky now to be eating a turkey sandwich sometime tomorrow morning. He gave it further thought and figured that probably wouldn't even happen if his brother-in-law Roger kept going back for seconds and thirds.

Detectives in the squad catch by times. Depending on how many detectives are working that day, you could catch for two hours, three hours, etc. For example, if there are four detectives working, it is broken into two hours each. Anything that happens in your two hours is yours. There had been times when he was the only one who caught cases all day because everything happened in his time frame. He went over to the RMP board and grabbed keys to unmarked car # 1550. It was a Black Crown Victoria and he liked its stereo. He yelled over to Rice who was in a deep conversation with Schieffman about who the Chief was fucking more out of overtime. He told Rice they had a guy stabbed, likely at Jacobi. Jacobi Hospital is a major trauma center and all the cops in the Bronx say "If I get shot, take me to Jacobi." Franco had witnessed amazing things done in the E.R for people whom he was sure were going to die.

They went out into the street and looked for the car. It wasn't in front of the precinct, and they started to walk around the corner. It was located all the way up 229th Street, almost a block away. Both Franco and Rice found this strange and when they got in they understood why. The car was a mess inside and the gas tank read empty. Detectives Murcer and Tompkins, the squad slobs, had the car before them on a stakeout. They apparently hit every bodega that morning and left coffee cups, empty chip bags, cigarette butts and both copies of the *Daily News* and *The New York Post* on the floor. Franco, being a bit of a neat freak said to Rice, "When I see those douche bags, I'm gonna fix their asses good." He was no doubt planning one of his practical jokes which he was a master of.

"What do you have planned?" asked Rice.

"It's gonna be a whopper," he answered, "you'll have to wait and see." So now they had to waste time getting gas before responding to the hospital.

Detectives are usually more conscious of keeping the car neat and gassed up for the next guys, but Murcer and Tompkins seemed to do this a lot. Franco even had a confrontation with Tompkins a while back about it. That time he got into the car that they had been using previously and he sat on a buttered roll that was left on the passenger seat. He had butter all over the leg of his suit pants. He went ballistic and ran into the station house to see if he could find one of them. He located Tompkins in the lounge up in the Squad. He held the flattened roll in his hand and hid it from sight behind his back. He asked Tompkins, "Did you guys have buttered rolls in the RMP?"

Tompkins replied, "Murcer had one but I didn't eat mine."

As Franco approached him he said, "Well I think you should have yours now." He then proceeded to shove it in Tompkins face forcing some of it into his mouth. Tompkins took a swing at him and that was just what Franco was hoping for. He side stepped the punch and landed a left hook to Tompkins' stomach. Tompkins went down on one knee and Franco walked away. He took a few steps and then turned and told Tompkins, "If you ever leave shit in the car like that again, I'll make you eat it." There were several other detectives in the lounge and no one said a word. They all liked Franco and thought he was a good guy, but they also knew he had a temper and a mean streak and he was not one to be fucked with. While he pumped the gas in the precinct driveway (all precincts have their own gas pumps), Rice cleaned all the garbage out of the inside of the car.

They hurried over to Jacobi Medical Center on Pelham Parkway. When they arrived, they went into the E.R. and were told that the stab victim was in surgery. They were directed to the victim's family who were in a waiting room near the lobby entrance. There were two uniform cops from the 4-7 standing across the room. At this point Franco and Rice had no information regarding what happened. They were directed to the mother of the victim. She was a short, fat white woman probably in her early sixties. She was wearing dirty sweatpants and a stained white sweatshirt that said *Frankie Says Relax* on the front. Franco thought *nice Thanksgiving apparel*. She was sitting next to her son who she introduced to the Detectives as Joey. Franco asked, "What is the name of your son who was stabbed?"

She replied "Anthony, but he wasn't stabbed he fell on the fork." They ascertained the needed information such as DOB (date of birth) and such and then Rice asked her, "Who stabbed your son?"

The mother hesitated and then said "He fell on the carving fork."

"He fell on the carving fork." Franco stated repeating the mother.

"Yes" she replied.

"Okay" Franco said "tell me from the beginning what happened."

Rice asked her son Joey to take a walk with him. The detectives wanted to separate them and get their stories without them hearing each other. Franco looked over at Rice as he was walking away with Joey and he noticed Rice had his arm around Joey's shoulder. *"Don't tell me this guy stabbed his brother on Thanksgiving,"* Franco thought. "One minute" Franco told the mother as he walked over to the two uniform cops across the way. "Are you guys here for this?" Franco asked.

"Yea" one of them stated. "We caught the job and when we got there the vic (victim) was unconscious and the mother said he fell on the carving fork. When we asked the brother what happened, he said he did not know. He was acting real weird and would not look us in the eye. The Sarge established a crime scene in the apartment just in case and told us to call the squad."

"You're the experts," said the other uniform cop who was new in the precinct and seemed to be a little sarcastic. Sometimes there is some tension between the squad and guys on patrol. The patrol guys sometime feel that the detectives drink coffee all day up in the squad room while they're out in the street catching all the shit. The truth is most detectives were in their position at one time and were promoted to detective because they were real good cops. It's kind of like you have to pay your dues.

Franco looked this young cop over for a second and asked "Do I know you?"

"I'm Mike Reilly," he stated.

"Are you new?" Franco asked, now determined to fuck with him.

"I'm new to the 4-7," he shot back "but not new to the job."

"Oh yeah, how much time you got on?" Franco asked.

"Five years," the officer boasted as if he should receive a medal or something.

"Five years," Franco said repeating him. "So that means you got fifteen more to go. Shit if I was you I'd slit my wrists."

Franco was making the point he had a long time to go and probably should keep his stupid comments to himself. He always felt the need to set people straight even from when he was a young boy growing up in the Bronx.

"Okay so tell me what you know," Franco demanded in a stern tone to the officer he had just chastised.

"Well, like he said," stated the officer, deferring to his partner, "we got this job, heavy bleeder on Matilda Avenue. When we got there, the aided was unconscious. His mother was there crying and his brother was sitting at the table eating turkey and other stuff. So we called for a bus (ambulance) and asked the mother what happened. She said he fell on the fork coming out of the kitchen; that he tripped over the saddle that separated the kitchen floor from the dining room. We asked the brother and he didn't even look up at us; he just kept eating. The Sarge thought it was weird or maybe he is just an EDP (emotionally disturbed person) so he told sector

Henry Ida to establish a crime scene and for us to take mother and son here."

"Where is the carving fork?" Franco asked.

"Back at the scene," Officer Reilly stated. With that Franco pulled out his cell phone and called the Squad. He spoke to Sgt. Muller and told him they might have a crime scene on Matilda and he needed detectives to get over there before the patrol guys fuck up the scene. He said it loud enough for Officer Reilly to hear. The Sarge stated he would send Owney and Price. *That was good*, Franco thought, *they both know what they're doing*.

"Make sure they safeguard and voucher the carving fork," Franco added.

Out of the corner of his eye, He saw Rice coming back with Joey. He sat Joey next to his mother and Franco knew the case was solved. Rice walked over to Franco and stated, "Wait 'til you hear this shit."

"I'm all ears," Franco said.

"Okay, so Anthony, the vic, who is the only one in the house who works, is at work until two o'clock. His mother has been cooking all day and Joey over there is real hungry. He said he was smelling his mother's cooking all day and wanted to eat. His mother told him they would have to wait until Anthony got home from work. He works at a bakery on Arthur Avenue, plus he was bringing home the bread. Joey talked his mother into carving the turkey so it would be ready to eat as soon as Anthony walked through the door. She agreed and carved the turkey. Apparently it is tradition in the family for each boy to eat a drum stick. So the mother covers the plate of turkey with tin foil and puts it on the table in the dining room. She goes back into the kitchen to prepare the other delights and low and behold, Joey can't fight the temptation and swipes a turkey leg. He goes into the bathroom and eats it. He throws the bone out the bathroom window and goes back to the couch to watch more of the football game. He's a big Cowboy's fan. So now he realizes he's still hungry and he goes over and swipes the other drumstick, goes into the bathroom and does the same as before. The turkey is all covered nice and tight with the foil. The mother puts all the other food on the table awaiting Anthony and the fresh Arthur Avenue Italian bread. Anthony comes home and they sit down to dinner. When the mother takes the foil off the turkey both drum sticks are gone. Anthony asked his mother, 'Where are the drumsticks?' and his mother is standing there staring at the legless turkey. Joey starts to laugh and tells Anthony he ate them because it took him so long to come home. All hell breaks loose and the two brothers start fighting. Anthony, according to Joey, punches Joey a couple of times and picks up the carving fork.

Joey, being well nourished, wrestles the fork away from his brother and plunges it into his chest in self defense."

"Self defense?" Franco exclaimed.

"That's what he told me," Rice responded. "He stated 'it was either Him or Me, so I chose me."

"We better let the Sarge know," Franco stated.

He called the Squad and gave them the update. Then they went over to the mother who by now knew Joey had let the cat out of the bag.

"Is there anything you want to tell us?" they asked the mother.

"Well I didn't want to see my son get in trouble," she explained.

"What about your other son?" Rice asked.

"Well, if he dies, it would not have changed anything," she said. "You can't un-ring a bell," she added. Franco stood there shaking his head.

"And if he lives?" Franco asked.

"Well, if he lives, which I hope he does, he's my first born," she continued, "then his brother will have to apologize and make it up to him."

No wonder this guy's a nut, Franco thought. *The apple doesn't fall far from the tree.* They got an update on the condition of Anthony and were told that he was in critical condition but that he was stable and not likely to die. Everyone was relieved and the detectives removed the mother and son to the 4-7 Squad to take written statements. The son was arrested for attempted murder in the second degree, assault in the first degree, and criminal possession of a weapon in the first degree. Rice took the collar and they finished up the processing at approximately 9:00 P.M.

Franco called his mother's house about fifteen minutes later and told his mom he was on his way home. She said, "Your sister Cristina was about to leave." She put Cristina on the phone and she said they would wait until he got there and hang out for a while. His younger sister, whom he affectionately called O.J. since she was a baby, would surely be waiting for him along with his wife and two sons C.J and Thomas.

His mother told him there was plenty of food left over, probably because she cooks for an army on holidays and his father was sitting on the couch watching the football game. Franco rushed home and when he walked into the house everyone greeted him with hugs and kisses. He thought to himself, *I have such a loving family, and although we don't always agree on everything, we don't stab each other with carving forks either.*

22

*What's in
the Bag?*

ONE OF DETECTIVE GIOVANNI FRANCO'S favorite things to do on a slow day
was to play a practical joke on a rookie who was assigned as the TS (telephone switchboard) operator. He would position himself far enough away
to be able to see the facial expressions of the officer but not be heard by
him. He would call the TS from another precinct phone and in a heavy Italian accent would explain his problem. It went something like this:

"Hello. Is thees-a the forty seva precint? My name is-a Luigi Pa-
trucci. I live-a at 4255 Seton Avenue. Datsa you precinct, right? Okay I was-
a drive-a my car down-a White-a Plains-a Road and I see-a dis black-a boy
a hitch-a hike. So-a I say-a to myself, 'Luigi, no pick-a up dis kid, he might-
a be-a drug-a addict.' But it was a rain-a, so I feel-a bad. I pull ova and he
get in-a my car in the front-a seat and I notice he carry a big-a black-a bag."

"He say, 'can-a you take-a me to-a Gunhill Hill Road?'"

" I say, 'sure im-a go-a that way.' I start-a to drive and I say-a to him,
'what-a you got in the bag?'"

"He get-a real nasty and he say-a to me, 'NONA YOU FUCKIN BUSI-
NESS, OLE MAN.'

" I say to myself, 'Luigi, you stupa son of a bitch, why you pick-a up
this-a fucka kid? '

"So I keep-a drive and I come-a to a red light. Across from me is-a
police-a car, face-a the other way. I was-a go a southboun and the police-a
they-a go-a nortboun. I try to make eye contact but they no look-a at me.
The lights turn-a green and I keep-a go.

"I say to the kid, 'I did not mean a nothin when I ask-a you, what was
in the bag. I was just make-a conversation.' I get-a to Two Eighteen Street

and there's a police-a man stand-a on the corna. I look at him but he no look at me.

"I say to the kid, 'That's a nice-a bag. Whata you gotta, basketball shoes in the bag or somethin?'

"He say to me, 'I toll you ole man, NONA YOU FUCKIN BUSINESS.'

"I say, 'Jesa Christ' to myself, *'this-a kid gonna kill you Luigi, shuta the fuck up*! '

"When-a I get-a to Two Dirteen Street, there' s-a two police-a man on the corner.

"I think a to myself 'Luigi pull-a the car ova by the police-a man and jump-a out.'

"As I slow-a down, the black-a boy, he jump-a outta the car. I drive away, and-a when I get-a home, I realize he leave-a the bag on the floor in the car. "

With that the TS operator who has been listening to the whole story without interruption, asks Franco, "Did you look in the bag?"

Franco responds, "A sure!"

The TS operator asks, "Well what's in the bag?"

And Franco responds, "NONA YOU FUCKIN BUSINESS!"

The TS Operator slams the phone down and looks around knowing he's been had. Usually there are several detectives in the area in on the joke and they all start laughing and pointing at the rookie. Franco inevitably would walk by with a smile on his face, and without saying a word would let the TS Operator know that he was the one who got him. Usually the rookie would vow to get him back, but that never seemed to happen.

23

Some Heads Are Gonna Roll

THERE'S NEVER A DULL MOMENT IN A squad room, and although there is always paperwork to be done, hot summer days don't really inspire anyone in that direction. Detectives sometimes amuse themselves by pulling practical jokes on one another. A favorite was the shaving cream in the phone trick. Detective Franco was notorious for this one. He would put shaving cream on the earpiece of his Lieutenant's phone and then call the Lieutenant's extension from his desk. He would then quickly walk past the Lieutenant's office door as he answered it. The Lieutenant would curse and scream as he got an earful of shaving cream and would vow to transfer the person responsible for this prank. Although all of the detectives in the squad knew it was Franco, no one would ever give him up. Everyone would just shrug and say "It wasn't me, Lu." The squad was a brotherhood that nothing, and no one, could ever sever.

With cases that had gone cold and few new leads, most of this day was spent in the squad with the guys. It was the height of the afternoon and the air was thick and humid. Franco hoped it would rain. The city streets stunk and a good soaking summer rain would wash some of the filth away, although Bronx streets are never truly washed clean. But the air was thick and heavy and Detective Franco could almost smell rain was near. He hoped it would be a thunderstorm. Loud thunderstorms in the Bronx tend to make people get off the streets, and he loved when the streets were empty.

"Franco! Franco!" Danny called, imitating the Bronx Chief of Detectives' tendency to call his name twice in a nasally voice whenever he was chastising him. "Drop your cocks and pull up your socks. We gotta go."

"Oh yeah, where we going, Chief?" Franco asked as his partner Danny Rice reached for the keys to vehicle 412 from the vehicle board.

"An anonymous call came from a woman who said there was a hit done in a basement apartment on Bronx Boulevard. She also said that there's a bad odor coming from that same apartment."

Franco sarcastically stated, "There's a bad odor coming from every apartment on Bronx Boulevard, but I guess we should check it out anyway. What's the number?"

"3514." Detective Rice answered.

"I know that building!" Franco exclaimed. "It's abandoned. An old Italian guy used to own it, but he died years ago when the precinct was still halfway decent. I guess he never had any family and the city just let it sit there and rot. The smell is probably a bunch of dead rats in the basement, but on second thought it might be legit, so we should probably head over there."

The two detectives made their way out of the squad and outside into the bright sunlight. As they were en route to Bronx Boulevard, they observed a dispute on the corner of Laconia Avenue and 215th Street. A livery cab driver was standing outside his car on the driver's side with a bat in his hand. He appeared to be of Hispanic descent and was screaming at two young Jamaican males. They both had dreadlocks and it seemed he was demanding payment for a ride. The driver took a wild swing with the bat that just barely missed one of the males. Upon seeing this, Franco and Rice jumped out of their unmarked police car and ran over to the dispute. Both detectives, in loud authoritative voices, identified themselves and demanded that the driver drop the bat. Franco drew his weapon and ordered all three men get on the ground.

As they approached the three individuals, one of the young men attempted to flee, but he was quickly subdued by Detective Rice and thrown to the ground. The driver explained in his broken English how he had picked up this fare on Fordham Road and brought them to the projects. When he told them the fare was eight dollars, they laughed and said, "Fuck you, have a nice day" and jumped out of the cab. Franco and Rice, knowing they had more important things to do, told the two individuals that the fare just went up to twelve dollars. They could either pay it or go to jail for Theft of Service.

One young man claimed he had no money and pulled his pockets inside out. The other reluctantly pulled out a twenty and handed it to Detective Franco. Franco handed the twenty dollar bill to the livery driver and told him to keep the change. A short protest from the individual with the twenty was nipped quickly as Franco told him that his bail would be a lot more than twenty dollars. The two young men were told to start walking and next time to take the bus.

The livery driver thanked the two detectives and promised only to pick up Spanish people from now on. With that settled, the two detectives laughed, got back into their unmarked car, and proceeded to Bronx Boulevard. Another case handled with no paperwork, no red tape, and no expenses to the taxpayers. As the detectives drove over to Bronx Boulevard, they laughed at the fact that if the driver had connected with the bat, he would have been the one going to jail. Sometimes it doesn't pay to be a hard working guy in the ghetto.

As they pulled up to 3514 Bronx Boulevard, the detectives' presence could be felt on the street. Men ducked their heads and averted their eyes to avoid the attention of these two ominous figures of the law in suits. And as far as the detectives were concerned, they damn well should.

The address they were summoned to was an abandoned building, just as Franco had thought. The basement apartment, where the hit supposedly took place, was locked. The smell was unmistakably death which seemed to be coming from right under the door.

"God, does it have to be so fucking hot? It stinks over here. I think I'm gonna puke," Danny groaned while covering his nose with his tie.

"I think you've smelled worse things. Just last night your wife's meatloaf in the microwave stunk up the whole squad room," Franco quipped.

"Yeah, you're right," Rice retorted, "Her meatloaf does smell like a DOA." They both laughed, but it was time to get serious. They knew there was something dead behind that door.

Franco checked if the window could be budged, but it appeared painted shut. The glass was too dirty to see through so it was impossible to know whether there was anyone inside or not. The detectives assumed the position at the door, guns drawn. Detective Franco forced the door open with his shoulder and entered high while Detective Rice entered low.

Their entrance to the apartment was met with total darkness. With the building being abandoned, it was obvious that there was no electricity and the detectives entering the basement from the bright sunshine could not see a foot in front of them. The few windows the apartment had were blackened with a dirty film, letting in not a sliver of illumination. Detectives travel light, unlike police in the bag or in uniform, so they had no access to flashlights. They had no choice but to wait for their eyes to adjust to the darkness.

Some Heads are Gonna Roll

Garbage littered the floor and they could hear scurrying, probably rats among the refuse. As the detectives moved, their feet clung to the sticky floor and made a peeling away sound each time they lifted them. They could barely see anything at all and had no idea what lay in store for them in this dirty smelly place. Both had their guns drawn and both kept their backs to the wall not knowing if the apartment was occupied. It was obvious from the smell that there was death in the room.

As their eyes adjusted to the darkness, Franco noticed what appeared to be a body or bodies against a rear wall. He motioned to Rice to follow and they quietly and carefully made their way towards them. It took a while to actually make out, but there were three bodies propped up against the wall, all apparently of Jamaican descent. It appeared to be a woman, a man, and a child, which made this call especially bazar. Crimes against children always occupy a special place in a detective's heart. But there was something off about the bodies. Detective Franco reached his hand out to touch the body of the man and to his shock the head toppled off and rolled across the floor.

"Holy shit!" Franco yelled but his shock soon turned to disgust as he realized two horrifying things. One: that this poor family had been decapitated, and two: that he had majorly screwed up the crime scene.

"Fuck! I can't believe I just fucked up this crime scene! The fucking head just rolled across the fucking floor. Now what the fuck do I do?" Franco roared. Uncharacteristically, there was no blood on the floor or walls in the immediate area of the bodies leading the detectives to believe that the bodies were placed there after they were killed.

"Pick it up," Rice told him matter-of-factly. "Put it back."

"Fuck me…like I really need to pick up this rotting head with my bare hands." But he saw no other way around it. They needed to call this in and Crime Scene would be there shortly so they had to get the head back to where they found it.

The decapitated man's head had dreadlocks which were extremely long, as if he had grown them since he was a child. Franco bent down and picked up the man's head. There were flies and maggots crawling all over it.

"This has got to the nastiest thing I've ever done in my life," Franco complained. As he attempted to place the head back on the corpse, he could hear Rice giggling behind him. "This isn't funny," Franco snapped. "This fucking head stinks like shit and my hands are going to stink forever. Maybe I'll wipe them on your suit if you keep laughing." With that, Rice didn't say another word.

As a man who washed his hands at least ten times a day, picking up a rotting head took some fortitude on his part, but Franco never walked away from his responsibilities, especially to fix one of his fuckups, and this was a major fuckup. Whatever it was he needed to do, he did. He obsessed about it later, but never while on a job.

The head belonged to a Rastafarian. Rastafarianism is considered to be a movement adopted by some Jamaicans. It proclaims Africa as the original birthplace of mankind and holds that the evil in society has always been white or Roman dominated. Rastas believe the use of razors, scissors, or combs are the work of the Romans and are therefore evil. They believe the book of "Leviticus" in the Old Testament supports the wearing of dreadlocks. All three members of this decapitated family sported dreadlocks.

So how ironic is it that Detective Giovanni Franco, of Roman descent, was attempting to maintain some dignity for this Rasta-mon who believed that Romans are the cause of all the ills of the world. Maybe if Franco had known how this Rasta had felt about him, he would have left the head where it rolled.

As he attempted to replace the head, he realized there was something else that was terribly wrong. The head belonged to a male Rastafarian, but the body belonged to a woman. Further inspection revealed that the man's body was topped with the head of a child and the child's body was topped with the head of the woman.

"They played musical fucking heads. These sick bastards," Rice said disgustingly.

"Yeah, well the game stops now, and this head needs to stay put." Franco carefully placed the man's head atop the woman's body, keeping his arms outstretched should it start to fall again.

"I think I got it," he said. "Phew, maybe not too much damage was done to the crime scene. I mean there's some blood splatter, but maybe nobody will realize."

Just as the words were out of his mouth, the man's head once again toppled, this time knocking the woman's head to the floor with it. The woman's head took a little bounce, while the man's head rolled full speed and smashed into the wall. Now there was blood splatter on the walls as well as the floor.

"Fuck!" Franco jumped back but did not avoid getting blood on his shoes.

"Nice job with the head," Rice said sarcastically.

"Fuck you," he replied as he again picked up the man's head, gingerly placing it back on top of the woman's body. "I don't see you doing anything to help. This is an Armani suit, you know."

124

"Now it's a piece of shit, we'll never get the smell out of either of our suits." Rice offered.

The woman's head still needed to be replaced and it was covered in a typical Rasta hat, a crocheted tam in the colors of the Jamaican flag: red, green and gold. Her hat was askew and needed to be adjusted. Franco decided to adjust her hat before placing it atop the body for fear that any adjusting later would again cause the heads to roll. Franco placed the woman's head back on the child's body being careful not to breathe or twitch or make any sudden movements. *Please*, he thought to himself, *just stay put.*

"I think I got it," Franco sighed.

Once it was determined the heads were in place, Franco asked Rice to call it in and he went to the door to get some fresh air. Rice followed behind, and warned, "You're not leaving me in this stinky fucking basement; we can safeguard the scene from the doorway."

Both men went outside and fresh air never smelled or tasted so good. Even though it was the Bronx air, which people would say was dirty, on this day, it felt like they were up in the country. The two men had noticed that the bright sunshine had turned to dark clouds and it was obvious it was going to rain soon; a typical afternoon summer thunderstorm was on its way. Rice called for Emergency Service to bring lights, Crime Scene to do their investigation, and the Patrol Sergeant and a sector car to establish and safeguard the crime scene. He also called the Squad because other detectives would need to come down to the location and canvas the area, knocking on doors, asking if anyone heard or saw anything. The Detective Duty Captain would also be showing up at some point. This was going to be a long drawn out, typical Bronx triple homicide. Franco called the squad room on his cell phone and told his Lieutenant they had a triple. The overtime was going to flow tonight.

As all the units starting arriving, Franco and Rice were directing them as to what they needed done. In the case of a Homicide, the detective catching the case is in charge of the crime scene, no matter what ranking officer comes to it. If the Chief of Detectives showed up, the detective whose case it is is still in charge and makes the decisions. There's a very fine line there, and most detectives will take the suggestions of the Chief and run with them for obvious reasons.

Franco was nervous, though. He had compromised the crime scene, and this was not the way he was used to working. He was considered one of the most meticulous and careful detectives, and he took his work very seriously. But he could not risk admitting the truth, so he hoped that his mishap would not be discovered. Besides, he would solve this case and bring the perpetrator to justice. He usually always did. That was all that mattered in the end, but at this moment he really wanted to wash his hands.

Outside there was a clap of thunder and the sky lit up with lightning. The dark room was illuminated momentarily but soon Emergency Service would have their lights and equipment everywhere. But for now, Mother Nature provided the light that was missing in this room. But some things would remain in the dark, such as Crime Scene's knowledge about what really occurred here after the detectives arrived. Rice, like Franco, would never give up a fellow detective and there was no doubt in Franco's mind that Crime Scene would remain in the dark about the toppling heads. And the much needed rain was coming, but there was no way that any amount of rain could cleanse what happened in this room, to this family or remove the stink that clung to the detectives' hands and clothes. Still the rain was welcome and Detective Franco walked outside with his head facing the clouds, feeling the raindrops on his face washing him, and his Armani suit, clean.

24

The Troll

IT WAS A HOT STICKY SUMMER DAY and Detective Franco was in no mood for bullshit. Yesterday had been tough with a grisly homicide and very few leads. His brain itched to get to the bottom of it. There weren't many cases that he couldn't solve, but this one was definitely a challenge, so when Pedro called in a panic, he did not want to hear it.

Pedro stammered and sputtered into the phone, "Detective, you told me I could c-c-c-call you, anytime…you're the only one I trust, puh puh please, you have to come to my apartment."

Pedro had been arrested by Detective Franco a couple of years ago for Disorderly Conduct. It wasn't a major case, just your run of the mill crazy, running amuk in the city without medication. It turns out Pedro had paranoid schizophrenia, but with proper medication, Pedro was able to hold a decent job and take care of himself. But every now and then he'd take a meds holiday and Franco would inevitably hear about it. It wasn't unusual for Pedro to be in a panic as that was part of his diagnosis. Sometimes he believed cats were aliens sent to earth to spy on him, and other times he insisted on purchasing all of the hair care products that the local Avon lady was selling, despite the fact that he was bald. But in each case, Pedro was essentially harmless.

"Calm down, Pedro. Why do I have to come down there? What is the problem?"

"Detective…there's a tr-tr-troll in my apartment. I have him trapped, please come and get him before he kills me."

Franco audibly laughed into the phone. "A troll, Pedro? What does he look like?"

He's tiny, with a big head and little hands with fat fingers. He kept

127

banging at my door, and I have him trapped now but he might escape. Please, Detective, you're the only one I trust."

Lucky me, Franco thought. With the thought that maybe a change of scenery would refresh his brain, and help him with his latest case, Franco called to his partner Danny. "I'm not calling this in," Franco told Rice. "Pedro is just off his meds. We'll bring him to the emergency room and let them take care of it."

"I don't know why we're going, but fine. I'm hungry anyway, let's stop for a hotdog."

Hot summer days in the Bronx have everyone out on the street, trying to escape from the oppressive heat of the apartments. There were people sitting on lawn chairs and empty milk crates in front of buildings, people sitting on stoops, and people hanging out on fire escapes. People even slept on fire escapes at night to get some air. Summer in a Bronx apartment building is stifling. "They come out like cockroaches from the woodwork," Franco's mom would say and it was somewhat true.

"Coco, cheri, rembo," called the ice vendor to the passing detectives.

"What's a "rembo?" asked Franco.

"Rembo" the vendor repeated in his thick Spanish accent. "Many color like rembo in the sky"

"Oh," laughed Franco, "You know what? Give me a large cherry," Franco said.

Danny declined. "I need real food" he said. The vendor scraped off ice shavings from the huge ice block and added the cherry syrup, the Bronx version of a Sno-Cone.

Pedro's building was a five story walk-up, and unfortunately Pedro was on the 5th floor. The detectives climbed the stairs, all the while Danny complaining. "I can't believe you brought me out here for this shit. This guy's a psycho....what are we investigating again? A troll? This is great! A troll! Let me tell you, there are a lot of fuckin animals in the Bronx, but I never saw a troll."

"Well, maybe today's your lucky day," Franco offered. "Besides, Pedro's a good guy and he trusts me. He's obviously upset, and someone needs to get him to the hospital. If we don't do it, it might not happen at all and I wouldn't want to see a couple of overzealous rookies show up here and Pedro wind up getting hurt."

Boom, boom, boom. "Pedro, open the door. It's Detective Franco." A series of clicks, at least eight, could be heard, each in succession of the other. Still Pedro didn't completely open the door as he peered out through a chain at the detectives.

"Detective Franco, Thank God it's you! Who's this guy?" Pedro motioned to Danny.

"He's my partner and he's cool; open the door Pedro." Pedro didn't look convinced, but he slowly opened the door. The apartment was neat and very quiet. There didn't appear to have been any type of disturbance or ruckus. But there in the corner was what appeared to be a closet door with a chair positioned under the doorknob to prevent it from being opened from the inside.

"Why is that chair there, Pedro?" asked Franco as he continued to lick at his cherry ice.

"The troll is in there, Detective. Please, be very careful. He's been banging at that door and screaming that he's going to kill me for days now."

"He's not banging or screaming now," Franco stated. Pedro just shrugged.

Danny sighed loudly, "Please can we get out of here?"

Franco approached the door and started to remove the chair. Still he heard no sound. *There's no one here, he thought. This poor bastard is off his rocker again.* But as he turned the doorknob, the door flew open with great force and a blur of a little body attempted to push past the detectives. As he ran, religious pamphlets and literature littered the floor. Franco reacted quickly despite his shock, as his cherry ice went flying into the air and pulled out his gun, ordering the creature to freeze. At the same time, Danny was doubled up against a wall laughing hysterically.

"He's a midget," gasped Danny, trying to catch his breath. "I can't believe you pulled your gun!"

"HE'S A TROLL!" screamed Pedro.

"I'm a Jehovah's Witness," the little man protested. "This crazy fuck opened his door and before I could even begin to tell him of God's goodness, the asshole shoved me in the closet, calling me a troll!"

"You ARE a troll!" Pedro continued to scream.

"I screamed and screamed for days, but he wouldn't let me out. I thought I was going to die!"

Franco took a deep breath and holstered his weapon. This would be funny, very funny, later. But right now he needed to get one very dehydrated little person, and one very distraught Pedro to the hospital. "Don't you guys travel in pairs Franco asked the little man?" "Yes we do, I was breaking in a new "brother" and I don't know what happened to him." "All I remember is hearing him scream as he ran off down the hallway; he probably never went back to Kingdom Hall."

Never a Dull Moment

Franco now needed to figure out a way to get these two to the hospital without anyone knowing. He never put them out to this location with Central dispatch. He decided to separate them, with his partner sitting in the rear of the squad car with Pedro, and the little fellow who he came to know as Ronald Manny in the front. Pedro was reassured that Ronald was just a short guy and not a troll. The ride to the hospital was uneventful. Giovanni took Pedro into the E.R. and told Danny to follow behind a few minutes later with the dehydrated Jehovah Witness. Both received the treatment they needed and as the two partners walked out of the hospital toward their squad car Danny shook his head.

"Never a dull moment Gio" Danny laughed. "I can't wait to tell the guys this one."

25

Wisdom

IT WAS A HOT STEAMY DAY in the Bronx and Detective Franco was swinging out for his regular days off. At this point in his career he had found working out in the precinct gym not only relieved the stress of dealing with the mutts, but it helped him stay in shape for the occasional donnybrook or riot that cops inevitably find themselves in the middle of when working in the Bronx slums. He was a big proponent of vitamin supplements and protein shakes. This one particular day, he found himself walking down the narrow stairway that leads from the detective squad room to the first floor precinct lobby. As he was coming down the stairs, a police officer with the last name of Wisdom was walking up. Franco was guzzling what was left of a half gallon of skim milk he had purchased earlier in the day to make his shake.

As the two passed each other on the narrow stairway, Officer Wisdom exclaimed, "Yo, Franco, that's nasty!"

With that Franco stopped drinking his milk and asked, "What are you talking about?"

As Officer Wisdom began to answer, Franco again began to drink. Wisdom's answer was both unexpected and hilarious.

He explained, "I can't drink that shit. I'm lactose can't tolerate."

Having a mouthful of milk at the time, Franco proceeded to spit it in the face of Officer Wisdom as his laughter was both uncontrollable and unexpected. Wisdom looked up at Franco as if he had been assaulted. He stood there with what appeared to be a gallon of milk running down his face, neck, and all over his uniform shirt. The contrast of the white milk against his very dark complexion was shocking. Franco was mortified as to what he did, but couldn't contain his laughter as he had never heard anyone use that term before. He apologized profusely, but the smile never left his face. As he wiped the milk off his face with both hands, Officer Wisdom explained what exactly "lactose can't tolerate" is. Franco, not wanting to insult him, pretended he never heard of such a thing, and asked if it's an actual medical condition. He stated it was, and it could sometimes be serious. With that he offered to pay for any dry cleaning bills Wisdom would incur. The two said goodbye on the stairway and when Franco got to the bottom of the stairs, he started laughing hysterically. Wisdom undoubtedly had to change his uniform because with the heat of the day he would have smelled like Parmesan cheese in no time.

26

George

THERE ARE SOME MAJOR THOROUGHFARES that run throughout the Bronx. Some stretch from Maine to Florida. One is I-95, which is commonly known in the Bronx as The New England Thruway. Along the New England Thruway, within the confines of the 47th Precinct, are several low budget flop house type motels that cater to the quick drug transaction or prostitution. One of which, *The Oasis Motel*, was the subject of Detective Franco and his partner's investigation. A homicide investigation they were conducting led them to this location early one chilly October morning. It seemed the suspect of this homicide investigation befriended the front desk clerk and was using one of the rooms in the rear as a hideout until he could make arrangements to flee the state. Detectives Franco and Rice, having gained this information, but not knowing for sure if it was 100% accurate, decided to stake out the motel. They positioned themselves in their unmarked car across the street, and could see with binoculars into the courtyard. Not knowing which room was being used, they mainly concentrated on the driveway entrance to the motel. There was only one way in and one way out. The detectives did not believe the perpetrator had a vehicle and they surmised he was most likely on foot.

They had staked the location out for several hours, and now found themselves at four o'clock in the morning, hungry and tired. They needed a bathroom break and wanted to get something to eat but couldn't leave the location unattended. Therefore, they called the Detective Borough and asked if they could get a couple of guys who were doing night watch to relieve them for an hour or so. Night watch consists of a group of detectives who are assigned to cover the whole borough of the Bronx from midnight until eight A.M. They are picked from several precincts within the borough and assigned there for the night. No one likes to get night watch duty because in the squad you worked either 8 to 4 or 4 to 12. Pulling night watch duty tends to screw up your body for several days because you work your regular 4 to 12, and then head down to the Homicide Task Force to cover the 12 to 8 tour. Sixteen straight hours investigating major crimes in the Bronx will wear on you. After an hour or so, two guys who usually work in the 44 Precinct Squad, a very busy house, came by to relieve them. Detective Franco handed them a picture of the suspect, gave them a brief rundown of the case, and then they exchanged cell phone numbers. Franco informed them that the suspect was probably armed and a three time loser. The detectives said they were just going to grab a quick bite and be right back. They thanked them for coming because it doesn't always work out so easily. The four detectives knew each other from working several cases over the years and they knew that Franco and Rice would do the same thing for them.

Franco and Rice drove off and headed southbound along the New England Thruway service road. This area was notorious for male prostitutes in drag, or as the cops called them, he/shes. These miscreants would dress in tight woman's clothing, wearing wigs and high heels, and for some reason, some men, especially out of town truckers, would actually think they were women and pay for their sexual services. As Franco and Rice were driving down the service road, they spot an eighteen wheeler pulled over to the side with its motor running. Franco, being the consummate ball buster, told Rice to pull over behind the truck.

"Come on," said Rice. "I gotta take a piss. Why do you have to fuck with this hillbilly?"

Franco looked at the plates on the truck and noticed it was from Tennessee.

"Because this poor bastard probably doesn't even know that he's getting blown by a man."

With that the two detectives laughed and exited their unmarked patrol car. Franco approached the driver's side and pulled himself up the two steps that led to the cab. Rice positioned himself on the passenger side of the cab. When Franco looked in, the cab was empty. He banged on the window and a middle-aged man wearing a John Deere baseball cap and looking a little bit like an older version of Brett Favre, stuck his head out through the curtain that separated the cab from the rear sleeping quarters of the truck.

Detective Franco identified himself and asked, "What are you doing in there?"

The man started to stutter and stated, "Uh, I was just taking a nap."

Franco asked, "Who do you have back there with you?"

George

The man went silent and Franco knew that he wasn't alone. He could hear Rice making funny jokes from the passenger side but couldn't make out what he was saying. All he knew was he was laughing.

Franco stated, "If I look back there and there's someone with you, you're going to jail for soliciting a prostitute."

The man stated, "We were just talking."

"Let me ask you a question. Are you gay?"

"WHAT?" the man said in a somewhat defiant voice. "Where I come from, I'm considered a ladies' man. Why would you ask me something like that?"

"I think you like men," said Franco. "Why else would you be in your truck at four in the morning getting a blow job from a man?"

"You're crazy Officer, This girl back here's name is Ginger and we wuz just talking."

When he hears the name Ginger, he knows exactly who's in the back of the truck. He's been working these streets for 18 years now and knows most of the he/shes by name. Ginger, or as Detective Franco calls him, George, has been a mainstay on the New England Service Road for several years. Franco thought to himself, *how anyone could think that that 6 foot 2 Amazon, with hands like Wilt Chamberlain, could be a woman is beyond me. But maybe in Tennessee, they grow them big.* Franco then demanded that Ginger and the man from Tennessee get into the front of the cab. The man obliged, and lo and behold, it was observed that he had his pants down around his ankles. He asked if he could get dressed, and Franco told him to "pull up his pants." Rice had climbed up on the passenger side of the truck and was watching through the window.

He demanded Ginger come up front. Franco knew from the sound of her moving around, she was getting dressed. She climbed into the front and when she saw Franco she looked at him with eyes that said, *Please don't tell him.* But he couldn't help himself.

"Hey, George, long time no see. " Franco greeted the beautiful Ginger. She was a mess, her wig was crooked, her lipstick was smeared, and her dress was wrinkled.

"Hi, Detective," she said in a very low, almost apologetic voice.

"So you are gay," proclaimed Franco to the ladies man truck driver from Tennessee.

"Not gay," stated the man once again. 'Why would I be with her if I was?"

Detective Franco looked over at Ginger and told the trucker to put on his interior light.

"Okay George, show 'em what you're packing."

Ginger, or George, as the detectives knew him, just shook his head and said "Detective please, I thought we were cool."

"Yeah we're cool," Franco said, "but he needs to know."

"How about I just leave?" George asked, in the prettiest most feminine voice he could muster.

'No you show him and then you can leave. And consider it a good deal that nobody's going to jail."

George slowly lifted up his dress and reached between his legs. Nothing was visible, but Franco knew the trick.

"Untape it," Franco demanded.

With that, George lifted his ass off the seat and you could hear duct tape being pulled. He then produced the biggest cock that both Franco and Rice had ever seen.

"Holy shit!" Rice exclaimed. Franco stared at the Tennessee truck driver and the look on his face was both shock and awe. He sat there with his mouth open and you could see his face get as red as a Jersey tomato.

"I knew you were gay," Franco told him. "Have a nice day."

Both detectives jumped down from the cab of the truck, walked back to their unmarked police car, got in and drove away.

"You're fucked up," Rice yelled at Franco. "But that was one of the funniest things I've ever seen in my life. If I had a cock like that, I certainly wouldn't be sucking dick on the side of the highway. I'd be making millions in movies."

Both men laughed and headed to the diner. They picked up four bacon, egg, and cheeses on a roll and four coffees, and headed back to *The Oasis Motel*. Along the way, they drove by where the Tennessee ladies' man had been parked. The truck was long gone, and they thought all was well. But one of the other he/shes was flagging them down while pointing towards an area of high grass across from where the truck had been parked. Rice rolled down his window and asked him/her, "What are you pointing at?"

"You need to go check that out."

Both detectives got out of their car and walked several feet into the high brush. Before they could see anything, they heard moaning.

"Oh, shit," Franco said. "I think George got fucked up."

"What did you expect?" Rice shot back at him. "The ladies man from Tennessee was pissed."

They went over and saw George lying on his back with several head wounds and a busted eye. He was conscious but hurting.

"You okay George?" Franco asked.

George

"You're fucked up, Detective," George complained. "I'm just trying to make some money." He sat up and held his head in his hands.

"You might have to take a week or so off," Franco shot back. "You want an ambulance?"

"No, man, you did me enough favors for one day. That crazy mother fucker had a pipe in his truck. I told him nobody would know about this, but I think he was mad because he kissed me."

"Okay whatever, "Franco said, "we gotta get going."

The men got back in their car and drove towards the motel. Rice looked over at Franco and said "Hey Giovanni, I thought I saw a he/she over there that looked like the Lieutenant."

"That's funny" Giovanni shot back, "because I thought the one in the purple dress looked a lot like the Chief."

"No," Rice said, "The Chief has bigger tits." They went back to the motel and relieved the two detectives from the 4-4. They gave them each a sandwich and a coffee and thanked them for coming by to help. At about seven o'clock that morning, the perp they were sitting on exited room 112 and was quickly apprehended. In his possession was the gun that was used in the murder and he, after hours of interrogation, gave them a full confession. It turned out to be a fruitful night, with a little fun thrown in as well.

27

Thumbs Up

HEAD BANGERS WAS A BAR THAT ATTRACTED a motley crew. There were gangsters from Arthur Avenue and City Island who hung out until the wee hours of the night. But *Head Bangers* also attracted detectives, who would steal away from their daily grind for a few hours of drinks and jokes. It was an unlikely mix, but the two groups usually coexisted peacefully and there were rarely any incidents between the two. The wise guys, although they strutted their stuff on the street, knew better than to piss off New York's Finest. The detectives just wanted a breather from their hectic schedule, so they really didn't give a shit if a few football ticket transactions took place. Besides Monday nights, along with the football game, was rib night. Rib night consisted of all the barbeque you could eat for $9.99. The cook, Eddie, originally from Barbados, took great pride in his barbeque chicken, ribs and pulled pork.

On this particular night, Detective Franco, along with three other guys from his squad, decided to go to *Head Bangers* for dinner and catch the first half of the game on T.V. When Eddie saw them enter the bar, he came over to them and greeted them with hugs and his usual big smile. Eddie was a small round faced man with a heavy West Indian accent and he was a bit of a cop buff. He would love to sit at the table and listen to war stories. Detective Franco, a while back, had deputized Eddie by placing Eddie's left hand on Franco's shield and raising his right hand. Franco made him repeat after him, "I swear to uphold the constitution of the United States of America and the constitution of the State of New York, so help me God." Franco then told Eddie, "You are now a deputy; you have to buy the next round." Although all the guys knew it was a joke, Eddie thought he was now an honorary member of the NYPD. Eddie hung out with the guys for a few minutes and then went back into the kitchen. He came out with a large plate of barbeque: chicken, ribs and pulled pork. The guys all started eating and complimenting Eddie on a job well done. Several pitchers of beer were consumed and it was getting to be that time.

Franco wanted to use the bathroom before they left. He walked into the bathroom, a small, cramped, dingy, area which contained two urinals and a toilet. Across from the urinal was a small white sink with a sign that said for employees to wash their hands. Franco took out his pen and wrote on it, *this means you, Eddie.*

As Franco washed his hands, a large white male, definitely Italian with black curly hair, entered the bathroom and was using one of the urinals. Franco, feeling he knew him from somewhere, stated, "You look familiar."

The guy looked back at Franco and asked, "My cock or my face?" He showed no facial expression so Franco was not sure if he was joking or fucking with him.

"I wasn't looking at your cock," Franco said.

"No, you don't know me," the guy shot back in a surly tone. Franco eyed him up and down for a second, letting the man know he wasn't happy with his comment and then he walked out of the bathroom and returned to join the other detectives at the table.

He told them what happened in the bathroom and one of the guys, Bobby Altieri, started to laugh.

"Maybe he's a homo," Bobby offered. Giovanni then walked over to the owner because he needed to know who this wiseass was. Lenny, the owner, after being told of the conversation in the bathroom, explained, "That's just Vinny, you can't take him serious. He's an actor."

"Oh yeah," Franco shot back. "What have I seen him in?"

Lenny proceeded to name several wise guy type movies depicting Italian mobsters and the like. Franco told Lenny, "He might play a mobster in the movies, but if he gets smart with me again, he's gonna have a problem, this is real life."

Lenny, feeling that there was some tension between the two, called Vinny over. He introduced Vinny to Giovanni and bought them both a drink. Lenny told Vinny that he had pissed Giovanni off and Vinny explained that he was only playing around. The men drank their drink and engaged in a short conversation, Vinny then returned to the far end of the bar where he had been sitting with some people. Giovanni went back to the table. A short time later, Vinny walked over to the table the four detectives were sitting at.

He told the other three detectives, "This guy here," pointing at Franco, "almost kicked my ass in the bathroom."

Never a Dull Moment

The three detectives looked at him and nodded their heads *yes*, pretty much affirming what would have been his fate. Vinny sent over a round of drinks for the guys and Altieri asked him to join them. As Vinny sat down at the table, one of the other detectives', Tommy Barbons' cell phone rang. It was the Squad Lieutenant. He was inquiring as to their location. Tommy told him that they had just stopped to get some dinner and were on their way back. The Lieutenant informed Tommy that they received a job of a girl who had been held hostage by some psycho who was going to use her as a prostitute. He had her trapped in his basement for several days, but she was able to escape and get to a phone. Apparently when uniform arrived, the perp was in the house, and ran out the back door. They're canvassing the area for him. Barbone got the address and told the guys at the table what was going on. They quickly paid the bill, said good-bye to Vinny, Lenny and Eddie and ran out to two unmarked cars.

The location of the house where this girl was being held hostage was right off Boston Road, less than one mile away from the bar. When they arrived at the scene, there were police cars everywhere. The girl had been removed to Jacobi Hospital to be physically examined. The Squad Lieutenant was on the scene and he directed Barbone and Altieri to go to the hospital to interview her. Franco along with his partner, Danny Rice, entered the house in question. They were directed by patrol to the basement and what they saw was shocking. This guy had concocted a sub-basement complete with a small mattress and a bucket of water. It had a trap door above it which was locked with a padlock. There was no light or windows and the area was only about 8 feet wide by 8 feet long. Somehow the girl had forced the trap door open and upon further observation by Franco, he could see the wood was rotted around the padlock. The Patrol Supervisor, Sergeant McCabe, informed the detectives the perp got away when patrol knocked on the front door. Apparently he went out the back and no one was covering the rear because the job came over as a woman calling for help. By the time they spoke to her, and ascertained what was going on, he was gone. The Sergeant also informed them that patrol was searching for him in the area, and the Bronx Task Force had been mobilized and was also assisting with the search.

Altieri called Franco on his cell phone and gave him an update after interviewing the girl at the hospital. He stated that the girl was from Oklahoma and wanted to come to New York to be an actress. She had gotten off the bus at the Port Authority, a busy transportation hub in Manhattan, and befriended a middle aged black man who told her he had connections in the movie industry. He took her to his house in the Bronx and then kept her captive in a hole in the ground in his basement, no doubt in an attempt to turn her into a prostitute. She stated she had been held captive for around one week, and during that time was forced to perform various sex acts on her captor. Altieri stated that she was only 18, very pretty and extremely naïve. He also added that he thinks he knows who this guy is.

"He walks around like a pimp." Altieri said. "If he's the guy I'm thinking of, he always dresses in very colorful, flashy clothes."

He said that people in the neighborhood think he's a psycho. He didn't know his name, but he said if he saw a picture of him, he would recognize him. The girl was being treated for sexual assault, exposure and dehydration and was being admitted to the hospital.

As Franco was about to hang up from Altieri, he heard a transmission over the radio that a uniformed unit was in pursuit of a possible suspect in this case. They jumped into their unmarked car and proceeded to the location where the uniform officers stated they were chasing the suspect on foot. It was only one block from the house, an area of both residential and commercial establishments. It seemed the uniform officer who was chasing him lost him in one of the yards.

Franco and Rice drove up and down several blocks in the immediate area where he was last seen. As they were driving down Boston Road at Corsa Avenue, Franco looked down a driveway and thought he saw something move behind a row of garbage cans. He told Rice to let him out by the corner and that he was going to walk down the driveway. Rice stated he would drive around the block in case the perp cut through to the other street. As Franco proceeded down the driveway, a transmission came over his radio which he had placed in his back pocket. This alerted the perp to his presence and the perp jumped up and ran further into the alleyway. There seemed to be nowhere to go because at the end of the alley was a ten foot high fence topped with barbed wire. Franco ran towards the perp who was now scaling the fence. He was thin and much younger looking than the man Altieri had described. He seemed to get up to the top of the fence in only a second or two. He threw his body over the top but his right hand got caught up in the barbed wire. His whole body was on the other side of the fence, except that his hand seemed to be caught. Franco gave his location over the radio and thought the perp was had. What happened next shocked him. The man pulled himself up towards his hand and while making a growling noise, bit his thumb completely off, freeing him from the barbed wire. He looked down at Franco from the top of the fence and spit his thumb out at Franco. He jumped back as the perp hit the ground on the other side of the fence and ran off. Franco frantically put the location over the radio again, as the man made a quick right hand turn disappearing completely from Franco's sight. Rice pulled up on the adjacent block

141

and ran towards Franco and the fence. Rice was on one side of the fence and Franco was on the other and Rice swore he never saw the guy come out into the street.

Franco then pointed to the thumb on the ground and asked Rice, "Do you know what that is?"

"It looks like a dead bloody mouse," Rice answered.

"It's that psycho's fucking thumb," Franco shot back.

"Thumb, what do you mean his thumb?" Rice asked.

"It's his fucking thumb!" Franco said. "He got caught up on the barbed wire and bit his thumb off to free himself. Then the sick fuck spit it at me, jumped down and ran off. You didn't see him?" Franco asked Rice.

"No, I wasn't exactly sure where you were in relation to my block, but he never came out into the street. There has to be 100 cops looking for this guy. How could he have gotten away again?"

"I don't know, but it's making us look bad," Franco shot back.

"Do we have to voucher the thumb?" Rice asked.

"Well, it IS evidence," Franco replied, "But I don't know where we would send it. Maybe the morgue can keep it until the case is solved."

"Oh, you're planning on catching this guy?" Rice asked Franco.

"He spit a bloody fucking thumb at me. You better believe I'm going to catch him."

28

Badge Bunnies

YOLANDA HERNANDEZ LOOKED IN THE MIRROR. She knew she wasn't a beautiful girl, not a classic kind of beauty anyway. Her nose was a little too wide, her waist a little too thick, her hair a little too kinky, and her accent a little too pronounced. But she knew she was hot. When Yolanda walked down the street, men gawked, honked their horns, and made their catcalls. But the men in the Bronx had very little to offer Yolanda, and she would toss her head away. Yolanda was a smart girl and had dreams of her own. She wanted it all … the house with the picket fence, the two and a half kids, and a sugar daddy to provide it all. But, the chances of finding a sugar daddy here in the Bronx were slim. Most of the guys Yolanda grew up with were already involved in either drugs or some kind of illegal activity. Now Yolanda wouldn't mind if the criminal activity they were involved in caused them great wealth, but it didn't. For instance, Tito, her ex-boyfriend, sold weed on the corner of 182 and Creston Avenue. He liked to flash a wad of cash, but Tito was small time. He might be able to buy some gold jewelry and some nice shoes for Yolanda, but Yolanda had bigger plans, and Tito couldn't fulfill them. In addition, the guys in the South Bronx, once they had a little money, thought they were God's gift. Instead of appreciating a fine woman like Yolanda, these guys wanted to snag as much sex as they could, and Yolanda wasn't buying this. She wanted a man who would be hers and hers alone.

One of Yolanda's friends, Priscilla, had started visiting the 47 Precinct during her spare time. She would bring the officers food, such as cod fritters or arroz con gandules and the officers would let her hang out for a while. Priscilla told Yolanda she had her eye on a hottie cop named Tommy, and she invited Yolanda to join her, as long as she stayed away from Tommy. Yolanda agreed, but in her heart, she knew all is fair in love and war.

In fact, Priscilla, with her little titties, would have been smarter not to place Tommy off limits since this just intrigued Yolanda even more.

Yolanda tried to decide what she would wear to visit the boys in blue. Her hair was in curlers, an effort to straighten out the kink. Most of the cops in the 47th were Italian or Irish and Yolanda knew their women rarely had kinky hair. She stood in her bedroom wearing a black lace DD bra and black lace panties while she oiled her olive toned skin with some cocoa butter. Her closet did not have the greatest assortment, but Yolanda was ingenious at making a sexy outfit from just a few basics. She chose a tight pair of jeans, so tight she had to lie down on the bed in order to pull up the zipper over her size twelve body. A little fat hung over the top of the jeans waistband, but that didn't bother Yolanda. *Something for them to hold onto to,* she thought. For her top, Yolanda chose a tube top and decided to ditch the bra. *Easy access*, she mused. Lastly, since she was short, Yolanda, found a pair of high heeled boots on the floor of her closet. They were beaten up and scuffed, but Yolanda didn't expect that anyone would be looking at her feet.

Priscilla had called Yolanda and said that she had made food for the detectives. Priscilla had fried plantains and lasagna, which when made in a Puerto Rican kitchen, tasted nothing like Italian lasagna. But Priscilla thought the officers would appreciate her flexibility in the kitchen and maybe could envision her flexibility in the bedroom as well. Yolanda, personally, didn't feel she needed to bring any food to win over any admirers.

The detectives at the 4-7 were used to neighborhood girls coming by and bringing them food. If the girls were pretty, they let them hang out in the Squad room for a while. If not, they sent them packing. The Badge Bunnies, as the officers called them, were cop groupies looking to snag a boyfriend or a possible husband. The officers knew the desolate area of the Bronx that these girls called home offered them little opportunity to meet a nice man. To these women, the precinct was like finding a gold mine, the opportunities were endless. But when you think about it, the whole situation seemed desperate and pathetic.

Detective Giovanni Franco received a call from the desk officer stating there were two Spanish girls at the desk who needed to speak with a detective. The Sergeant who was on the phone said, "It looks like they have some food and they're pretty good looking." Giovanni announced to the guys in the squad that two badge bunnies were on their way up.

Yolanda and Priscilla's heels clicked as they walked into the squad. "Hola," Priscilla called. "Mira what I have for you." She proudly placed the lasagna on Tommy's desk and pointed to Tommy. "I make this for jou. Lasagna. Jou favorite."

"My favorite?" Tommy asked, pointing to himself and laughing. Priscilla didn't really do much for him and he wasn't sure about her lasagna either, but he did like the looks of her friend. Ever since she walked into the squad, she hadn't taken her eyes off of him. Tommy, recently divorced and a distinguished looking man in his late thirties, was intrigued.

"Who's your friend?" Tommy asked as he looked at Yolanda. Priscilla scowled and rolled her eyes, but Yolanda paid her no mind. "I'm Yolanda," she answered as she looked at Tommy and licked her lips.

Green light, Tommy thought. He looked over at Mulligan, a detective who was assigned to the 4-7 Squad about the same time as Giovanni. Mulligan raised his eyebrows and let out a low whistle. The other detectives in the room stopped typing and hung up the phones to observe the activities before them.

"Um Priscilla," Mulligan said, "Why don't you cut me a piece of that delicious lasagna?" He motioned to Tommy to get out while he could.

"Of course," Priscilla replied as she hurried into the detective's lounge to get utensils. She had been in there before. Tommy took this opportunity to make his move with Yolanda.

"You want to see the interrogation room?" Tommy asked Yolanda. Yolanda stared deeply into his eyes and nodded.

"Okay," Tommy said, acting the tour guide. "This here is where we question suspects when we…"

"Where do jou sleep?" Yolanda asked.

"Sleep?" Tommy asked incredulously. *Do I even have to work for this*, he thought?

"Um there's a dorm room here, for when we stay over. He showed Yolanda the cinder block room. It was dark with four bunk beds and no windows. The door had a dead bolt on it, which Yolanda immediately locked.

I guess I don't, Tommy thought, answering his own question.

Yolanda sank to her knees and slowly unzipped Tommy's pants.

When they were done, they both adjusted their clothing and walked out of the dorm as if nothing had happened. Their return to the squad was met with an icy cold stare from Priscilla.

"Eres puta!" Priscilla screamed as she lunged for Yolanda, calling Yolanda a whore in Spanish.

The guys in the squad started jeering, anticipating a sexy scuffle between the two. "I got twenty bucks on Priscilla," Mulligan called out "She could always kill her with that lasagna." Mulligan grabbed his neck with both hands and imitated choking sounds. Tommy quickly placed himself between Priscilla and Yolanda to avoid an all out cat fight, but Yolanda didn't even flinch. She kept her head up and just looked at Priscilla. Priscilla had her chance with Tommy, but he just wasn't interested. Yolanda got what she came for and Priscilla would just have to deal with it. Yolanda was right; she didn't need any lasagna, just a big sausage.

29

Stay in School, Fool

THE BASS WAS LOUD AND TREVOR COULD FEEL IT reverberating through his body. He loved that feeling; it was like your heart was beating outside your chest and it made Trevor feel more alive than ever. It was especially meaningful tonight because the bass was beating to HIS music, to HIS sounds. The Community Center was filled to capacity and the crowd was swaying and dancing to his music. It was a dream come true. Ever since he was a little boy, Trevor knew he wanted to be a musician. When family came over, Trevor would grab any object that could substitute as a microphone, such as his mother's hairbrush, and start singing or rapping. His family would cheer, as families always do, but surprisingly, Trevor was actually pretty good. Trevor knew he could never be the kind of musician who rapped about "hoes," "thugging" or killing. He had never held a gun in his hand and hoped he never would. He felt rapping about such negative things was disrespectful to his people and he hated when his fellow black brothers used the power of their gift of music to perpetuate hate, and in his opinion, to sell out. "I'm not a stereotype." Trevor would say, "I'm a man and I try to be the best man I can be. And I hope that I can set a good example for others like me."

Trevor knew hateful violence-filled lyrics sold CDs and filled concert halls, but Trevor also knew this was the easy way out. It was much easier to sell anger and hate than to sell conscientiousness and responsibility. No one wants to stand up and do the right thing. No one wants to take a stand. You risk becoming a punk or a bitch. But Trevor took that risk and tonight it appeared to pay off. The Community Center was packed and people were screaming his name. Trevor decided to open with his favorite rap, *Stay in School, Fool:*

Never a Dull Moment

Yo Yo Yo Put Yo hands together
Now ya know what I say
It ain't no lie
Stay in school fool if ya wanna be fly
Don't believe da hype
Put down the crack pipe. Ya need an education
Ya need to learn
Like the sun above yo head needs to burn.
Self-respect is the ticket
It's yo only way out.
I can't tell ya how to do it, but I can tell ya why
If you drop out you become a statistic and that's no lie
You know you might just die. Everyone will say
He was an aspiring whatever but now he ain't shit
He made some fast money, the street was his tit
But the police had other plans for him
So now he's doing a 12 ta 20bit
And his baby daughter don't know the next time she'll see him
He ain't got no life, would you really want to be him?
He ain't got no future
He left school for the big plan
He was the big man
The man with da plan
But now he ain't shit
You should have stayed in school fool
Stayed in school fool
Stayed in school fool
Stayed in school fool
Stayed in school fool
Stayed in school fool

The crowd sang along with the catchy chorus, bobbing their arms and heads. *Stay in School, Fool,* was a crowd favorite, and probably his biggest hit, but Trevor also had some very serious songs that were written to help guide young people through the chaos of their lives. *Stay in School, Fool* gave Trevor the hook to get the masses listening, so later they would pay attention to his other songs which provided even deeper messages. And that was Trevor's main purpose; to provide a solid foundation for the young black male in the ghetto to live their lives. But young black males weren't the only ones listening to Trevor's music. There were women everywhere, scantily dressed, eyeing him up and down.

Any other guy would use this type of fame to his advantage, but these women didn't tempt him. He had his woman and she was the love of his life, his angel. She stood by him through the hard times, through the dates at McDonald's because he didn't have enough money to bring her somewhere fancy, through the freezing car rides when his heater was on the fritz, and through the *Dollar Store* presents when it was all he could afford. And, she never complained, because all she really cared about was being with him. Trevor reciprocated that feeling, and also wanted to give Darlene more, because she deserved more. He caught Darlene's eye and she smiled up at him from her corner spot on the floor. His heart belonged to Darlene; he knew it and she knew it and soon everyone else would know it when they announced their engagement. Trevor hadn't proposed to Darlene yet, but he knew she would say "yes." Then his life would be damned near perfect. Trevor had even written a rap entitled *Destiny* especially for Darlene as his love for her was hard for him to contain. Later that evening, as he performed his final encore, he dedicated it to her, as Darlene blew him a kiss from the audience.

> When I think about my destiny
> I ponder what will happen to you and me
> Sometimes the visions are so cloudy I just can't see
> But I know deep in my heart my girl you will always be
> I think about our life together and I sing with glee
> About the perfect life for you and me
> Our baby will be born and it will know
> All the love two people can give we will surely show
> This beautiful creation will thrive and we will show
> How it's suppose to be done, not just for show
> But love from the heart to enrich a family
> You and me together for all of eternity
> It's not just my dream, it's my destiny.

Maybe Trevor's luck was changing and maybe fame and happiness would be a part of his destiny. Growing up had been difficult. His father had split when he was just a baby and his mom was forced to work two jobs just to put a small amount of food on the table. Trevor hated the fact that his mother had to leave her job in the school cafeteria only to go and clean office buildings at night, and he vowed that one day he would make it up to her. She would come home so tired; every bone in her body seemed to ache, but still she'd sit and listen to Trevor ramble on about his day, and she'd smile and look at him lovingly, telling him he was a wonderful son. She taught Trevor to respect life, women, God, and himself and he loved her for that. His mother had helped make him the man he was today. Trevor rapped about getting a college education, loving family and respecting women, working hard to succeed, being a father to your children, and obeying the law, all lessons he learned from his mother, lessons he took to heart.

As Trevor's tribute to Darlene ended, the crowd showered him with applause. Trevor bowed, waved to the crowd, blew a kiss to Darlene and exited backstage.

30

Chicken and a Coward

DARLENE AND TREVOR'S BROTHER LYLE went backstage to congratulate Trevor on a job well done. The crowd was still going wild and when they saw Trevor they could tell from the look in his eyes that he knew the crowd got his message, to live a positive life as young black men. The first thing he did when he saw his brother and Darlene was to give them a big hug. He then called his mother on his cell phone. He told her how well the concert went, and that they would be home in a little while.

They were going to drop Darlene off first because she had class early in the morning, and then Trevor and Lyle would stop and get something to eat. He told his mom not wait up for them, and he would see her in the morning.

"I love you, my son," his mother breathed into the phone, "You've made me so very proud."

"I love you, too, Mama."

The three walked out to Trevor's car, amid handshakes, high fives and hugs from some of the crowd who had stayed to congratulate him. A few people in the crowd actually asked for his autograph and he couldn't believe it. Trevor had never given an autograph before and he wasn't actually sure how to do it. He wasn't sure if he should include the person's name, or just sign his.

From out of the crowd stepped a well dressed man who introduced himself as a record producer from a well known label. He handed Trevor his business card and told him he had Trevor on his radar for quite some time. He further stated they were willing to offer Trevor a record deal and

151

asked if he was interested. Lyle, standing next to Trevor, kept hitting him with his elbow and couldn't control the big smile on his face. Trevor tried to play it cool although his heart was pounding. The producer whose name was Isaac Ward told Trevor he didn't need to make any decisions that night and asked if he could stop by his office in the morning to speak with his people. Trevor said he would and the two shook hands.

"You did a great job tonight," Mr. Ward told Trevor. "We need more young black men like you to get out a positive message." Trevor found this ironic because the main clientele of this record label was gangsta rap. They set up an appointment for 10 A.M., before saying their goodbyes.

As Trevor, Darlene and Lyle walked towards Trevor's car, Darlene turned to Trevor and said, "You're going to be rich."

"I don't know about that," Trevor replied, "but maybe I can get a car that starts on the first try."

As they got into Trevor's rusty, old car, it was shocking how different it was from your average rapper's vehicle. It was a beat up green Toyota Tercel with 180,000 miles on it, a far cry from the Cadillac Escalades and Hummers the other rappers drove. But, Trevor didn't care, because he was floating on air. He got his message out and everyone seemed to love it. He actually felt as if he made a difference tonight and it seemed to be paying off.

Off they went. The first stop was Darlene's house. Trevor walked Darlene to her door while Lyle waited in the back seat. As they approached the front door, Darlene gave Trevor a big kiss. She told him how proud she was of him and with that the porch light came on. She knew it was her mom waiting up for her. The front door opened and her mother was standing there with a big smile on her face. Darlene's mother loved Trevor for the person he was and for the way that he treated her daughter. She gave Trevor a hug and asked how everything went. Darlene didn't give him a chance to answer as she told her mother it was the best concert she had ever attended. Darlene's mother then reminded Darlene she had school early in the morning and that she should get upstairs to bed.

"I'm 19 years old Mom and you treat me like a baby," lamented Darlene.

"You'll always be my baby; now get your butt to bed," her mom teased.

With that Trevor kissed both women on the cheek and said good night. As he walked off the porch, he turned to Darlene and called after her, "When I see you tomorrow, our lives will be different."

Unbeknownst to Darlene, Trevor had been saving for months and had bought her an engagement ring. He was going to give it to her tonight, but didn't feel he had the right words, an odd thing for a rapper. Trevor wanted to sleep on it so he could come up with exactly the right thing to say. He hadn't told anyone yet, but now he was about to ask Lyle to be his best man.

When he got back to the car, Lyle had gotten into the front seat. As Trevor drove off, he turned to Lyle and asked, "What would you think if I told you that I wanted to marry Darlene?"

Lyle responded, "She's a good girl; she'd make a great wife, but how are you going to support her with both of you going to college?"

"Well, I think she'd agree we both have to wait until we graduate even if I get this record deal. I just want her to know I intend to marry her. I've been saving up for months and I bought her this ring."

Trevor had reached inside his jacket pocket and took out a box. He handed it to Lyle and asked him to open it. As they pulled up to a red light at the corner of 222nd Street and White Plains Road, Lyle opened the box. It contained a single diamond set on a gold band. The diamond looked red as it was reflecting the light from the traffic signal on the corner. As the light turned green, the diamond changed color again.

"It's beautiful," Lyle exclaimed. "She's going to love it. Does Mom know?"

"No, you're the only one I've told so far."

As Lyle handed Trevor back the ring, he closed the box and put it back inside his jacket pocket. "Would you be my best man?" Trevor asked Lyle. "Of course" Lyle shot back without hesitation." "This has been a perfect night Trevor exclaimed. "I'm starving," Lyle stated. "How about we get some chicken?"

"Sounds good to me," Trevor said, "How about *Kennedy*?"

Kennedy Fried Chicken, unlike the better known *Kentucky Fried Chicken*, tends to exist in poor inner city neighborhoods only. Someone would be hard pressed to find a *Kennedy Fried Chicken* in a wealthy suburb. Given their location, many *Kennedy Fried Chicken* establishments serve their clientele from behind bullet proof glass.

"That's good. It's right up the block from the house. You think mom would want something to eat?" Lyle asked.

"No, I told her not to wait up for us when I spoke to her before."

They pulled over to 232nd Street and White Plains Road stopping in front of *Kennedy Fried Chicken*. The night was cold and the wind was howling as they exited the car. There was a large patch of ice in front of the store's door and Trevor alerted Lyle, warning him, "Be careful, it's slippery."

The brothers entered the *Kennedy Fried Chicken*, went up to the counter and placed their orders. The restaurant was empty except for one shady looking character standing off to the side that appeared to be waiting for his order. He was very small in stature, standing no taller than five feet. He had a thin build and was wearing a black and white leather eight ball jacket. His eyes looked glassy but seemed to light up when he noticed the chain around Lyle's neck. Trevor had already placed his order and Lyle was speaking to the Indian man behind the counter. When Lyle was done, he turned and faced the eight ball jacket wearing customer. As Trevor looked at him, he thought how stereotypical that jacket was, because it seemed to be very much in fashion in the ghetto.

This shady person approached Lyle, and said, "Nice links," referring to the chain around Lyle's neck, which his mother had given him for Christmas only five days before.

"Thanks," Lyle replied, but uneasiness came over him as he felt this person was sizing him up and not actually complimenting him. Suddenly the young man reached into his waistband, pulled out a gun, and pointed it at the two brothers as he grabbed the chain off Lyle's neck. Lyle ran past him, and as he ran for the door of the restaurant. The gunman pointed his weapon at Lyle's back. Seeing this drama unfold before his eyes, Trevor pushed the gun wielding man, causing him to be shoved into the wall.

Lyle was able to run out of the store and out of harm's way, since Trevor's push had given Lyle enough time to escape. But, it seemed to also have sealed Trevor's fate. As Trevor attempted to run out of the restaurant, he got just outside the doorway and slipped on the same patch of ice that he had alerted his brother to as they entered the restaurant moments before. He landed flat on his stomach and tried to get up but his feet slipped out from under him. The gunman, who had chased him out of the restaurant, shot him point blank, two times in his back. The gunman stepped over Trevor's body as he lay on the cold ice covered sidewalk, and fled south on White Plains Road, disappearing out of sight.

Lyle, who had run around the corner, hearing the gunshots, ran back to the location and saw his brother Trevor lying in a pool of blood. Lyle knelt beside his brother, taking his hand, and screamed frantically for someone to call 911. The street seemed uncharacteristically empty, with only one livery cab driver parked across the street in front of the diner. Lyle comforted Trevor, telling him he was going to be okay but Trevor knew different. He told Lyle to roll him over on his back, which he did. Trevor looked up at Lyle and asked him to please take care of Darlene and Mom.

Lyle pleaded, "Don't talk like that; you'll be able to take care of them. The ambulance is on its way and you're going to be okay." *Please God*, Lyle prayed, *please let him be okay.*

Trevor squeezed Lyle's hand and told him, "No, you're going to have to do it. You're going to be the man of the house now. I love you."

"No Trevor, Please...." Lyle begged.

Trevor's eyes then closed and Lyle could hear a deep gurgling sound as a rush of air filled his brother's body. Trevor was no longer squeezing Lyle's hand and Lyle knew it was the end. He screamed his brother's name as he buried his face in his brother's chest, sobbing uncontrollably. He did not leave that position until the police arrived on the scene and had to pry him off his brother. A sheet was placed over Trevor's body as Lyle was taken to the 47th Precinct by the detectives on the scene for questioning.

31

The Investigation

THE ALARM CLOCK BLARED AS Detective Giovanni Franco rolled over and hit the snooze button. He looked at the clock and it read 6:30 A.M. This would be his last day tour and he hoped it would be an uneventful one because he needed to do some shopping when he got home tonight for the big New Year's Eve party he was throwing at his house the next night. The day was December 30, 1995, and as he stumbled out of bed, he could hear his two young boys talking in their bedroom. They were eight and three at the time and he could hear them fighting over what to watch on TV As he walked into his sons' bedroom, he asked in a stern voice what the TV was doing on so early in the morning. He didn't really care, but sometimes he felt he needed to project an air of discipline to keep his boys on their toes.

"It's Christmas break," his son CJ replied, "We're on vacation."

With that Giovanni gave his son a look as his little guy Thomas asked, "Did it snow last night? I want to build a snowman. Mommy said if it snowed, you would stay home from work and help us build a snowman."

Giovanni walked over to the window and pulled up the shade illuminating the bedroom and both boys squinted from the sunlight.

"No snow," Giovanni, replied. "Lucky me, guess I'm going to work today." Then he got down on the carpet of the bedroom and started wrestling with his boys. They were getting out of hand and he could hear his wife yelling from the bedroom that she didn't need to get up yet. The two boys started giggling and Giovanni had an idea.

"Let's go jump in the bed with Mommy." They were more than happy to oblige. So all three kids ran into Giovanni's bedroom and dove onto the king sized bed. All three started tickling mommy as she pretended to be very angry with them. Giovanni snuck out of the bed and went to take a shower leaving behind an early morning ruckus.

After his shower, he returned into the bedroom and all three were snuggling under the covers. He kissed them goodbye and headed out to work.

When he arrived at the precinct, he noticed several cars from night watch parked in front, along with two crime scene vehicles and three news vans parked across the street. It didn't take all his years of experience or a rocket scientist to figure out something had happened on the midnight tour. As he walked up the stairway to the detective squad, a crime scene detective was walking down and as they passed, Franco asked, "What do you got, Billy?"

"Some kid was shot on White Plains Road last night. DOA. His family's upstairs and they seem like nice people."

"That sucks," Franco replied. "Five days after Christmas. Never a dull moment in the 4-7."

As Franco entered the detective squad room, the place was packed. There were detectives everywhere, and one detective from night watch who he didn't know, was sitting at his desk. Franco hated when other detectives sat at his desk but he understood there was limited working space. Diplomatically he placed his newspaper and coffee on his desk and then went and signed in the sign-in log. When he returned, the detective sitting there had already moved. The Lieutenant called Franco into his office along with some other day tour detectives and they were briefed on the case. When Franco looked at the catching sheet, his worst fears came to light. It was his case. Night watch just does a preliminary investigation until the catching detective comes in in the morning. Although they were very thorough, there wasn't much to go on yet. He was told the kid who got shot was a good boy and came from a respectable family. He was also told that his mother, brother and girlfriend were in the Detective's Lounge awaiting his arrival.

Franco hated catching homicides that occurred on night watch, because he couldn't get a good feel for it. He did not respond to the scene when it happened, and always felt there was some piece of evidence someone might have overlooked, but if he had been there, he might have noticed it: a possible witness, a plate number, or some type of other physical evidence at the scene that someone else might think was unimportant. Now he had to go deal with a family of distraught individuals and they would expect, as usual, the case to be solved already. He had a bad feeling about this one. All he knew was a kid was shot in front of a chicken joint He had never even been inside that *Kennedy Fried Chicken*. He knew it was during the commission of a robbery and he remembered hearing about a law change that went into effect that stated, *if you kill someone during the*

157

commission of a robbery it is considered murder in the first degree, punishable by the death penalty; the governor had just signed it into law.

Taking a deep breath, he picked up his coffee, and made the long trek past all the detectives' desk to the door of the Detective's Lounge. When he opened the door, he observed a well dressed middle-aged black woman sitting at the lunch table. She had blood shot eyes and next to her was a young boy who was about 18 years old, holding her hand. Off to the left, in a chair, was a young girl, who also looked to be in her late teens and she was sobbing into her gloves. Detective Franco introduced himself and the woman stated that she was Trevor's mom. He conveyed his condolences to the family and asked the young man whom he knew was a witness, what happened. He said his name was Lyle and explained how his brother had performed at a community center that night and he had been a singer. After the show, they went to get some food right up the block from their house. This guy with a gun grabbed his chain, but he was able to run out of the restaurant. His brother tried to run out and must have slipped on the ice in front of the restaurant. He didn't actually see the man kill his brother because he had run around the block. He heard two shots, ran back to the store and saw his brother lying on the pavement. He further stated that he saw the guy who grabbed his chain running down White Plains Road. He then lost sight of him as he tended to his brother.

As Lyle was reenacting the incident, his mother and would have been sister-in-law were sobbing uncontrollably. Detective Franco always puts himself on the spot in cases like this and then he hates himself for doing it later. But he looked into Mrs. Webb's eyes, took her hand, and told her, "I know it's no consolation, but I promise you, I'll get this guy."

She stood up, hugged him and cried, "My boy was a good boy. He's never been in any trouble and actually he raps about positive role models for young black men. How ironic that a young black man took his life this morning."

Then Darlene called out Trevor's name and walked out of the lounge crying. Lyle ran after her trying to console her.

The door to the lounge opened and Detective Rice popped his head in. He called, "Giovanni, the ME's office is on the phone." He excused himself and went to take the phone call. He was told a family member needed to come down to positively identify the body and the bloody clothes that were vouchered. Also there was personal property that needed to be returned to the family. The ME, who Franco was quite friendly with due to other homicide cases he's worked on, informed Franco that there was an engagement ring inside the jacket pocket of the deceased. As Franco was speaking to the ME, Lyle and Darlene went back into the lounge to be with

Mrs. Webb. Franco hung up the phone and went back to speak with them. He asked if anyone was aware of a ring inside Trevor's jacket. Lyle put his head into his hands and started to cry.

"What's going on, Lyle?" his mother asked.

Lyle looked at Darlene and said, "Trevor was going to ask you to marry him today. He showed me the ring last night. He had it in his jacket. All three then started to cry and they hugged each other for comfort.

Detective Franco was visibly affected by this emotional scene and felt he needed to walk out of the room at that moment. When he came back a few minutes later, he informed the family someone had to go and identify the body at the morgue and pick up Trevor's personal property, a wallet, watch, and Darlene's ring. He gave them his business card and directions to Jacobi Hospital where Trevor's body lay in the morgue. He walked them down to their car which was parked around the corner from the precinct, and they noticed the three news vans that were apparently not there when they came into the precinct last night.

A woman with a microphone approached as they were walking up the block. She was trailed by a man with a large camera on his shoulder. "I don't want to talk to anyone, please Detective," Mrs. Webb implored.

"You don't have to talk to anyone," Detective Franco stated. He walked towards the woman with the microphone, stopping her in her tracks. The camera was not recording yet. Franco told the three to keep walking towards their car. He stood in front of the woman and scolded her, with a disgusted look on his face, "You can't be serious. These people just lost a loved one. Can you respect that?"

"I'm just doing my job," the woman replied.

"Well, they have nothing to say," Franco answered.

He was not a big fan of the media and found on numerous occasions they reported on events where he was, and their rendition didn't match his memory. Franco turned his back to the woman and walked towards Mrs. Webb's car. He told her if they needed anything to call him. Then he looked at Lyle and said, "If you remember anything that you think can help me, please let me know," and handed Lyle his card.

Sadly, the three drove off, on their way to the morgue to identify Trevor's body. As Franco walked back into the precinct, the detective from night watch who was leaving told him there was one possible witness, a 911 caller who called from his cell phone. He told Franco the information was upstairs in his report. *Good*, Franco thought, *at least there's something to try to work on here*. He thanked the night watch detectives for their help as they were all getting ready to go back to their command and sign out.

Franco went up to his desk and read the report that included the 911 call. It was a local guy and Franco told Detective Richie Talia to take a ride with him as he wanted to see if he could locate this possible witness. They arrived at an apartment building on Olinville Avenue. When they knocked on the door of apartment 3A, a middle aged heavy set Puerto Rican man answered the door. They asked if he was Ramon Gonzalez and he nodded yes. He had not given his name to the 911 operator, but they traced him through his cell phone records. They asked if he had called 911 last night about the shooting at the corner of 232nd Street and White Plains Road and he reluctantly answered yes. Franco asked him why he didn't give his name to the 911 operator when she asked, and he explained he didn't want to get involved but he also didn't want that moreno to get away with it. Moreno is slang Spanish people use to describe black people.

Franco asked, "You call him a moreno like you know him."

"I've seen him around before," the cabby stated.

Franco thought, *okay then he can identify him if I catch him.* He didn't want to put too much pressure on the cabby; he just asked him what he saw. He stated he was parked in front of the diner on the corner across the street from the *Kennedy Fried Chicken.* He sits there late at night picking up fares that come off the train. He saw somebody run out of the restaurant and slip on the sidewalk. Then he saw somebody else stand over him and shoot him in the back twice. He said he slid down low in his seat so to not be seen by the gunman. Although he thought about driving off, he was afraid that the guy would shoot at him.

"So, if you saw him again," Franco asked, "you would know him, right?"

"I would know him Detective, but I don't want to be involved," the man replied.

"Well, you know what?" Franco offered, "that kid who got shot was a good kid. Never been in any trouble. And if that was your son, you would want somebody to get involved, right?"

The cabby looked down at the floor and nodded his head yes. Franco told him he would try to keep him out of it the best he could, but he might need him to look at some pictures at some point.

The rest of the day was spent with Franco rounding up all of his informants that he had on the street for years. People he either cut breaks for or people who owed him favors from situations that were considered big to them but no big deal to Franco. Neighborhood drug pushers, pick pockets, and numbers runners who owed him a favor or two. Franco, being in the same precinct for the last twelve years, had established many contacts in the street. They weren't good people, but if they thought their information would keep Franco off their backs, they would sometimes come through for him.

Franco knew he had one thing in his favor. The description of the perp was unique. He was very short and thin and the cabby said he had seen him around. If the cabby saw him around, other people must have seen him around, too. He hoped he was a neighborhood skell who might go around bragging about what he had done. Franco also had a detailed description of Lyle's chain and he was going to canvass the neighborhood pawn shops with Detective Talia to see if anyone had tried to sell it. There wasn't much to go on at this point, but he was hoping for a break. He really didn't want to cancel the New Year's Eve party planned for tomorrow at his house but he also knew that this was much more important.

As Franco described the perp to one of his CIs (confidential informants) the CI said, "That sounds like Lingo."

"Who's Lingo?" Franco asked.

"He's this light skinned black dude that everybody says is crazy. I heard he bought a gun a while back and he's been showing it to everyone in the street."

"When was the last time you saw him?" Franco asked.

"About a week ago," the CI replied. "He was fucking with this homeless woman on the corner and he turned over her cart, spilling her bottles out into the street. She was cursing at him, and he lifted up his jacket and showed her the handle of his gun."

Franco took the CI into the precinct and got him some lunch. He told him "I'm gonna see if I can locate a picture with that nickname. You don't know his real name do you?"

"No," the CI says, "Lingo is his street name; I don't even know what it stands for."

The CI sat in the detective's lounge watching T.V. as Franco frantically looked through all the nickname books the squad had compiled throughout the years. But, this proved to be a dead end. Then he entered the name Lingo in the nickname computer database that's compiled throughout the entire NYPD. He got four hits. One was a man arrested in his 50s for a sexual assault in the East Village so he was eliminated. Another was a man who stood six foot two and he was arrested for selling drugs in Brooklyn so he was gone too. The third one was listed as a short thinly built perp who was arrested for an assault two years prior but the arresting officer had entered him as being Hispanic. He was arrested by Transit PD for an assault that occurred at the Gunhill train station which was within the confines of the 47th precinct. For his address he was listed as domiciled. Franco felt this was his man. The arresting officer could have been duped into believing this person was Hispanic being he was light skinned. He just wished he had an address to go along with it.

He pulled up the case on the computer and retrieved the arrest photo of that individual. Then he took that arrest photo and put it into a photo array with five other light skinned males in their early 20s. He showed it to Detective Talia pointing at photo number two and stated, "I think this is our boy."

"Let's hope so," Talia said, "I felt terrible for that family."

"Well let's find out," Franco said as he walked back into the lounge where the CI sat.

Franco tossed the photo array on the table in front of where the CI sat and asked, "Tell me if you see your boy Lingo in there."

As the CI looked down on the photo array, his eyes widened as he stared at photo number two.

"That's him," the CI screamed. "That's that little piece of shit."

"What number?" Franco asked.

"Number two man," the CI said.

"You beez the man," Detective Talia said to Franco as the two high fived.

"Yo, I ain't gonna have to testify or nothing in court, right?" the CI asked.

"No" Franco said, "you're not a witness. I just wanted you to tell me who Lingo is."

"So, you owe me then, right?" the CI asked.

Franco walked over to him as he sat at the table, and said "Yeah I do owe you," and smacked him on the side of his head. "Do you want me to give you everything else I owe you?"

As the CI rubbed his head, he said, "No that's okay, I guess the sandwich was good enough."

Franco put his hand on the CI's shoulder and thanked him for his help. "I guess I won't be breaking your ball for a while," Franco said. He and Talia then drove him back and dropped him off a few blocks from his house. CIs don't like to be seen with the police and prefer to be dropped off a few blocks away.

Franco turned to Talia and said, "We're not going home today until we find this scumbag."

32

Two in the Bush

THE SUN WAS SETTING AND THE TEMPERATURE was dropping quickly as a cold front out of Canada had taken over the city. Detectives Franco and Talia were on their way back to Olinville Avenue to show the cabbie the photo array. They made the trek up the three flights of stairs to his door and knocked on it several times but there was no answer. Franco had noticed a brown Chevy Impala with livery plates parked across the street from the building and he was pretty sure that it was the cabbie's car. He knocked several more times but no one answered. Franco took his cell phone out and dialed the cabbie's cell phone. From the hallway he could hear it ringing inside the apartment and he knew that Mr. Gonzalez was home. He shouted through the door, "Don't make this hard on me, Ramon, I just need to show you something, it will only take a minute. If I have to go down to court and come back with a warrant, I will arrest you as a hostile witness. Then everyone in the neighborhood will know that you are cooperating with the police." Franco said it loud enough so that Mr. Gonzalez could hear and maybe a couple of his neighbors too. With that, the locks on the door started clicking and the door opened. Mr. Gonzalez stood in the doorway in boxer shorts and a tee shirt, rubbing his eyes. He stated he was sleeping and didn't hear anyone knock. Franco and Talia looked at each other and gave the usual glance that they give when they knew someone was bullshitting them.

"I'm not hostile," Mr. Gonzalez stated. "I'm just tired. I worked all night and have to go back in two hours."

"This will only take a minute," Franco shot back as he walked past Mr. Gonzalez and into his apartment. The cabby closed the door quickly as if to shut out any neighbors who might be looking through their peepholes.

Franco told Mr. Gonzalez, "I'm gonna show you six photographs and you tell me if you see anyone who you recognize."

With that he handed Mr. Gonzalez the photo array, and told him, "you're not a very good liar so if you recognize someone, I'll know it." Mr. Gonzalez looked down at the photos and his eyes went right to photo # 2. The cabby didn't say anything, but both Detectives knew that he saw the perp.

"It's okay Ramon, you can tell me," Franco assured him.

The cabbie looked up at him and stated, "Number two is the guy that shot that boy. But I really don't want to be involved Detective."

Franco had the cabbie sign the back of the photo array stating that # 2 was the person wanted in connection with this homicide. He informed him that the District Attorney would need to speak with him at some point. He further informed him that he would need to testify in front of the Grand Jury, but neither the suspect nor his lawyer would be present. It would only be Bronx residents who had been called for jury duty and the DA asking questions. The whole process would take less than 10 minutes. This would only happen if the suspect was ever caught. They thanked him for his cooperation and told him they would be in touch. The cabbie didn't seem very happy about the whole situation, but hey, that's life in the Bronx.

So Franco and Talia got back in their car, knowing they had a definite suspect to try to locate. They then went to the home of the victim to see if Lyle, the victim's brother, could identify the suspect. When they arrived at the small one family stucco house Franco took notice of the freshly painted porch and manicured bushes in front. Even though it was late December the house had a warm feeling to it. It was nothing he could put his finger on but it seemed more like a home and less like a house. A chill came over him as they rang the bell and waited by the front door. Mrs. Webb came to the door and greeted the detectives warmly. Franco introduced Talia to Mrs. Webb and she stated she noticed him in the squad room. Franco asked if Lyle was home and she stated he was and invited the detectives in. They entered the living room and the smell of fresh pine hit Franco's nose. Off in the corner was a real Christmas tree tastefully decorated with several opened gifts underneath. It gave him a sick feeling knowing that this family would never feel the same about this time of year again. Mrs. Webb called up the stairs to Lyle and he came down. He greeted the detectives with a handshake and Franco told Lyle he wanted him to look at some pictures.

"Did you catch the person who shot my boy?" Mrs. Webb asked as her voice seemed to crack.

"No not yet Mrs. Webb but were working very hard to do just that."
He found it odd that she said the person who shot her boy, guess she
couldn't get the words KILLED to come out of her mouth. *Maybe she will
never be able to face that fact* he thought. So the detectives took Lyle into the
kitchen away from Mrs. Webb and Franco handed him the photo array.

"Tell me if you see anyone who looks familiar to you Lyle," he stated.

As Lyle looked down at the photo array a look of pure anger distorted
his face. He pointed to photo # 2 and stated, "That is the guy that did it."

Franco hated to do this to Lyle but for legal purposes he needed to.

"That is the guy that did what Lyle?"

"That is the guy who shot my brother."

Franco had to correct Lyle as he was not actually present when his
brother was shot. Although it was understood, he did not see this person
shoot Trevor. All he could speak about was his chain being robbed. Once
Franco explained this, Lyle stated, "that is the guy who pulled a gun on
me and my brother in the store, snatched the chain off my neck, chased me
outside and was running away after I heard two gunshots and came back
to see my brother lying on the ground shot."

Talia looked at Franco and said, "This kid is going to make one hell of
a witness."

Mrs. Webb walked into the kitchen and stated, "I heard what you
gentlemen were talking about. Can I please see the person who shot my
baby?"

She had tears in her eyes and against his better judgment Franco handed Mrs. Webb the photo array. "Number Two Mommy," Lyle exclaimed as
Mrs. Webb's eyes focused on photo # 2.

"So that's him," she exclaimed, "he looks so young, he looks like a
baby."

"A very dangerous baby," Franco replied.

With that, Mrs. Webb said something Franco, in all the years he had
been investigating homicides, had never heard from a victim's mother.
Mrs. Webb handed the photo array back to him and stated, "I will pray for
his lost soul."

"You're a better person than me," he told Mrs. Webb as the two detectives said their good-byes.

The detectives were now off to the Kennedy Fried Chicken to show
the photo array to the owner who was working when the murder happened. The night watch detective who interviewed him at the scene stated
in his report that he was not very cooperative and stated he could not I.D.
the perp but they would try anyway.

Franco and Talia arrived at the location and were told the owner was in the rear of the store doing paperwork. They were buzzed in behind a bullet proof glass partition and lead down a short hallway into a very small office. They were introduced to Mr. Kamal who instantly told them he did not see what happened and that it happened outside his store. The detectives found it strange that there were no cameras in the location and when they asked why, he stated it is too expensive.

"Bullet proof glass is cheap?" Franco asked Talia as he gave the owner a look of disgust. Franco and Talia knew he was lying and was sure he saw Lyle's chain get snatched at the very least. They told him they had some pictures to look at and handed him the photo array.

He looked at it briefly and quickly stated, "No I don't recognize anyone."

Franco, losing his temper stated, "You didn't even look at each face, but that's okay I have some other faces for you to look at later on today. I'm going to have the Board of Health here to see how many violations they can find in this filthy pigsty."

"Let's go Richie," Franco said as he turned his back on the owner and started to walk away. "Thanks for all your help you are truly an upstanding citizen sir. Oh by the way are you a citizen? Well we'll find out about that too. I love when people come to this country to make money but don't have the common decency to do the right thing when someone gets murdered, maybe next time it will be you or someone you care about."

Franco was so angry he needed to leave at that moment fearing he might do something he would regret.

The detectives hit several pawn shops in the neighborhood hoping that the perp would try to sell Lyle's chain, but that proved to be negative. They left a copy of a photo of Lyle's chain and contact information for the detectives.

It was now dark out and Talia commented how much the temperature had dropped. "It's got to be in the teens," he stated as they drove back to the precinct to see if there were any further developments in the case.

As they were walking up the stairs to the detective's squad room, Franco's cell phone rang. They had showed the picture of Lingo to several people on the street that they trusted with that information. One of them, a hardware store owner named Ralph, who had been in business at the same location, White Plains Road and 226th Street, for many years and was a personal friend of Franco's, was on the line stating that he was pretty sure he had just seen the guy in the picture walk up 226th Street towards Barnes Avenue. The detectives ran back out of the precinct, jumped in the car and headed towards 226th Street. They canvassed the area for approximately one hour but didn't see the suspect. As they were driving west on 222nd Street, Talia saw a guy who had given him good information a few times in the past.

He told Franco, "Pull over. Let's talk to this guy. He knows everybody on the street."

They showed him a picture of Lingo and he stated he saw him go into a house yesterday on 224th Street.

"Are you sure?" Franco asked him?

"Yeah I'm sure," he stated. "Everybody knows that crazy mother fucker around here."

He further stated that he didn't want people to see him talking with the detectives so he asked them to pick him up down the block on Bronx Boulevard by the park. He would be down by the river and being that it was cold and dark, no one would see him get into their car. He didn't know the address that he saw the suspect go into, so he needed to show the detectives the exact house he was talking about.

Franco wasn't too happy with letting him walk away like that, but Talia assured him that the guy was cool. So they drove down to the river and after a few minutes he came up behind their unmarked car and jumped into the back seat.

He lay down on their back seat the whole time he talked. He gave them a brief history of Lingo because he had known several things he had done throughout the years. There was the time he lit a woman's cat on fire, another time when he dumped a gallon of paint on a sleeping homeless man at the train station, and one time when he sprayed Raid bug spray in a girls' face because she wouldn't go out with him. He said even though he was small, people in the neighborhood were scared of him and afraid to call the police because they were fearful of what he might do to them. He said he heard about the shooting in front of the chicken store, but didn't know Lingo was involved. He asked if there was a reward for any information about him and he was told that there wasn't.

"I guess you're just helping out because you're a good citizen," Franco informed him.

"No he's helping out so that I don't fuck with him," Talia added.

The informant directed the detectives to the house on 224th Street that he had seen Lingo go into yesterday. They drove by the house causally as he pointed it out trying not to make it obvious. Franco was able to catch the address out of the corner of his eye. It was 736 East 224th Street, and it looked to be a three family house. It was made of brick which was usual for the houses in the neighborhood, a sign of a time gone by when the neighborhood was predominately Italian and most of these houses were built by Italian masons. They had since all moved out and now the neighborhood was predominately Jamaican with some Hispanics thrown in.

They dropped the informant back off at the park and went into the precinct to give a brief update to the Lieutenant, took a piss then hurried back to the location. They parked their car on 223rd Street approximately a block and a half away from the house. Franco and Talia went through a backyard on 223rd Street and made their way across from the house in question positioning themselves in the bushes of a house directly across the street. They crawled the last fifty feet on their hands and knees because the bushes were only two feet tall and they did not want to be seen. They lay on the cold dirt behind these bushes, on their stomachs and observed the house in question. The Lieutenant had another unit positioned north of 224th street on Barnes Avenue. Now the waiting game began.

Talia looked over at Franco and stated, "We have no idea if he's even in the house and I'm freezing. This could take forever."

Franco shot back with a whisper, "It's all we got to go on right now."

So the two detectives lay on their stomachs, freezing, and observing this house. Neither one of them was dressed for this as they were both in suits and neither had on a bullet proof vest. Talia was visibly shaking as the cold air and even colder ground consumed his body. Franco was playing mind games, telling himself how it was a nice sunny summer day. He thought about Trevor's mother and the pain that he saw in her eyes and he kept telling Talia, "That poor family, we're all they have right now."

Franco's feet were numb and he kept blowing into his hands to try to get some circulation going. He told Talia, "If we get into a shootout with this guy, I'm not even going to be able to feel my gun."

Talia stated, "Why don't we have a couple of the guys go to court and get a warrant?"

But Franco knew no judge would ever give them a warrant based on a sighting by some street mutt twenty-four hours ago which was actually before the murder was even committed. It had only been eighteen hours since the homicide and he saw no choice but to lie on the cold ground and wait.

There was one light on coming from the second floor and he could see shadows going past the window occasionally. The window appeared to be covered with a blind and sometimes Franco thought he saw a space in the bind, as though someone was looking out. Most of the time the two detectives concentrated on the front door and they planned what they would do if he either came to the house or left it. If he arrived at the house, they would alert the unit parked at Barnes Avenue and rush him before he could get inside. If he left the house, that would be a little more involved. It would depend on which way he went on 224th Street. If he went east toward the other unit, they would alert them and have them cut him off while they trailed from behind. But if he went west towards White Plains Road they would be left on their own to try to grab him before he fled. It had been over three hours now that the detectives were lying on this cold frozen ground and it started to really take a physical effect on them. Talia joked about symptoms of hyperthermia and Franco felt like his ears were about to fall off.

"A suit from Syms is definitely not winter stake out apparel," Franco chuckled as he tried to keep Talia's spirits up, but it was starting to become a serious situation and they didn't know how much longer they could lie out there in temperature that had to be hovering around ten degrees at this point. It was now ten o'clock at night and the street was very quiet. An occasional car would pass by or someone would walk by with their dog, let it pee, and then hurry back into their house. All of a sudden a yellow cab pulled up in front of the house in question.

"Oh God," Talia whispered, "Please let this cab be for him."

"From your lips to God's ears," Franco shot back. "My balls are frozen."

The cab waited approximately a minute, then beeped its horn several times. The front door of 736 opened up and Franco's heart was pounding. His mouth became very dry as he starred at the open doorway. Out from the house emerged a very small person wearing a black and white eight ball jacket, the same jacket that was described as being worn by the suspect in the homicide. This person was also wearing blue jeans, red sneakers, a hoodie tied very tight around the face and what appeared to be a wool cap underneath. It was hard to make out any facial features. The detectives knew they had to make a decision as to what to do, and they had to decide now.

Talia said, "That's him. Let's grab him before he gets into the cab!"

Franco wasn't so sure. "I don't think it's him," Franco said.

"What!" Talia said with an exasperated tone. "He's wearing the exact same clothes as the perp."

"Yeah but something's not right. Just wait a minute." Franco begged.

"He's going to get away," Talia warned as the person opened the rear door on the driver's side of the cab.

"No let's let him go. I'll radio to the other unit. And once the cab is off this block they can stop it. I don't think it's him." Franco insisted.

"It's him!" Talia exclaimed. "How can it not be him? He's dressed exactly like the perp!"

"Something's just not right, Franco continued, "There was a large bulge underneath his hood, like a ponytail or something, and his walk, there's something funny about his walk."

"It was probably just his hat underneath his hood, and what do you mean about his walk, you don't know how he walks" Talia said with exasperation as Detective Franco radioed to the unit that was parked one block up and off the corner and instructed them to stop the yellow cab that was about to drive by their location.

As the cab drove away, Talia looked over at Franco, pointed his finger, and stated, "You fucked up. We could have grabbed him. Now we have to hope that the other guys will stop him. And what if he has the gun on him? Somebody might get hurt. We could have taken him easier because he had no idea we were here."

"I don't think it was him," Franco calmly repeated as Talia just shook his head in disgust.

Franco got the impression that Talia thought that he hesitated because he was fearful. Or that he wanted to let the other unit grab him due to the danger aspect, which made him feel angry and defensive. Franco considered himself quite brave and although nothing was said he sensed Talia was silently questioning his manhood. Approximately forty-five seconds after the cab drove off; the front door of 736 opened again and out came another small individual wearing a dress covered by a pink woman's coat, women's shoes and a pink and yellow wool hat tied tight around the face. This person walked to the sidewalk, looked to the left and then to the right, then started to walk west on 236th Street, the same direction that the cab went in.

"That's him," Franco told Talia.

"No fucking way, that's a girl!" Talia cried.

"It's him wearing girl's clothes, stupid," he shot back, although he was not 100% sure.

With that the two detectives got up on their knees and Franco said, "I'm going to go up along our side of the street staying low behind the cars. You run across and get behind the trunk of one of the cars. If he sees me and doubles back, you can intercept him."

As Franco ran down the five steps of the house they were hiding in front of, he noticed how his whole body was extremely stiff and couldn't believe how painful it was to get his body to move. His feet and hands were frozen and nothing seemed to bend or move the way it should.

The individual in the dress briskly walked up the block, with Franco following across the street, going from car to car and trying to stay below the roof lines. As he got even with the suspect, he pulled his gun and made a mad dash across the street feeling his hamstrings tightening, no doubt from lack of blood flowing through his body. He slammed the individual up against an apartment building wall. He hoped to God it wasn't a girl because this had lawsuit written all over it. A second later Talia arrived by his side, and they had both hands behind the suspect's back. As they turned the suspect around, they recognized him as Lingo and Franco ripped the stupid pink and yellow hat off his head.

As he was being handcuffed, Lingo looked at Franco, and stated, "You dirty rat," making reference to a Jimmy Cagney line from the 1931 movie, *Blond Crazy*. He was searched for a weapon but none was found on his person.

Over their radios the detectives were told that the cab had been stopped and it contained one female dressed in men's clothing.

Franco stated over the radio, "We got him," and asked them to take the female suspect to the precinct.

Franco requested a sector car to come to the location to transport them and their perp back to their unmarked car which they parked on 223rd Street. After getting into the unmarked car, Franco was gloating and felt it necessary to break Talia's balls. "So Richie, if you thought the first one was a guy, and this one was a girl, I'd hate to see you at four in the morning at one of the local watering holes. Tell me, how many times have you woken up in the morning with some cock lying next to you?"

Lingo, finding this extremely funny laughed out loud until Talia turned around and smacked him in his mouth. Again he repeated his famous quote, "You dirty rat."

Talia stated "I got to give it to ya, Gio, you can tell a little cross dresser when you see one. Guess you've woken up with a few of those yourself."

33

The Interrogation

AS FRANCO AND TALIA PULLED UP IN FRONT of the precinct they knew Lingo
was going to catch all hell for the way he was dressed. They didn't care, he
was a cold blooded murderer and Franco was kind of looking forward to
it. It would be a small payback for the terrible deed he committed. Before
they got out of the car, Lingo asked if they could go by a hospital or shelter
to get him some clothes.

"Yeah right," was all that Franco could mutter as he started to laugh.

"You can't let me go to Central Booking dressed like this," Lingo
stated.

Talia turned to Franco and said, "Why don't we go by the little girls
department in Macy's and buy him a pretty dress."

"I'm already wearing a pretty dress," Lingo shot back, "anyway
Macy's is closed its night time I need men's clothes."

"If you were a man you wouldn't have shot that poor kid in the back,"
Franco informed him.

Lingo just put his head down and didn't respond.

The detectives removed him from the rear seat and started walking
him up the fifteen stairs that lead to the front entrance of the precinct. There
were several cops standing on the landing in front of the door and when
they saw Lingo, they started whistling and making catcalls.

You could see the anger on Lingo's face as he told one of the cops to
go fuck himself.

With that, Franco, who was gripping Lingo's handcuffs which were
behind his back, lifted them straight up, causing him severe pain. He
stopped walking and whispered in Lingo's ear, "If you disrespect anyone
inside this precinct, you will regret it."

Lingo apologized and said, "I look ridiculous. It's embarrassing."

The Interrogation

Franco told him, "You shouldn't wear girls' clothes."

With that they entered the precinct and the three of them walked up the stairs to the detective squad. When they walked into the squad room, all eyes were on Franco and his prisoner. He walked Lingo over to the holding pen, a twelve x twelve cell with bars, uncuffed him, and put him in the cell.

Franco knew if he was going to get a confession he had to work quickly because once word got out on the street, it was possible that an attorney would call and inform the detectives not to question his client. Franco and Talia went into the Lieutenant's office and updated him on the details of the investigation and arrest. Just then, the female suspect who was picked up by the other unit was brought into the squad room. When Franco saw her he asked the detectives to take her into interrogation room # 2 so that he could keep them separated and take her statement. But his main concern was Lingo and what he had to say.

So Franco and Talia removed Lingo from the holding cell and brought him into interrogation room # 1. This room contained a table and two chairs. You could see into the room through a one way mirror from the hallway, and sometimes other detectives would watch Franco attempting to get a confession. Sometimes it was quite comical with the antics and stunts he would pull, and how he would go about it. But today he didn't feel like he had anything special up his sleeve; he was just going to approach the suspect head on.

So Franco sat Lingo down on one of the chairs and read him his rights. He had him sign a piece of paper with those rights written on it, stating that he understood them, and was willing to speak to the police. After Lingo signed the paper, He removed it from the table and he began to question Lingo.

He informed him that he was under arrest for the murder of Trevor Webb on December 30 1995. At first Lingo claimed he had no idea what Franco was talking about.

With that Talia, who had been standing off to the corner, interjected, "You better not disrespect this detective; I've seen him kill people in this room."

Lingo looked at Talia, attempting to gauge some type of facial response, but Talia just stared back at him blankly.

"Okay Lingo, We're going to try this again. First of all, where did you get that stupid fucking nickname and what's your real name?" Franco asked.

Lingo explained that his grandmother used to call him that but he never asked her why. He stated that she basically raised him, that he didn't know who his father was and his mother was a heroin junkie. He had been out of school since eighth grade and his grandmother did the best she could, but she was old and lived alone. He's basically been in the streets since he was a young boy.

"My fucking heart bleeds for you." Franco responded. "I feel so bad maybe I'll ask the court if I can adopt you."

With that Franco got real close to Lingo and as they came nose to nose, told him "You killed a good boy and ruined his whole family's lives because you needed to be a tough guy on the street. But you're not a tough guy, you're a coward."

He went on to tell Lingo, whose real name was Marvin Davis, a little bit about his victim. He told him how he was an up and coming rap singer who rapped about young black men making it in the ghetto, how it was important to stand up, make something of yourself and go to school. He especially told him how he preached about black on black violence.

At this point, Lingo seemed to get teary eyed and Franco wasn't sure if it was an act or if he was actually getting to him, but he figured this was the time to run with it. He told him how his victim was about to ask his girlfriend to marry him that day, how he was in college planning his future, and how he had a heartbroken mother and brother who, today, would be making funeral plans for him. He was attempting to lay as much guilt as possible on Marvin.

After about an hour of constant bombardment from Talia and Franco about how he killed such a good kid for absolutely no reason, Lingo turned to Franco and asked, "How can I make it better?"

That's what Franco was hoping to hear. He told him, "You can't change what you've done, but you can be a man for the first time in your life, accept ownership of it and let everyone know how sorry you are, if you are sorry."

At this point Marvin started to cry and went on to say that he was truly sorry and doesn't know why he does some of the things he does. He said he feels as though no one cares about him and he lashes out, out of anger and frustration.

Franco told Marvin he was going to take a statement from him about what happened that night, he could sign it and Franco would give it to the DA, and maybe he wouldn't be viewed as such an animal. Maybe the family might someday find it in their hearts to forgive him, and maybe a jury would look at him with some sympathy.

Right before Franco started to take Marvin's statement; he told Marvin what Mrs. Webb had said to him when he showed her Marvin's photo.

"Do you know what this woman said when I showed her your picture? She said you look like an innocent baby and that she was going to pray for your lost soul."

By now Marvin was weeping uncontrollably, stating he was sorry and wished he could take back what he had done. Franco told Talia to go get Marvin a soda and Marvin asked if he could have a cigarette.

Although smoking wasn't allowed in city buildings, sometimes rules would be bent for necessary outcomes. So Talia came back with a soda and a cigarette and Franco started the long process of taking Marvin's confession for murder.

Marvin started off by explaining his horrible childhood and was no doubt looking for sympathy leading up to his actions on December 30th. He explained the situation with his mother, and the father that he never knew; how his grandmother raised him, but couldn't control him and how he was in the streets since he was a little kid. He also mentioned his size, or lack of, and how he needed to do crazy things on the street to gain street cred. He felt if people thought he was crazy, they would respect him and wouldn't fuck with him. He stated he was always doing crazy things to get people's attention.

"Okay Marvin, let's talk about last night," Franco stated. "Why were you in Kennedy Fried Chicken?"

"I sometimes hang out in there when it's cold and sometimes the guy behind the counter will give me a piece of chicken. I don't think he likes me being in there but I think he feeds me to prevent me from causing problems."

"So you intimidate the guy into giving you chicken," Franco asked.

"Yeah," he stated.

"Alright so what happened when the two boys walked into the store?" He asked.

"Well, they came in and they looked soft. The first guy ordered his food and he was looking at me funny. When the second guy ordered his food, I saw he had a nice big fat gold chain around his neck. I said, *nice links* to him and he said *thanks*."

"Did you have a gun?" Franco asked.

"Yeah it was tucked in my pants and my jacket was covering it."

"Where did you get the gun?" He asked.

"I bought it from a guy on Canal Street in Manhattan. Chinese dude."

"Where's the gun now?" Franco asked.

"I went to City Island and threw it in the ocean 'cause I knew you guys would be looking for me."

"Okay you're going to have to show me later on where you threw it.

Now let's get back to the chicken store. So the two guys ordered their food and then what?"

"So the guy with the chain, he looks real scared, like he knows I'm going to take him off.

So I walk up to him. Pull out my jammy."

"Your gun?" Franco asked.

"Yeah." Marvin stated. "You don't know what a jammy is?" Marvin asked.

"I know what a jammy is," Franco answered, "but the DA might not so you got to speak English, not Ebonics."

"Yo, you funny detective."

"Okay so what happened next, Marvin?"

"So I pulled out my GUN, and grabbed the kid's chain. He ran away from me and the other guy pushed me into the wall."

"Did he push you because you were pointing a gun at his brother?" Franco asked.

"Oh that was his brother?" Marvin asked.

"Yeah Marvin that was his brother. Were you pointing the gun at the kid whose chain you took?"

"Yeah I guess I was detective."

"So his brother pushed you to try to stop you from shooting him in the back."

"Yeah."

"Okay what happened next?"

"So he ran out of the store and I chased him. But he got away."

"Why would you chase him if you already had his chain?" Franco asked.

"I don't know, sometimes I do stupid shit."

Franco just shook his head.

"So what happened next?"

"The guy that pushed me tried to run out but he slipped on the ice in front of the door of the store. So I came up behind him and . . . you know."

"No I don't know Marvin. Don't stop now. You're right there, bro. You'll feel a lot better once you say it."

Marvin started crying and Franco thought *I hope he doesn't clam up now.*

"Take a drink of your soda." Franco urged. Tears and snot were running down Marvin's face as he wiped his nose with the sleeve of his dress. "What did you do when the boy slipped on the ice?" Franco asked.

Marvin, looking down at the ground, stated in a low voice, "I shot him."

"How many times?" Franco asked.

"Twice," Marvin answered.

Franco, who was writing down everything Marvin was saying, put the pen down and put his hand on Marvin's shoulder.

"It's okay, Marvin. You've had a rough life. At least you're sorry for what you did. Hopefully, his family will forgive you someday. Is that important to you, that they forgive you?" He asked.

Marvin looked up at Franco and nodded his head yes.

Franco read Marvin's statement back to him and asked if it was accurate. He said it was and Franco asked if he felt better now that he had told what he did. With that, Marvin stood up, leaned over the table, and hugged Detective Franco.

After their embrace, Franco asked Marvin to sign the statement, which he did. It was dated, and signed by Franco and Talia also.

A short time later, Franco had Marvin show him where in City Island he had thrown the gun. The next day, Franco along with Emergency Services and Harbor Unit had the area drudged, but the gun was never found. Detective Franco notified the homicide DA on duty that an arrest was made in this case and the homicide DA, who only handles homicides, responded to the 47th precinct. She prepared the necessary paperwork and when she was informed there was a written confession, asked Franco if he thought the perp would make a video, confessing to his crime.

Franco went over to the cell where he had put Marvin and he was lying on the bench sleeping like a baby, apparently his conscience was clear and he was feeling better about life. He woke Marvin up and informed him that the DA was there and wanted to speak with him. He also told Marvin that this was his chance to come off as remorseful and given the fact that this case warranted the death penalty, this was a way for Marvin to save his life. The Governor of NY had signed the death penalty into law recently and this case certainly met that criteria.

Marvin was asked if he would do a video confession and Franco told him, "You just need to tell the DA what you told me. The only difference is that there's a camera videotaping it. It will be played in court and when the family sees how upset you are, maybe they'll ask the judge to go easy on you. I can't make you any promises, but sometimes if they see you as remorseful, they don't think of you as such a monster."

"I'm not a monster, Detective," Marvin answered back. "I'm just a confused 19-year-old kid who never had anybody love him."

Marvin agreed to make the video and the DA's video unit set up their cameras and recorder in the Lieutenant's office. DA Cheryl Goldberg and her video photographer sat in the Lieutenant's office as Franco and Talia walked Marvin into the room. He was not handcuffed, but his eyes were red and bloodshot and you could tell he had been crying. Everyone was introduced on video and the date and time were recorded. Marvin gave a full video confession explaining in detail, his every action as the DA asked him question after question. She had read his written confession before-hand and was filled in on any other details from Detectives Franco and Talia before her questioning started.

At 11:45 P.M. on December 30th after Marvin had given a full video confession, he was taken back to the holding cell, and when Franco asked him if he was okay, he gave him a huge hug again. Franco didn't mind so much except that Marvin got snot all over the lapel of his suit jacket. When he showed it to Talia, Talia shot back, "A small price to pay for a murder one confession and 9 hours overtime."

A short while later Marvin was processed and transported to Central booking. The three said their good-byes with Marvin shaking Franco and Talia's hands. Marvin looked Franco in the eye and stated, "Even though you arrested me tonight, you treated me like a man."

Before they went into Central Booking Franco had a little surprise for Marvin. He had run over to the hospital emergency room and got him a set of scrubs and slippers. He tossed them into the back seat, uncuffed Marvin and let him change out of his dress. Marvin thought Franco was doing him this great favor, but in fact Franco needed the clothes as evidence. Marvin was brought into central booking and handed over to corrections.

Franco and Talia went back to the 47 squad to voucher the girl's cloth-ing that Marvin was wearing along with Marvin's original clothes that he wore at the scene of the murder which were now being worn by his girl-friend Shameeka Williams. They were removed from her and she was al-lowed to have someone from her home bring her clothes.

When they got back to the precinct, they interviewed Shameeka who gave them a complete statement as to how Marvin told her what he had done and asked her to switch clothes with him. He also told her to call a cab and to take it someplace close so it wouldn't cost much money. With her wearing his clothes, the police would stop her if they were watching him or the house. If they didn't approach her as she was getting into the cab, then he felt the coast was clear and he would leave on foot in her clothes. They were to meet back at the house at midnight if everything went okay.

In the meantime, he was going to try to get together some money so he could go down south and stay with a cousin until the heat blew off.

She was crying uncontrollably the whole time the detectives spoke to her. You could tell she wasn't a bad person; she just got involved with the wrong guy.

She had no criminal record and the Detectives knew they could use her as a witness against him. So with being arrested hanging over her head, the DA informed her she would have to testify at the Grand Jury and if it ever went to trial, and she reluctantly agreed.

She was arrested on a misdemeanor, obstructing governmental administration, which would be enough to hold over her head until trial time came. She was given a desk appearance ticket and was allowed to go home.

It was now 2:30A.M. December 31st, New Year's Eve Day, and the Detectives would have to come back in the morning to testify at the grand jury along with the cab driver Mr. Gonzalez, Lyle, the chicken store owner Mr. Kamal, and Shameeka Williams.

At three o clock in the morning the detectives arrived at Mrs. Webb's house. They knew it was late and felt terrible about waking them up but Lyle would have to know about coming to court and Franco and Talia really wanted to tell Mrs. Webb that they arrested the person who killed her son.

They rang the bell and a light came on in the hallway. Mrs. Webb came to the door and the detectives apologized for coming there so late but they didn't want to do this over the phone. They informed her of the arrest and told her Lyle would need to come to court in the morning. Lyle came downstairs and when he was told of the arrest, he shook both detectives' hands. Mrs. Webb started to cry and called the detectives her two angels. She said, "It's only been one day and you guys already caught him you truly are NY's finest."

The detectives slept at the precinct that night and had to be up at 8A.M. They picked up Lyle and sent car services for the chicken store owner and Shameeka Williams. The cab driver stated he would get there on his own. Everyone testified, even the chicken store owner. It turns out that he had a remarkable turnaround in his memory. No one knows for sure why, but maybe it had something to do with Detective Franco's kind words about being an upstanding citizen. Or maybe he felt it was his civic duty. Most likely it was because of the threat of the Board of Health stopping by for a visit, and possibly being deported. Whatever the reason, he became a very valuable and cooperative witness for the prosecution.

Marvin Davis was indicted on one count of murder in the first degree, one count of manslaughter in the first degree, one count of robbery in the first degree, one count of criminal possession of a weapon in the first degree, assault in the first degree, menacing, and reckless endangerment. He would stand trial in approximately one year.

34

The Trial

FOURTEEN MONTHS HAD PASSED SINCE Franco and Talia last saw Marvin. He had been doing his time on Riker's Island, NY's 413 acre, main jail complex, located in Queens, N.Y. It is where offenders who cannot afford or did not obtain bail, are held. The ADA who was prosecuting the case, Sid Baron, contacted Franco and Talia and had them come in for trial preparation. Franco testified on numerous homicide trials in the past that ADA Baron was the lead prosecutor on. He was a bit eccentric. For instance, he had a large number of exotic birds that he kept in his Manhattan apartment. From what Franco was told, he was known as the bird man in his neighborhood but he had a reputation as one of the best trial attorneys in all of New York City. He also had several assistants who would help him with legal research and case law. As the two detectives entered ADA Baron's office, he greeted Franco warmly and Franco noticed that he seemed to have aged since the last time the two saw each other. Detective Talia had never met ADA Baron and Franco introduced Talia as "the kid they put me with that night," drawing a chuckle from Talia.

The three started discussing the case and were going over the DD-5s (detective reports) when there was a knock on the office door. ADA Baron called out, "Come in." The office door opened and standing in the doorway was Mrs. Webb, Lyle and Darlene. Lyle seemed to have grown and looked much like a man. He was dressed in a suit and his hair was close cropped and neat. Mrs. Webb was wearing a dark blue dress and appeared to have aged ten-fold. Darlene was wearing jeans and a black sweater and she seemed scared. When Mrs. Webb saw Detective Franco she walked over to him, and as he stood up to greet her with a handshake, she gave him a hug. "Did you get my Christmas card, Detective?" she asked. She had sent a Christmas card to the precinct with a short note, wishing all of the detectives well and at the bottom she inscribed a message to Detective Franco that read, "Detective, I hope you and your family are fine and this Christmas season brings you much joy." He had taken it and kept it in his locker and looked at it often, wondering how a woman who had lost her son during the holiday season could muster the mental energy to send anyone a Christmas card. But he knew she was a special woman the moment he met her.

She said hello to Detective Talia and remembered his first name was Richie. Franco introduced all three to ADA Baron. He stood up, and shook all three of their hands. The office was quite cramped now, so Franco and Talia made their way into the hallway and allowed ADA Baron some one-on-one time with the family. As Franco was walking out into the hallway, Lyle called to him. He stopped and Lyle walked over and said, "Darlene has never really gotten over my brother's death. She didn't want to come today because it's like reliving everything all over again."

Franco nodded his head and said "it's going to be real hard on everyone but it's the only way to get justice."

He also told Lyle that he needed to be strong for his mother and Darlene, and Lyle nodded and shook his hand. "That's a real nice suit," Franco said. "Maybe my partner Richie can borrow it when he has to testify. The suits he wears look like they came from the Salvation Army." Franco was attempting to add some humor to a very tense and stressful situation.

Talia responded by saying, "And maybe you can borrow Mrs. Webb's dress."

Lyle shot back, "It might be a little big in the hips for him."

Franco responded, "You better not let your mother hear you say that, Lyle," and all three laughed.

Franco and Talia walked down the hall to visit other DAs that they knew, and came back a short time later. When they arrived back at ADA Sid Baron's office, Mrs. Webb was crying. They had been discussing Trevor and how Mrs. Webb was going to describe him to the court. Although Franco and Talia didn't hear any of that conversation, they pretty much knew how it went. ADA Baron ordered lunch for everyone which was delivered by the local deli. The rest of the afternoon was spent discussing strategy for the trial with some levity thrown in, mostly of Franco making fun of Talia. The whole day was very stressful and this case seemed to wear on Franco more than usual.

When he got home that day he went out of his way to spend some time with his two boys who were now nine and four years old. Although he hated video games, his boys loved them and he sat in their room for hours watching them play. A few times he thought back on Trevor and his family and became a little melancholy. Then he got a great idea. "How about we all go to Friendly's for dinner?" The boys loved Friendly's, not so much for the food, but for the big ice cream sundaes that came with their meals. So now they had to convince their mother of the nutritious value of the meal that was awaiting them. She seemed to be okay with it as she got home late from work and wouldn't have to cook dinner. At dinner Giovanni thought how lucky he was to have his family intact, safe, and happy.

Two weeks had passed since everyone was down at the ADA's office discussing the case. It was now time to pick a jury and get on with the process of attempting to send Marvin away for the rest of his life.

ADA Baron had already informed Franco and Talia that the Bronx District Attorney, Ron Jackson, was not willing to seek the death penalty in this case although it was absolutely warranted. The District Attorney's position is an elected one and most people in the Bronx would not look upon the sentencing to death of a young black man as favorable the next time Ron Jackson was up for election. Politics always comes into play at the higher levels of government, and the people who really matter are used as pawns in the big scheme of things.

Although Franco was in favor of the death penalty, he did see a certain human element in Marvin and deep down was happy that the death penalty would not be sought. When you have a personal connection to the case it's not so easy to just say, *kill the bastard*. In a private conversation with Mrs. Webb, she revealed to him that she would not want Marvin to die. She stated that she felt sorry for him and, again called him a lost soul. Although it seemed that she had forgiven him in her heart, she did want him punished for his actions and she relayed to Detective Franco that life in prison would be okay with her.

The date was March 15, the Ides of March, and Franco and Talia were down at ADA Baron's office while the jury for this case was being selected. Both the defense attorney and the ADA have to come to an agreement on prospective jurors. They are both allowed to eliminate jurors after being interviewed. Peremptory challenges are permitted for both the defense and prosecution; it allows the attorneys to reject potential jurors who may have bias without giving a reason. Both the defense and prosecution are allowed twenty peremptory challenges. So after two days of jury interviews, the jury was selected; twelve jurors and two alternates. The trial was set to start on Saint Patrick's Day, March 17, 1997.

Everyone met in ADA Baron's office on that morning and, because there were so many people, a conference room was reserved. It was located on the 4th floor of the Criminal Court building across from all the ADA's offices. It was your typical conference room with a large table surrounded by chairs and with several speaker phones. Everyone was there: Detectives Franco and Talia, Detective Bobby Marcone from the Crime Scene Unit, Mrs. Webb, Lyle, Darlene, the cab driver Mr. Gonzalez, and the chicken store owner, Mr. Kamal. No one discussed their involvement on that faithful night in front of anyone else. Each was interviewed separately by ADA Baron, who was sporting a green tie with white shamrocks for the occasion. Detectives Franco and Talia were present during much of the interviews. ADA Baron would take the witnesses over to his office, and go over their testimony as far as what he was going to ask them idvidually. It was a tedious but necessary process.

Franco asked who the judge was that would be presiding over the trial and he was told it was Judge Weinstein. Franco had testified on several homicide trials in which Judge Weinstein had presided in Supreme Court. He found him to be a no-nonsense but very fair judge. He would pretty much follow the letter of the law not making outrageous decisions that could be challenged in an appeal. He was an older grey haired gentleman and Franco felt comfortable testifying in front of him. Well, as comfortable as can be expected testifying at a homicide trial in Supreme Court. He took great pride in his trial preparation and testifying skills. It is always a very stressful situation, and he would go over every aspect of the case for days on his own time. To the point where he would basically have the facts of the case memorized. He would read the case folder over and over again, and attempt to anticipate the questions the defense attorney might ask. He would also attempt to learn as much about the defense attorney as possible from ADA's who opposed him on trials. He would also speak to other detectives that testified on cases where he was the defense attorney. He would do his "homework" as they say. He felt he never wanted to be embarrassed on the stand for not being prepared.

The first witness for the prosecution was Detective Bobby Marcone of the Crime Scene Unit. Detective Marcone had twenty-two years with the N.Y.P.D., the last twelve of them assigned to the Crime Scene Unit. He had salt and pepper hair and a ruddy face. He had a raspy voice, no doubt from the two packs a day habit he had since he was fifteen years old. He was known as a through investigator and Franco was always happy with his work when he was the Crime Scene Detective assigned to his other investigations. He testified about the murder scene and spoke about the pictures that were taken and the ballistic evidence that was recovered at the scene. He told the court that there were twenty-seven photos taken of the scene, and these photos were placed into evidence, and marked Peoples Evidences # 1 through # 27, including photos of the victim as he lie dead on the sidewalk. There were no objections from the defense. Marcone also testified that the chicken store and surrounding area were dusted for fingerprints and that there were no matches to the defendant found. Finally he testified that there were two 9 millimeter bullet shell casings found at the scene. They were located six feet seven inches and seven feet two inches from the front door of the store on the sidewalk. These shell casings were photographed and vouchered as evidence. The shell casings were entered into evidence and marked Peoples Exhibits # 28 and # 29.

The next one up on the witness stand was Lyle, the victim's brother. He testified about where they had been that night (community center) and spoke about his brother and the subjects he rapped about in his music. He then testified to having his chain snatched off his neck at gunpoint, being chased outside of the store, hearing two gunshots, and then coming back to the front of the store and seeing the defendant fleeing the scene south on White Plains Road. He testified to identifying photo # 2, in a photo array that was shown to him by Detective Franco, as being the person who robbed him at gunpoint. He also positively identified the defendant in court as being the person who robbed him at gunpoint that night. The photo array in question was placed into evidence and marked People's Exhibit # 30. The defense attorney inspected the photo array and then stated that he had no objections.

The defense attorney, who was very high profile and known in his circle as being a bulldog, took this case pro bono, because of the media attention it had gained and the fact that it was the first murder in the first degree trial since the Governor had signed the death penalty into law. His name was Kenneth Bagelman and he was known to belittle witnesses and try to get them to lash out at him, making them appear unstable, and unprofessional. He was especially rude and disrespectful to police witnesses. He would try many tactics to get them to lose their cool. He would do this walking a fine line between appearing confrontational, drawing the objection of the prosecutor, and coming across as being smarter than everyone else. But in this case he needed to walk a tightrope between those tactics and appearing compassionate towards a family who had lost a loved one, especially a loved one who was considered such a good kid with no criminal record.

The defense attorney, when it came time to cross examine Lyle, only asked a few brief questions. It's a very touchy situation and the defense attorney does not want to appear callas to the family in front of the jury. So he asked simple questions, like what time they got to the chicken store and things like that. These questions really didn't have much impact on the case. The defense attorney seemed to want to be done with this witness as quickly as possible. Lyle's testimony on direct examination with ADA Baron was very compelling. The jury seemed to be quite affected and moved by it.

Next up was Darlene, with ADA Baron asking her questions about her relationship with Trevor, and the plans they had discussed for the future. She broke down in tears several times when she spoke about how much she loved him, and how he died with an engagement ring inside his jacket pocket, which he was going to give to her the next day when he was to ask her to marry him. She also testified about how they had discussed finishing college before getting married, and then starting their careers and family. She told ADA Baron and the ladies and gentlemen of the jury how a re- cord producer had offered Trevor a recording contract that night after his appearance at the community center, and how their lives all of a sudden seemed to be too good to be true. She spoke about what a good man Trevor was, how he rapped about positive black role models and doing the right thing as far as treating women, and taking care of your responsibilities, especially when it came to children. She broke down in tears several more times and her testimony went on for almost an hour on direct examina- tion. Several women and even a few men in the jury seemed to be visibly affected by her testimony and the bailiff had to bring over some tissues to the jury box for them to wipe their eyes.

When it became time for Darlene to be cross examined by Mr. Bagel- man, the high profile attorney, all he could say was, "No questions, your honor." Darlene was excused from the witness stand and fourteen pairs of sad eyes in the jury box watched her walk out of the courtroom.

The defense attorney, Mr. Bagelman, asked the judge for a brief recess to discuss some facts with his client, but it was obvious he needed a break himself. There really wasn't much for him to rebut.

When the trial resumed, approximately half an hour later, the next witness up was the chicken store owner, Mr. Mohammed Kamal. He was sworn in and began his testimony by describing how the defendant, who he identified in court, would hang out in his store all hours of the night, causing trouble for his customers. ADA Baron asked him if he ever called the police to have him removed and he stated, no, that he had to work there every day and he tried to not have trouble with him. He was then asked what he had witnessed on December 30, 1995. He described the in- cident as two boys coming into the store and ordering food at the counter. He then stated that he saw the defendant approach one of the boys, pull out a gun and pull something off his neck. He thought it was a chain. He further stated that the boy who had his chain taken ran, and the defendant pointed a gun in his direction. The other boy pushed him against the wall and also ran out of the store with the defendant chasing after him. The boy who had pushed the defendant slipped on the sidewalk and the defendant ran up on him and shot him twice in the back. He said he ducked behind his counter which is encased in bullet proof glass and then retreated to his back office where he locked himself in. ADA Baron asked him if he called the police and he stated "no." He was then asked by ADA Baron if the person who shot that young boy was in court today. Mr. Kamal stated that "he was", and pointed to the defendant. ADA Baron asked that the identification be recorded by the court. ADA Baron had no further questions for this witness. It was now time for him to be cross examined by Mr. Bagelman. It seemed that Mr. Bagelman had taken his kid gloves off as he approached the witness box, rolling up his shirt sleeves.

"You didn't call 911 did you, Mr. Kamal?"

"No."

"And you never called the police on my client?"

"No."

"But you say he would cause trouble in your store all the time."

"Yes he ask people for money sometimes."

"But you said he would scare your customers. Why didn't you call the police to remove him?"

"I afraid of him."

"But he's a little guy, Mr. Kamal," as Mr. Bagelman gestured a small height person with his hand.

"Yes but he crazy."

"I object to that answer, Your Honor. Mr. Kamal, as far as I know, is not an authority on who is crazy and who's not. You don't have any professional psychological background, do you, Mr. Kamal.?

"No."

"And this happened in front of your store, not inside… the shooting?"

"Yes."

"Isn't it true that you were already hiding behind your counter before the shooting occurred?"

"No, I standing behind the counter when the boy chased the other two boys outside."

"And there are no cameras in your store, right Mr. Kamal?"

"No, no cameras."

"Now why is that? You have bullet proof glass and you state that crazy people like my client hang out in your store, harassing you, but there are no cameras. If you were scared, wouldn't you install cameras?"

"I can't afford it," Mr. Kamal responded.

"Now this was about two in the morning and it was dark out, right Mr. Kamal? And you're looking out from your lit store into the darkness. Isn't it true that you actually never saw my client shoot anyone, you just heard two gunshots?"

"No I think I saw him," Mr. Kamal said.

"You THINK, so you don't know."

"I am not good with English language. I saw him run out with gun in his hand, then I heard shots, then a saw flash then I saw boy lying on ground."

"But you didn't actually see my client point a gun at that boy, did you Mr. Kamal?"

"I'm not sure, I confuse."

Yes Mr. Kamal it does appear that you are confused.

"Okay so now I get the picture. You saw my client rob someone, no one is disputing that fact. But you never saw my client shoot anyone. We don't know what happened after they ran out of the store, do we?"

"I'm not sure. Everything happened very fast. But he had gun in my store, so I think he shot the boy."

"Again, Mr. Kamal, you think but you don't know. You can only testify to things you saw, things you know. So I'm going to ask you one more time. Did you see my client shoot anyone in front of your store on December 30, 1995 at two in the morning?"

"I think he shot him, but you are making me confuse."

"I'm not making you confused, Mr. Kamal. YOU are confused and you cannot tell this jury that you witnessed a homicide if you did not. That is perjury and you can go to jail. Did you see my client shoot that young man?"

"He chased him outside with the gun in his hand, the boy fell down and then I heard *boom, boom.*"

"I guess you didn't see him shoot him, Mr. Kamal."

"In fact isn't it true that a detective showed you a photo array that contained a picture of my client and you told the detective that you did not recognize anyone in that photo array?"

Mr. Bagelman walked over to the court officer and asked for the photo array that was marked Peoples exhibit # 30. The same one that Lyle had identified of the gunman. He held it up high and in a loud deep voice stated:

"You didn't see anyone in this group of pictures that you recognized did you Mr. Kamal?"

"Well I did know the boy in the picture"

"You did?"

"Yes"

"But you told the detective you did not recognize anyone in the pictures."

"Were you lying to the detective Mr. Kamal?"

"Yes."

"So you lied to the detective?"

"Yes, I was scared and did not want to be involve."

"So you lied about something as important as someone being killed."

"I was scare."

"Did you lie to the detective Mr. Kamal?"

"Objection!" ADA Baron exclaimed as he stands up and states, "It's already been established that Mr. Kamal was not truthful with the detectives when they showed him the photo array Your Honor."

"Sustained, move on Mr. Bagelman."

"One more question Your Honor."

"So Mr. Kamal now that we have established that you're a liar, how do we know you're not lying now about anything you have told us today?"

"I tell the truth."

"Well I'm sure you told the detectives you were telling the truth when you said you did not see my client in these pictures"

Again Mr. Bagelman held up the photo array for all to see.

"If you lied then you're probably lying now."

"Objection!"

"No further questions Your Honor."

Now it was time for ADA Baron to redirect the testimony of Mr. Kamal. After the prosecution asks its questions, the defense attorney cross examines and then the District Attorney has the right to ask additional questions, which is called redirect.

"Mr. Kamal, did you see the defendant with a gun?"

"Yes."

"Did you see him rob that boy of his chain?"

"Yes."

"You saw this?"

"Yes."

"It was done in front of you as you were watching through the bullet proof glass."

"Yes sir."

"And then you saw the boy who got robbed of his chain run out from your store. Is that correct?"

"Yes."

"And then the second boy who you said pushed the defendant, you saw him run out from your store also?"

"Yes."

"And the man that chased him had a gun in his hand."

"Yes."

"You saw this with your own eyes looking thru the bullet proof glass?"

"Yes."

"And the defendant ran after him with the gun in his hand."

"Yes."

"You saw him run outside with a gun in his hand, is that correct?"

"Yes."

"And how much time had passed from the time that you saw him run outside, till you heard *boom boom*?"

"Seconds."

"Seconds? How many seconds Mr. Kamal?"

"Maybe two."

"Two seconds. So let me get this straight, you see the robbery…you see the defendant with the gun in his hand…you see him chase the boy that pushed him out from your store…You see him slip on the sidewalk directly in front of your store…you can see all of this through the window…two seconds later you hear *boom boom*."

"Yes sir."

"Okay Mr. Kamal."

"Now let's address the photo array."

"Mr. Kamal did the detectives show you this photo array?"

ADA Baron holds up Peoples Exhibit # 30

"Yes."

"And when they showed it to you did you recognize anyone in it."

"Yes."

"And who did you recognize?"

"That boy."

Mr. Kamal pointed to the defendant sitting at the defense table

"Objection! Your Honor identification has already been established of my client by this witness."

"Overruled I believe the prosecutor is establishing a basis for Mr. Kamal's actions when the detectives had him view the photo array. I'll allow it but keep it brief counselor."

"Yes Your Honor."

"Mr. Kamal when the detectives showed you this photo array did you recognize anyone"

"Yes."

Again Mr. Kamal points to the defendant.

"And why did you tell the detectives that you did not recognize anyone?"

"Because I was scared that if he found out I tell on him he would come back and kill me."

"Objection!" "Your Honor please."

"Sustained." "Ladies and gentleman of the jury, please disregard Mr. Kamal's last answer and strike it from your memory."

"Continue Mr. Baron."

"So you lied to the police because you were afraid."

"Yes."

"But now you are here testifying, why is that?"

"He should not get away with what he do."

"No further questions Your Honor."

"You may step down Mr. Kamal," stated the judge.

It was now 12:30 P.M. and Judge Weinstein decided it would be a good time to recess for lunch. He instructed the jurors to not discuss the facts of the case with each other or anyone else and told them to enjoy their lunch and be ready to get back to work at 2:00 P.M. The jury was dismissed and left the courtroom escorted back to the jury room by two armed New York State Court Officers. After the jury was out of the courtroom the other occupants were instructed to please stand and the judge exited the courtroom. After he was gone all other members of the room left.

ADA Baron arrived back in the conference room where all the witnesses were waiting. Franco and Talia were there with Mrs. Webb, Lyle, Darleen, Mr. Gonzalez and Mr. Kamal. Mr. Kamal asked ADA Baron if he was needed anymore as he had to get some sleep before going into the store tonight. ADA Baron stated he was finished and that he could leave. He asked Mr. Kamal to be available by phone if anything arose. As he was leaving the conference room Mrs. Webb walked over to Mr. Kamal and hugged him. She thanked him for his help. This was the first time the two had spoken and Mr. Kamal wished her good luck and told her to stay strong. She nodded as her eyes filled with tears. Mr. Kamal turned and gave a wave to the others in the conference room as he left. Detective Franco gave him a thankful nod as the door closed behind him.

Because witnesses who have not yet testified cannot be present in the courtroom Detective Franco had no idea how it was going. Franco turned to ADA Baron and asked, "How is it going?"

ADA Baron stated, "It's going real well so far." Detective Marcone,

Lyle, Darleen and Mr. Kamal did a great job." this prompted a smile from Mrs. Webb. Lunch was ordered with Franco and Talia ordering corned beef sandwiches.

As Franco joked, "All us Irish people eat corned beef on St. Patrick's Day prompting Talia to respond, "You're about as Irish as an enchilada." Lunch was eaten and now it was time for Mr. Gonzalez the cab driver to walk over to Supreme Court with ADA Baron and testify.

Mr. Gonzalez was sworn in and was visibly nervous. After only a few questions asked by ADA Baron, Mr. Gonzalez requested a glass of water. His hand shook as he brought the paper cup of water to his mouth. Mr. Gonzalez testified that on December 30th 1995 at the time in question he was working as a livery cab driver. That he was parked across the street from the Kennedy Fried Chicken store. He was parked in the bus stop in front of the diner. He stated he would park there at night and pick up fares that get off the train. He described the area and told how the elevated train runs above White Plains Road. He described the weather as extremely cold and windy. When asked by ADA Baron what he saw in regards to the homicide the dialog went like this:

"Mr. Gonzalez, did you see someone run out of the Kennedy Fried Chicken on December 30th at approximately 2 A.M. and slip on the sidewalk?"

"Yes."

"Can you describe for the court what you saw.?"

"I was in my cab and saw some commotion in front of the store. I saw a boy run out, and then I saw another boy run out and slip. Then someone ran out after him and shot him after he slipped.

"How many shots did you hear Mr. Gonzalez?"

"Two."

"And what happened next?"

"I got down real low in my car and called 911."

"And what did you tell the 911 operator?"

"I said someone got shot on East 232nd Street and White Plains Road."

"And then what happened?"

"I hung up."

"What did you do next?"

"I drove off and made a quick right turn onto 233rd Street."

"And then?"

"I worked the rest of the night down by Gunhill Road."

"Did you have an occasion to drive back by East 232nd Street again that night?"

"Yes."

"When?"

"About an hour later I had a fare that needed to go from Gunhill Road. train station to Boston Road. After I dropped her off I drove by the chicken store to see what was going on."

"And what did you see?"

"There were police cars everywhere and cops in the street. They had the whole side of the street blocked off with yellow tape."

"What did you do then?"

"I went home and went to sleep."

"Now Mr. Gonzalez, did you have an occasion to view a photo array related to this case?"

"Yes."

"And who showed you that photo array?"

"Detectives Franco and Talia."

"And did you recognize anyone in that photo array from the night of the homicide?"

"Yes."

"And who did you recognize?"

"The person who shot the boy."

"And what number was his photo in the array?"

"# 2."

ADA Baron asked the identification by Mr. Gonzalez be marked into evidence Peoples Exhibit # 31.

No objection by the defense.

"And Mr. Gonzalez do you see the person who shot the victim here today?"

"Yes."

"And where do you see him?"

With that Mr. Gonzales points to Marvin sitting at the defense table in a gray sweater and black slacks.

"That's him."

ADA Baron exclaims "Let the record show that Mr. Gonzalez has identified the defendant, Marvin Davis, as being the gunmen in connection with the death of Trevor Webb.

"Noted," states Judge Weinstein.

"No further questions Your Honor."

Now it was time for Mr. Bagelman to cross examine the witness:

"Good afternoon Mr. Gonzalez."

"Good afternoon."

"You stated that you saw a commotion in front of the Kennedy Fried Chicken store on the night in question?"

"Yes."

"And you stated you saw a boy run out of the store, then another, then another after that. Then someone slipped, and then someone got shot?"

"Yes."

"And in all this commotion—that was your word was it not? "Commotion"—you saw my client shoot someone."

"Yes."

"Your Honor I would like to read the court the definition of the word "commotion" as stated in Webster's New World Dictionary.

"Objection Your Honor" declared ADA Baron. "I believe the ladies and gentlemen of the jury are familiar with the word 'commotion.'"

"I'll allow it counselor, objection overruled."

As Mr. Bagelman reaches into his leather briefcase and removes a hard bound copy of Webster's Dictionary all eyes are on him as he thumbs through it arriving at the word he was seeking.

"Commotion: 'Violent or tumultuous action or activity, noisy disturbance or mass confusion. "Mass confusion: 'violent or tumultuous activity.'"

"So Mr. Gonzalez you want us to believe that from your car, parked on the other side of White Plains Rd at two in the morning, on a dark street, you were able to see my client's face while there was, in your words, mass confusion and tumultuous activity occurring hundreds of feet away from you?"

"I saw him."

"Do you wear glasses Mr. Gonzalez?"

"Yes."

"Were you wearing them when you witnessed this incident?"

"I'm not sure."

"You're not sure?"

"Are you mandated to wear glasses by the D.M.V. when you drive?"

"Yes."

"But you don't know if you were wearing your mandated glasses?"

"I don't remember."

"You don't remember if you were wearing your glasses but you do remember my client?"

"Yes."

Mr. Bagelman shakes his head from side to side with a disbelieving look on his face.

"Okay Mr. Gonzalez you told the court earlier that you called 911 is that correct?"

"Yes."

"And you told the operator what happened?"

"Yes."

"Did you give the operator your name?"

"No."

"No?"

"Did she not ask you for your name?"

"Yes she asked but I hung up."

"You hung up on the 911 operator after you just witnessed a shooting?"

"I was scared."

"You were scared?"

"Well you weren't too scared to call."

"And then you told the court that you went back to the scene about an hour later?"

"Yes."

"Did you stop then and tell the police that you were a witness?"

"No."

"No?"

"Why not?"

"I didn't want to be involved."

"So what changed your mind?"

"Well I didn't really change my mind, the detectives found out that I called 911 and they came to my house and told me…"

"Objection! The conversation with the detectives is hearsay Your Honor."

"Sustained."

Judge Weinstein speaking to the witness instructed him as follows:

"Mr. Gonzalez, you may not speak about your conversation with the detectives, just tell the court what happened when the Detectives came to your house."

"Okay the Detectives came to my house and showed me the pictures and I picked the guy out, and they made me sign it."

"They made you?" asked Mr. Bagelman.

"Well I mean they told me to sign it."

"So you didn't want to sign it?"

"No I don't mean that, I saw the guy in the picture and they told me that after you pick someone out you sign the back, I don't know."

"So the detectives find out who you are, come to your house and show you some pictures?"

"Yes."

"Did they ask you why you did not give the 911 operator your name?"

"Yes."

"Did you feel that they were angry at you for not giving your name?"

"Yes."

"So did you feel obligated to maybe make them not angry at you anymore?"

"Objection." ADA Baron responded. "Counselor is leading the witness Your Honor!"

"Sustained."

"Okay Mr. Gonzalez, so you signed the photo array and that made everything better in your eyes with the Detectives?"?

"Objection."

Judge Weinstein, chastising Mr. Bagelman states" You know better than that counselor, I will have none of that in my court."

"Objection sustained."

Judge Weinstein instructs the jury to disregard the last question by the defense.

"Now you stated it was very cold and windy that night is that correct?"

"Yes."

"Isn't that perfect conditions for your windows to fog up?"

"They were not foggy."

"Well you can't remember if you had your prescription glasses on but you do remember that your windows were not foggy?"

"Yes I remember they were not foggy."

"Okay Mr. Gonzalez, only a few more questions and we'll be done."

"Cab drivers in the Bronx get a lot of tickets from the police do they not?"

"I guess sometimes."

"And it would be helpful for someone in your line of work to be friendly with the police so maybe you will get a break when you get pulled over?"

"Objection," insisted ADA Baron.

"Sustained."

"Do not answer the question" the judge instructs Mr. Gonzalez.

"Okay Mr. Gonzalez, one last question, since you identified my client in that photo array, have you received any moving violation summonses from the police?"

"Objection Your Honor what possible relevance does that have to this case?"

"I'll allow it. You may answer the question."

"No."

"So since you've identified my client you have not received any tickets?"

"Objection. He's already answered the question."

"No further questions, Your Honor."

Mr. Bagelman's cross examination of Mr. Gonzalez took the better part of the afternoon. It was now 5:45 P.M. and Judge Weinstein recessed the court for the day. He once again instructed the jury not to discuss this case with anyone and told them to be back at court at 8:00 A.M.

35

The Trial (Continues)

IT WAS NOW MARCH 18TH AND Detectives Franco and Talia arrived early at ADA Baron's office. It was around 8:30 A.M. and they were greeted by ADA Baron and his assistant Kim Cohen. She did a lot of his research on case law, and was responsible for all the paperwork involved in the case, most importantly ordering lunch. She was a very attractive woman in her early 30s and she wore tight skirts that showed off her shapely legs and round butt. Richie Talia seemed to not be able to keep his eyes off of her as she moved around the small office. This prompted remarks from Giovanni when she was out of earshot of how he better keep the case folder on his lap and not stand up. Richie actually asked Giovanni to please not make fun of him while they were in her presence as they drove down to court that morning. Now you would think that he would know better, because once a cop hears that something bothers you, he would usually be relentless. But Giovanni had a real liking for Richie and he kind of looked at him as his little brother. He did make one comment to him, though, in the car on the way down. As Richie was talking about how hot Kim was, Giovanni told him, "You're lucky I'm married, 'cause if I wanted her, there's no way you'd get her."

Richie laughed and made some kind of comment about Giovanni being old. Richie was in his late twenties and Giovanni was thirty-four.

When Giovanni heard the word "old" he made a muscle and grabbed Richie's hand, trying to put it on his bicep. As Richie was driving the car, it swerved and he called Giovanni a homo. Giovanni had a grip on Richie's

197

hand and when he heard the word "homo" he pulled Richie's hand towards him, attempting to put it on his crotch.

"I got your homo right here," he told Richie. Richie pulled his hand away so fast he actually banged it on the steering wheel prompting a big laugh from Giovanni.

As the two arrived at the courthouse, there was a squeegee man on the corner of 159th Street and Sheridan Avenue where the detectives usually park. He came over to the unmarked car on Giovanni's side with a dirty rag in one hand and a dirty bottle of water in the other. Giovanni rolled down the window and told him, "Don't come near the car." The squeegee guy, dressed in layer upon layer of clothing, none which seemed to have been washed in the last 40 years, stated, "I won't clean your windows if you give me a dollar," prompting Giovanni to tell him, "I won't break your face if you won't clean the window." The squeegee man gave Giovanni a big smile and Giovanni noticed that there wasn't a tooth in his mouth. They had picked up two bagels and a couple of cups of coffee on the way down and Giovanni hadn't eaten his bagel yet. He tossed it to the squeegee guy and said "If you can figure out how to eat this with no teeth, you can have it." Richie just shook his head and laughed, stating, "You're fucking crazy Gio."

They went upstairs to the 4th floor to meet ADA Baron. As they entered his office, the ME (medical examiner) was going over the autopsy reports. He was explaining to ADA Baron the actual cause of death, and they were talking in technical medical terms.

Giovanni joked to Talia. "This is over your head, you better wait in the hallway," prompting a giggle from Kim Cohen.

As Richie gave Giovanni a dirty look, Giovanni put his hand over his mouth and said, "Oh I forgot, sorry."

Franco then turned to Kim Cohen and stated, "I was only kidding; he's really very, very smart." She smiled back at Franco as Talia shook his head and walked out into the hallway. After about a half hour, ADA Baron and the ME walked over to Supreme Court for his testimony.

The ME testified that upon autopsy of Trevor Webb, it was determined that he died by means of homicide. The cause of death was cardiac arrest caused by one bullet that entered through his back and severed his heart. The second bullet which also entered through his back perforated his right lung and lodged in his spleen. He testified to massive blood loss and trauma to his upper region. It was a cut and dry testimony with ADA Baron asking only a few questions. The bottom line was Trevor was killed because he was shot. The ME, when asked how long someone could live with those massive injuries, stated, "no more than a minute or two." This coincided with Lyle's testimony of how he held his brother's hand as he lay bleeding on the sidewalk. He also testified that the injuries upon examining the entrance wounds to the body were made at a close range by a firearm the caliber being 9mm. The ME's report and death certificate were entered into evidence as People's Exhibits # 32 and # 33.

Upon cross examination, Mr. Bagelman only asked a few brief questions like, "were the bullets that were removed from the body fingerprinted?" and "could the doctor tell who fired the weapon that killed the deceased?"

The ME looked at Mr. Bagelman with sheer disbelief as he answered, "No."

The question was so ridiculous that ADA Baron decided not to even object. There wasn't much Mr. Bagelman could dispute in this case in relation to the autopsy or the ME's testimony. The ME's testimony was complete and he exited the courtroom.

Shameeka Williams, the girlfriend of the defendant had been cut a deal, and her testimony against him was leverage against her charges of obstructing governmental administration. Basically what is commonly known as aiding and abetting. She was reluctant when ADA Baron spoke to her by phone. She stated she had moved on with her life, and just wanted to forget about the whole thing. She was now in her second semester at Bronx Community College. She informed him that she was studying to be a veterinarian and that before this incident she had never been in any trouble. ADA Baron was having none of her sob story and he explained to her that he would prosecute her to the fullest extent of the law if she did not cooperate with this prosecution. She reluctantly agreed. They made arrangements for her to come in and see him after all the other parties were gone, as to not cause a stir with the family. ADA Baron had met with her in his office when just he and Kim Cohen were present. They went over her testimony and she seemed bright and articulate.

After she left his office ADA Baron told ADA Kim Cohen, "she is going to be very damaging to the defense, she paints a picture of the defendant's mindset after the murder." ADA Baron had alerted the Webb family by phone that evening that she was on the witness list. She would be testifying after the M.E.

As the court officer called Shameeka Williams' name out in court, as the next witness, the court doors opened and in walked the defendant's former girlfriend. She was smartly dressed in a business suit pinstriped in blue. She had her long hair pulled back in a ponytail tied with a dark blue ribbon. Her shoes were black with a slight heal. She looked professional. Not what you would envision a street punk's girlfriend to look like. It seemed she had moved on.

As she was sworn in by the court officer, she looked over at the defense table and made eye contact with Marvin Davis, the defendant. He knew she was on the witness list as it is mandatory that all witnesses' names be given to the defense beforehand. His eyes seemed to be pleading with her not to hurt him.

She looked away as she stated "I Do" referring to the court officer's question, "Do you swear to tell the truth, the whole truth so help you God?" as her right hand was resting on the bible. With that she took her seat as ADA Baron approached her.

"Good morning Ms. Williams"

"Good morning"

"Ms. Williams, how long have you known the defendant Marvin Davis?"

"Two years"

"And how long had you dated the defendant prior to him being arrested on this case?"

"About nine months, but we were not boyfriend and girlfriend I was kinda just talking to him"

"Can you explain what you mean by, 'Just talking?'"

"He would see me in the street and he would try to talk to me and sometimes I would hang out where he was hanging out, but he was not my boyfriend. He became my boyfriend in October of 1995."

"So you were friends for several months, then became a couple in October, and he was arrested at the end of December, so you were dating when he was arrested?"

"Yes."

"I'm going to draw your attention to the evening of December 30th 1995"

"Were you with the defendant that night at 736 East 224th Street?"

"Yes"

"And who lives at that address?"

"My mom and my grandmother"

"And why was Marvin Davis there"

"Objection Your Honor" yelled Mr. Bagelman. "The prosecution is asking for an opinion Your Honor"

"I'll allow it" stated Judge Weinstein.

"He was hiding from the police"

"And you knew the police were looking for him?"

"Yes"

"And did you know why the police were looking for him?"

"Not at first."

"What do you mean, not at first?"

"Well, at first Marvin told me that the police were looking for him because he robbed some kid."

"So when did you find out the whole story as to why the police were looking for him?"

"Well he was acting real scared and I knew he had done bad things before and he never seemed to care about the police."

"So how did you find out the whole story?"

"Well he started talking about me putting on his clothes and calling a cab, to see if the cops stop me, and he was going to wait and he wanted to wear my clothes to trick them. That's when I made him tell me the whole story."

"So he wanted you to wear the clothes he was wearing the night of the shooting and call a cab, go outside to see if the cops knew where he was hiding?"

"Yes."

"And where was your family, did they know what was going on?"

"No they were home but they had no idea."

"So did you agree to help him?"

"I did but not for the reasons you think."

"Oh I never said why I thought you helped him, but since you brought it up why don't you tell us."

"Well once he told me what he had done, I became very scared of him and I just wanted him out of my house."

"And what did he tell you he had done?"

"Objection. Your Honor, any conversation these two might have had is hearsay," asserted Mr. Bagelman.

"Sustained" barked judge Weinstein, "Do not answer that question Ms. Williams"

"So what did you do next Ms. Williams?"

"I put his clothes on and called a cab, and told them that I wanted to go to the Baychester train station."

"Why there?"

"Marvin wanted me to not go far. We were to meet back at the house if everything went well."

"So what happened next?"

"He put on my dress and my coat, and my hat and shoes, and he kept looking at himself in the mirror asking me how he looked."

"Did he ever say he was sorry for what he had done?"

"Objection hearsay."

"Sustained."

"Did he appear to be feeling sorry for what he had. . . .?"

"Objection Your Honor."

"That's enough of that counselor, Judge Weinstein bellowed at ADA Baron.

"Then what happened?"

"The cab came and I got in, and then we got pulled over when the cab turned the block."

"And what happened next?"

"There were like six cops with their guns out pointed at me in the back seat of the cab. They pulled me out of the cab and handcuffed me."

With that Shameeka Williams began to cry. The judge motioned for the court officer to bring her some tissues. She asked for a glass of water which was also given to her.

ADA Baron—— feeling he had made his points, and had established the defendant as a manipulative, cold blooded killer—stated "No further questions."

It was now Mr. Bagelman's turn to cross examine the witness. He paused for a moment, looked over at his client and approached the witness stand.

"Just a few questions Ms. Williams."

"You were arrested that night were you not?"

"Yes I was."

"And what was the final disposition of your case?"

"I don't understand the question."

"Well you were arrested for obstructing governmental administration were you not?"

"Yes."

"So were you found guilty or not guilty?"

"The case is still pending I believe."

"The case is still pending you believe?"

Have you been promised that your case will be dropped if you testify here today?"

"Objection!" bellowed ADA Baron.

"You may answer the question" stated judge Weinstein.

"Well ADA Baron told me that if I did not cooperate with this case that I would be in trouble with my case."

"No further questions" exclaimed Mr. Bagelman in a loud voice signifying some type of victory.

"May I redirect?" asked ADA Baron to Judge Weinstein.

"Go right ahead," stated the judge.

"Ms. Williams, were you promised any special treatment, or promised that your case would be dismissed if you testified here today?"

"No."

"No further questions" stated ADA Baron in a loud voice no doubt meant to mimic that of Mr. Gabelman.

"You may step down," Judge Weinstein stated to Ms. Williams. As she did she looked at Marvin Williams as she passed by the defense table. He looked up at her and shook his head in disgust.

The judge sensing some outward tension decided it was a good time to recess. He directed everyone to be back by 2:00 P.M. ADA Baron walked back to his office with the Webb family. He explained to them that Detective Franco would be the next to testify.

Detective Franco would be the next witness on the stand and they hadn't fully gone over his testimony yet. ADA Baron had a lot of faith in Franco and did not school him to the extent that he normally does with other witnesses. Franco, on the other hand, never feels 100% confident that he is fully prepared. The whole time that the ME was on the stand, Franco was at ADA Baron's office, pacing back and forth.

He kept checking his watch—a 1943 Bulova which he picked up at a garage sale in his neighborhood for one dollar. ADA Baron who dabbled in fine timepieces, upon seeing it several years ago, commented on its rarity. He actually looked it up in a book and showed it to Franco. It was rectangular and encased in 18 karat gold. He offered Franco 1800 dollars for it at the time, and he told him it was worth in excess of $2000. What made it valuable was the fact that it was made by hand, during WWII and was solid 18 Karat gold. When Franco told ADA Baron he paid $1 for it at a garage sale, his jaw dropped. Franco wore this watch whenever he would testify on a homicide and considered it good luck.

Now as he paced the hall in front of ADA's Baron's office, he repeatedly looked at it and what was only a short time, seemed like forever. As ADA Baron came into view, Franco walked over to him and asked, "Are you going to prep me or what?"

"You're a seasoned detective," ADA Baron shot back with a big smile on his face.

Nothing ever seemed to rattle him.

"I'm glad you're so confident, Sid," Giovanni shot back. "I heard this guy's a real scumbag. Who knows what he's going to ask me."

"Remember, Detective, we're the good guys and we're doing God's work." With that he gave Franco a big smile and said "Let's head down to Supreme Court."

"Wait," Franco protested, "you didn't prep me yet."

"You know this case backward and forward Detective. We spoke about it at length last week."

"But I don't feel comfortable; let's just go over my testimony. Tell me what you're going to ask me."

"The usual stuff, Detective. We'll talk about how you got the case, the investigation and the identification that led up to the arrest, the arrest itself, and the confession."

"You make it sound so simple, Sid."

"I've been doing this a long time, Giovanni. This is a tight case; you did a great job. Just tell the story of how you did what you did. You'll be fine. Now let's go down to Supreme Court. We don't want to keep the judge waiting."

Talia wished Giovanni good luck. As they were walking down the hallway, out from the elevator came Mrs. Webb, Lyle and Darlene. They exchanged a brief greeting and Giovanni explained that he was off to testify. Mrs. Webb gave him a hug and whispered in his ear, "Trevor's depending on you." *Nothing like pressure*, Giovanni thought to himself, as a rush of adrenaline ran through his body. All five of them stepped into the elevator and off they went.

When they arrived at the courtroom, Franco was made to wait in the hallway until he was introduced to the court. It was only about ten minutes, but it seemed like forever. He could feel his mouth becoming dry and thought to himself, *I'm not ready for this*. The large wooden double doors opened and an older court officer with a white handle bar moustache motioned for Detective Franco to enter the courtroom.

Supreme Court courtrooms are quite impressive not only in size but in style. This one in particular was adorned with beautiful mahogany woodwork on all the walls with pictures of past Supreme Court judges wrapping around the expansive room.

As Detective Franco made the long trek to the witness stand, his name was announced and he could feel all the eyes of everyone in the courtroom upon him. The room was packed with onlookers; there was actually a class of college students in attendance along with many members of Trevor's family and a large amount of media. There was a woman off to the right who was doing a sketch and Franco thought to himself, *Holy shit, look at all these people*. Something came over him at that moment and he told himself he needed to be aggressive and deal with this. He looked over at Mr. Bagelman and sized him up quickly. *He's a little shit*, he thought to himself. *Can't be more than 5'6", and he doesn't look all that smart. Who would wear a brown double breasted suit with grey wing tipped shoes and a red tie with a matching red handkerchief? Not to mention the bad* Just for Men *dye job. He's obviously trying so hard to look the part. Okay Gio, just tell the story like Sid said, you've testified many times before. This guy's nothing to worry about.* He then had a thought which made him chuckle to himself, *hey it's a murder trial, but I didn't kill anybody. What am I so worried about?*

With that he took his place in the witness box and was told to raise his right hand and put his left hand on the bible. He swore to tell the truth, the whole truth, and nothing but the truth, so help him God. As he stated, "I do," he was looking directly at the jury and made the sign of the cross. When he was told by the judge to be seated, he greeted the court with a "good morning" and as they responded in turn, he smiled. He wasn't overly religious or anything, he just thought it went over well with the jury. He was dressed in a black pinstripe Armani suit, crisp white shirt, with a pale yellow tie and shiny black shoes. His hair was short from a haircut he had received the day before with a touch of gel in it to keep it neat. He wore a neatly trimmed goatee and looked quite handsome.

As ADA Baron approached Detective Franco, he also greeted him with a "Hello Detective how are you today?"

"Fine," Detective Franco answered and ADA Baron began his questioning:

"Detective, please state your rank, name, shield number and command for the court."

"Detective Giovanni Franco, shield # 4328, New York City Police Department's 47th Precinct Detective Squad."

"Detective how long have you been a member of the Police Department?"

"Fourteen years."

"And how long have you been a Detective?"

"Eight years."

"And your current assignment is the Four Seven Detective Squad?"

"That's correct."

"Okay now on December 30th 1995 did you have an occasion to investigate a homicide that was committed in the confines of the 47th Precinct?"

"Yes."

"And where did this homicide take place?"

"In front of 4565 White Plains Road."

"And that is at the corner of East 232nd Street and White Plains Road?"

"That's correct."

"And you were the lead investigator assigned to this investigation?"

"Yes I was."

"And did you have an occasion to make an arrest in regards to this investigation?"

"Yes I did."

"And who did you arrest in connection with this homicide investigation?"

"Marvin Davis."

"And Detective do you see the person who you arrested in connection with this homicide investigation here today in court?"

"Yes."

As Detective Franco points to the defendant sitting at the defense table, ADA Baron states. "Let the record reflect that Detective Franco has identified Marvin Davis, the defendant, as the person arrested in connection with this homicide investigation."

Judge Weinstein states, "So noted," as the stenographer (an attractive woman, with a nice smile and big blue eyes named Tiffany) types away, recording everything that is being said in the courtroom.

"Now Detective, please give the court a brief understanding of the events that lead to this arrest."

"I was working a day tour on December 30th 1995. When I arrived at the 4-7, I was informed that a homicide had occurred during the midnight tour. We catch cases by times, and according to the catching sheet, it occurred in my catching time. I was briefed by the night watch Detectives and my Lieutenant and then started my investigation."

"Can you explain for the court what you mean by night watch detectives and what is their function?"

"Sure, well night watch is detectives from various precincts within the Bronx who are assigned to cover the whole borough from 12 midnight to 8 A.M. Any investigation that would be assigned to a detective that occurs in that time span, the night watch detective would respond to and do a preliminary investigation. At 8 A.M. precinct detectives who are working the day tour are then assigned the case based on catching time."

"Okay Detective so what information did you obtain from the night watch detective?"

"There wasn't much info in the beginning. The only thing the night watch detectives had was a description of the perp which was somewhat unique."

"What do you mean by unique, detective?"

"He was described as a light skinned black or Hispanic and was very small in stature, no more than 5 feet tall and no more than 100 pounds. He also had information about who called 911."

"And what did you do with this information detective?"

"Well as far as the small perp went, I drove around to many of my street connections describing the shooter."

"And did this amount to anything?"

"Yes one of my CIs told me it sounded like a guy he knows from the neighborhood named Lingo."

"What is a CI Detective?"

"A CI is a confidential informant whose identity is kept confidential but is registered with the police department."

"And is Lingo his first name or his last name Detective?"

"The CI told me it was his nickname."

"Okay Detective so then what did you do?"

"Well then myself and Detective Talia went back to the 4-7 precinct detective squad and looked thru the nickname books."

"And what is that detective?"

"Those are books that are kept on file in the detective squad room. Whenever you have a person who you arrest, who has a nickname, you log it in for future reference."

"So is that where you found Mr. Davis, Detective?"

"No the nickname logs had no one by the name of Lingo in them."

"So then what did you do Detective?"

"I entered that name, Lingo, into the nickname database which is a computerized list of all people arrested in New York City with their nicknames."

"And what happened with that Detective?"

"I got four hits."

"What do you mean by hits?"

"I mean there were 4 people who used the nickname Lingo who were arrested by the NYPD."

"So then what did you do Detective?"

"I checked each one and only one matched the physical description of the perp in this case."

"So what did you do next?"

"So I pulled up that person's arrest report and found that he was arrested for assault."

"Objection, Your Honor," Mr. Bagelman declared.

"Sustained." Judge Weinstein directs Detective Franco to only speak about what he did.

"Okay Detective so you pulled out this person's arrest report and what then?"

"Well like I said, one matched the physical description so I obtained the arrest photo from that arrest and I prepared a photo array containing that photo."

"And what did you do next Detective?"

"I showed it to my CI."

"And did he identify anybody in the photo array?"

"Yes he identified photo # 2 as being who he knew as Lingo."

"Now did you have the CI sign the back of the photo array, Detective?"

"No I did not."

"And why is that?"

"Because he was not a witness in this case; he was only helping me identify who he thought I was describing to him."

"So what did you do next Detective?"

"I went to find the 911 caller that night watch had traced through his cell phone records."

"And who is that Detective?"

"Mr. Ramon Gonzalez."

"And did you locate Mr. Gonzalez, Detective?"

"Yes I did."

"And did you have an occasion to show Mr. Gonzalez a photo array containing Mr. Davis's picture?"

"Yes I did."

"And did he identify anybody in that picture?"

"He identified photo # 2 as being the person who shot the victim."

"And did he sign this photo array, Detective?"

With that ADA Baron hold up the photo array and shows it to Detective Franco.

"Yes he did. He signed it on the back."

"Okay Detective so what did you do next?"

"I took the photo array and brought it to Lyle Webb."

"And did he identify anyone in the photo array Detective?"

"Yes he did, he identified photo # 2 as being the person who robbed him of his chain."

"And did Mr. Webb sign the back of the photo array?"

"Yes he did."

"What did you do next Detective?"

"We went to Kennedy Fried Chicken and showed the owner the photo array."

"And what were the results of that?"

"He stated he didn't see what happened; that it happened outside."

"And did you believe him Detective?"

"OBJECTION."

"SUSTAINED."

"Okay Detective, so what did you do next?"

"We had just arrived at the precinct to give the lieutenant an update on the case, and I received a cell phone call from a friend of mine who owns a store in the precinct. After a brief conversation with him, we responded back to the area of East 222nd Street and White Plains Road."

"And then what happened?"

"Detective Talia saw someone in the street who had given him information in the past and we stopped and showed him the picture of Lingo."

"And what was the result of that?"

"He stated that he knew him and had seen him go into a house the day before."

"So what happened next?"

"We met him in the park because he didn't want to be seen speaking to us. He got in the back seat of our unmarked patrol car and directed us to a location on 224th Street."

"Do you remember the address Detective?"

"736 East 224th Street."

"So then what did you do?"

"We dropped that guy off back at the park and went into the precinct to give the Lieutenant a brief update. We asked for another unit to park around the block as backup and proceeded back to 224th Street cutting through a backyard on 223rd. We made our way through the backyard and positioned ourselves in the front yard of 739 East 224th Street hiding behind a row of bushes."

"And where were these bushes Detective? Can you describe the area where you were hiding and who you were with?"

"We were up from the street about five steps. There was a wall that ran the length of the property and we were lying on the ground behind a row of short bushes. I was with Detective Richard Talia and we were looking directly across the street at 736 East 224th Street."

"And that was the house that the person told you he had seen the suspect enter the day before?"

"Yes."

"And you and Detective Talia were lying on the ground?"

"Yes."

"And what were you wearing?"

"We were each wearing a suit."

"And what were the weather conditions on this night Detective?"

"The temperature was around ten degrees and it was very windy."

"And you stated there was another unit assisting you on this stakeout?"

"Yes there was."

"And who was that and where were they positioned?"

"We had another unit in an unmarked car parked on Barnes Avenue just off East 224th Street."

"And do you recall who was in that unmarked car Detective?"

"Yes it was Detective Randy Broomfield, Detective Maureen Green, and Sergeant William Sutherland."

"And did you have any communication with that unit?"

"Yes we communicated by walkie-talkie."

"Okay Detective so what if anything happened next?"

"So after several hours of observing this residence, a yellow cab pulled up in front and after about a minute began to blow its horn."

"And what happened next Detective?"

"The front door to 736 East 224th Street opened and an individual walked out, walking towards the yellow cab."

"And can you describe for the court, Detective, what this individual looked like?"

"The person was black, short, and was wearing a black and white leather 8 ball jacket, blue jeans, red sneakers with a hoodie on pulled tight to its face and there appeared to be a wool hat underneath. The hat was pulled down low, almost covering the person's eyes."

"Okay Detective and can you describe what the shooter was wearing the night of the homicide?"

"He was wearing a black and white 8 ball jacket, blue jeans and red sneakers."

"Okay Detective, so what did you and Detective Talia do next?"

"Well we felt that this person who was walking towards the cab wasn't the shooter. There was something that just didn't seem right."

"Can you explain to the court what you mean by that?"

"Well it was just a feeling that we got that the person was wearing the shooter's clothes to see if any police would approach as they entered the cab."

"So what did you do?"

"We radioed to the other unit that there was a yellow cab coming west

210

on East 224th Street and I instructed them to stop the cab and detain the person in the back seat after they got off the 700 block of 224th Street."

"And why did you do this Detective?"

"So that if someone was looking out the window of 736 they wouldn't see the police stop the cab."

"Okay Detective so what if anything happened after that?"

"Less than a minute later the door to 736 East 224th Street opened again and out came another individual."

"And can you describe this individual for the court?"

"This person was black, short, and was wearing a pink woman's coat covering what appeared to be a flowered dress, with pink woman's shoes and a pink and yellow wool hat pulled down low on the person's face."

"And how could you tell the person was wearing a dress, Detective if it was covered by a coat?"

"The coat was ¾ length and the dress was almost down to the person's ankles."

"Okay Detective so what, if anything, did you do next?"

"Well we observed this individual walk out to the sidewalk, and then this person looked first east towards White Plains Road then west towards Barnes Avenue, as if they were looking for someone or something."

"Objection. The detective is not a mind reader, Your Honor; he does not know what this person was thinking."

"Sustained. Just tell the court what you observed Detective," stated Judge Weinstein.

"Yes Your Honor," Detective Franco replied.

"Okay so I saw the person walk out to the sidewalk, look to the right, then to the left and then proceed to walk west on 224th Street towards Barnes Avenue."

"And what happened next Detective?"

"We came out from our location, went down the stairs, and I started going west on 224th Street on the opposite side of the street from where the individual was walking."

"So you were following him Detective?"

"Yes I was going up 224th Street trying to hide behind cars that were parked on the south side of the street."

"And where was Detective Talia?"

"Detective Talia had run across the street and positioned himself behind a parked car."

"And was he also following this individual towards Barnes Avenue?"

"No."

"And why is that Detective?"

"Well we had discussed beforehand our strategy and we figured if he saw me and doubled back towards White Plains Road he wouldn't know Detective Talia was there and he would be able to intercept him."

"So what happened next?"

"As the individual got in front of an apartment building, at 752 East 224th Street, I ran across the street and apprehended him."

"And was Detective Talia also present?"

"Yes he got there a few seconds later."

"What happened next Detective?"

"Well I had this individual up against the wall with his face towards the wall. We handcuffed him and turned him around and I observed his face."

"And who was this who you apprehended Detective?"

"Marvin Davis."

"And did Mr. Davis make any spontaneous utterances?"

"Yes he did."

"And what did he say?"

"He said, 'You dirty rat.'"

"Excuse me Detective, could you repeat that?"

"He stated, 'You dirty rat.'"

"And what did you take that as meaning Detective?"

"I was not sure, I know it's a quote from an old James Cagney movie, but I did not know why he said it to us."

"Okay Detective, so what happened next?"

"I radioed to Sergeant Sutherland and asked if they apprehended the person with the 8 ball jacket. He stated that they had and they were parked around the block. He further informed me that that person was a female."

"What happened next Detective?"

"I asked Sergeant Southerland and Detectives Broomfield and Green to remove the individual to the precinct."

"What did you do next Detective?"

"Well we had already searched the individual that we apprehended and I radioed for a sector car to transport us back to our vehicle that was parked on East 223rd Street."

"And you say that you searched this individual. Did you recover anything of an evidentiary nature?"

"No."

"Detective do you know who came to transport you back to your car?"

"Yes it was Officers John Englert and Sal Pascente.

The Trial (Continues)

"Okay so what happened next?"

"They brought us to our vehicle and we transported the perp to the stationhouse for processing."

At this point Judge Weinstein recesses for lunch and directs all parties to return to court at 2:00 P.M. He instructs the jury not to discuss the case.

Detective Franco and ADA Baron walk back over to ADA Baron's office. As they're walking Franco asks ADA Baron, "So how am I doing so far?"

"You're doing fine," he responded. "But remember the hard part comes when Bagelman starts cross examining you."

ADA Baron looks at Franco with a smirk on his face knowing that Franco is always a little unsure of himself. "And don't forget this, Giovanni, Trevor is depending upon you, he said, quoting Mrs. Webb.

Giovanni looked back at Sid with a puzzled look and said, "That's what Mrs. Webb told me."

"I know, I heard her," was his response. "I figured let's get the acid moving around in your stomach before lunch." And with a smile on his face, he put a hand on Giovanni's shoulder, as if to assure him that everything would be fine.

Uncharacteristically, Giovanni declined lunch and sat in ADA Baron's office, reading his homicide folder over and over. He was again trying to anticipate questions that the defense attorney would be asking him in a few short hours.

Now was Talia's turn to break Franco's balls. When he saw that he wasn't eating, he stated, "You could have ordered a sandwich anyway and let me have it."

Franco responded, "Why, so you could give it to Kim and make believe that you bought her lunch? She's the one who orders food so she would have known that you're full of shit."

With that Kim looked up from her desk and smiled at Giovanni. "You're never going to learn," Giovanni told Talia. "You can't fuck with me and if you continue to try, I'll tell Kim what I saw the last time I saw you come out of the shower in the locker room."

"Well why were you looking?" Talia asked.

"Because all the guys told me that I wouldn't believe it if I saw it."

"You're right," stated Talia. "It IS unbelievable."

"I agree," Franco shot back. "It reminded me of when my son was four years old."

With that Talia knew this war of wits was a losing battle. But Franco

213

just couldn't let it die. Franco looked Kim right in the eye and stated, "I'm only kidding Kim, it was huge. Actually the biggest thing I've ever seen in my whole life." And then he winked at her.

Seeing this Talia picked up his diet coke and walked out of ADA Baron's office with the sound of Kim, the pretty office assistant, laughing in his ear.

Two o'clock was quickly approaching and ADA Baron and Detective Franco walked back over to Supreme Court. As the two entered the courtroom, Franco made eye contact with a female cousin of Trevor's who he had met several times at the precinct after the murder. She seemed to pal around with Lyle and it was obvious that they were very close. Her name was Ruthie. She was in her early twenties and had a classy way about her. She acknowledged Franco with a warm smile and he smiled back, thinking to himself how pretty she was. The trauma that this murder caused was all the more evident to Franco as he looked around the courtroom and saw many members of Trevor's family present. It wasn't the typical homicide that he was used to testifying at, where one drug dealer kills another and no one really seems to care. The courtroom was packed with onlookers and you got a sense that most of them had a personal connection to the family.

Detective Franco took a seat in the first row behind the prosecutor's table. A hand reached out from behind him and touched his shoulder and as he turned around to see who it was he was greeted by Trevor's grandmother. He had only met her once before at Mrs. Webb's house. She whispered to him, "Jesus loves you and so do we. For you and your partner to lie on the cold ground for hours to catch that boy tells me about your dedication and what good men you both are." She then took Detective Franco's hand, looked him in his eyes, and said "Thank you."

It was an awkward moment for him because he was trying to go over the testimony in his head before he had to get back on the stand. He gave her a small smile and nodded his head. With that everyone was told to rise and Judge Weinstein entered the courtroom.

Detective Franco's name was called and he walked back up to the witness stand, clutching his homicide folder. The judge informed him that he was still under oath and Franco acknowledged him. ADA Baron continued his questioning from earlier that day.

"Okay Detective so we were speaking about the apprehension of Mr. Davis On December 30, 1995. Can you tell the court if Mr. Davis made any admissions to you?"

"Yes sir."

"And what was that?"

"He made a written confession to me in the presence of Detective Talia that evening."

With that ADA Baron held up a two page confession that Marvin Davis made to Detective Franco. He handed it to Franco and asked if he recognized it. Franco stated that he did.

"And what is that Detective?"

"That's the confession that I took from Mr. Davis in the interview room on December 30, 1995 (While testifying Detective Franco would call the interrogation room the interview room so as not to have it sound so forceful)."

"And Detective how do you recognize that document as being the confession made by Mr. Davis to you?"

"It has his name, his date of birth, his signature, my name, my shield number, my signature and Detective Talia's signature."

"Okay Detective can you read that statement made by Mr. Davis to the court?"

At this point Detective Franco began to read the confession.

I don't know why I do some of the things that I do. I think it's just because there's a demon in me sometimes. I feel like no one cares about me and it's been like that since I was a little kid. My mother left me and I don't know who my father was. My grandmother tried to raise me but she was old and couldn't control me. I was always very small and on the street when you're small you need to act crazy to get respect. I don't think I'm really crazy, I just act crazy sometimes. Sometimes I do things and then feel bad about it later, like this time with that boy. I didn't want to shoot anyone, but when they ran away from me, I felt they were dissing me so when I saw the kid with the chain in the store, I wanted to take it. After I took it and he ran, I got mad. Then the other guy pushed me and that made me even madder, so I chased him and then I shot him. I don't know why I did it, and I wish I didn't, but there's nothing that I can do now, except say I'm sorry.

As Detective Franco finished reading the statement, a woman screamed out, Lord Jesus!"

Franco looked into the crowd and saw it was Trevor's grandmother. She was weeping uncontrollably and several members of Trevor's family were speaking and carrying on. Judge Weinstein slammed his gavel down several times telling the audience members that they needed to be quiet. He stated, *order in the court* on two occasions. The emotions that were running through the courtroom were very high and Judge Weinstein again reprimanded no one in particular and everyone in general as he slammed his gavel down one more time and stated that if there are any more outbursts everyone will be removed from this court and not allowed back in.

There were several family members hugging each other and crying and Franco felt a chill run down his spine as the total senselessness of this crime became so blatantly evident. Even the murderer realized that there was absolutely no reason to shoot Trevor and everyone in the courtroom could feel the stupidity of the defendants' actions. The judge, sensing he was losing control of his courtroom, demanded a recess at that moment and called both the defense attorney and the prosecutor to his bench. He had the court officers clear the courtroom of all spectators. He told Detective Franco to stay seated along with the jury. Once all spectators were gone, he instructed the jury to not let any emotions of any spectators influence their decision making in this case.

When court resumed, everyone was allowed back in, and they had been instructed by the court officers as they each walked into the court room of proper behavior and that any outbursts would not be tolerated. It was a touchy situation because all of the court officers felt for the family of Trevor and they didn't want to come off as being mean or cold, but they also had a job to do and order needed to be kept. Franco heard one court officer basically pleading with each person as they entered the courtroom. He said something like, please I know this is hard on everyone, but the judge will make everyone leave if it happens again. Please try to control yourself when you're listening to the testimony.

They were all good people, but their emotions were getting the best of them because it was such a senseless act. Almost every one of them to a person apologized, for causing a disruption. Judge Weinstein again entered the court, and everyone was told to rise. He again instructed the onlookers that outbursts would not be tolerated and if it happened again, the rest of this trial would be held behind closed doors. You could sense the sympathy in his voice, but he also had a job to do, and could not have any further disruptions. He had to assure that the jury was not influenced by the emotions and only used facts to decide the outcome of this case.

So as Detective Franco resumed his testimony, the confession was entered into evidence as People's exhibit # 34. There was no objection by Mr. Bagelman but as Mr. Bagelman looked at the document he seemed to get bright eyed as if he discovered some type of discrepancy. Franco seemed to be the only one who noticed the reaction of Bagelman's face as he looked at the confession. Franco was thinking, what could he have seen, that almost seemed to make a light bulb go off in his head?

At that moment ADA Baron stated that he had no further questions for Detective Franco.

Oh Boy here we go, Franco thought to himself as Mr. Bagelman adjusted his tie and opened his top shirt button. *This guy's got nothing, Gio, he's all smoke and mirrors. You got a kid who shot somebody twice in cold blood and gave you a written confession. What could he possibly say to get him off? He's just trying to get you nervous.*

With that Mr. Bagelman approached Detective Franco and with a big smile on his face greeted him like they were long lost buddies.

"Hi Detective Franco how are you today," Mr. Bagelman exclaimed.

"Fine," was Franco's response, almost like he knew he was being set up for something. His questioning started very matter-of-factly.

"So Detective you say you didn't respond to this shooting scene did you?"

"No I did not."

"And this happened at 2 A.M., is that correct?"

"Yes."

"And you didn't arrive at the precinct for work until 8 A.M. is that correct?"

"Yes."

"So six hours went by before you even started your investigation?"

"That's correct."

"And isn't it true that the first several hours are the most important in a homicide investigation?"

"Objection! Counselor is asking for the Detective's opinion, and not a factual answer."

"Sustained. You don't have to answer that Detective."

"Okay Detective, but six hours did go by before you started to conduct your investigation, true?"

"That's correct."

"And you were the lead investigator is that correct?"

"Yes."

"And you testified that the night watch detective just did a preliminary investigation, is that true?"

"Well they conducted their investigation until it was handed over to me."

"But detective, you testified to this court that they just did a preliminary investigation. These are your words are they not 'just a preliminary investigation?'"

"Well, what I meant was they conducted their investigation until I got there and then the case was turned over to me."

"So Detective, how would you define preliminary?"

"Preliminary is like the beginning."

"Okay the beginning, so the night watch detectives, they began your investigation for you. Is that what you're saying?"

"Well they began the investigation for the NYPD. I was assigned the case when I came in to work. I don't believe they knew who was catching the case at 8 A.M."

"Detective I detect a bit of sarcasm in your voice."

"Objection."

"Detective Franco is just trying to answer the question Your Honor, states ADA Baron."

"Sustained. Counselor, move on with your questions we all know what preliminary means."

"Yes Your Honor."

"Okay Detective, the night watch detectives did a preliminary investigation six hours before you got to start your investigation on this case, then you were assigned, as the lead investigator. Is that correct?"

"That's correct."

"And you further testified that there wasn't much to go on, in your words, when you first came in."

"No what I said was there wasn't much to go on except for the 911 caller's information and the eye witness's statement who happens to be the victims' brother, counselor."

"Okay Detective, so when you got in at 8 A.M. and received this case as the lead investigator, you had one witness and a 911 caller's information."

"Yes."

"And in the span of fourteen hours you had this whole case solved, with a confession by my client, all in one big happy package for the DA."

"Well I never thought of it like that, but yeah I guess I did."

"UNBELIEVABLE." "VERY IMPRESSIVE"

"Objection your honor. The defense is attempting to influence the jury with a statement, not a question."

"Sustained. I will have none of that Mr. Bagelman," stated Judge Weinstein. He also directs that Mr. Bagelman's outburst be stricken from the record and further directs the ladies and gentleman of the jury to disregard it as if it was never said.

"Okay Detective let's move on. Did you have an occasion to take a pedigree of my client?"

"Yes I did."

"And can you tell the court how tall my client is?"

"Four feet eleven inches."

"And what does my client weigh?"

"Ninty-five pounds."

"Wow pretty tiny wouldn't you say Detective?" as Mr. Bagelman out-stretches his hand, showing the height of a short person.

"I guess."

"And how tall are you Detective?"

"Objection! What possible relevance could the Detective's height have to do with this case your honor?"

Mr. Bagelman responds, "it has a lot of relevance. Please allow me some latitude in the questioning of this witness and I'll tie it all together in the end Your Honor."

"I'll allow" stated Judge Weinstein, but keep it relevant to this case. You're on a short leash counselor. "Objection overruled."

"Answer the question Detective."

"Six feet."

"And what do you weigh detective?"

"220 pounds."

"Okay Detective so here you are six feet 220 lbs interrogating my client who you say is four feet eleven, ninety-five pounds is that correct?"

"Yes."

"And you look like a pretty strong guy. Are you involved in any kind of sports?"

"Objection, Your Honor what could this possibly have to do with this case?"

"Judge please, I stated I would tie it all in."

"Overruled, I'll allow it, answer the question Detective."

"I play football."

"And that's on the NYPD football team?"

"That's correct."

"And how long have you been on that team?"

"Fourteen years."

"Fourteen years! Wow. So you're battle tested."

Detective Franco answered, "Is that a question? Am I supposed to answer that?" as he looks at Judge Weinstein with a bewildered look on his face.

"No Detective you don't need to answer that. Mr. Bagelman, I warned you, short leash ask relevant questions."

"Yes Your Honor."

"Okay Detective so you played football for the NYPD for fourteen years and that's tackle football correct?"

"Yes."

"And you wear a helmet and shoulder pads and leg pads?"

"Yes."

"And football is a very violent game is it not?"

"Objection."

"Sustained."

"Okay Detective did you play football in high school?"

"Objection."

"Overruled, I'll allow it."

"Yes."

"And I bet you won some awards didn't you?"

"Objection."

"Sustained."

"Okay but you would consider yourself a good football player wouldn't you?"

"Objection. The question calls for the Detective's opinion."

"Sustained."

Judge Weinstein looks at Mr. Bagelman and states, "you're at the end of your leash, you've made your point, the Detective is a football player. Move on."

"Okay Your Honor, did you play any other sports in high school Detective?"

"Objection."

"Move on Mr. Bagelman," states the judge.

"Sorry Your Honor I'm trying to make a point here."

"Detective did you play football in college?"

"Objection."

"Overruled, I'll allow it."

"Yes."

"Wow it's pretty hard to make a college football team, isn't it?"

"Objection."

"Sustained."

"All right, one more question with regards to sports, when you're dressed in your football uniform and you look in the mirror, do you look intimidating?"

"Objection."

"Sustained."

"That's enough Mr. Bagelman," Judge Weinstein instructs.

"Okay Your Honor." Detective, back to my client. "You stated he gave you a written confession. Is that correct?"

"Yes it is."

"And you were in a room with just you and he for quite some time you testified is that correct?"

"Well we were in the room for about one hour."

"Okay Detective, and in that hour was my client allowed to make a phone call?"

"He didn't ask to."

"That wasn't the question. Detective, was he allowed to make a phone call?"

"Objection Detective Franco testified that the defendant didn't request to make a phone call."

"Sustained."

"Detective could my client have made a phone call if he asked to?"

"Yes."

"Really?"

"Objection Your Honor."

"Question withdrawn Your Honor."

"Detective did you read my client his Miranda warnings, commonly known as his rights?"

"Yes I did."

"And did he state that he understood them?"

"Yes he did."

"But in his statement that he gave to you, didn't he tell you that he sometimes thinks he's crazy?"

"Yes he did."

"So would you think that someone who thinks they're crazy can understand their rights?"

"I believe he said that he sometimes feels that he's crazy."

"And wouldn't you think at that moment detective that you should stop questioning him and seek some kind of psychological evaluation for him?"

"No I didn't think to do that."

"You didn't think to do that or you didn't want to do that?"

"Objection."

"Overruled, I'll allow it."

"It didn't occur to me."

"Well you testified that he was wearing women's clothes, do you feel that's normal, Detective?"

"Objection. Counselor is asking for the Detective's opinion."

"Sustained."

"Okay Detective so here we have this little guy come out of a house wearing a dress and a pink hat and pink shoes and that seems totally normal to you?"

"Objection."

"Okay Detective just a few more questions and then I'll let you go. It seems to me from looking at you that you're a pretty big and strong guy and I would think that your background in sports would sometimes involve violence and intimidation."

"Objection."

"Sustained."

"Okay Detective I'm going to ask you straight out because I can't take this farce anymore. Did you have any physical contact with my client while you were in the "interview room" for an hour? You being six feet tall and 220 lbs, and him being four feet eleven and ninety-five pounds and you wanting him to confess to this crime?"

"Objection."

"Sustained. Rephrase your question counselor so as to not make it accusatory."

"Detective do you want us to believe that you, at no time, had any physical contact with my client?"

As Detective Franco attempts to answer the question, he put his head down and spoke softly as he stated, "Well I never said I didn't have ANY physical contact with your client."

"What was that Detective? Excuse me!" as Mr. Bagelman sprang to life. "Can you repeat that in a louder voice for the court what you just said. I don't think they all heard you."

Detective Franco looked up and looking right into Mr. Bagelman's eyes stated with a regretful tone,

"Well I didn't say I never had ANY physical contact with your client."

"OH REALLY!" stated Mr. Bagelman. "Well why don't you tell the court exactly what physical contact you did have with my client."

A stunned silence came over the courtroom as Detective Franco spoke.

"Well once your client finished making a video confession to the ADA, he seemed so relieved that he came over to me and hugged me, getting tears and snot all over my suit. "

"WHAT?" exclaimed Mr. Bagelman. "I object to that answer Your Honor, that's not what I was talking about."

Laughter filled the courtroom as it was obvious that Mr. Bagelman had taken the bait and that Detective Franco was playing a high stakes game of cat and mouse with him, which Franco undoubtedly won.

"Your honor," exclaimed Mr. Bagelman, "that was not what I meant."

"Now Mr. Bagelman, you know never to ask a question that you don't already know the answer to. They teach you that in your first year of law school. Are there any further questions for this witness?"

With a stunned look on his face, Mr. Bagelman softly said "no" as ADA Baron stood up.

ADA Baron asked that the video confession be marked into evidence and Judge Weinstein deemed it People's Exhibit # 35.

With that, Judge Weinstein recessed the court for the day instructing the jury not to discuss the case with anyone. The jury was escorted out of the courtroom by two Supreme Court officers and after they were gone, Mr. Bagelman requested a sidebar with the judge. He was protesting the manner in which Detective Franco answered his last question and was visibly upset.

Judge Weinstein had not yet made a decision on his ruling in connection with the Huntley hearing. A Huntley hearing is a pretrial hearing in New York State. Huntley provides that a defendant may challenge the voluntary and lawful nature of any statement made to the police. If the prosecution intends to use the statement at trial the prosecution must inform the defense of its intention. The defendant has the right to a Huntley hearing in front of the judge to determine whether the statement can be used at the trial. Factors that the judge will consider include whether the defendant waived his/her Miranda rights, whether the defendant was in legal custody of the police, or whether the police used unfair tactics such as coercion, or false promises, to the defendant. The judge must also consider whether he feels, beyond a reasonable doubt that the defendant gave the statement of his or her own free will. The judge must find voluntariness beyond a reasonable doubt, before the confession can be used at the trial. The judge must rule that the statement or confession was obtained properly and voluntarily under Miranda. If that is the case, the statement or confession can be used by the prosecutor at trial regardless of whether the defendant testifies on his own behalf or not.

Judge Weinstein informed Mr. Bagelman in a low but stern voice that his decision to allow the video confession was a proper one due to the fact that the defense opened the door to the subject by his questioning of Detective Franco. He further informed Mr. Bagelman that his method of questioning Detective Franco while legal, was somewhat unethical and he told Mr. Bagelman, off the record, "it looks like you got what you deserve. I'll see you gentlemen in the morning."

Mr. Bagelman walked back to the defense table, with his head down knowing that a very damaging piece of evidence against his client would now be viewed by the jury tomorrow. Not only did they hear his client confess to a senseless murder that was written down, and read to the jury by Detective Franco, now they would get to see his client on video, describing how he killed the defenseless victim. Because he made the cardinal sin of attorneys, he damaged his case, and his client's chances. He asked a question of a witness without knowing the answer. He thought he caught Franco in a compromising situation. He thought Franco was about to admit to some type of wrong doing, that would shed doubt on the validity of his testimony. He thought he wore Franco down, In fact what looked like a strong case, with an eye witness and a confession, just got even stronger with a video of his client confessing to this senseless murder to come. In his attempt to discredit the investigating Detective and shed some doubt on the entire case, he screwed up. He got played, the same way he was used to playing witnesses. He was used to turning their words around; used to making them seem not so credible even when they were. Well this time he met his match and his courtroom antics backfired on him. He might just have dug himself a hole which not even his theatrics, big words and fancy suits could help him climb out of. As Detective Franco was instructed by Judge Weinstein to step down from the witness stand, he glanced over at Mr. Bagelman and gave him a faint smile. ADA Baron stood as the court officer instructed all the occupants of the court to stand as the judge exited to his chambers. Franco and ADA Baron were walking down the aisle toward the exit, after gathering their belongings and Giovanni was aware that Mr. Bagelman was walking directly behind them. As they got to the two huge wooden courtroom doors Giovanni held the door open and ADA Baron walked through. As Mr. Bagelman approached, Franco looked Mr. Bagelman in the eye and said "You know he did it, but you're trying so hard to get him off, I don't understand it."

Bagelman turned to Giovanni as he walked past and said "I'm just doing my job."

Franco replied "I could never do your job."

With that Bagelman replied, "And I could never do yours."

As the three men walked toward the elevator on the 7th floor Mr. Bagelman stated, "You and your partner did one hell of a job Detective."

This took Giovanni completely by surprise. All he could think to say was "thanks."

The next morning found Franco arriving at the Precinct at 7:30 A.M. When he walked into the Squad room there was a note on his desk to call Mrs. Webb. As he picked up his desk phone he realized that he knew her number by heart. As he dialed it a strange feeling came over him. It rang three times and a woman answered the phone, "hello."

"Good morning, this is Detective Franco; "I had a note on my desk to call Mrs. Webb, my I speak to her please?"

"Hi Detective this is she."

"What can I do for you Mrs. Webb?"

"Detective I just wanted to tell you that my mother passed away last night in her sleep."

A chill came over him as he heard the grief in Mrs. Webb's voice. He thought to himself, *how much more can this women deal with.*

"I'm so sorry Mrs. Webb" he stated as he could feel his mouth go dry and at that point he was at a loss for words.

Feeling his uneasiness Mrs. Webb replied, "Well Momma, as we called her, thought the world of you and Detective Richie. I think the stress of losing her grandson and having to relive it this week in court was too much for her to take. I know she will be watching over us today in court. My brother is flying in from Virginia to take care of the arrangements, and he will meet us sometime today at the court house if he gets everything taken care of in time."

Franco could not think of anything to say to this women who exhibited remarkable strength, in the wake of such trying and stressful times. All he could muster was "I'm so sorry Mrs. Webb, I'm sure she will be there with us."

Mrs. Webb replied, "My family has been through so much in the past year, I'm sure the Lord has his plan." "Now Momma is with Trevor, she can watch over him in Heaven like she always did here on Earth."

With that all Giovanni could muster was an "I'm sure she is."

Then Mrs. Webb replied, "We will see you at ADA Baron's office at nine."

"Okay Mrs. Webb."

A few minutes later Talia entered the Squad room. Giovanni motioned for him to come over to his desk.

"Mrs. Webb called, her mother died in her sleep last night."

"Holy shit! "What else is gonna happen to these poor people."

"I know right, unbelievable, That is one strong woman."

A few minutes later the detectives were on their way down to court in an unmarked car.

There was a solemn mood in the car with the news of Mrs. Webb's mother's passing, and all that she had been through. Usually the two Detectives are in pretty good spirits pointing out funny looking people and unusual occurrences along their route: like the toothless hag on the corner selling oranges, or the squeegee guy with urine in a bottle and dirty newspaper trying to clean car windows as they stop for red lights on the corner. But today the mood in the car was that of sadness toward all the despair and unfairness of a cruel world. Both detectives just seemed a little out of it, and were uncharacteristically quiet on the ride down.

At the intersection of East 161st and Park Avenue, Franco observed a Hispanic man pushing another guy up against a fence. It appeared he had some type of object placed in the man's back, possibly a gun. Franco told Talia what he saw and said "swing a U-turn at the corner."

Talia protested saying "We need to get to court; we are on a Homicide trial you know." Franco answered back with an angry tone, we might be preventing a homicide, or better yet enabling one if we don't stop."

Talia swung the unmarked car around at the intersection and came up quickly on the two individuals who were still up against the fence. The individual who had the other guy pressed against the fence turned his head when he saw the car coming in his direction. At that moment he fled on foot north bound on Park Avenue running through an abandoned lot covered with high grass. Franco jumped from the unmarked car and gave chase. Talia seeing this yelled to him, "We don't have radios." Referring to the fact that because the Detectives were on their way to court for a trial, they did not carry walkie-talkies, thus they had no way of communicating with other police officers in the area. They would basically be on their own, in a potentially dangerous situation without any communication or back-up. Franco didn't respond as he ran through the abandoned lot in pursuit of the suspect. Talia seeing this also gave chase. He knew Franco was not going to let the suspect just run away. As they were chasing the suspect, he made a turn on 159th Street and proceeded east bound. *This guy can run* Franco thought to himself as he continued the pursuit in his Blue pinstripe suit and shiny wing tip shoes. *Not exactly running attire* Franco thought. The individual they were chasing, after turning right and now running southbound on Third Avenue, threw something over the fence of a lot next to a bodega. Franco, who was quite winded by now after chasing this person several blocks, yelled to Talia to go get what he threw. This would mean that Franco would now be completely alone chasing this suspect as Talia searched for whatever he threw.

The suspect was slowing down considerably as he was getting tired also. Suddenly the suspect made a mad dash across Third Avenue, which is a very wide street with two lanes of traffic going both north and south. As the suspect attempted to run across the four lanes of traffic, a livery cab traveling northbound slammed on his breaks and, as his car screeched and smoke came up from his rear tires, he struck the suspect with great force. This caused the suspect to be hurled up over the vehicle's hood, striking the windshield which immediately caused it to shatter as the suspect flipped over the skidding gold Chevy impala and came crashing down onto the pavement. As Franco ran across the street a crowd already began to gather. The suspect was unconscious and bleeding from his mouth. The crowd was screaming about him being chased into traffic.

Detective Franco called 911 on his cell phone and requested an ambulance and some additional units for crowd control. He then attempted to administer first aid the best he could without any medical supplies. He ensured that no one moved the suspect for fear that he most likely had a head, neck, or back injury. He ordered people to back up and asked for someone to get a blanket to put over the suspect. The suspect most likely was going into shock. He then phoned Talia and told him of his location and what happened. Talia informed Franco that he had not found anything in the lot. Franco responded "we better find whatever he threw Richie, I doubt the guy he had up against the fence is still there after all this time. If we don't recover some evidence I'm fucked. This guy's hurt real bad."

With that Richie stated I'll call ESU and have them do a grid search.

"Okay good" was Franco's response.

Just as Franco hung up, his cell phone rang, it was ADA Baron. "Where are you guys?

"We're heading over to Supreme Court." Franco explained what happened and ADA Baron was not very understanding.

"Why would you get involved in something today, you know we are in the middle of a Homicide trial."

"I'm sorry Sid."

"We saw a guy who looked like he was robbing this other guy at gunpoint, he ran and I chased him, then he runs into traffic and gets hit by a car."

ADA Baron responded, "Jesus H Christ!"

At that moment all Franco could think to say was "I thought you were Jewish Sid?"

You're killing me Detective. I'll try to get a postponement, keep me posted."

"Okay" was all Franco muttered.

As some sector cars pulled up Franco's phone rang again, it was Talia. "I found a gun" Talia screamed into the phone.

"Oh great what kind?" Franco asked as sweat poured off his forehead and into his eyes.

"A little black .22, you know one of those Saturday night specials."

"Secure it and don't let anyone touch it, we need to send it down to the lab for ballistics and to be printed," if this guy's prints are on it, I should be okay."

"Is it loaded" Franco asked.

"Yeah just two bullets though"

"Two bullets is loaded, good enough for me" Franco replied.

Talia stated "I'll go back and get the car, then I'll come get you."

"Okay Richie, but first go back to the scene and see if our victim is still there."

"Okay" was all Talia said as he hung up.

Franco kneeling alongside the suspect heard sirens in the distance; he could tell they were that of a sector car and not an ambulance. Over the years he became very familiar to the slightly different sounds that distinguished the two. Within a minute or so there were several sector cars at his location and he felt relieved as the crowd had become quite large and very hostile toward him. No one actually tried to get physical with him, but he could hear their comments. They were saying things like "fucking white mother fucking cops, always fucking with us," as if they had any knowledge of the situation. Franco wanted to yell out, "Yeah, he was robbing one of you with a gun, you stupid mother fucker, and I risked my life to protect one of you stupid mother fuckers." But he knew it was useless and unprofessional, so he pretended not to hear the nasty comments and idle threats.

As one of the patrolmen approached him, Franco identified himself and explained the situation. The 44th precinct was a close house and the cops there did not take any shit from the mutts in the street. Within minutes the crowd was cleared to almost a block away, and the ambulance was pulling up to the scene. A Lieutenant from the 44th who heard the 911 transmission arrived on the scene and pulled Franco aside and asked what had occurred.

As Franco was explaining, Talia pulled up on the scene and exited the unmarked car holding the recovered gun with his pen through the trigger guard as to not destroy any possible prints. He made it a point to allow the crowd to see it as he walked past them on his way over to Franco and the Lieutenant. Franco looked at the gun briefly and then told Talia to put it away. Talia then put it into his front jacket pocket. Franco then walked over and identified himself to the ambulance attendant and paramedics. He informed them that the aided was under arrest for a possible robbery, and definitely weapons possession along with other charges. He wanted to obtain the persons I.D. He asked if they could look through his clothes to see if he had any I.D. One young ambulance attendant told Franco "we need to get him to Lincoln stat." He was referring to Lincoln Hospital, a trauma hospital on East 149th Street. "Just check his pockets please," Franco pleaded. "No can do" the attendant shot back as he closed the ambulance door.

"Fucking scumbag" Franco shot back as the ambulance sped off with sirens blaring. "What the fuck are they doing? Franco yelled out aloud. "Someone has to be with the prisoner, he's under arrest." With that Franco yelled to Talia to follow the ambulance to Lincoln and stay with him until he can get everything sorted out. Talia was not happy as he handed Franco the gun and walked over to the unmarked car.

The patrol sergeant from the 44th was now on the scene along with several more sector cars. It was quite a site. Franco went over to him and filled him in on the situation. He looked familiar to Franco and it seemed the two had done night watch together when the sergeant was a detective. He explained what had transpired and informed the sergeant. that he was on a homicide trial in Supreme Court. The sergeant feeling for his situation told him, "You should have never got involved."

Franco thought to himself *"If one more fucking person says that to me I'm gonna shoot myself."*

The sergeant offered him a ride back to the precinct to begin his paperwork on the arrest, but he explained that he had no idea who he was arresting. He explained that his partner was on his way to Lincoln Hospital to obtain this person's identification, and then they would have to have a cop sit on him, because until he can be released from the hospital he is considered a hospitalized prisoner and has to be guarded twenty four hours a day.

The sergeant shook his head as to say "I know you are fucked."

The precinct in which the hospital is located has to guard the prisoner; therefore Franco would be making some enemies today. Then once the prisoner is stable enough to be released Franco will have to process the

229

arrest and take the prisoner to Central Booking for processing. By the looks of the prisoner, he might be in the hospital a very long time. If that's the case then they would have to do what is known as bedside arraignment. That is when the prisoner is too injured or sick to be removed to court for processing so he gets arraigned in the hospital. It is a lengthy process that is very involved and Franco was wondering to himself *what he has done to deserve all this stress and aggravation.*

As he continued to speak to the sergeant, Franco's cell phone rang. It was Talia calling on his way to Lincoln hospital. "What's up Richie? Franco asked. Did you catch up to the ambulance; Franco could hear the ambulance's siren blaring over Talia's cell phone. Yeah I'm right behind them, were pulling into the E.R. entrance right now. I almost forgot to tell you . . .

"What's that?" Franco asked.

"I went back to the scene but our Vic was long gone. "I asked around but nobody saw nothin."

"How typical," was Franco's response. "I better get a ride to the 44th."

He still needed to prepare a complaint report for the initial incident, an aided card for the prisoner struck by the livery cab, and voucher the gun. He had to send the gun to the lab and request ballistics and prints. He also needed to obtain the driver of the livery cab's information and prepare an accident report. He spoke to the driver who was a sixty-nine year old Dominican man. He was very shook up by the whole incident.

Thank God he has a license Franco thought, or I'd be doing more paperwork.

As Franco told the sergeant he would take him up on the ride to the 44, his cell phone rang again, and it was ADA Baron.

"So what's going on Detective?"

Franco filled ADA Baron in and ADA Baron stated "the judge gave us till 1:00 P.M. He said you better be in this courtroom at that time or you will be held in contempt."

"Like I don't have enough fucking stress." Franco replied.

"Well I suggest you do as instructed Detective," ADA Baron replied.

He looked at his watch and it read 10:35. Less than three hours and I don't even know who this perp is. Franco called Talia on his cell and informed him what ADA Baron said.

"Looks like you might have to take this collar Richie" said Franco.

"You saw it go down, you chased him, you got him run over, and you want me to take the collar?" Let's see how much we get done by the time you need to be in court."

"Okay" I know it sucks to stick all this paper on you but you did recover the gun."

"Yeah, what a mistake that was," Richie replied.

"Tell me you love me Richie."

"You know something Giovanni."

"What's that Richie?"

"You're a real good cop, and you see things in the street that other cops including myself don't even notice, but you don't know when to let things be.

"I mean so yeah the guy pulled a gun on the other guy, but maybe he deserved it, maybe he caught the guy fucking his wife, maybe the guy molested his kid for god's sake, we don't know. Maybe it was not a robbery, maybe the scumbag did something and the guy with the gun was trying to scare him, taking things into his own hands. You know these people don't always call us; sometimes they take care of shit themselves. Maybe the guy in the hospital was a good guy looking out for his family and the guy we thought was the victim was a fucking scumbag rapist or worse.

"We knew we had court, and not just any old bullshit case but a fucking homicide. A homicide of a good kid who wasn't bothering anyone, and was killed by a real piece of shit. He should have been our priority; we should have driven down here with blinders on and made sure we did the right thing by him."

Franco thought for a moment as silence filled the phone. He then gave this response. "You might be right Richie but I go with my gut a lot, and my gut told me that the guy with the gun was not playing, his face told me he meant business. If we just kept going, and I pretended to not have seen anything, then I find out there was a shooting there or a homicide no matter what the reason, I would have a real hard time dealing with that."

Franco sensing that this conversation was getting way to deep and out of the ordinary for the two partners decided it was time to get back to their usual ball breaking and joking mode, told Richie.

"You know Richie if I stop seeing things in the street and reacting to them, their not going to keep calling your name and handing you awards at next year's medal day."

With that the two partners had a good laugh and the seriousness of their conversation vanished. They both brought very important skills to the table and together they made one hell of a team.

Detective Talia got stuck taking the collar that day and Franco did all the paper work involved except for the ballistics on the gun. Franco arrived at ADA Baron's office at 12:45 P.M. and was informed that the Judge had instructed that they be in his courtroom ready to go by 2:00. Seems ADA Baron lied to Giovanni about the time to ensure he would be there on time.

When Franco found out he had been lied to he remarked "Perps lie to me, now the DA lies to me also. What's this world is coming to?"

ADA Baron had ordered Franco a tuna on a roll for lunch from the local deli and got one for Talia also. When told Talia had to take the collar they made, ADA Baron stated "you screwed the kid over."

All Franco could do was shrug his shoulders.

36

The Trial
(Video Confession)

AS EVERYONE LEFT ADA BARRON'S OFFICE AND headed across the street to
Supreme Court, Detective Franco and ADA Baron were walking a little
ways ahead of Mrs. Webb and her family. As they approached the corner
of the Grand Concourse the light was red to cross giving the Webb family
an opportunity to catch up. As they did Mrs. Webb reached for Giovanni's
hand and stated "It sounded like you had a very interesting day already,"
referring to the early morning arrest and all that was involved. Giovanni
looked her in the eye, and she could see that he was not only physically
tired but also mentally exhausted.

"You look so tired Detective."

"I'm okay" he assured her.

"I think you need a vacation" she said with a faint smile. "This trial
has been exhausting for everyone," Mrs. Webb muttered as the light turned
green and the group made its way across the street to the Supreme Court
building.

"You are a remarkable woman" Franco told her in a low voice, not
wanting the rest of the group to hear for some reason that he realized was
unknown to him, as he said it.

"Your son is murdered, you have the stress of reliving it through this
trial, and your mother passes away in her sleep, in your house during all
of this, and you are concerned that I look tired."

Mrs. Webb looked Giovanni in the eye and stated "The Lord has his
plan, who am I to question it?"

As the group made its way in the elevator to the seventh floor courtroom, they observed Mr. Bagelman in the white marble covered hallway outside the two huge wooden doors to the courtroom. Mr. Bagelman acknowledged Mrs. Webb with a nod, but seemed to ignore the rest of the group. As a burly court officer with a handlebar mustache opened the door and held it for the group, Mrs. Webb along with Lyle and Darlene walked into the courtroom first, as ADA Baron and Franco followed behind. Franco knew he would not be allowed to stay in the courtroom while any of the court proceedings were taken place. He might be recalled to testify on some matters that could arise during the testimony of other witnesses. Although only the video confession was still to be played to the jury he was not allowed to be there. He walked the group over to show support and to be available should he need to be recalled.

He could have waited in ADA Baron's office for the group to come back, but he was nervous and amped up, from all the events of the day, and the anticipation of the jury finally seeing the video confession of a cold blooded killer. Not only did they get to hear the written confession that he had obtained from the killer when he read it to the court, but now they would get to watch how this cold blooded killer with no regard for human life, describe how he gunned down a young, promising, defenseless, young man in the prime of his life. And try to somehow justify it because he had a rough life.

Giovanni knew that this would be the hardest part of the trial for the Webb family to go through, and he felt he needed to be as close to them as physically possible.

After what felt like an eternity, Franco found himself making his way over to the huge closed courtroom doors. He stood in front of them almost like he was guarding the courtroom, but in reality he was trying his hardest to hear what was going on inside. Although it was a good try, it was quite a feeble attempt, as he could not hear a sound. Time seemed to pass very slowly and Giovanni found himself looking at his 1943 Bulova watch every few minutes. At one point he checked it to see if it was still ticking because he couldn't believe how the time was dragging.

Inside the courtroom was a different atmosphere entirely. The jury looked on intently as ADA Baron entered the video, Peoples Exhibit # 35, into the video machine and focused the light emitting from it on a large white projector screen across from the jury box, and alongside Judge Weinstein's bench. Everyone sat in anticipation as ADA Baron made some preliminary remarks as to the content and the circumstances that led up to this video being made. Mr. Bagelman and his client Marvin Davis just sat at the defense table with blank expressions on their faces.

Judge Weinstein informed the jury that they should refrain from making any comments or sounds of any kind during the playing of the video. He also directed those demands to everyone else in the courtroom. He also addressed the family of the victim and stated if they would like to step out of the courtroom before it is played they should do so now. No one from the Webb family moved, and in fact all three, Mrs. Webb, Lyle, and Darleen all turned their heads and stared at the defendant Marvin Davis. It was like they were telling him they could handle whatever was on that tape. With that ADA Baron took a long slow walk back over to the tape machine and pressed play.

The video began with an Assistant District Attorney named Cheryl Goldberg in the Lieutenant's office of the 47th precinct's detective squad, stating the date and time, (December 30th 1995, 11:15 P.M.) She introduced to the camera, the people present in the room. They were Detective Giovanni Franco, Detective Richard Talia, the video Technician Robert Lancer, and the court reporter Kristin Nappi. ADA Goldberg asked Detective Franco to bring the defendant Marvin Davis into the room. Franco is seen exiting the room and returning approximately one minute later with Mr. Davis. ADA Goldberg introduces everyone in the room to Mr. Davis and then reads him his Miranda warnings. There is a large portable clock sitting on the desk where Mr. Davis is seated. Court reporter Kristin Nappi is typing away on her stenographer's machine documenting what is being said and by whom. Video technician Lancer is filming as ADA Goldberg asks Mr. Davis if he is willing to make a statement and wave his rights. He states he was. ADA Goldberg, after obtaining his full name, date of birth, and address, simply asked "So Mr. Davis what happened on the morning of December 30th 1995 in the Kennedy Fried Chicken store on East 238th Street and White Plains Road in the Borough of the Bronx?

Marvin went on to tell a chilling tale. It sounded like this:

"I was hanging out in the chicken store when these two dudes come in. They was looking up at the menu on the wall and I seen the links on one of them." ADA Goldberg interrupts, "Links I don't understand Mr. Davis."

"I seen one of them had a big gold chain on."

"Oh go on."

"So I says to him, nice links." "He says "thanks." I think he was scared 'cause he looked over at the other dude. So I got close to him and pulled out my gun as I snatched his chain. He saw the gun and runs out the store. The other guy pushed me, and I got mad that he put his hands on me so I chased him out the store and…." Marvin paused just like he had when giving the written confession to Detective Franco.

Franco chimed in, "Its okay Marvin tell the ADA the rest."

With that Marvin continued, "Then I shot him."

"How many times?" ADA Goldberg asked.

"Twice," was his answer.

At this point Marvin must have remembered what Franco told him about wanting to seem remorseful and sorry because he started to cry.

ADA Goldberg asked him if he wanted something to drink and he declined.

She then asked him where he shot the individual and he stated "In the back."

He was now weeping as he sat in one of the office chairs. He put his hands to his head and stated, "I don't know why I shot that boy, I just go crazy sometimes." The jury along with the rest of the onlookers in the courtroom sat in stunned disbelief.

Mrs. Webb was holding Lyle's hand and they both had tears streaming down their faces. One elderly black woman on the jury looked over at Mrs. Webb and Lyle and just shook her head. Darlene sat there with her face buried in her hands, she wept ever so quietly, and although Judge Weinstein could hear her, he made no attempt to reprimand her.

The video continued with Marvin giving a sob story about his childhood and how bad he had it as a kid. None of what he said after that seemed to matter. He also explained how he hid out at his girlfriend's house and tried to get away dressed like a girl. He explained it in such a way as to make himself seem like a genius, but the way it sounded in court was that of a desperate fool.

He ended his statement with these words:

"If I could take it back I would, I'm sorry I shot that boy. I guess he was just in the wrong place at the wrong time."

In Marvin's sick mind he was showing remorse, but to the people in Supreme Court part B that day Marvin Davis was nothing but a cold blooded killer.

At that point both the prosecution and the defense stated they rest. Meaning they had no further evidence or witnesses to supply to the court. Judge Weinstein recessed for the day and instructed both sides to be in court tomorrow with their closing arguments.

37

Closing Arguments

EVERYONE WAS BACK IN ADA BARRON'S OFFICE the next morning in anticipation of the trial finally being over. It had taken its toll on everyone, especially the Webb Family. They had been through so much and hopefully they could get some closure. ADA Baron sat quietly at his desk going over his notes, that he prepared last night, for his closing argument.

Franco was on his cell phone talking to his nine year old son C.J. who was home sick from school. He was telling his dad about the Teenage Mutant Ninja Turtles episode which he had seen that morning in which one of the turtles, Donatello, had saved a damsel in distress and brought her to safety deep in the sewers of New York. He told his dad that Donatello was like his daddy because he saved people in New York City. His son, C.J., was teasing him comparing him to a giant turtle. They spoke for several more minutes then Giovanni explained to C.J. that he had to go back to work. C.J. asked if he could bring some Italian ice home after work because his throat hurt. Sure was the answer but only if you share it with your brother Thomas. He replied, "Okay Daddy see you later alligator."

"Love you Baby."

"Love you too Daddy."

Mrs. Webb looked over at Giovanni and commented on what a beautiful relationship he had with his baby boy. Giovanni just smiled at her knowing at that moment she was thinking about Trevor.

ADA Baron explained to all that his closing argument would consist of all the facts that were brought to light in this case. The act itself, the subsequent fleeing from the scene, the hiding out in his girlfriend's house, his feeble attempt to trick the detectives by dressing up as a girl, his apprehension, and his written and video confessions. He informed Mrs. Webb that it is cut and dry, and for them to not worry about the verdict. He also stated that Judge Weinstein was a no nonsense judge who would not feel sorry for the defendant when it came time for sentencing.

The group again made their way over to Supreme Court and entered the courtroom. All except for Detectives Franco and Talia. They were still not permitted in the courtroom during this time. They waited patiently in the large hallway. The elevator doors opened and out walked Mr. Bagelman. He saw the two detectives standing off to the side but did not acknowledge them. He opened the large wooden door to the courtroom and stepped in. The door closed behind him with a solid thump reminiscent of workmanship from days past.

Franco commented " Bagelman has a defeated look on his face."

Talia replied, " He doesn't lose too many trials, this is gonna fuck up his batting average."

Franco gave a slight smile and warned Talia, "Yeah well everyone thought O.J. was guilty and we saw what happened there." Franco referring to the recent 1995 murder trial of football great O.J. Simpson, who stood trial for killing his wife Nicole Brown Simpson and her friend Ronald Goldman. His attempted escape was captured on television as ninety-five million television viewers witnessed the slow police chase as they pursued O.J. in his white Ford Bronco. The subsequent 133 days of televised courtroom testimony turned countless viewers into Simpson trial junkies. Everyone seemed to have an opinion and it was basically split along racial lines. The overwhelming amount of forensic evidence seemed to suggest that there was no doubt as to his guilt, but on October 3, 1995 at 10:00 A.M. EST the verdict was "NOT GUILTY" as 91% of all televisions in the United States were glued to the scene unfolding in that California courtroom. Talia replied, "Yeah well that little piece of shit is no O.J., and he confessed so he's fucked."

"Bronx jury" Franco shot back, "you never know." Franco really didn't believe that he would be acquitted but he didn't want to jinx it. He was quite superstitious about such things and was not taking any chances.

As ADA Baron went through his summation, he depicted Marvin Davis as a heartless, ruthless, cold blooded killer. He described in detail the senseless murder, the attempt to deceive the police dressed as a women, his attempted escape, his apprehension and subsequent confession. He told the ladies and gentlemen of the jury in no uncertain terms that the world was now a better and safer place with this killer off the streets. He also told them that it was their duty as good citizens to ensure that he never experience the privilege of freedom. He went on to explain how in the wake of this senseless tragedy countless lives were changed forever and none for the better. He explained how a promising young man who did all the right things was taken away from the ones he loved, and the ones who loved him before his life really ever began. He told them how lucky the world was to have had a young man like Trevor, though be it only for a short time. He described how many lives and hearts he touched, and how he strived to make this world a better place, not only through his words, but through the way he lived his life. He credited Mrs. Webb for how she raised her sons and how it was their duty to give her the justice and closure she deserved. That maybe somehow she would someday be able to move on with her life at some point. He told them that this might be the most important decision they ever make. He implored them to do the right thing for Trevor, his family and the people of New York and find this cold blooded killer Marvin Davis guilty of FIRST DEGREE MUDER. He then in a low tone simply said, "Thank you."

ADA Baron walked back to the prosecutors table and sat down.

Judge Weinstein exclaimed "Mr. Bagelman, as the defense attorney approached the jury box."

"Ladies and gentleman" he stated, "this young man is a confused lost soul. He had the cards stacked against him from the moment he was born. No one wanted him, and even worse no one cared about him. His Grandmother did the best she could but even she was not thrilled to be burdened with his existence. He felt it from a very early age. Felt no one cared and no one loved him. Yes he admitted to doing something horrible but let's not blame him for the situation he found himself in. He feels genuine remorse for what he did as evidenced by his video confession. He stated he would take it back if he could. I believe this terrible tragedy actually changed my client for the better, as he now fully realizes how his actions can have a devastating impact on others. I'm asking you today to find it in your heart to consider the lesser charge of manslaughter in the first degree. With that my client can prove over time that he can be a productive member of society and someday make a difference in someone else's life. He can then at some time in the future be eligible for parole and for the first time in his life become a productive member of society."

"Thank you."

A stunned silence permeated through the courtroom. Was Bagelman serious? The jurors were looking at each other with blank stares. No one knew what to make of this closing argument. In fact it was no argument at all. Mr. Bagelman seemed to change his strategy, and it might just work. It seems he figured they heard him confess in a written statement, they saw him confess on video. He sounded like a heartless animal stating that poor Trevor was just in the wrong place at the wrong time, so what argument could he come up with to convince the jury his client was innocent. At this point it was damage control, and it might just be brilliant. If he could get just one juror to feel sorry for his client or feel that he can be rehabilitated maybe they would find him guilty of the lesser charge of Manslaughter 1.

Judge Weinstein instructed the jury to retire to the jury room and begin their duty of deciding the fate of Mr. Davis. He gave them specific instructions as it applied to the law in this case. He told them that they would stay sequestered until a verdict was reached, and that if they could not reach a decision by the end of the day, they would be removed to a hotel for the evening in the company of Court Officers. The court clerk Amanda Nappi, who has a younger sister who also works for the District Attorney's office as a court reporter, and who documented Marvin Davis' video confession the night of his apprehension, bellowed "ALL RISE" as the judge made his way off the bench.

The jurors accompanied by two armed Court Officers exited the courtroom through a side door. Several of them appeared to look back toward the audience where the Webb family was. One older black women looked directly at Mrs. Webb and appeared to ever so slightly nod. Mrs. Webb reached for Lyle's hand and they slowly walked toward the exit of the courtroom following ADA Baron and his assistant Kim Cohen. When the courtroom doors opened Detectives Franco and Talia were waiting in the lobby just outside the door. Franco made his way over to ADA Baron and asked, "How did it go?"

ADA Baron whispered, "He's going for the Man 1, referring to Bagelman's decision to forgo the usual plea for an innocent verdict and try to convince the jury to consider Manslaughter in the first degree.

"Can he do that?" Franco asked. "Let's talk about it in my office," was ADA Baron's response.

The group made its way over to the elevators and were standing there when Mr. Bagelman exited the courtroom. He saw them standing there and made his way to the stairwell. Although they were on the 7th floor, he probably decided the elevator ride would be awkward for everyone involved. As the group made its way into the elevator they filled it to capacity. There was Franco and Talia, Mrs. Webb, Lyle and Darleen ADA Baron and Kim Cohen. There seemed to be an awkward silence as the group rode the elevator to the lobby of Supreme Court. When the doors opened Franco held the door open as all the occupants exited. Mrs. Webb gave him a slight smile as she was the last to exit. At that moment Franco realized just how much she appeared to have aged since he first met her just over fourteen months ago. It gave him a really bad feeling in the pit of his stomach. *This fucking piece of shit has taken so much from this woman,* he thought to himself referring to Marvin Davis. They walked back across the street to ADA Baron's office, without anyone speaking. Franco could sense that the entire group was spent. He really wanted to say something to break the eerie silence but could not think of anything to say.

When the group entered the Criminal Court Courthouse where ADA Baron's office was located, a cop named Capone, who Franco knew from the 47th Precinct, ran over to him and asked him if he heard about the Citibank that had been robbed that morning on Boston Road in the 4-7. It seems that the robber armed with nothing more than a note and his finger under his coat, demanded that all the tellers put money into a black garbage bag. Well, two of the tellers gave him the dye packs, which are radio controlled incendiary devices that detonate, and when they explode cover the person holding the bag with a red dye that can't be washed off. He was caught a few blocks away covered in dye and visibly shaken. When the group heard this story they each laughed aloud and the awkward silence was broken.

Franco, for good measure asked Capone, "With a name like Capone, are you sure he's not one of your distant relatives?" referring to the notorious Al Capone. The group had another chuckle and proceeded to ADA Baron's office to eat lunch and wait for the verdict.

38

The Verdict

AFTER EVERYONE GOT SETTLED IN, Kim Cohen passed around the menu of a local deli that supplied lunch for the DA's office. The DA fills out a voucher that is approved by the Bureau head, and the deli gets paid on a monthly basis. So as everyone was deciding on what to eat, ADA Baron began to explain the jury deliberation process, and what to expect as far as time is concerned before they reach a decision. He was saying that sometimes the verdict could take days when other times it is fairly quick as in several hours. He explained that he has been doing this for many years and that there are too many variables to try to predict how long before they come back with a verdict. As everyone made their selection off the menu and Kim Cohen called the order in to the deli, Franco and Talia excused themselves and proceeded to make their way down the long hallway which runs through the 4th floor of the DA's office. They were trying to locate one of the DA's that they heard was running a March Madness college basketball pool.

As they entered his office Franco's cell phone rang. It was ADA Baron. "What's up Sid?" Franco uttered and then he let out a very loud, "No fucking way. O.K. we're coming," was all he said, as he hung up and told Talia, "Can you believe this, they have a verdict." Franco looked at his watch, it had only been forty-seven minutes since they went in to deliberate. *Forty-seven minutes he thought to himself, 4-7 maybe it's an omen.* As the two detectives made their way back to ADA Baron's office they could see Mrs. Webb, Darleen, and Lyle walk out with ADA Baron and Kim Cohen. They all had their coats on. As Franco approached ADA Baron he asked him, "Is this crazy or what?" ADA Baron responded, "I've never heard of such a thing, get your coats, let's go."

The group made their way back to Supreme Court and back up to the 7th floor. They all entered the courtroom. The defendant Marvin Davis was seated at the defense table with Mr. Bagelman and two burly Court Officers standing directly behind them.

ADA Baron and Kim Cohen made their way to the prosecutors table and sat down. Mrs. Webb, Darleen and Lyle took seats in the front row of the audience behind ADA Baron. Mrs. Webb sat in the middle between Lyle and Darleen. She held each of their hands for comfort. Franco and Talia sat one row behind the Webb family with Franco occupying the seat on the isle.

The Court Clerk Amanda Nappi stood at the Judge's bench and bellowed "ALL RISE." As she did, Judge Weinstein entered from his quarters located behind his bench and took his seat. The Court Clerk then instructed the audience to "BE SEATED."

Judge Weinstein instructed one of the Court Officers who was assigned to escort the jury to have them enter the courtroom. As he opened the side door the twelve jurors and two alternates entered the courtroom and took their seats in the juror's box. All eyes were upon the jury as they made their way to their seats. When they were all seated, Judge Weinstein instructed the defendant Marvin Davis to stand and face the jury.

The Judge then asked the foreperson, a black women in her mid-fifties, if the jury had reached a decision?

She stood and stated "We have." She then stated in a slow, deliberate, monotone voice, "We the People of the State of New York find the defendant Marvin Davis GUILTY of the charge of MURDER IN THE FIRST DEGREE, so say us all."

The Webb family stood and held each other as they all were weeping and sobbing. There were some cheers heard in the rear of the courtroom and Franco turned to see where they came from. There was a group seated in the last row and Franco did not recognize any of them. He later found out they were from Mrs. Webb's Church group. He turned to Talia and smiled, the two partners shook hands as Franco put his arm around Talia and gave him a hug.

"Good job Gio," Talia shot back.

At that moment Mrs. Webb turned to face Franco and Talia and stated, "You two men are my angels, you will always be in our hearts and in our prayers." She had tears running down her face.

Lyle turned to face the detectives and stated, "My brother's life will always have meaning because of you." Darleen looking on was so overwhelmed all she could do was nod her head.

The audience became louder and Judge Weinstein banged his gavel to return the courtroom to some semblance of order. He understood that there was an extreme amount of emotion being released and the observers were just overwhelmed by it. In a half-hearted stern voice he exclaimed, "Order, Order." He brought his gavel down one more time and the courtroom was silent, except for the muffled sounds of people sobbing in the audience.

At that moment Franco looked over at Marvin Davis seated at the defense table. He had sat back down and had his face buried in his hands. Mr. Bagelman sat next to his client writing something on a legal pad. Franco wondered if he was writing anything at all, or was it just some nervous doodling. The Judge excused the jury and then stated that sentencing will be set for April first at 10:00 A.M.

How fitting Franco thought, *let this fool be sentenced on April fool's day.*

The Judge then demanded that Marvin Davis be remanded to Riker's Island Correctional Facility until that date. As Marvin Davis was led away in handcuffs, he seemed to actively seek out Mrs. Webb in the audience with his eyes. When she looked back at him he mouthed the words, "pray for me."

Franco looked at her for a reaction but did not see one. It left Franco with an eerie feeling. Was Marvin Davis working Mrs. Webb? Was he trying to get her to feel pity for him before sentencing? Or was he genuine and feeling remorseful for the first time in his life. Franco was skeptical by nature, and had a hard time believing that a psycho killer like Marvin could ever change. Well it really wasn't his problem anymore. He did his job and did it well. Marvin Davis would be going away for a very long time.

39

The Sentence

APRIL FIRST SEEMED TO COME VERY QUICKLY as Franco and Talia had been working several shooting cases that seem to be occurring on almost a daily basis. Most were drug related and did not seem to give the detectives the same rush of adrenaline that a "real" shooting or homicide did. These types of cases, although serious and certainly felonies, were sometimes referred to as "Misdemeanor shootings, because no one really cared if a drug dealer got shot. They never cooperated with the investigation, and if an arrest was made, would never be located again when the case went to trial. Both detectives were looking forward to this day, and the closure it might bring them, but especially the Webb family.

Sentencing was scheduled for 10:00 A.M. but Franco knew from past cases that the Judge probably would not be ready until closer to 11:00. He phoned ADA Baron when he first got in and was told to be there before 10:00 A.M. When he protested and stated "the judge won't even be there before 11:00", ADA Baron seemed to become more upset then was his nature. Franco feeling some tension promised to be there on time.

This he thought would only give him an hour or so to think of a good "April Fool's joke" to play on one of his fellow detectives. He decided that the Squad Sergeant would have to be his latest victim as he observed the Sergeant's car keys sitting atop the Sergeant's desk. *This is too easy*, he thought as he engaged the Sergeant in some idle chit chat as he so professionally swiped the keys right from under the Sergeant's nose. He ran down to the boss' parking lot and located the Sergeant's car. A white 1977 Cadillac Eldorado that this particular sergeant, a very Italian guy in every stereotypical way, named Ralphie adored. Ralphie was a throwback to a time, when neighborhoods were ethnic, especially Italian neighborhoods. Everyone knew each other. You lived upstairs from your parents or uncles and aunts in the same house, and you shopped at the corner Italian Meateria, and you dated the Italian girl down the block. Family was the most important thing you had. The guys loved Sergeant Ralph, he looked out for them like they were his family, and Sergeant Ralph loved his car. He even had a white raccoon tail hanging from his rear view mirror as a symbol of a long gone era. So Franco jumps in the white Eldorado and started it up. *Now where should I put it* he thinks to himself. *I know I'll put it in the garage under the precinct* he decided. The precinct garage was used to house vehicles that were involved in crimes and were awaiting crime scene to come photograph them, or dust them for prints. Franco knew that at 4:00 P.M., when the Sergeant's tour of duty was over, he would freak out when he went out to the lot and discovered his car was missing. Best part of it was he knew the Sergeant would assume the car had been stolen and would be running around losing his mind. Franco would be back from court and the sentencing by then so if things got crazy he could always re-cover the missing vehicle in the garage and be the hero. Also, the Sergeant would have no way of knowing that Franco had anything to do with it. He was down at court all day. *What a brilliant idea* he thought. So Franco pulled the Sergeant's prize possession around the building and placed it ever so gently in the precinct garage. He went back up to the Detective Squad room and placed the keys back on the Sergeant's desk with him only a few feet away speaking to the Squad Lieutenant about overtime and how they had to keep it down in a precinct that was leading the city in homicides at the time.

Franco grabbed the keys to one of the unmarked detective squad cars off the vehicle board and signed it out. He grabbed his Homicide folder that had the name Trevor Webb on the front and noticed how beat up the cover looked. He took the folder and placed it inside a clean, fresh homicide folder that had no writing on it. He knew he would be seeing the Webb family and did not want that folder staring them in the face with Trevor's name on it.

Franco yelled to Talia who was at the far end of the Squad room speaking to a suspect that was in the holding pen. He had been arrested on the midnight tour by two uniform cops and was the subject of some strong arm robberies of elderly women coming back from the check cashing store after receiving their assistance checks. It looked like Talia was making some headway getting some information for the Robbery detectives who had seemed to strike out with obtaining a confession. Franco walked over and told Talia that they needed to be down at court by 10:00. Talia gave him a strange look as only about a half hour or so ago Franco had told Talia that there was no hurry getting down to court, and that the judge would be taking his time because the judge always picks the day of sentencing on a day where his calendar is empty and that's the only thing he does that day. He must be available for any appeal motions by the defense and all that.

As if reading Talia's mind Franco told him "I know what I told you, but I spoke to Sid and he was pissed when I suggested that there was no hurry getting down there. He sounded uncharacteristically annoyed so I told him we'd be there on time.

"Okay," Talia shot back, "just give me a minute."

With that Talia went over to the far wall and removed the cell key from the wall. He went over to the cell and unlocked it. He escorted the suspect to the interrogation room. Franco stood outside the interrogation room and watched through the one way mirror. The suspect was speaking to Talia and Talia handed him a cigarette and lit it for him. After his cigarette Talia grabbed a legal pad and had the suspect write something on it. He also signed the bottom of it as did Talia. They both got up and Talia exited the room with the suspect and returned him to the holding pen. After locking him in the cell, Talia told the suspect, "I'll be back in a bit." With that he motioned to Franco "let's go."

Franco gave him a strange look as they walked out of the Squad room.

"What was that all about?" Franco asked. "He confessed to two robberies that went down this week."

"I thought he wasn't saying anything to anyone about them." was Franco's response.

Yeah well he saw me smoking and asked me for a cigarette. I said, 'I'll give you a cigarette if you tell me what you did.' He said 'Okay' I didn't think he was serious so I brought him in the box and gave him a cigarette. He told me about two that he did near the check cashing place on Laconia Avenue and 226th Street.

"So why did he tell you and not the cops that locked him up," Franco asked.

"He said they were nasty to him and roughed him up. He also said that they really didn't ask him about the robberies, all they kept telling him was he's going to jail. So I figured I'd be nice to him and give him a cigarette and see what he has to say."

"I guess I'm rubbing off on you" Franco shot back. "You know I knew somehow you would figure out a way to take credit for this confession," Talia said.

Both partners laughed as Talia walked into the Robbery Squad and handed the catching detective the pad with the suspect's brief statement on it. "Be nice to him, and give him cigarettes and he will tell you everything" was Talia's advice to the Detective.

"Okay," was his response as the detective looked over at Franco with a puzzled expression on his face.

Franco found this as an opportunity to break some balls. "You better check out the name on that confession, it is April fool's day you know" With that both Franco and Talia walked out of the Robbery Squad room.

As they made their way down to the squad car and headed to court, Franco informed Talia of the prank he pulled on Sergeant Ralphie.

"You shouldn't have done that Giovanni, you know how much he loves that car."

"That's what makes it a great prank Richie. He will freak out thinking someone stole his prize possession."

"Yeah well he might have a heart attack."

"Yeah well I didn't think of that" was Franco's response, with a slightly nervous chuckle.

As the two detectives drove down to Supreme Court for the sentencing, their conversation turned to the Webb family and all that they have been through. Franco wondered how Mrs. Webb felt when Marvin Davis asked her to pray for him as he exited the courtroom.

"She should pray that he goes to hell," was Talia's response.

"Yeah well she's a special kind of person," Franco said. "I could see her praying for him. I could also see her telling the judge that she has forgiven him."

"I don't think so Gio. He took away her child for no reason. People don't forgive that," was Talia's response.

"Well we shall see" Franco shot back. The conversation turned to ADA Sid Baron and the mood he was in when Franco spoke to him.

"He is usually so mild mannered," Franco stated. "Maybe someone pulled an April fool's prank on him today."

"We shall see" Talia shot back, mimicking Franco.

The ride down to court was uneventful, and at one point Talia warned Franco not to observe anyone committing any street crimes where he might need to jump out of the car and chase the perp into traffic. They both had a laugh and Franco who was driving this time, informed Talia that if that happens again, he'll just run the perp over to save some time. "We are on a schedule you know" he said.

As they pulled up to the courthouse there was a dirty looking, apparently homeless man selling parking spots. Franco motioned with his hand for the guy to move out of the space. He stubbornly refused and yelled out, "five dollars for the spot." Franco again waved with his hand for the man to get out of the street. Again the man dressed in a long dirty overcoat and orange sneakers defiantly stood his ground and yelled out "five dollars bitch."

"Oh shit, here we go," Talia exclaimed while looking at Franco with a pleading expression. "Let it go Gio, PLEASE" requested Talia.

"Bitch? Bitch? I got your bitch right here" stated Franco as he exited the unmarked car and walked toward the homeless man. "This is a city street MOTHER FUCKER, if you don't move now, I'll move you permanently," stated Franco as he got in the face of this filthy, smelly, miscreant.

"Yo April fool, fool" was the homeless man's response as he hopped up onto the sidewalk and walked away muttering something inaudible. As he walked away he turned and pulled out a wade of money from his right front pants pocket and waved it at Franco. "How much you got?" he asked Franco as he continued down the street.

Talia began to laugh, but Franco was not amused.

"Do you believe these assholes gave this guy money to park on a city street?" he asked referring to no one in particular. "This fucking city is going to be the death of me" he continued.

"Or the death of someone else," Talia shot back. They got back in the car and parked it.

They made their way up to ADA Baron's office and were met by his assistant Kim Cohen in the hallway right outside his door. She had a distressed look on her face. Franco asked what was wrong and she informed them that ADA Baron's apartment building sustained a fire over the weekend and he lost everything. She went on to explain that all his exotic birds had perished in the fire as well. She stated "he has no family, they were like his children."

"Why is he here today?" Talia asked.

"This job is all he has now, he is very sad, I just wanted you guys to know because I know you joke around and all, he seems so depressed and I'm not sure if he will tell you."

"Okay Kim, thanks" Franco replied. When they entered his office he was not there. Mrs. Webb, Lyle and Darleen were sitting in there speaking softly. When they saw the detectives they each smiled and greeted them.

Mrs. Webb gave them both a kiss on their cheek and stated "Hi my Angels" which drew a smile from them both. Lyle shook both their hands with a firm shake and Darleen smiled and said "hi." They made some small talk about how Lyle was doing in school and how Darleen was progressing in college and in her new job at Madison Square Garden. Darleen had accepted a paid internship in their marketing department and stated "she loved it."

Franco joked that when she becomes a big shot there she can get him some Rangers and Knicks tickets. Lyle chimed in that he would like Knicks tickets in a luxury suite. "Well if you're getting a suite we can all go," Franco replied.

At that moment ADA Baron entered his office. He greeted the detectives and informed them that the clerk will call when they are to come over to the courtroom. He said it should be in a few minutes. Franco looked at his watch and it read 9:40 A.M. ADA Baron sat at his desk working on some paperwork and took an occasional phone call. At 10:20 A.M. the phone rang and it was Amanda Nappi the court clerk requesting their presence in the courtroom for the sentencing.

The group made their way across the street to Supreme Court. On their way Richie Talia told the group about the run in Franco had that morning with the homeless man selling parking spaces in the street. He embellished the story a bit to make it sound like the homeless guy got the best of Franco. He told them that when he got out of the car and approached the guy, the guy smacked Franco, twisted Franco's arm behind his back, and made Franco pay double to park the unmarked car. Franco just rolled his eyes as the group had a good laugh.

As the group entered the courthouse they made their way to the courtroom on the 7th floor. Franco opened the double wooden doors and held them open as each entered. Talia was the last to enter and Franco stepped on the back of his shoe causing his foot to come out of his black loafer. Franco then walked past Talia as he sarcastically apologized. "Sorry bro," he uttered with a slight smile. "You always have to get the last laugh," Talia whispered.

The joking ended as a side door to the courtroom opened and out walked Marvin Davis accompanied by two Court Officers. They escorted him to the defense table in handcuffs where his attorney Mr. Bagelman was seated.

Talia and Franco took their usual seats one row behind the Webb family. ADA Baron and Kim Cohen were at the prosecution table.

The court clerk asked all to rise as Judge Weinstein entered the courtroom from his quarters behind the bench. All the spectators took their seats after the judge sat.

Judge Weinstein addressed the Webb family and asked if anyone cared to say anything to the defendant. Mrs. Webb raised her hand and Judge Weinstein asked her to stand. She proceeded to state the following:

"When I was told that my first born baby was murdered it was like my world came to a screeching halt. I could not breathe and I could not think. I felt like I was inside a nightmare where I had no chance of waking.

I pictured the killer in my mind, and for some reason envisioned him as a large, older man with a worn, scary face. Then I saw your photo. I could not believe that this young boy I was looking at was my son's killer. I began to question my faith, surely if there was a God he would not allow someone to take my baby from me. My boy was a good and kind boy. Do you even know his name? Do you? His name was Trevor, Trevor Webb. He was named after his grandfather who came to this country from Jamaica and worked sixteen hours a day to support his family. My son Trevor adored his grandfather. That was my dad. Well he is with his grandfather now thanks to you. God says that we must forgive so I will forgive you, but I will never forget the empty, cold feeling you have put in my heart. Remember his name, Trevor Webb."

With that Mrs. Webb sat down.

Franco looked over at Lyle and Darleen and they were sobbing. He then looked at Marvin Davis and he had his face in his hands. Judge Weinstein asked if there were any other family members who wanted to say something. Both Lyle and Darleen declined.

With that Marvin Davis was told to stand. The judge addressed him as follows:

"Mr. Marvin Davis, you have been found guilty of Murder in the first degree by a jury of your peers. This senseless act that you have committed has had a profound impact on many individuals. You took it upon yourself to decide the fate of a young man that you did not know, nor did you care how many lives you would affect by your deed. You are a coward in every sense of the word. You have blamed society and anyone you can think of for your situation. Mr. Davis the blame lies in the mirror. Your brazen acts throughout your young life disgust me. You are not a man, no sir you are a shameful little boy with no conscience and no civility. By the power vested in me by the State of New York I hereby sentence you to spend the remainder of your pathetic life in prison without parole.

Marvin Davis was escorted out of the courtroom and never looked back at the Webb family. The side door opened and he was gone.

The Webb family were still weeping as the court clerk demanded that all rise. Judge Weinstein exited the courtroom to his quarters and Mr. Bagelman sat at the defense table waiting for everyone to exit the courtroom. Talia looked over at Franco and realized that he had been crying as well. It made him very uncomfortable, and he choose not to comment. As they walked out of the courtroom Franco headed straight to the bathroom located halfway down the hall. He splashed some water on his face and then went back out into the hall to rejoin the group.

As he approached the Webb family Mrs. Webb gave him a big hug and whispered in his ear. "It's okay to cry, you're a good man. You and detective Richie could not have been kinder or more understanding throughout this entire ordeal. I will always keep you in my prayers." With that she went over to Talia and hugged him as well. She said something to him but Franco could not hear her.

Lyle was shaking ADA Baron's hand and Darleen, who was so quiet, and shy throughout all these months stated to Franco, "Trevor is watching us right now, I know he is." With that Franco smiled and nodded his head. Mrs. Webb was now talking to ADA Baron off to the side and Franco heard ADA Baron say that they should go back to his office so Bagelman could leave the courtroom.

Franco thought, *Bagelman, what a shitty job. Representing the scum of the earth. I could never do it, no matter what it pays. In hindsight Bagelman didn't seem so bad. He did what he had to do to represent his client, but he showed the Webb family respect. He tried to screw Franco with the whole "did you have any physical contact with my client shit and you're a big, strong football player, you must have beat my client bullshit" But all in all, he said the detectives did a good job and he knew his client was fucked.*

The group headed back to ADA Baron's office. Franco and Talia said their goodbyes once they got to the front of Criminal court where their car was parked. They wanted to get back to the precinct to see if the Sergeant had discovered his car missing yet. They all hugged and shook hands as they departed. ADA Baron thanked them both for an excellent job and stated that he was going to write a letter commending them for their work on this investigation to the Police Commissioner. He never did mention the fire at his apartment building or the loss of his birds and his property.

As the two detectives walked to the unmarked car there was a note on the windshield that Franco read aloud, "YOUR LUCKEY I DIDN'T KICK YOUR FUCKING ASS BITCH BITCH BITCH." Franco smiled as he put the note in his pocket. All he said to Talia was, "he spelled you're and lucky wrong."

When the two arrived back at the precinct Franco pulled over on the side of the precinct and looked in the garage window. There sat the Sergeants car, nice and shiny. "Okay Richie it's still there." Franco checked his watch it was 2:50 P.M. Enough time to head to the Cozy Cottage for a sandwich. The Cozy Cottage was a sandwich shop on Boston Road. It was frequented by many civil service types. Sanitation had a garage down the block and along with the Fire department, the cops and EMS workers the place was a gold mine. They opened for breakfast and lunch and were closed by 3:00 P.M. The food was always fresh and the price was right. If you want to know where to get good food in New York City eat where you see, ambulances, fire trucks, police cars and garbage trucks parked outside.

So the guys picked up a couple of brisket wedges and headed back to the squad room. When they arrived all seemed normal. There were two perps in the holding cell from a collar that Owney made for an assault. He was getting ready to go down to Central booking with Vinny Price. Franco looked into the sergeant's office and saw Sergeant Ralph at his desk doing paperwork. He walked in and asked, "What's up Sarge?"

He replied, "Just trying to get the Chief to approve overtime for Owney and Price."

"Good luck," was Franco's response. Franco went over to his desk and put his sandwich down. He sat down and called Talia who was sitting at his desk on the other end of the squad room eating his lunch. "He has no fucking idea," Franco told him.

"Don't involve me in this," was Talia response.

"Pussy," was Franco's reply as he hung up the phone.

Four o'clock came and Franco walked past the sergeant's office and observed the Sergeant packing up his briefcase for the end of his tour. Franco went over to the coat rack and put his coat on. He timed it so they would leave together and walk down the stairs to the first floor together. As the sergeant walked out of his office. Franco walked over to the sign in book and signed out for the night. "Wait up Sarge I'll walk down with you," he uttered as he looked back at Talia who was shaking his head at Franco. He gave Talia a devilish grin as he waved goodbye and shouted, "See you tomorrow guys" to the remainder of the detectives left in the squad room. "Later Franco" was the usual response.

As they descended the stairwell The Sergeant asked Franco "How did the sentencing go?" It was sad Sarge, the mother and whole family are such nice people."

"What a fucking shame," was the Sergeant response.

"Yeah well he gave him life without the chance of parole."

"Good for that little piece of shit, only problem is now we have to feed the cock sucker for the next seventy years," said the Sergeant.

"Yeah I know," said Franco.

As they got to the bottom of the stairs and walked outside, Sergeant Ralph made a right to go to the supervisor's parking lot. Franco was walking with him as though he was cutting through the lot to East 229th Street where Franco's car was parked. All of a sudden the Sergeant had a blank look on his face. He stopped in his tracks and did a pirouette turning completely around. He did this twice and came to a stop putting his hand to his chin as thought he was posing for the statue THE THINKER.

"Where the fuck is my car" He exclaimed.

"Where did you park it?" Franco asked with a straight face.

"Right fucking here were I always park it," was his response. "It's gone" the Sergeant exclaimed.

"Are you talking about your Eldorado" Franco asked.

"Yeah I'm talking about my Eldorado, what the fuck, someone stole my fucking car right out of the fucking precinct lot, these mother fuckers," the sergeant yelled.

With that the sergeant ran back into the precinct. He informed the Lieutenant on the front desk that his car had been stolen. He requested auto crime respond over the radio.

Franco feeling it was getting a little out of hand suggested that they walk around the precinct that maybe the Sergeant didn't park where he thought he did. But the Sergeant was having none of it.

"I know where I parked," he bellowed as he dismissed Franco with his hand and got on his cell phone. "Well I'm going to look around the precinct anyway," Franco told him.

Franco went out the front door of the precinct and walked around to the back door. He waited several minutes and could see the Sergeant through the large windows that cover the doors. The Sergeant was frantic and had a small crowd of cops around him. Franco then walked back to the desk and told the Sergeant there is a white Eldorado downstairs in the garage.

The Sergeant made a mad dash out the door and down the driveway. Franco followed behind him. When the Sergeant got to the garage doors and looked in he immediately knew he had been had. Now the question was by who. He was pissed but you could also tell he was relieved. He asked Franco straight out, "Did you have anything to do with this?"

"I was down at court all day Sarge, remember?"

"Yeah that's right, well when I find out who did it they're going to be transferred to the 123rd," referring to the 123rd Precinct located at the very tip of Staten Island.

"It's a pretty funny April fool's prank you must admit," Franco said.

"I don't think so," was the Sergeants response.

The Sergeant then told Franco, as he opened the garage door and walked around his car inspecting it for damage, "I guess whoever did it got me pretty good." He had a smile on his face.

He was feeling Franco out trying to get him to admit it, but he didn't take the bait. Instead he responded, "Yeah I wish I had thought of it."

It seemed like months that the Sergeant was trying to figure out who pulled this April fool's prank on him, and although Talia was the only other person who knew Franco did it, Franco knew his secret was safe.

40

We Will Never Forget

MONTHS TURNED INTO YEARS AND Detective Giovanni Franco continued to work his cases in the 47th Precinct Detective Squad. With 18 years on the job, he had seen and heard it all. Not even the most horrific crime scenes seemed to rattle him. He had turned into what cops called a "HAIR BAG" he'd seen it all and done it all in his mind. He worked his cases in a meticulous almost robotic fashion. He had his craft down to a science. He had become very proficient at solving homicides and procuring confessions from suspects. He was solving cases at an extremely high rate. During this time he was awarded several citations for excellent police work and received recognition, not only from his department, but from other departments and police organizations. His children were growing like weeds. C.J. his oldest son was now fourteen and his youngest Thomas was now eight.

He found himself working long hours trying to build up his overtime as he would be eligible to retire in two short years. He seemed to be at work much more than at home and this always gave him a bad feeling deep down inside.

During this time he missed several family functions because he was either scheduled to work and could not get off, or he got stuck at work because he caught a shooting or a homicide and could not leave. He even missed his son Thomas's 8th birthday party because a deranged maniac stabbed several people in the lobby of a local hospital and he caught the case. The suspect fled the scene and Franco tracked him down late that same evening.

Although he was excelling at his craft, he felt he was neglecting his family. Through no fault of his own, he felt he was growing apart from them, especially his boys. This feeling seemed to have him in a foul mood much of the time, and he found himself growing impatient, and even downright nasty, when dealing with individuals during the course of his investigations. He even found himself becoming short with the very people he loved and missed. It was becoming a vicious cycle.

He realized this one day when he came home after a very long and stressful day. This particular day involved attempting to get a confession from a father who had murdered his infant son, because he would not stop crying. He pulled into his driveway and there were toys and his son's bike spewed all over, and he could not pull his car in. He jumped out of the car and entered his house. He found his son Thomas sitting on the couch watching TV. He went over to his son, grabbed him by the arm and dragged him outside, all the while screaming at him to clean up after himself. His son was crying and at that moment it hit him. He was burnt out. He went into his bedroom and began to cry. He was so upset at how he reacted to his baby boy. The stress of his job, dealing with the scum of the earth was turning him into someone he didn't like. Turning him into someone he didn't even know.

A short time later he went out into the living room and apologized to his son, who with unconditional love in his heart simply said "It's Okay Daddy.

The next day he was back to work doing an 8 to 4 tour of duty in the Squad. It was a bright, clear, perfect September day. The air was crisp and there was not a cloud in the sky. He arrived at work at about 7:45 A.M. and signed in the log book located in the Lieutenant's office. He made himself a cup of coffee and went over to the file cabinet to retrieve the homicide folder of the infant that was killed by his father the day before. The father had been arrested by Franco's partner Vinny Price who had to go down to the Grand Jury to testify. Franco wanted to go over the case to ensure that nothing had been missed. Price had not arrived for work yet. The Squad room began to fill with detectives arriving for their day tour. There was the usual banter between the guys, and discussions about sports and current events. Vinny Price walked in and he was in his usual surly mood. He complained about having to go down to court and testify at the Grand Jury. He posed an interesting question to no one in particular as he made this statement:

"I got this piece of shit who killed his own kid because he wouldn't stop crying. He confesses to the murder, but we have to go through all this bullshit that will cost the city, and the state, god knows how much. A fucking bullet costs forty cents. Why not just shoot him in his fucking head and leave him out with the trash?"

It seemed, although everyone in the room knew the answer, no one disagreed with his simplistic overview of the situation.

Franco engaged Price in some conversation about the case folder and some paperwork that seemed to be missing. He informed Franco that he was going to do it before he left to go down to the Grand Jury.

"You want to take a ride down to court with me?" he asked. "They might need you."

"I didn't get notified," was Franco's response. "Besides if they do need me maybe they'll bring me down on my RDO". "OVERTIME MY BOY," Franco shouted, causing some of the detectives in the room to laugh aloud.

This brought a smile to Price's face and his bad mood seemed to be washed away.

The Squad room became quite active as detectives were now at their desks working on their individual cases. The sound of typing and phones ringing filled the air.

A uniformed officer from the Precinct brought in a perp that he caught breaking into cars on Jerome Avenue near the # 4 train station.

This area was a target for thieves as they would observe people park their cars, and then walk to the train station to head down to their jobs in Manhattan. The thieves knew they had plenty of time to do their dirty work as the owner of the vehicle would be gone all day.

This particular "Brain Surgeon" broke into a brand new BMW while the vehicles owner went into the corner store to purchase the newspaper. The vehicle owner realized he forgot his cell phone in the car and went back to get it. The thief made the mistake of not waiting until he heard the train pull out of the station before he broke the passenger window and entered the vehicle rummaging through it looking for anything of value. He found the cell phone plugged into the charger but unbeknownst to him, the owner had arrived at the vehicle and began screaming for help as he held the door closed, and would not let the thief escape.

Apparently this cop was down the street and was alerted to the situation. He and his partner responded and arrested the suspect. The cop was inquiring if a detective could interrogate this suspect as there had been several break-ins of vehicles on this strip recently and the Precinct Commander was getting a lot of pressure from the Community Board. Detective Owney motioned for the cop to come over to his desk. He told the cop to put the perp in the cell and he'd be with him in a minute.

It was now approximately 8:50 A.M., and one of the detectives that was in the detective's break room began shouting for everyone to come see this. As the detectives filled the break room there was live footage, on the TV, of a commercial airplane striking the North tower of the World Trade Center. They kept showing the footage over and over. The information on the bottom of the screen kept scrolling stating it was American Airlines flight eleven and that it struck the North Tower at 8:46 A.M. The detectives watched in disbelief as the footage was repeated over and over. They stood there almost frozen and watched this iconic symbol of the world financial mecca burn.

Within minutes the phones in the Squad room were ringing off the hook.

The Lieutenant came into the Squad room and ordered everyone into uniform and informed the Detectives that intelligence information seemed to suggest that this was no accident, but that of a terrorist attack upon the city. All the detectives ran down the two flights of stairs to the locker room located in the basement. There were cops everywhere gathering their things. The detectives dressed in record time and then ran back up to the Squad room. When they re-entered the Squad room the Lieutenant informed them that a second plane had struck the South Tower at 9:03. The men made their way back to the break room and watched in disbelief as the footage of both plane strikes were played over and over.

By this time the entire North Tower building was engulfed and people were breaking windows and waving with their clothing or anything they could find to get someone's attention. The detectives stood by helplessly as the Lieutenant informed them that city buses had been mobilized by the MTA and were responding to all precincts to bring the detectives down to the scene. This would be the LARGEST CRIME SCENE in NEW YORK CITY HISTORY.

Within minutes there were several buses parked in front of the precinct. Franco along with the rest of the detectives in his Squad boarded the bus. The Lieutenant and Sergeant Ralph sat in the front as the bus was about 3/4 filled. The bus driver stated that he had instructions from his supervisors to not leave until the bus was filled to capacity.

The detectives began screaming at the driver and some even threatened him telling him to drive now. He did as he was told and headed to the West Side Highway. Franco looked at his watch and it read 9:40 A.M. The Highway Patrol Units had all the entrances closed and they had emptied all traffic off the highway and on to the city streets. There were no vehicles on the highway except police cars, ambulances, fire trucks and city buses carrying detectives and other police personnel. It was the most eerie sight to see nothing but first responder's vehicle in a huge caravan speeding down this three lane highway in the middle of rush hour.

The Lieutenant stood up and announced that he wanted all his men to stay together upon their arrival. He informed them that communication could be effected and that the radios might not be operational. The men didn't seem to really care what he had to say at that moment. Their country had just been attacked and although they had no idea who was responsible they wanted to respond and somehow get revenge. The conversations were that of, "Those poor people, and I wonder who the fuck did this." Some speculated it was Muslims of some sort. All seemed to agree.

Franco sat uncharacteristically quiet as his mind was racing. He was trying to envision what he would be encountering when he got there.

The bus was flying down the West side highway, and they had just passed Chelsea Piers. As they got closer to the scene they could see smoke in the distance. They were now only a few blocks away and one of the detectives commented that it seemed like the entire area was engulfed.

There were police check points that had been established throughout lower Manhattan, and only first responders were allowed beyond them. As the bus made a left hand turn onto Canal Street, the Trade Center was visible from the bus. There was only one tower standing. The Lieutenant received information over his radio that the South tower had collapsed at 9:59 A.M.

There was a sense of disbelief inside the bus as all the detectives came to the realization that thousands of people must be dead. Franco looked at his watch and it read 10:09 A.M. As the bus made a right, it came to a stop at the final check point on Hudson Street. The Lieutenant instructed the bus driver to open the doors of the bus. The Lieutenant and Sergeant exited the bus with all the detectives following them. There was a thick plume of smoke heading down the street toward the detectives. Franco stepped around the Lieutenant and hurriedly marched into the smoke, towards the remaining tower, unaware of the horror that awaited him.

THE END

About the Author

Charles J. Longi is the author behind this debut novel *Never a Dull Moment, The Chronicles of a New York City Street Cop*.

As a retired, highly decorated twenty year veteran Detective of the NYPD, he chronicles some bazaar and captivating experiences in this edgy and raw tale told through the eyes of the main character Giovanni Franco.

Charles worked various assignments within the NYPD, both in uniform, and in *Plain Clothes*. He was promoted to the rank of Detective Investigator and was recognized for his outstanding work by being inducted to The New York City Police Department's prestigious Honor Legion in 1993.

Upon retirement, he transitioned his talents and expertise to the private sector, accepting a position as the Director of Security at a prominent private college, and continues in that capacity today.

Charles's unique and distinctive writing style and storytelling ability is evident as he paints a picture of events that will entice and hook you, leaving you craving for more.

Charles lives with his wife Sharon and their 160 pound Italian Mastiff dog *Capone* in the suburbs of New York.